43

DEAD RECKONING

Per Anna

Grazie per Venuta

Lawrence Battersby

A NOVEL BY

LAWRENCE BATTERSBY

Tre
Cappelli
Editions

First Published in Great Britain in March 2024 by
Tre Cappelli Editions
Copyright © 2024 Lawrence Battersby

Paperback ISBN 978 1 913332 01 3

A CIP catalogue record for this book is available from the British Library.

Printed and bound in Great Britain by Clays Ltd, Elcograf S.p.A.

MIX
Paper | Supporting responsible forestry
FSC
www.fsc.org
FSC® C018072

Cover picture licensed through Alamy Ltd, UK

Cover design by Audrey Beauhaire

IN MEMORIAM

NOTICE

Whilst every character in this novel may correspond to a real historical person, may share vital dates, and may even have been in a certain place at a particular moment, *Dead Reckoning* is a novel of historical fiction. It is inspired by several real historical events, but it is not reportage of such events. It is, at best, a work of empathetic imagination.

PREFACE

THE DEFINITION & PURPOSE OF

DEAD RECKONING

"Dead Reckoning allows a navigator to determine their present position by projecting their past courses steered and speeds from a known past position.

Also, to determine their future position by projecting an ordered course and speed of advance from a known present position.

The present position is only an approximate position because it does not allow for the effects of <u>leeway</u>, <u>current</u>, <u>helmsman error</u>, or <u>gyro error</u>.

Dead Reckoning helps in determining sunrise and sunset; in predicting landfall, sighting lights and predicting arrival times. It also helps in predicting which celestial bodies will be available for future observation.

Thus, the navigator should carefully tend his Dead Reckoning plot and update it when required, especially use it to evaluate <u>external forces acting on his ship</u> and consult it to avoid potential navigation hazards."

Adapted from: Chapter 7, of the New American Practical Navigator from Nathaniel Bowditch, published in 1902, and adapted from page 189 of the eighth edition of John Hamilton Moore's The Practical Navigator, published in 1784.

PART I

SUNRISE

1933

Convergence of the Twain

Alien they seemed to be
No mortal eye could see
The intimate welding of their later history
Or sign that they were bent
By paths coincident
On being anon twin halves of one august event.

— THOMAS HARDY

1

LILY

Honiton, Devon.

Lily's smile was warm and her thoughts were fertile. As soon as Edgar hauled his sea-legs off the train and placed his feet on the station platform, she made certain he knew why. Well, she was forty-four years old and the next time he would be home on shore-leave it would surely be too late.

'They came back,' she told him discreetly.

'Who did?'

'Not who. What!'

'Ahh…I see.' Edgar cuddled her tentatively like he did when his bones ached.

'They hadn't really gone. It's Mother Nature giving us one last chance.' She smiled with the confidence of someone who had spent time in the company of nature's gods and goddesses and in a certain manner it was true.

'Well, that's interesting.'

'I knew you'd be glad.' She pecked him on the cheek. 'Your mother was my age when you were conceived.'

'I'd forgotten.'

'Well, now you've been reminded. How are you feeling?'

'To tell the truth. I'm awfully tired. I'm afraid it'll be an early night for me.'

'Me too, then.'

Edgar shook his head. 'Did you forget?' he asked doubtfully. 'We've got the early train up to London in the morning. Jacob and Johanna are already up there. It's June's turn for a visit.'

She had half-hoped her news and enthusiasm might have pushed off June's "turn" for the ritual. 'No, I've not forgotten. Friedrich's going to drive us to the station to catch the five o'clock flyer.'

'He's still here, then?' Edgar replied. 'There's no need for him to do that. Anyway, won't your parents need him around the farm?'

'He's got the weekend off. Apparently, he's got business of his own up there.'

Edgar grimaced and groaned a little as he picked up his suitcase from the platform.

'Fine. It'll be an early night.' Lily winked. 'We'll keep our energy for when we get back.' She looped her arm through his and they walked like that all the way from Honiton station platform to her car. They were in the privacy of the parking lane when she held him close and pushed herself against him.

His smile grew large.

She wondered if he was reconsidering his plans for the night. But nothing else expanded. When you have been in nursing for more than twenty years you notice these kinds of things. All the same, after they got home, they paused in the garden. They held hands and looked at the sky, vast and rich with clouds in shapes that spoke to her.

'It's beautiful, she said.'

'It has a certain contemplative majesty.'

'You think so?' She peered again at the sky and wondered what was up there that she could possibly have missed.

'Tranquil,' he elaborated. 'A classic Devon land sky, languid, just hanging around being passive.'

Lily thought of her father, her grandfather, her brothers all toiling under land skies that were often violent. Storms. Colours that changed in seconds.

'Passive?' she asked and did not hide her doubt.

'Meditative then. Like *Crossing the Bar* .'

His analogies were usually of that kind. Poetic, or nautical, or Welsh. Sometimes all three. It had been part of his attraction. Lily, however, was practical, a farmer's daughter and as English as any rose. Her own analogies were climatic or cyclical. She supposed that had been part of her attraction.

'They couldn't be like ocean skies,' she teased.

'Well,' he said and sighed. 'Ocean skies have more in common with *The Iliad* or *The Odyssey*. But you know all of that.'

'Do I?' She continued to tease him as she pressed his hands and watched the "contemplative land sky" change shape. She felt the tension flow out of his bones and float away. The clouds came together and formed new shapes. She saw babies. They had gilled necks and webbed feet and little boy-bits. Clouds of sea-children. Pods of sea-cadets. The sky was suddenly full of them.

'Look Edgar.' Can you see what your contemplative sky is telling us?

'I've no idea.'

'None at all?' Her voice sounded small.

'Sorry.'

'Why don't men have the bloody menopause?'

'You're a nurse.' He pulled her closer. He held her tightly, and he spoke quietly and calmly. 'You know the answer.'

That was Edgar. He brought tranquillity when waters were turbulent and composure when chaos threatened

***

In India, it had been the first thing she had noticed and came to love about him. After what had happened to her, she decided she could not wait to marry him. She did it out there. Her Mam had been vexed that her only daughter had got married in India. Worse, she had married a sailor and returned home alone with a modest ring on her finger, and an immodest bun in her oven.

'How could he let you come all the way back on your own?' Mam had asked.

'I'm almost thirty years old, Mam!'

Lily had needed to work on Mam. She talked ceaselessly about her "Edgar." She had shown Mam photograph after photograph of Edgar. Mam barely flickered at the photographs. As far as Mam was concerned, Captain Edgar Moulton was a phantom, and his seafaring family even more so. Worse, they came from an odd church, one that Mam frequently confused with another.

She knew that until Mam could see Edgar with her own eyes he might as well not exist. She passed six miserable weeks waiting for Edgar to return from India. There were moments when she wondered if her mother had been right; would Edgar turn up after all? But turn up he did, and Lily did not have to wait over-long for a reaction from her Mam.

'He's awfully calm,' Mam whispered when Edgar had gingerly arisen and headed away to visit the farmhouse bathroom. 'Is that because he's a Methodist?'

'No Mam. It's because he's a Master Mariner.'

'If you say so, dear,' Mam conceded and settled into the warm seat Edgar had just vacated.

'You should have seen how composed he was in India,' Lily repeated for the umpteenth time and tried to sound matter-of-fact. 'Our ship was a sitting target. Most days we were all scared shitless.'

'What did you say?'

'Scared witless, Mam.'

Mam wasn't fooled. Her face turned to stone.

'It was Edgar that kept everyone's morale up.' Lily sounded proud. 'When we were at our lowest ebb, Edgar would have us gather around and quietly recite a poem or tell a story and we'd all feel certain we would see our homes again.'

'Oh, I like how he talks,' Mam answered. 'He's like one of those theatre-hall hypnotists you keep hearing about. Takes his time though. You'd think he had all day to finish whatever it is he has on his mind.' Mam took out Grandfather's cup. For years the superficially cracked heirloom had been on display in their glass-fronted cabinet. It had followed them to every farm they had ever leased. This was the Selfe family's Arthurian monument, and it had waited for someone worthy like Captain Edgar Moulton to come and claim it from its resting place. Mam wiped the cup clean. 'I doubt he'd be much use on a farm, though.' Her voice was prim and steadfast. 'How long does he need to pee?'

'Not everyone's cut out for working on a farm,' Lily riposted.

'I know that,' Mam answered. 'What use would he be if he ran around like a fool when he needed to be phlegmatic? None. He wouldn't be worth a fig.'

'That's right, Mam.' Lily's relief sounded its own note.

Mam patted Lily's belly, 'And we know he can get excited when he's supposed to.'

'Mam!'

'No need to blush.' Mam's eyes sparkled. 'I suppose he's going to be well paid now that this foolish war is ended, and he's got his old job back.'

'Did I tell you Edgar was decorated in India?' Lily asked, remembering her grandfather's often repeated epithet of how courage in the tank beats money in the bank.

'Decorated?' Mam answered. 'You make him sound like a spare room.'

Lily laughed. 'You know perfectly well what I mean.'

'As were you when it comes to that, my dear.' Mam looked Lily squarely in the eyes. 'They don't give those medals out for fun. Do they?'

She had been serving aboard HMHS Salta almost twenty months when it hit a mine on the way into Le Havre. They had practiced what to do. But their rehearsals had been on calm seas, with composed comrades and sufficient time to react. Their reality had been far from that: a stormy sea with panicked comrades and minutes to act. There had been, perhaps, ten-minutes between hitting the mine and HMHS Salta brutally listing and then sinking. Barely time to take a life jacket from the rack and tie it tightly. Lily had been one of only two nurses to survive. Nine of her colleagues drowned, along with forty-two of the medical corps and crew members. Afterwards, they had sent her immediately out to India, straight into the path of Edgar.

'No, I've not forgotten,' Lily spoke softly. 'It's not something one forgets,' she added.

'Anyway, I suppose he makes you feel secure.'

'So, you like him, then?' Lily whispered her question urgently as she heard the flush and the whoosh of water leaving the cistern in a rush.

'Maybe he'll do.' Mam moved crockery around the table. 'It depends how much he likes Devon.'

It turned out he liked Devon a great deal. The bun in the oven, Elizabeth, was delivered in the front room of Edgar's ancestral home, a redbrick, semi-detached house in Wavertree, Liverpool. But they moved back to Honiton before Elizabeth was one year old and found a farm cottage in walking distance of Mam.

***

The following morning, just as daylight traversed Devon they took their seats aboard the flyer. Lily tried to keep the others awake with a running commentary on the magnificence of the light that touched the land, warmed the beasts, brought everything to life and could be seen clearly through the carriage windows.

She was thwarted.

Hardly fifteen minutes passed before Friedrich, Edgar and June closed their eyes and dozed off. Her intentions on quizzing Friedrich about his own plans for his short stay in London came to nothing.

Her family, adopted lodger included, slept and missed the wonder until she gently woke the three of them, one-by-one as the train slowed and pulled into London, Paddington station. Except for Lily, the Devonians emerged from the train with the trepidation of dormice leaving a hibernation

Whilst Friedrich carried June to the taxi queue, Lily carried her aspirations for the weekend close to her chest, and Edgar carried their weekend valises.

In the taxi-cab they hushed so that June might return to her dreams and they only woke her as they pulled into the courtyard of the Savoy and it was time to kiss Friedrich goodbye.

'Good luck, June,' Friedrich said with enthusiasm.

Lily directed the taxi-cab driver to their own lodgings, a modest hotel, located significantly closer to the epicentre of Edgar's universe and where they intended to rapidly deposit their luggage and arrive at the the London Naval Museum sufficiently early to be at the head of the queue.

Plan accomplished, Edgar arranged the taxi fare whilst Lily arranged June's headband. It would be a long day, but at least she would see Johanna. She had been looking forward to that because Johanna told her things that Edgar liked to hide away.

2

FLORENCE

Westbourne Street, London.

When her doorbell rang, Florence was about to cremate a magazine article. Written by Ursula Bloom it was entitled *Tragic Women of Fifty*. She threw the offending piece on the hearth and went to answer the call. She was surprised to see her daughter, Dorothy standing with her nose in the air and her unfashionably shod feet on the doormat of the third-floor apartment.

'*Ciao figlia.* I thought we were meeting later at *La Società*?'

'Something's smoking.'

'Come in and close the door, dear.'

'What's burning?'

Florence shuffled back and stood in front of the nascent fire. She randomly tore several more pages from the *Weekly Dispatch* and threw them atop. She knelt and blew to encourage the flames. Satisfied that Bloom's sorcery had disappeared in a puff of smoke, she answered absently, 'it's just an old magazine.'

Dorothy folded her jacket, deposited it with her handbag on the settee and joined her mother at the hearth.

Florence held her hands out over the fire. 'I was chilly.'

'In July?'

'Wait until you get to my age.' Florence sounded rueful. 'Anyway, give me a proper hug,' she insisted. 'And a proper kiss and tell me why you're here.'

'I thought I'd go with you to the solicitor. Also, I wanted to get your opinion on something before we go to the club, later.'

Florence forced a smile. She wished Dorothy would be more respectful. It was not "the club," it was *La Societa* . And what further opinion could she want? Florence had given her opinion on everything of importance. *Unless. Of course.* Dorothy was thirty-two years old. All of her friends were already long since married. She had seen some positive changes in Dorothy recently. However, she partly feared what it was Dorothy might want to obtain her opinion on.

'You're going through with it?' Dorothy asked. 'This time you're serious?'

'I've never been more serious.'

It had been fifteen years since the hog had left. Ten years since she had given up moping for the return of the swine. The moment had arrived to go "through with it." Time to give up rotting on the vine. She had no intention to be like those tragic women she had read about in the article. No one, whether friend or enemy, kindred or kin, would stand in her way. She consulted the clock on her mantlepiece. 'I'm grateful, dear, but I don't need anyone to come with me.'

'I'm sure dad will be cooperative. He'll probably be relieved.'

She did not care whether her estranged hog would be relieved or not. It was not up to him. He had long since installed himself in his tawdry sty in East Barnet. A banal, two-up, two-down pebbledash construction that resembled every other house in the street. Yes, she had finally been to see it: a chocolate-box dwelling whose façade the hog, with his signature lack of imagination, had screwed a wooden sign onto and named "*Mia Bella*." No doubt his sexy young sow would have considered that to be as unique and sincere an expression of the hog's assessment of her peerless beauty as any man of his age would be expected to make.

For the first years of their marriage the hog used to call Florence the exact same thing. And she used to call him *Il mio bello*. Twenty years ago it was *la mia bella* this and *il mio bello* that. Even when she was pregnant and particularly when she was breast-feeding Dorothy. When Florence looked back on it, she was certain the hog had already begun his philandering back then. He was probably busy being breast-fed himself in East Barnet, or somewhere similar.

'I'll be the one to be relieved.'

'I suppose nothing good came out of your marriage.' Dorothy sounded sad.

'Certainly, something good came out of it. You and a passion for Italy.'

'But you loved Italy before you met dad.'

'True,' Florence acknowledged, and remembered how when she had first met the hog he mistook her for a full-blooded Italian.

***

Later, as she sat in the stuffy waiting room of solicitor W.B.D. Shackleton alongside Dorothy, she listened to the traffic from the street and the rhythmic typewriter tapping of Shackleton's secretary. She studied the secretary, a young woman not unlike Dorothy, which is to say someone who had the potential to make a lot more of her looks if only she made an effort.

She considered recounting the kernel of Ursula Bloom's perspicuity to both younger women, but a well togged, ginger moustachioed man exited the solicitor's office. He smiled at them all, and especially at Florence. She smiled back and decided to share the essence of the article at some other moment. It might even be better if, in due course, the youngsters learnt that lesson for themselves.

The secretary told Florence she could go into Shackleton's office. Florence insisted that Dorothy remain in the waiting room. She crossed the threshold and placed her hat on the lawyer's shiny, oak, hat-stand, and she sat down on one of his tasteless, green-velvet-covered armchairs.

'What brings you here?' the breezy Mr. Shackleton asked.

For a moment she was unsure where to start. Had he not read her letter? She thought of riposting something witty: the usual: sex appeal (someone else's), the beauty and eternal youth of a young temptress. Except of course when she had snuck out to *Mia Bella* she had seen for herself. There was eight years difference between Florence and the young sow, but when she had glimpsed her estranged husband's floozie, she concluded that despite her youthfulness, the scarlet lady was no oil painting. Perhaps she had been prettier when she and the hog had first rooted. But it could not have been her beauty that kept the hog so firmly tied up all these years in East Barnet.

'It's just time,' she answered, and that was close enough to the truth of what had taken her there to his office.

Shackleton's eyebrows chevroned. 'In your letter you mention it's been fifteen years since you separated from your husband.' The lawyer tapped a finger on the letter which lay on the desk.

'Why bother with a divorce now?'

'What if I'd like to get married?' Florence lowered her voice.

'Do you?' Shackleton seemed startled.

'I didn't say that I did,' Florence corrected her over-direct lawyer. She wondered where the female lawyers were. One of them would have suited her better. One of them would not have been asking the silly questions this one did.

'By the way, Mrs. Lantieri, there's no need to whisper.'

'I wouldn't want to be overheard.'

'You needn't worry about that,' Shackleton assured her, and pointed. 'That door is built from solid oak. And what about your estranged husband does he want to remarry?'

She frowned and shook her head. 'I suppose so. I mean he did.'

It was true that she no longer knew whether the hog still wanted to marry his floozie. When he first left Florence, he had definitely wanted to remarry. But since she had never given him "just cause," and was "without fault." He would have needed her submission to a divorce and for that he could have gone to hell. But the circumstances had changed. She assumed the hog would still wish to get married. He had better because she expected Shackleton's fees to be paid by him.

'It's a simple matter of procedure,' Shackleton said. 'But it takes a while longer when it's the wife that initiates the process.'

'Really?' Florence said quickly. 'But he's been living with her fifteen years.' For the first time, she regretted she had not acquiesced when the hog had initially suggested the means by which they could divorce. It had been too raw a moment. And back then she had not yet read Ursula Bloom's article nor met the person who had recently asked her if she had a spare room to rent.

She rose to leave the solicitor's office. 'I'm counting on you to do whatever you can to speed things up.'

Florence stepped into the waiting room which, in addition to Dorothy, now held two other women. She detected the distinctive odour of *lilas pourpre*. She could not help herself. She tutted. It was much too heavy a perfume for an aspiring sophisticated city woman like her only child, Dorothy. *She's probably wearing it to spite me,* she thought and she remembered an evening six months previously when she had told Dorothy *lilas pourpre* gave her the odour of a farm-girl desperately trying to mask hours of toil mucking out the stalls, or some old biddy dressed in a sack and marking her card at Bermondsey bingo hall. Dorothy's response had been to say nothing but disappear the following weekend and waste another three-shillings-nine-pence buying another bottle of the stuff.

Florence had wondered why, until she remembered Fortunato had recently told Dorothy that she smelled interesting. "It's not exactly a compliment," Florence had responded when Dorothy told her. "If he had told you that you smelled sensual, that would have been a compliment." But evidently, being "interesting" was quite sufficient for Dorothy.

Florence had not failed to notice that since then her daughter had rediscovered the cultural programme of *La Società* and had started coming back there every month. Likely because she could occasionally "bump into" Fortunato. She had even begun taking Italian lessons, which was worse than pointless since she was fluent from the moment she could speak.

As they walked away from Shackleton's office, Dorothy finally asked, 'I wanted to ask you about Fortunato.'

'Is that why you've been coming along and taking all these Italian lessons at *La Società*?'

Dorothy giggled.

'I had hoped you would aim a little higher,' Florence scolded.

'Why, what's wrong with Fortunato?'

'I mean a hotel banqueting assistant manager.' Florence was on the brink of punctuating with her fingers.

'We're talking about the London Savoy here,' Dorothy answered as though that made Fortunato a Duke and her a prospective Duchess.

'You know he was a waiter on a transatlantic liner?'

'What about it?'

'He shared a bunk-room with several other sailors,' Florence delivered what she hoped would be a *coup de grace*, and she winked. 'For two years!'

Dorothy looked glum. 'Are you suggesting what I think you might be?'

'I'm just saying,' Florence answered softly. 'Haven't you ever wondered how come he's still unattached?'

'You seem friendly enough with him.' Dorothy stopped walking and turned toward Florence.

'Do I?' Florence replied, and her face reddened. 'Well, he's been through a lot.'

'How come you know so much?'

Florence shrugged. 'He's usually early for his appointments and he chats a lot. Been coming back often too.' She avoided Dorothy's stare.

'Yes, I've noticed that. He seems atypical in his interest in oral hygiene. Wouldn't you say?'

Florence cleared her throat. It was perhaps a mistake to work in the same dental establishment as her daughter. But it was not her fault if Dorothy had the wrong ideas. Dorothy ought to stick to someone her own age. Not someone who had fought in a war. They were never the same after a war. Dorothy ought to consider someone with better prospects. 'Anyway, I thought you liked that other chap, Charlie Churchman. He seems more your type, modern, and he's awfully fond of you.'

'Maybe you're right,' Dorothy said but sounded unsure as she restarted them on the route home.

The discussion, and the day too, had gone better than Florence feared it might. She had given Dorothy good advice and had, herself, taken a step toward something she knew that she deserved. She imagined herself about to re-bloom, and the days and nights ahead of her suddenly held great potential. There was no harm done, and Charlie Churchman definitely had better financial prospects than Fortunato Picchi, who was so poorly paid he was looking for cheaper lodgings.

3

INGEBORG

Savoy Hotel, London.

Ingeborg loitered in the corridor. Through tall, colourfully paned restaurant windows she spotted Günther and Bert already situated at the breakfast table. Around them, every table had been set with a similar floral-patterned teapot and matching crockery of cups and saucers. It was as though a geriatric home had chosen to visit London for the weekend.

Günther spotted her and he mouthed, '*wo ist Friedrich?*'

'He's not here yet,' she mouthed back. She pointed at Günther's breakfast plate where a forlorn poached egg, a single slice of bacon and a thin finger of toasted bread had been artistically placed some ten minutes previously. 'Yummy,' she mimed and rubbed her belly.

Bert took the opportunity of Günther's distraction to tip the contents of Günther's plate into his own dish. It was to be expected since Bert had already eaten his own breakfast and his appetite could never be less than Günther's. In an instant, Günther entered a tug-of-war to recover his breakfast.

Though she had paid her own way, their laddish games

provoked a pang of regret. Had she done the right thing joining them on this trip? On the other hand, it was hardly a secret what Günther's plans were. She still did not know what her own response would be. Perhaps she would accept. Perhaps she would politely say, "it's not the moment."

The light was low, but she snapped another grainy memory before she turned away and resumed her search for Friedrich. She wandered up and down the corridor and casually observed the other guests on their way to the breakfast room. They were, for the most part, the same docile elderly couples: posh old women with pearls, and bald men with liver freckles and creaking brown brogues whom she had met the prior night. She watched the couples slowly canter toward the breakfast room and she was reminded of a herd of genteel bovines in some hushed English pastoral landscape. She had become engrossed in watching the seniors and had not noticed Friedrich had strolled up behind her.

He tapped her on the shoulder.

She jumped. 'Creeping Jesus.'

He was dressed as though he might have been a regular client of the Savoy. 'Good morning, Fräulein.' He placed a brown leather Gladstone bag on the floor next to his feet and asked her in a peculiar accent, 'where's Cain and Abel?'

She supposed Friedrich's crusty English accent was for the benefit of the Savoy staff, or perhaps to impress her. '*Guten Morgen*,' she answered. 'They're finishing breakfast,' she added and before he could protest she snapped a photograph of him then briskly strode toward the breakfast room. They had almost reached it when Günther and Bert came through the swing doors.

'Friedrich, good to see you.' Günther hugged Friedrich and proffered him the room key he held in his hand. 'You can leave your bag in our room.'

'Thanks,' Friedrich replied.

Bert gave Friedrich a ritualistic crushing that masqueraded as a handshake. It was a habit he had begun several months previously when he had turned twenty-two years old. 'Shalom,' he said and squeezed harder. 'Who'd have imagined us, meeting here?'

Friedrich barely winced. 'Since we are meeting here, you could just as well call me Fred.'

'Fred?' Ingeborg tilted her freshly brushed blond-bob hairdo.

'They have a weakness for the diminutive form here,' Friedrich answered.

'Does Friedrich sound too foreign for them?' Günther asked.

'Much too alien,' Friedrich said playfully. 'My landlady confuses it with fried rice, and therefore, "Fred" it is.'

The friends laughed and Ingeborg took another photograph.

'She's gathering memories for Mother.' Günther placed an arm around Friedrich's shoulder. 'We've already got our taxi ordered. It's not too late to come with us if you change your mind.'

'Are you joking?' Friedrich picked up his bag. 'I'm starved. We'll see each other later.'

'You look different' Günther said. 'What have you done to yourself?'

'What do you mean?'

'For a start,' Günther answered, 'I've never seen your hair that long. Nor seen you dressed like a banker.'

Friedrich did look odd. All the way from his perfectly knotted tie to his shiny cufflinks and fancy pants waistcoat and jacket.

'Fred the bohemian banker!' Bert spoke through a mouthful of hot croissant. 'That's what Bea would call you.'

'Listen to Bert-the-Dancer,' Friedrich replied rapier-like.

Bert winced.

They all knew how much Bert despised dancing, especially ballet. However, Bea had chosen the perfect nickname for him: dark complexion, high cheekbones — for a male — and snarled up lips that always seemed to be caught in the act of hiding a thought.

Inevitably, Bea had called him, "Nijinsky," and despite Bert's protests, it stuck.

Ingeborg leant in and whispered, 'any news of Bea?'

'She's still in Vienna,' Friedrich answered and you could see in his face that wore all-of-the-worries-of-the-world that Vienna, with his girlfriend, was where he wanted to be.

A quietness fell over the quartet.

'Vienna's a good place right now,' Bert said.

'Safer than a lot of other places,' Günther added.

'I suppose it is,' Friedrich answered. 'At least she's not alone. My parents and sister are with her.'

***

Ingeborg had been present right at the beginning when Friedrich had latched on to Bea in the beer-house near the Academy. Although Bea was a year ahead of Friedrich and she had many options, somehow it was the pale-faced, first-year medical school student from Stralsund who summoned the confidence to ask Bea for a date. Bea had been quick to answer, "ok, why not?"

For the following eighteen months, Bea, the loudest, most colourful and wittiest art student to occupy any beer house lounge in Leipzig, tottered through the city streets as though she was a slightly inebriated Shakespearean female lead and, on her arm, cast in the role of Benedick, was the unassuming Friedrich.

Bea had nicknames for them all: Nijinksy for Bert, and Day-Dreamer-Lena for Ingeborg because Ingeborg reminded her of Lena Dietrich in *The Ship of Lost Souls*. — Ingeborg had gone to see that film three times and although she considered the comparison a flattering exaggeration, she took to styling her hair in the same manner Lena did — and from then on Bea addressed her as Lena or Dietrich.

When Günther showed up *torse nu* for their art-life classes, Bea nicknamed him Ulysses on account of him being a sailor. "Heh Ulysses," Bea called out, "want to come to my party?" When Günther seemed to hesitate, Bea winked and added "Lena's going to be there." Bea had omitted to mention that an admirer of Ingeborg's would also be there. But, in Bea's opinion, that other chap: the Somnambulist Banker as she had nicknamed him, was not the man for Ingeborg. "Dump the somnambulist," Bea had repeatedly told Ingeborg, "Ulysses is more your type." Until then, Ingeborg had wondered if Bea secretly had a soft spot for Günther.

***

Günther stepped back, as though he wanted a different angle from which he could better admire the peculiar combination of Friedrich's three-piece-suit and long hair. 'I'd pay to see Bea's expression if she could see you now.'

'Me too,' Friedrich replied.

Once again, they all heard his sadness.

'Anyway, how is my favourite Leipzig couple?' Friedrich said and embraced Günther and Ingeborg in sham gaiety. 'How are things in Leipzig?'

Ingeborg exchanged looks with Günther. She could have answered: well thanks to Günther's mother I have a job. And thanks to *Herr* Hitler, Günther has a job. It is considerably below his qualifications but it is better than unemployment. She might have added, Leipzig is not what it used to be. But none of that would be news to Friedrich because he and Bea would not have needed to disappear if Leipzig had remained what it was.

Leipzig was certainly lonelier since Bea and Friedrich had needed to escape. But at least Bea was safely hidden in Vienna and thanks to the Jewish Refugee Committee, Friedrich was now safely hidden in England. Everyone missed Bea's silly sobriquets and everyone missed Friedrich and all the other medical students whom the JRC had spirited away. Ingeborg could have said all of this, but instead she found herself at a loss for words.

'We're fine,' Günther said. 'But Leipzig is tense.'

Bert licked the last remaining crumbs from his thumbs. 'You know,' he said and shook his head, 'I don't think you should allow them to call you Fred.'

'I'm sure it's not out of disrespect,' Ingeborg asserted.

'It's not that,' Bert insisted. 'He doesn't look much like a Fred.'

'How do you imagine a Fred might look?'

'I'm not certain,' Bert answered. 'But in my mind, I'm seeing something different. Probably more country bumpkin than country squire.'

Friedrich smirked. 'Well, if you could see what I do for work.' 'You're assisting someone in Harley Street. Correct?' Ingeborg asked. 'Finishing your medical studies, right?'

'Where did you hear that?' Friedrich sounded surprised. 'Was it Bea? She knows I'm still waiting for the British Medical Association to recognise my existing studies. I can't take up accredited study or work in a hospital here until they allow it.'

'Then, what work are you doing here?' Ingeborg asked.

'Currently, I'm picking potatoes.'

'You're a potato picker?' Günther tilted an ear as though he had not properly heard. 'Medical students pick potatoes here?'

'The BMA are worried about foreigners,' Friedrich replied. 'If the situation changes maybe I can go back to medicine. Meantime, I pick potatoes and round up cows.'

'And what about the National Gallery?' Ingeborg asked. 'Part-time guide in the Prussian Art Section? Is that true?'

'I've not seen you look that serious before Ingeborg,' Friedrich said. 'Bea would never forgive me if I didn't keep that up.'

'Otherwise, all her efforts on you would have been wasted,' Bert said.

'Which reminds me,' Günther said, 'Clara sends her love.'

'How is your mother?' Friedrich asked.

'She's coping,' Ingeborg answered in Günther's place.

Clara was the beacon that brought them all together. She had taught Bea and Ingeborg. She had secured Ingeborg's role at the Academy of Fine Arts. And since Günther now spent most of his time in Kiel, hundreds of kilometres from Leipzig, she made sure that Ingeborg was not lonely.

'Mother would have loved to come here with us,' Günther added.

Bert walked ahead to the hotel exit.

For a moment there was a silence, until Bert returned. 'No sign of it.' Bert sounded impatient. 'What are your plans for today?'

'It's the twins' birthday,' Friedrich replied. He turned to Ingeborg. 'If you can get to the synagogue earlier you might join their little party.'

'The twins?' Bert asked, perplexed. 'What twins?'

'That's partly why I'm all suited up,' Friedrich answered. 'I'll be having cake with Günther's cousins. I owe them a lot.'

'You have cousins in the JRC?' Bert turned to Günther and sounded confused.

'Not first cousins,' Günther said. And with less haste he added, 'and they're not members of the Refugee Committee either, although they know people who are.'

On the hotel concourse the brakes of a taxi-cab squealed loudly. Bert stared for the source of the noise.

'Maternal side,' Günther spoke falteringly. 'Mother's aunt's family. Like cousins once-removed. Or maybe twice-removed.'

'Plenty of us like that,' Friedrich said.

'Like what?' Bert asked.

'Once or twice removed,' Friedrich let the hurt twist his lips for a moment. 'Stateless is becoming all the rage.'

The taxi-cab engine thunked repeatedly and whilst the taxi-cab made a turn of 180° Günther handed two envelopes to Friedrich. 'These are for the twins, from their Aunt Clara.'

'Maybe see you later, then,' Friedrich said. He popped the envelopes in his jacket pocket. 'You have the address? Portland Street. In front of the synagogue. Around five o'clock?'

'I doubt we'll be finished by then,' Günther replied, saving Bert the trouble.

'I don't think tea with cousins-once-removed, nor even high Prussian art will deprive Günther and Bert of their moment of divine worship,' Ingeborg teased. 'We'll be lucky to see them back here in time for dinner.'

'They could join us at the National afterwards. It's open late,' Friedrich said.

'If we're not there by closing time,' Günther replied, 'we'll see you back here.'

In unison Günther and Bert hugged Ingeborg and Friedrich and then hurried away to their waiting taxi.

Günther and Bert's plans for London had never taken any account of a potential visit to the National Galleries or the Royal Academy. They had always been clear to Ingeborg about their own intentions: a full day spent in Greenwich, worshipping in the churches of their own choice — the Naval Museum and the Royal Observatory. Their numinous would occur when they could gaze in awe at artefacts with names as peculiar as Muller's Cosmosphere and the Astrolabe.

'Your bag can wait. Let's have breakfast first,' Ingeborg said. 'Eat as much as you like. It's all on us.' She led Friedrich back toward the breakfast room. She felt some relief. Perhaps she and Friedrich might talk more candidly there. They breezed in and took their seats. Newspapers fluttered like monochrome muletas at the adjacent tables and the elderly English couples continued to ignore each other.

Friedrich poured tea whilst Ingeborg nervously flattened a

napkin. 'The truth is they're all over Leipzig now,' she whispered. 'They're taking over everything.'

'That's what they said about us.'

'You shouldn't joke, Friedrich. They've even kicked Willi Geiger and Hugo Steiner-Prag out of the Academy.'

'Bea will be disappointed. What's their problem with those two old fogeys?'

'Same problem as with you,' she answered.

Friedrich shrugged. 'Didn't Steiner-Prag do a Mendelssohn?' he asked, and something weighed his words down.

Ingeborg had friends and neighbours who had "done a Mendelssohn." Even children were busy being converted to whatever religion or sect might offer sanctuary and permit them to be sent out of the country. But the National Socialists were making it difficult. When looking for that lack of purity, they had ways to trace right back to your great-grandparents. Steiner-Prag had been a Christian for thirty years, but because he could not go back in time and convert his parents and grandparents they threw him out of the Academy. Same story for Willi Geiger.

'Have they been invited to practice their art in Dachau for their own protection yet?'

'Not yet,' Ingeborg answered.

He looked at her as though he felt sympathy for her. 'It's some form of psychosis that has taken over. Not only in Germany and Italy. Spain, Portugal, and Hungary all have their versions of it you know,' he whispered and looked around to ensure none of the locals were listening. 'It's here too. And they're also in denial. They think it'll all calm down. That everyone will wake up and then all of us "refugees" can go back home.'

'Maybe they're right,' Ingeborg said. 'Perhaps there will be a wake up and everyone will be able to go home.'

'Home? Where's home for me? There's none of my kind left in Stralsund.'

'You could stay here. Make a new home like Günther's cousins, twice-removed.'

He stopped his arm in mid-flight, a slice of cold toast in his hand. 'The Neufelds are smart, they saw what was happening. They came here a few years ago. They didn't wait until they couldn't finish their studies or practice their profession in Germany.'

There was a silence between them before he spoke again. 'Anyway, I've decided to leave here and go to Vienna.' His hands shook as he poured the dregs of the teapot.

'You shouldn't do that.'

'I've got to complete my medical degree somewhere. And if things do get worse in Vienna at least I'll be able to get Bea and the family out.'

'And if they don't want to leave?'

'I'll stay there with them.'

'Then Bea will be stuck with you after all?' Ingeborg grinned.

'And Günther will be stuck with you.'

'I suppose he will.'

'Bea always said you preferred Mariners to Somnambulists.'

Ingeborg laughed. 'But no one ever asked me if I preferred Mariners to Medical Students.' She reddened a little at the low-hanging cloud of discomfiture that drifted over them.

They both appeared to be looking for the door marked *Ausgang* when Friedrich broke the silence. 'Bea always said the Somnambulist Banker would wake up one day and come looking for you and ask you to marry him.'

'He'd better do it soon then because Günther's got a job and Clara's got prospective mother-in-law ideas and I'm feeling all round enamoured.'

'Bea also said you were more in love with Clara than you were with Günther.'

'Tell Bea I miss her.'

'I will,' he assured her and twirled a teaspoon in his teacup.

'I suppose if things do get difficult in Vienna you can always come back here and pick potatoes.'

This time Friedrich laughed. 'That'll be me. Picking potatoes with surgical precision.'

'They can put that specialty on your medical degree,' Ingeborg replied.

4

THE WATCHAMACALLIT

Naval Museum, London.

As soon as the museum doors opened, Lily announced she would make a short visit to the ladies' room. Before disappearing, she left the necessary instructions with her rotund but beloved husband, Edgar, and their boyish daughter, June. 'I know where I'll find you. Don't move.'

Fifteen minutes elapsed before Lily stepped out of the ladies' toilet. She adjusted her pleated linen skirt and meandered in the direction of the "leading exhibit." Her husband and daughter were located precisely where they should have been. In the meantime, they had been joined by Jacob and Johanna and a little group of acolytes. Lily veered behind a minor exhibit and surreptitiously observed. Like a school of fish, the group had gathered in a semi-circle and gawped in wonderment and nodded their heads in synchrony at the object held in the large purpose-built glass display cabinet.

If the "leading exhibit" display had contained a mark2 autoclave promising increased theatre-mobility and reduced sterilising times, Lily would have sidled up and had her nose against the glass with the little group of gawpers. But it was a *whatchamacallit*, some ancient nautical artefact of explicable interest to the kedger community but holding barely an incidental interest to Lily. If she could only have remembered what the gadget was called, or even what its purpose was, she may have waded in amongst them and confidently added a comment or two. Instead, she contented herself with an appreciative look at Edgar, who had returned rather tanned from his three-month cruise.

Although Edgar's wardrobe contained a cornucopia of smart and casual, dark clothes, specifically selected by Lily to flatter his portly silhouette, it was true that nothing did the job so well as his uniform. He looked handsome in his Blue Star Line captain's uniform and she had happily conceded he ought to wear it on this visit. However, it had taken some maternal authority to ensure June was not similarly dressed. June's interest in the navigator's dress code seemed an omen. She would be the one to pass her father's disguised test. Edgar never talked of their museum trip ritual in exactly those terms. Likely, he never even thought of it in those terms either but Lily knew better. This ritual trip to the naval museum was only about two things: firstly, it was Edgar's chance to meet up again — in the usual place — with Jacob Burfeind his distinctively bearded almost brethren friend and captain of the *Adolph Woermann*, and secondly it was their chance to learn whether Lily had succeeded in producing a future seafaring Moulton, a task which she had not yet accomplished and which continued to distress her.

Edgar had his hand on June's head, as though to reassure himself that none of the ancient mariner's knowledge he stuffed in there was in danger of seeping out, but he seemed not to be fully concentrated on June. He had turned to address Johanna Burfeind, the smartly attired wife of Jacob. He was so distracted he succeeded in knocking June's hair-band off-kilter and poor June was so absorbed in lapping up everyone's attention she had not yet registered that her blue fabric tiara of forget-me-nots was lopsided.

Several of the gawping foreigners, also German by the sound of them, seemed enthralled by whatever it was Edgar was telling them. All the while Edgar regaled his audience with his stories of ancient navigation and ghostly navigators, the group pointed excitedly at the darn *whatchamacallit* and were utterly transfixed. The gadget had rendered them all giddy. Even Johanna Burfeind bobbed around excitedly and knocked June's little tiara hairband further off-centre.

Finally, Lily stepped out from behind the display cabinet. She coughed robustly and smiled in Edgar's direction and then she pointed her boss finger to the door marked "Tea Room," and strode toward it. She expected Johanna to follow soon, and Edgar and the others would, after a while, meander in too. She naturally assumed that several of his newly acquired foreign fan club would come plodding along behind him. It happened every visit: amiable friends, Edgar and Jacob, would invite anyone that might qualify as a navigator a.k.a. kedger to join them for tea.

In the meantime, Johanna remained with the others. Lily had the Tea Room to herself. She gathered up half a dozen menus and immediately turned one over. Edgar would be delighted. Printed on the back, they had retained the odd illustrations and the kedger's code. She consulted a board containing that day's list of "specials." Half a dozen types of cake, including ginger cake. All was good in the world. Cake made Edgar happy. Any kind of cake would suffice, but considering her plans for when she got him back home, ginger cake was especially perfect — regardless of what her brothers might think.

According to her brothers, Edgar had returned to her a little less "lithesome" this particular shore-leave. Even if she might have agreed with them, there were no circumstances in which she would ever confess it. "We're all knocking on," had been her response.

"Some of us are less prone to double chins," her older brother insisted. "A random genetic accident," she reminded them. Thus, there would be plenty of cake, especially ginger cake, and she expected Edgar to know why. She had dropped him plenty of hints.

Eventually, the others drifted noisily into the Tea Room.

Although Lily had been surprised that Johanna had not come in earlier, she thought she understood the reason why. She saw at-a-glance how much Johanna was enraptured with June. As were the latest members of Edgar's fan club who tagged along. It was not often that one came across a five-year-old English girl as authentically enthused by all things nautical. At that age neither of June's older sisters could name and tie half of the knots that June could.

Lily rose and welcomed the group. She distributed the cafeteria menu that had so captivated Edgar and Jacob on their last visit. She waited for their reaction, whilst Edgar enthusiastically introduced the newest members of his fan club to her.

'This is Günther and Bert,' Edgar said as the two young men pulled up enough seats for all of them. 'They're countrymen of Jacob's.'

'I suppose it was Jacob who dragged you gentlemen out to the museum,' Lily remarked.

'Not at all,' Jacob defended himself. 'We just met. They're here on their own pilgrimage.'

Lily liked that a new generation of kedgers, younger and easier on the eye, could be as interested in the Naval Museum as older salts like Edgar and Jacob. Whilst Günther and Bert took it in turns to kiss her hand, she noticed neither man wore a wedding ring. 'Nice to meet you, both.' She smiled broadly and pointed to a large advance plate of ginger cake already on the table. 'I thought you all might like some of this whilst you're waiting.'

Johanna shook her head. The ginger cake would not be for her.

Instead, she consulted a menu amongst the pile spread on the table.

Meanwhile, June had evidently already decided what she wanted. 'Can I have two donuts?' she asked. 'And milk.' And then she turned the menu over and blurted, 'look everyone it's got Muller's Cosmosphere on it.'

They turned over their menus and Lily realised, beyond the definition of *Dead Reckoning* and several busy illustrations of planets and stars and tides and ships and monsters, there was an illustration of the lead exhibit: Muller's Cosmosphere. The darn *whatchamacallit* had been there all that time under her nose.

'Mum, it's great here,' June said.

'And we've barely started,' Edgar added.

'Calm down, dear,' Lily said, perhaps to June, perhaps to Edgar.

'Daddy's friends want to join in the quiz.'

'I thought they might,' Lily answered and sighed. She hoped they could at least order tea before they launched into a discussion of things she found unintelligible. Fortunately, a waiter came to take their orders. After the orders were taken, Lily said, 'I imagine June roped you in to help her with her dad's quiz?'

'Your daughter doesn't need our help,' Günther, the blond foreigner said. His English was impeccable and his voice a rich baritone, like an opera singer. 'I think she knows more than us,' he added and laughed.

'Possibly.' Edgar said.

Lily recognised a pride in Edgar's eyes. She had seen a similar pride, or was it anxiety, when it had been the turns of June's elder sisters, in that same tearoom, undergoing that same ritual. Would it end differently this time?

***

In the absence of a son, Elizabeth had been the trailblazing Moulton daughter; the first of their three surviving children to make the trip up to London. Elizabeth had been just as keen to try and please her Daddy. She had revised her list of nautical terms on the train journey up. And when it came to the mid-tour quiz in the tea-room, Elizabeth had seemed undaunted too: "I'm ready, Daddy," Elizabeth had said. "All right Elizabeth, darling," Edgar had reassured. "What's a funnel?" he asked. Elizabeth had paused and then answered, "a hill where you go to have fun?" Edgar gently laughed and Lily had too. "No, sweetie, not a fun-hill a fun-nel." Lily had known there was little chance that Elizabeth would correctly answer more than a few of Edgar's remaining questions concerning anything nautical. Nevertheless, it was plain, Edgar had enjoyed Elizabeth's attempts and there was a bonus: they had met Jacob and Johanna for the first time on that trip.

Five years later, it had been Cilla's turn. Lily was the one to insist, not Edgar. Same place. Same routine. June was only two years old, back then, and Lily was already pregnant with the next applicant. Thus, should Cilla, like Elizabeth before her, not make the grade, there were reserves in abundance: June and whomever was in the belly. A boy, perhaps? On that occasion too, Lily had gone immediately to pass time in the Tea Room — she had chatted with Johanna and they read magazines and ate peculiar cheese and jam sandwiches and she had learned things from Johanna about Edgar. Things that she did not know if she believed. Johanna had said Edgar does not care about having a son. Who needs another Moulton, heavy with the obligation to go to sea and all that goes with it? Lily could not see it that way. She supposed Edgar was pretending not to care whilst still desperately hoping his wife would produce a son. When Edgar and Jacob showed up with Cilla, Lily had not dared to imagine that Cilla's answers would be as creative as they turned out to be. "How about the stern, Cilla, darling, can you remember what that means?" Edgar had asked. "I know that one," Cilla answered and she had run on the spot with excitement. "Excellent," Edgar answered. "What does it mean?" Cilla sniffed and tilted her head as though it was all too easy. "Stern means angry." Cilla said. Lily had laughed uncontrollably and thought her waters would burst. At least there was June and another candidate growing in the belly. Lily's pregnancy ended in a miscarriage. Edgar had been at sea. She had pretended the gender was unknown.

***

Now here they were, back in London and all hope rested on her energetic daughter, June who seemed eager to begin, and her own feeble menstrual cycle which seemed eager to end.

'All right, June,' Edgar said. 'What's the purpose of the Crow's Nest?'

'Don't be silly, Daddy. I know you're teasing me. You want me to say, it's where crows lay their eggs.'

'Well?' Edgar asked. 'What is it?'

'You know what it is. It's a lookout.' June's blue eyes sparkled with chutzpah.

'But wait a minute,' Edgar replied, 'do you know which particular mast it's fitted on?'

Günther, whispered something to June.

'Yes, Daddy, it's on the Main Mast,'

'*Ja!*' there was a collective shout from June's supporters as Jacob, Johanna, Günther and even Bert, the shorter, quieter, darker skinned fellow also winked and gave a thumbs-up to June.

June winked back and nodded with such vigour her crown of forget-me-nots finally dropped off.

Johanna picked up June's crown and sat it back on her head.

'Can I ask your sea-cadet a question?' Günther asked and whispered the question in Edgar's ear.

'That's a great one,' Edgar said.

'All right, young lady,' Günther asked, 'where's the Poop Deck located?'

June scratched her arm. Then sniffed haughtily. She turned to face Edgar. 'He means the Bridge, doesn't he?'

'*Ja!*' Another shout from June's supporters and this time Johanna clapped as though relieved and hugged June.

Jacob unwrapped a replica of the contraption they had all been giddy for and popped it on the middle of the table.

'Look Mam,' June said, 'it's a little Muller's Cosmosphere.'

The others seemed fascinated. Lily feigned an interest. 'It's unique.' She nodded approvingly.

'It's a full working model,' Edgar said.

'I knew that,' Lily said. 'It says so on the box.'

'Thanks to Edgar,' Jacob said, 'these boys just received a lesson in how to operate it.'

'They don't teach this anymore in the modern schools of seamanship.' Günther held the Cosmosphere tenderly in his hands.

'We still get taught the theory, though,' Bert said. 'But nowadays no one knows how to handle these old instruments. Radio Direction Finder, RDF, is what it's about now.'

Lily exchanged a look with Johanna who sipped her tea and pretended to studiously read the back of the menu.

I'm not following them either,' Johanna said and grinned. 'I'm just re-reading the kedger's code.' She held up the menu as though to establish an alibi for tuning out.

Lily was reassured to realise that RDF meant as much to Johanna as it meant to her. She had an urge to lean in closer to Edgar and whisper that she was impatient for him to handle an "old instrument" when they got home. She resisted the urge but chuckled at her own audacity.

'What's so amusing, dear?' Edgar asked.

'I'll tell you later.' Lily sipped her tea and watched and listened whilst Edgar explained afresh some other element of how the gadget worked.

Lily tuned in and out whilst one of the others would ask a question and Edgar would manipulate the object or point at it or scrawl something on the back of the menu.

One moment they talked about geometry, the next moment they talked of the celestial system and then she heard them become enthused about RDF again, but when their conversation inevitably turned to the navigator's code, Lily smiled. Finally, a matter she knew plenty about: *Dead Reckoning*. After fourteen years of being married to Edgar, she knew perfectly well what the kedgers' code was. It was more than a metaphor for how to live your life. It was a philosophy of sorts for those who choose to be an actor and not a spectator in their own lives. Who amongst them knew more about that than she did? Perhaps only Edgar.

'It's simple.' Edgar took a pen to his own copy and circled the terms: *Leeway, Current, Helmsman*, and *Gyro* — 'you choose a few terms, then replace them with your own and you'll have a kedger's code for living.' He held the menu up for the others to see.

Jacob smiled mysteriously at his two countrymen and then whispered something to Johanna.

A kedger's code?' Günther asked doubtfully.

'He means navigator,' June interjected.

Edgar grinned. 'I'm surprised you lads haven't already picked that up, given all the time you've served on British merchant vessels.'

Günther shrugged and exchanged looks with Bert.

Jacob had already begun to replace the words with his choice of German words, which were probably the same as last time. He folded his copy and put it in his trouser pocket.

'What do you have?' Günther asked Jacob.

'Everyone has to do their own,' June said crossly.

'How can it be a navigator's code, if every navigator has to have their own version?' Günther sounded perplexed. '

'That's the point,' Edgar said. 'It has to *belong* to you.' Günther squinted at his copy and pursed his lips, as though ideas might be forming.

Edgar looked over the top of Günther's menu. 'I'll leave my telephone number here on your copy,' Edgar said. 'Call me if you ever need help creating your own.'

Lily chuckled. Edgar had given their number out again.

'I see what it is,' Günther said in the manner of someone who expected an enigma to be more of a challenge. 'It's about knowing where we are and how we got here, right?'

'Me too,' Bert said and completed his own substitutions for the encircled terms and pocketed his copy of the menu.

'No,' Lily said because she knew what it all meant to Edgar. 'It's not about knowing where you are but who you are.'

'We'll bring our children here in the future,' Bert said as though annoyed he had not figured it out. 'They can even do Captain Moulton's quiz.'

'I doubt they'd do as well as June.' Günther smiled at June.

'What do you have?' Lily asked. 'Boy or girl?'

Bert squirmed on his seat. 'Neither. I don't even have a girlfriend. Günther's always been the lucky one.' Bert shot a glance at Günther. 'But that's how things are in Germany. First you have to find a job and then, if you're fortunate, like Günther, you find the girl.'

Lily cast a look somewhere between sympathy and consolation at Bert. 'Well, I wouldn't leave it too long.' She placed her arm around Edgar's shoulder. 'You've got to act when the chance is there.'

'It won't be long,' Günther said. 'We're expecting Bert's employment offer to come through any day,' and he looked fraternally into Bert's eyes.

'You shouldn't leave it too long either,' Lily addressed Günther. 'If you know what I mean.'

'I don't intend to. But my girlfriend's not in a hurry.'

'Pity you didn't bring her with you,' Lily answered. 'We could have had a little word. Right Johanna?'

Johanna put down her teacup, and quietly said, 'yes.'

'There's no chance she'd come here,' Bert said. 'She's not entirely smitten by all things nautical, is she?'

Günther looked at his watch. 'She's more interested in art.'

Bert also looked at his watch. 'Probably on her way to meet Friedrich about now.'

Lily leant across the table as though she was alone with Günther and asked him quietly, 'do I understand there's some competition?'

Apart from June, who still concentrated on the illustrations on the back of the menu, the entire group laughed aloud.

'Absolutely not.' Günther locked eyes with Bert. 'Friedrich's a good friend. He has his own fiancée in Vienna.'

Small world. Lily knew someone called Friedrich who also had a fiancée in Vienna. Lily passed around the ginger cake.

Johanna declined cake for herself but took two slices for Jacob.

Bert accepted a small slice.

Günther seemed hesitant.

'You'd better not wait too long,' Lily suggested softly. 'Otherwise, someone else will have it.'

'Message received,' Günther said.

5

GOLEM TRIPLETS

Portland Street, London.

Ingeborg stood opposite the synagogue in Portland Street. Friedrich had described it as "Gothic style" and that had been enough to guarantee she would want to get there early and sketch it. She had taken two photographs before she sensed she was not the only visitor interested in the view. At the street corner a trio of men loitered.

All three men wore baggy black trousers and black turtle-neck jumpers. They had short, greased-back hair. Two of them dark headed and the other fair headed. Ingeborg had become used to seeing fascists in Leipzig and this British version seemed to carry little menace. For one thing, it was broad daylight and locals walked unmolested in the street. Nevertheless, the triplets' interest in the church made her uneasy. She pretended to be aiming at nothing in particular and clicked the camera in their direction. Clara's Kodak Retina was not top of the range and the snap was probably out of focus. Better to memorise some markers: the fair haired one was thin, tall, and clean shaven. Of the dark headed fellows, one of them was also tall but thuggish, the other one rather short. And there was something comedic about the shorter one. Both wore a moustache. What would Bea have called them? Ingeborg was still wondering about sobriquets when the triplets left the scene.

She returned the camera to her bag and removed her pocket sketch-pad. She held the pad expertly in the crutch of her left arm and began outlining. She was engrossed in her sketch and had pushed the black-jumpers out of her mind when in the periphery of her vision, the trio reappeared and headed in her direction.

They stopped by her side, as though interested in what she was doing. The fair haired one got close and looked over her shoulder. She stood her ground. She smiled at him and noticed a scar that ran from his ear to his mouth. Had he not been disfigured he could have been handsome.

'Waiting on someone, love?' Disfigured asked her and his voice was mellow and confident, as though a question of that type ought to be considered innocuous.

Ingeborg considered it none of his business. She ignored his question. She returned her sketch-pad to her bag and waited for a car to pass before she strode across the road. There was no need to look back, she heard from their laughter that the three men had followed her.

On the opposite pavement, two elderly women paused to look in her direction. Ingeborg smiled hopefully but the elderly women ambled away. She quickened her pace and walked toward the synagogue. She stopped abruptly in her tracks.

The triplets did likewise.

Ingeborg turned to face them. She folded her arms purposefully and slowly. Her heartbeat sped involuntarily and unevenly. She looked them over: three cankered golems. Suppose she had to pick them out in an identity parade? Disfigured. Thug and what about the short one? His clothes belonged to another body: jacket sleeves that reached his knuckles and trousers gathered under his pot belly and a perfect little version of a Hitlerian moustache that seemed to have been drawn on his face. He appeared more circus clown than storm trooper and except for his sneer, which held a menace equal to that of Disfigured and Thug, he was comical. But Ingeborg felt as afraid of Comical as she did of Disfigured and Thug.

'I asked you if you were waiting on someone, love.' Disfigured's tone had lost its mellowness.

'I'm not your love,' Ingeborg spat the words.

'You could be,' Disfigured answered, grinning. 'A pretty lady like you.'

'Leave me alone.'

'Waitin' on your boyfriend?' Thug sneered as he spoke. 'Why bother? We could 'ave kids. Nice, Christian ones.'

The door to the church opened and family by family the congregation emerged.

'Haven't your Nazi friends told you about the GVE yet?' Ingeborg dared to ask Thug.

'What the hell are you talkin' 'bout blondie?' Thug snapped.

'It's the new law brought in by your dear German cousins.' She smiled saintly.

'What's she on 'bout?' Thug asked Disfigured.

'I'm talking about the *Gesetz-zur-Verhütung Erbkranken*,' Ingeborg spoke through clenched teeth. 'It's expressly for people like you,' she added. 'Didn't you know? People like you and your badly dressed friend, the mentally defective, the physically disabled. You're not allowed to have children anymore.'

'That's nasty,' Disfigured replied but laughed as he stepped between Thug and Ingeborg.

If any of the cankered golems had had sufficient empathy, they would have seen how cheap Ingeborg felt in citing the GVE law. In Leipzig they would likely have killed her for saying it.

Church leavers continued to stream out. Several of them swarmed around Ingeborg and blocked the golems from her sight.

An adolescent boy and what appeared to be his twin sister started to shout, 'piss off! fascist gits.'

The triplet of black-jumpers left.

Other strangers from the church emerged and asked Ingeborg if she was all right. Friedrich appeared and she learnt from him that it was Günther's cousins, twice-removed, who had shouted "piss off." Ingeborg thanked the twins for their bravery and snapped a photograph of them together with Friedrich. She promised to send a copy of the photograph when she returned home. More of the congregation arrived. After a few minutes of introductions and more people asking if she was fine, they asked her what things were like back home. A calmness had settled over them when Friedrich reminded Ingeborg of their rendez-vous at the National Gallery

'How far is it?' she asked.

'We could walk there in twenty or thirty minutes.'

'Or take a taxi?' she replied hopefully before she remembered that Friedrich was working as a potato picker and not a student doctor. 'I'll pay.'

'We'll see if we can find one on the way,' Friedrich suggested.

They walked along Great Portland Street looking for a taxi-cab. There were none. They arrived in Oxford Street where lots of taxi-cabs waited and served lengthy queues that barely moved.

'We're half-way there,' Friedrich said. 'We may as well keep walking. Unless you don't feel like walking anymore.'

If she had foreseen her pilgrimage would have covered such distances, Ingeborg might have worn more comfortable shoes.

'Halfway?'

'At least.'

'All right,' she replied without enthusiasm, 'we'll keep going.'

Ingeborg and Friedrich had reached Shaftesbury Avenue when Ingeborg first noticed them. 'Don't turn around now,' she whispered, 'those men from outside the synagogue, I think I saw them.'

'Follow me,' Friedrich answered and quickly crossed the road.

Ingeborg followed. Friedrich picked up the pace and she did the same. She felt her palate parch and become sandpaper.

Friedrich turned into a bustling lane full of restaurants where oriental signs hung above every other door. 'Chinatown.' He laughed. 'Buffoons are not welcome here.'

'Buffoons?'

'British Union of Fascists,' he answered. 'Buffoons! Everyone knows that.'

She looked around. Chinatown was crowded. There was no sign of the Buffoons.

Friedrich took her hand. He led her into a narrower, emptier street. He seemed to have read her thoughts: 'Don't worry, we lost them ages ago.'

Ingeborg barely had a moment to consider his reassurances when she heard footsteps behind her and instinctively knew to whom they belonged.

'There they are!' a Buffoon called out.

'Run!' Friedrich shouted and took off.

Ingeborg took flight too but this time she was unable to keep pace with Friedrich. The Buffoons gained on her. She heard them breathe harder as they got closer. Friedrich was twenty metres ahead of her and waited at the turn into a side street. She ran toward Friedrich but saw in the distance ahead of him several other figures had appeared. *Ambush* The Buffoons had chased them to precisely where they wanted them.

A hand yanked her hair. She spun to the ground. 'Leave me alone,' she shouted and from the corner of an eye she saw that Friedrich had stopped running.

'Not so brave now are you, blondie?' Thug taunted her and

held a knife in his hand. Comical and Disfigured ran past her toward Friedrich and she heard a scuffle as they confronted him.

'Empty your pockets, Jew boy,' Disfigured shouted.

Ingeborg was on her knees.

Thug started a circling motion with the blade in front of her face.

She heard coins fall to the ground and then Friedrich's kippah flew past. She tried to get up off her knees.

Thug pushed her back. 'If you want to keep those cheeks unscarred and those eyes in their sockets, you'll get that camera out of your bag.'

Ingeborg did not want to give any gratification to them but she cried as she looked at Thug's sneering expression and it dawned on her that he would probably cut her face, whether she surrendered the camera or not.

6

NOT DRESSED FOR IT

Red Lion Street, London.

They walked together to their respective appointments at *La Società*. Florence reflected with a degree of contentment upon her own plans for the afternoon and evening. She would deliver her class: *English-for-Adult-Learners* and afterwards, she would gather with the other members of the *circolo* and they would take their usual stroll to attend their monthly art appreciation club at the Empire Café.

She looked forward to these evenings in the company of Fortunato and their mutual friends, Maria and Renzo the proprietors of the Empire Café. Also, there would be Giovanni Ferdenzi and his youngest son, Ernesto; and then, of course there was always Decio Anzani. She would enjoy excellent food and if they could keep Decio clear of politics there was excellent cerebral nourishment too.

The Empire Café would be the perfect place to celebrate her awakening from self-imposed sentimental hibernation. There she would uncork several bottles of prosécco, and also uncork the shady news about Fortunato. On that last point, she felt guilty that she had not yet informed Dorothy.

'There's something I wanted to mention to you,' Florence said as they reached the door of *La Società*.

Dorothy fumbled one-handed in her handbag. 'Later, when we're in the club,' she said and pushed open the door.

Florence shivered at the expression "the club." She was amongst those members inclined to refer to their social institution as *La Società* . It implied a vague yet agreeable level of sophistication and an acceptable whiff o f d istinction. It bothered h er t hat some younger folk casually referred to it as "the club." In her mind, the term evoked mainly dancing or society games. Not that she was averse to either. Since it had been his habit to refer to the old premises in that manner, she blamed the hog for Dorothy's continued use of the colloquial.

They entered together and Dorothy immediately hurried in the direction of the toilets.

Florence followed.

Inside, a group of women huddled in front of the long mirror situated above the sinks. It was not the moment to talk. Florence weaved through the huddle and searched a free cubicle, leaving Dorothy to compete for a mirror spot.

'*Ciao, come va?*' several women asked Florence and Dorothy without turning from the mirror.

'*Bene grazie, voi?*' Florence replied as she stepped into a cubicle.

'*Anche bene,*' the women declared.

On the exterior, the toilet cubicles were painted red, white, and green, because even in the ladies' room the *patria* was not particularly subtle. But, on the interior, the cubicles were painted a calming shade of beige. Florence hung her coat and handbag on a peg and she sat down. The chatter from the women on the other side continued and was as entertaining as always.

'*Dove sono i bidet?*' a newcomer asked.

'Bidets? They don't even have them in Buckingham Palace,' someone laughingly responded.

'But you'd think they'd have them in here,' the newcomer complained with apparent affront and as a measured afterthought added, 'I mean we're in London, not some backwater, and this place is supposed to be a little bit of Italy.'

Florence had no idea whether Buckingham Palace had bidets or not. She had never thought about it. Nevertheless, she found herself in agreement with the newcomer's sentiment: *La Società* deserved bidets. She would bring it up at the next meeting. The ladies' room emptied and Florence emerged. She was searching haphazardly for her compact when cold fingers tapped lightly on the side of her neck. She might have screamed had a cloud of *lilas pourpre* not proclaimed that Dorothy had reappeared.

'I didn't hear you come back in.' Florence turned casually toward the mirror and continued her application.

'I hadn't gone out,' Dorothy said. 'By the way, there's no need to go preening yourself like that.'

'What would you know?'

'You look fine.'

'You don't say.'

'For a woman of your age.'

'What age would that be?'

'Don't go fishing, Mother,' Dorothy answered. 'Everyone says, you'd easily pass for ten years younger.'

Layers of tiny lies. Dorothy always knew when to trot them out. All the same, Florence appreciated her daughter's attempts at reassurance. In *La Società* there was limited room for a middle-aged, borderline divorcee to compete. Even the old Italian grandmothers who called *La Società* their second home seemed more glamorous than she did. And the stakes were increasing.

'Ten years younger?'

'Fifteen, in the dark.' Dorothy giggled.

It was the giggling. Florence could have been willing to swallow ten years younger. Plenty of others had said the same. She could, near enough, pass for forty-something years old. But trying to pass for thirty-something, that would be too brazen. 'You're such a liar.'

'No, I'm not,' Dorothy answered. 'Anyway, the light in here is always dimmed.'

Florence smiled. She knew how to take advantage of the light. She was ready to apply all of the witchcraft she had learnt at *La Società*. Italian women knew all the secrets. Their mothers had passed along nature's tricks to them and in turn they had happily passed them along to Florence, and there was never a more diligent student. Florence was willing to pass them along to Dorothy, but Dorothy seemed not to care or was simply unable to grasp the importance of it. Start with the perfect face-tint and judiciously selected colours. Always insist upon fashionable, flattering cuts and shiny accessories selected to subtly draw attention away from places where attention shouldn't linger. Those were the minimum weapons. The advanced weapons? Pay attention to how youth moves, how it sounds, and especially how it smells.

Certain women had successfully decrypted all of this and no matter the light conditions in *La Società* they held tenaciously onto their youth. It was they whom Florence most admired. And it was they who had recently introduced her to *Wrinkola*, which promised to reduce your wrinkles in forty-eight hours. It was not cheap, but one could not expect eternal youthfulness to come for free. It was a tragedy that some younger women, and Dorothy was one of them, had been blessed with natural good looks but remained blithely willing to wave those youthful looks goodbye without a struggle. Dorothy seemed content to look older than she was, and act older too. She certainly smelled older since she had taken to wearing that perfume.

Mother and daughter strode out of the ladies' room to their

respective classes: Florence as teacher of English and Dorothy as redundant star pupil in Italian.

'Have you seen your father recently?' Florence remembered to ask.

Dorothy shook her head. 'No, why?'

'I'm curious.'

'Isn't that an understatement?'

Florence shrugged. She liked being noted for her curiosity, especially when it concerned her estranged husband. She always made time to hear about Dorothy's charlatan father, or his young floozie. 'I wondered what car he was driving,' Florence asked.

'I'm not often in father's company these days,' Dorothy sounded haughty.

Florence liked that her daughter was not impartial on the matter. All the same, she would have been content for some insights: especially financial. Big car: Big wallet. But news had trickled out. Although the hog was the swarthy son of a cheese importer, a fact she used to consider exotic, and for two generations his family had a near monopoly on imports from Gorgonzola, apparently business had not been too good during the past ten years. It seemed the hog had to find other, less remunerated, work. It was rumoured he was a travelling salesman for the Remington Typewriter Company.

Florence would have pursued the conversation with Dorothy except that the kitchen door swung open and Fortunato and Renzo stepped out, their arms full: jugs of water, wine, and grissini. '*Ciao*, Florence. *Ciao*, Dorothea,' Renzo said and asked, '*come va la famiglia?*'

Always the same question from Renzo: How is the family? How are you and your children and your brothers and sisters and your parents and your grandparents? One might pass half-an-hour talking with Renzo about *famiglia*. Firstly, those members that were alive and then all of those who had passed away but were sorely missed. Then, once he had exhausted all branches of family, it would be food and then the piccolo. Renzo was Fortunato's best friend and a fellow lover of the piccolo, fellow creator of culinary delights and father of Fortunato's godson. In Fortunato's eyes, Renzo's sole fault was that his passions did not extend to include Arsenal football club.

She took a few grissini and snapped them. 'All good. Is it possible to chill a couple of bottles of *prosécco* to take with us tonight?'

'What are we celebrating?' Fortunato asked.

'Tell you later.' She fluttered her eyelashes and wondered if her mascara had been well applied.

Dorothy had remained at Florence's side and spluttered, 'maybe I'll come along tonight.'

'I didn't know you had an interest in art.' Fortunato looked doubtfully at Dorothy.

'Me neither,' Florence answered and grinned. 'We can't wait for you though.'

'I know.' Dorothy smiled at her mother and seemed on the point of curtseying.

'Don't forget to bring a subject to draw.' Florence sounded harsh. "Inventions that Changed the World." That's our theme for tonight.'

'I'll bring one of grandpa's pocket-watches.'

Florence had forgotten that Dorothy carried one of her grandfather's timepieces around with her. It was the perfect object for that evening's theme. It heartened her to be reminded that her daughter had been the only grandchild to show an interest in grandfather's vocation. Dorothy had never previously manifested any interest in art or art-history, but she could certainly name the parts of any pocket watch: pins and wheels and microscopic springs, as well as dials and hands.

'I have to go, mum.' Dorothy smiled warmly at Fortunato and she pointed upstairs. 'My classes are starting.'

Later, when Florence had finished teaching her English-Speaking classes to her enthusiastic older learners, she descended to search for Fortunato and whatever part of their *circolo* had shown up. She found Fortunato and Renzo tucked away in the corner in deep discussion with Decio and Giovanni. This pleased and worried her at the same time.

Fortunato held the two elder men in deep respect. He revered those who perfected their creative skills and dexterity, and Decio, the dapper anarchist cum Honorary President of LIDU — International League of Rights of Man — earned his keep as one of London's best known master tailors. He revered those who treated their animals kindly, and Giovanni Ferdenzi, the senior member of the London tribe of that name, was one of the last generation of car-men in London and he postponed his retirement until that of his dray horses. Decio and Giovanni were receptacles of the wisdom that a prior generation of immigrants had amassed and that appealed to Fortunato almost as much as their shared loathing for fascism and Mussolini.

But what were they up to?

A pot of coffee and a pot of orzo sat on their table and several brochures lay haphazardly across it. As Florence approached, the quartet stopped talking. Decio gathered up his brochures and stuffed them into a side pocket of his trench coat. As she took her place in the manner of a butterfly on a thorny branch, Fortunato pulled up a seat for her between himself and Renzo and kissed her on both cheeks.

'The usual?' Decio asked and reached for the pot of orzo.

'Thank you.'

'I hear we're going to be celebrating tonight,' Decio said. Florence looked inquiringly at Fortunato who did not return her gaze but instead he rubbed his hands together and looked at them with curiosity as though they belonged to someone else. She pushed back in her seat and stretched her legs out under the table. Her foot struck an object which she did not need to see in order to recognise it as a bag of brochures. She gently placed her foot against it and pushed the bag away toward Decio's side of the table.

Fortunato ceased his hand wringing. 'Decio noticed me putting the *prosécco* aside, for later.'

'A small legal matter I've finally decided to take in hand,' Florence said. 'I thought I'd celebrate it with you all at the Empire.'

'Always important to get your affairs in order,' Decio said. 'Seems to me as good a reason as any to celebrate.'

Florence smiled at Fortunato. 'Also, I've decided to rent my spare room to Fortunato.' She held Fortunato's quizzical expression and before he could frame the unspoken question she answered it. 'Yes, including Billy and yes for an affordable rent.'

Fortunato kissed Florence's hand. 'How did you manage to convince the rental agent?'

'Easier than you can imagine,' Florence answered. 'His wife's a dog-lover. When I took Billy for his walk yesterday, she came along too. I gave her the lead and we talked about how dogs are more faithful than men.'

Giovanni almost sputtered his coffee.

'Smart move.' Decio grinned appreciatively at Florence.

Florence looked directly back at Decio. 'That provides us with two reasons to celebrate tonight.' Under the table she gave the bag another little push and whispered, 'by the way, you're not supposed to be using the premises of *La Società* for political purposes.'

'Those are my supplies,' Renzo said.

'And mine too,' Giovanni added.

Decio raised his eyebrows and gazed at the ceiling in innocence.

Florence leant into the centre of the table and asked ironically: 'Art supplies? For tonight's class?'

Fortunato leant over also. His head touched against Florence's and he whispered, 'if we don't ask any questions, we won't make liars of anyone.'

With a push of his foot, Decio returned the small sack of brochures to Florence's side of the table. 'There's nothing to hide here,' he said, 'especially not from you. Do you remember that article I showed you a couple of weeks ago?'

Florence remembered it well. She had gone to Decio's place to drop off a blouse that needed adjusting. She had ended up in the League's offices complimenting him on his article warning of Mussolini: '*The Menace of Fascism*,' she replied. 'What about it?'.

'Well, I've found a way to get around our distribution problem.'

She looked at the other three figures of the *circolo* and thought she might laugh aloud. Had Decio become so desperate he had recruited Renzo and Giovanni to go around the country sticking up posters and delivering brochures? Fortunato would do it without question. She assumed he had already volunteered for it. But Renzo and Giovanni? That was difficult to believe. Crockery would fly in the Empire Café if Renzo had been turned by Decio into some kind of activist. Worse, if Fortunato had allowed it. Worse still if he had encouraged it. If Decio's distribution situation was that bad then maybe she should volunteer to help. And what of Giovanni's wife? That woman lived on the edge of a heart attack and had a permanent dread of the fascist secret service. The news that they, *Ovra* agents, were with apparent impunity killing anti-fascists outside of Italy was enough to worry others less fragile than Mrs. Ferdenzi.

'How?' she asked.

'We've made a little political breakthrough,' Decio revealed. 'I think you'll be impressed when you hear about it.'

'More than a little one.' Fortunato sounded a touch too smug.

But whatever breakthrough they had made, given Fortunato's delight, she supposed she ought to be pleased.

Decio shuffled in his seat and looked around with narrowed eyes, like a fox coming out of his den. 'We'll need you to cause a little diversion when we leave here.'

'Why me?'

'So that Renzo, Giovanni and his boy can slip away.'

'Which boy?' Florence asked.

'Ernesto, of course.'

'Ernesto?' Florence repeated loudly and betrayed her concern. 'Where is he anyway?' she asked. 'And what's all this "slipping away" nonsense? I thought we were all going to the Empire?'

'We are,' Decio said. 'Don't worry about Ernesto. We can hardly have our art appreciation meeting without our young maestro.'

'Well, are you going to tell me or not?' Florence pressed. 'What is this little diversion about?'

Decio redid his fox routine and spoke quietly, 'the Labour Party have agreed to distribute our brochure amongst their League of Youth membership, as soon as we can get the necessary copies to them.'

'That's great news,' Florence said, probably too loudly.

'Since we can't allow *Ovra* agents to know about any of this until it's too late for them to call their political friends and put pressure on,' Decio said, 'I've concocted a plan to distract them. I've split the brochures into three bags. Giovanni, Renzo, and Ernesto will take one bag each.'

'Why Ernesto?' Florence asked, her voice strained. Florence was fond of Ernesto. He was talented and it was his enthusiasm that made their art appreciation evenings such a joy. Also, he was too young to be involved in any of this.

'I know what you're thinking.' Fortunato placed his hand over Florence's. 'But this was Ernesto's own idea.'

'And don't mention that to his mother,' Giovani whispered. 'Otherwise, I'll be in worse trouble than usual.'

'When we get outside,' Decio said, 'we can expect the usual couple of *Ovra* agents.'

'And?' Florence shrugged.

'We'll walk together for say fifty metres.' Decio continued, 'Make sure they're following us. We'll talk loudly and argue about tonight's class. That's when you collapse, or trip over.'

'Collapse?' Florence asked dubiously.

'Fall on the ground,' Decio demonstrated with his hand, the back of which gently slapped against the table.

'I'm not falling on the ground. I'm not dressed for it. Why don't you fall on the ground yourself?'

'Well, I'm hardly dressed for that either.'

It was true. Of their *circolo*, Decio was always the best dressed. He modelled his own work, and therefore nothing short of impeccable ever sufficed. No matter the circumstances, no male at *La Società* ever wore better pressed suits or more pristine trench coats than Decio.

'Well, I'm not falling to the ground,' Florence insisted.

'Could you come over all faint then,' Decio asked. 'Fortunato could hold you up.'

Florence wondered if Decio had not led her there on purpose. She shook her head vigorously as though Decio had asked too large a favour. Gradually, her shaking slowed. 'All right.'

'Good,' Decio answered. 'And whilst Fortunato's holding you up, Renzo will loudly offer to go for water and he'll head back in the direction of *La Società*. If he's not followed he'll walk right past it.'

'And if he is followed?' Florence asked.

'He'll go inside and get a jug of water. Probably wait a while in there,' Decio answered. 'Meanwhile, Giovanni will suddenly remember he forgot his exhibit for tonight's class.'

'What sort of first-aid will I be receiving whilst all this is going on?'

Decio and Fortunato exchanged glances.

'I could manage a shoulder massage,' Fortunato said.

'That'd do,' Florence replied.

'Whilst you're having your shoulder massaged,' Decio said, 'Ernesto will quietly saunter off in another direction.'

'I see,' Florence said. 'What about us?'

'Who?'

'You, me and Fortunato.'

'We'll simply go to the same place we go on this day and this time every month.'

Decio's plan seemed sound. The two *Ovra* agents would have to choose whom they should follow. One of them might follow Decio and Fortunato and Florence. That would leave only one agent to decide whether to tail Renzo, or Giovanni or Ernesto. Either way, the *Ovra* agents were certain of a pointless walk around London and in any case they would finally all end up at the Empire. Meantime, either Renzo, Giovanni or Ernesto would be free to casually deliver Decio's brochures to the Labour Party offices on Smith Square.

Florence hoped the *Ovra* agents would follow Renzo or Giovanni and ignore Ernesto, whose mother was known to have a weak bladder as well as heart. 'Not the dumbest of plans,' she acknowledged. 'Let's get a move on. I can tell you are all in the mood for danger.' She added because she could not have guessed what was to come shortly thereafter when Fortunato would insist that they take a side street they usually avoided.

7

THIS IS A BERETTA

A back street, London.

Eyes closed; Ingeborg fumbled in her bag for the camera. She waited to feel the blade slice her cheek open and blood spurt agonisingly from her face. Instead, she heard steps and someone call out.

'*Porca puttana,*' an angry voice shouted.

She reopened her eyes.

Thug froze. He stopped circling her face with the knife.

'Put the blade away,' the voice ordered. 'Big, brave man that you are.'

Thug stepped away but did not let go of his weapon.

She remained on her knees and turned toward the enraged man who could be her saviour.

Disfigured had Friedrich on the ground in an arm-lock. Friedrich's face pushed against the cobblestone and his nose bled.

Comical was standing immobile, adjacent to Disfigured, who appeared equally transfixed by the appearance of the two men and one woman who had materialised behind him.

The enraged potential rescuer appeared to be in his thirties. He had a clear view of them all and held a pistol in his fist which he pointed at Thug's head. His accomplice was debonairly dressed and considerably older, perhaps around fifty years old. He stood a little further away and rocked perkily back-and-forth on his heels. He had the appearance of a mature cockerel that had happily stumbled into a cockfight. He had a hand inserted into a pocket of his light-coloured trench-coat and seemed to be pointing something through the pocket at Disfigured.

Several paces further back, an elegant lady stood statue-like in heels and wore a fashionable cloche hat. Her demeanour and dress were more suggestive of a cocktail than a cockfight. The lady watched the scene intently, apparently unafraid of whatever drama might unfold in front of her.

The enraged pistol holder gestured with the pistol making it clear he had a line of sight on all three golems. 'Fascist cretins.' He sneered and the atmosphere became charged.

Comical hurriedly thrust his arms further into the air.

Pistol holder stared at Thug. 'Why don't you come over here and try your blade on me?'

Thug shuffled his feet and looked expectantly toward Disfigured as though awaiting some sign.

'Keep your eyes on me,' Pistol Holder shouted at Thug. 'I want you to see who's pulling the trigger.' The pistol holder's face transformed. There was a wildness about him. He seemed to become angrier by the second.

Ingeborg felt hairs rising on her neck.

The older man stepped slightly forward. His hand remained in his trench-coat pocket but the shape protruding from there became clearer. He had a weapon tucked away. He grinned broadly.

'Who the hell are you?' Disfigured asked.

Before the older man could answer, Pistol Holder interrupted. 'All you need to know is this is a Beretta,' he said it matter-of-factly and glared even more insanely as he gesticulated with the pistol. 'And this is the last time any of you will hear me asking him to drop the knife.'

Thug loosened his grip on the knife. It dropped onto the road.

The elegant woman walked forward and addressed herself to Pistol Holder, 'shoot the fool, amore. Personally, I'd shoot all three of them.'

Thug tentatively kicked the knife further away.

Disfigured breathed deeply and noisily.

The gracefully attired woman continued, 'you'd only be doing your civic duty.'

'Funny that,' Disfigured's voice squeaked, 'we thought we were doing the same.'

Ingeborg heard a click as the pistol was swivelled and pointed at Disfigured's head.

'Dearie me,' the elegant elderly lady said. 'You've upset him now. If I were you, I'd run off home whilst I still had the opportunity.'

Disfigured continued holding up his hands. 'We're going, we're going.' He signalled to Thug and Comical.

The golem triplets walked backwards. They had barely gone a hundred-metres when they paused and began shouting. 'Wops and Jews go home.'

The Beretta was pointed afresh in their direction, but the Buffoons ran before a shot could be fired and were soon out of sight.

When it was clear the Buffoons were not returning, Ingeborg led a small explosion of euphoria. Her hugs were fulsome. Her cries were blissful and her laughter seemed to have been infectious.

The elegant lady assisted Friedrich to his feet. She led him to a low garden-wall and called out to the now becalmed Pistol Holder, 'pass me your handkerchief, Fortunato.' She took the handkerchief and extracted a small flask of water from her handbag and she helped Friedrich clean himself.

Meanwhile, the trench-coat wearer introduced himself and the others. 'I'm Decio.' He pointed to the pistol holder. 'And that's Fortunato, and over there's Florence.'

'Thank you, Mr. Decio.' She tripped over her words. She thanked her rescuers repeatedly. 'Thank you! Thank you!' But they all spoke to her at the same time.

'*Non era niènte,*' it was nothing. '*Era una piacére,*' it was a pleasure.

She hugged and kissed Decio and Fortunato on both cheeks. She told them they were musketeers. She told Fortunato, 'your mother is fearless.'

'She's not his mother,' Decio corrected Ingeborg quietly and he chuckled as though he found her error amusing. 'She's his landlady, or soon will be. Florence calls everyone *amore.*'

Ingeborg covered her mouth with the back of her hand. Apologising would simply make it worse. Nor did she know what to say.

'Where were you going?' Florence, the prospective landlady, asked her sharply.

'To the National Portrait Gallery.'

Albeit a little pale, Friedrich had rendered himself presentable. He thanked Florence and he stooped a little as though embarrassed by all the fuss, or perhaps because he had been unable to save himself and Ingeborg. 'Maybe, I should get you safely back to the hotel,' he said.

'I'd listen to my boyfriend, if I were you.' Florence popped the bloodied handkerchief into her handbag and then closed the bag with a loud snap of its brass clasps.

'He's not my boyfriend,' she replied. 'Hopefully, my boyfriend's on his way to meet us at the Gallery.'

'An excellent choice, by the way,' Decio declared.

'Would you like to come with us?'

'I'm afraid we can't,' Florence answered brusquely. 'Our friends are waiting for us.' She looked at Fortunato and her tone softened. 'We're going to be late.'

'Maybe you can join us?' Fortunato suggested.

'You're forgetting.' Florence adjusted her hat. 'Her boyfriend's waiting for her. We should all get a move on.'

In the midst of their backslapping, Decio pulled his "pistol" from his coat pocket and unrolled it until the others saw that it was not a pistol at all but simply some tightly rolled up brochures.

She felt her jaw drop.

Friedrich laughed.

'What did you think it was?' Decio asked.

'I don't know about anyone else,' Friedrich said. 'But I believed it was what you pretended it was.'

'It's something much more powerful than that.' Decio flattened the creases on one of the brochures. It was entitled *The Menace of Fascism.*

As though he wished to out-jest his friend, Fortunato held out his pistol and pulled the trigger. 'This hasn't worked in years.'

'You're all crazy,' Ingeborg said.

'And late,' Florence reminded them all.

'You go ahead, Florence,' Fortunato said. 'Decio and I will catch up.'

Florence smiled at them. 'I'm afraid I'll have to leave you both in the capable hands of your musketeers.'

She shook hands with Florence. 'We'll never forget this. We're lucky you came when you did.'

Friedrich took Florence's hand and kissed it. 'We're most grateful.'

'You can thank him.' Decio nodded in Fortunato's direction. 'If it was not for Mr. Picchi, we wouldn't have come down here at all.'

Fortunato simply shrugged at having been exposed.

'Why did you come down this way?' Ingeborg asked. Her curiosity and gratitude evident.

'Don't ask him,' Decio said. 'He doesn't even know why he does it. It's some old unwritten Picchi code he lives by. He'll say he looked down this alley and knew "something wasn't right." Other people, you and I for instance, we would walk on by. We would run a mile in the other direction. But not Picchi. He loves looking down dark alleys and sticking his nose in. Isn't that right, Fortunato?' Decio sounded serious, as though this particular reproach was not infrequent.

They all stared at Fortunato, even Ingeborg herself. It was as though they awaited some rebuttal or defence against Decio's summation.

But Fortunato only grinned and when no one else seemed ready to speak in his defence he said, 'there's no code. We've all seen what happens when people don't pay attention to the way the world is turning.'

The mood turned serious.

She was drawn to observe Florence and her reaction to her future lodger. Florence had been adjusting her clothes but had stopped when Fortunato began to speak. She saw in Florence's eyes, a sadness and pride. That was the moment she first understood it: Florence was the one who knew why Fortunato Picchi was the way he was. Only Florence understood what unwritten Picchi code he held in his conscience. And that, in Ingeborg's calculations, was much more than any "landlady" could know.

As though she had become aware Ingeborg had been observing her, Florence swivelled abruptly and pointed back up the alleyway. 'I'll tell you where I'm turning. Back the way we came. Friends are waiting for us.' She took several steps before pausing to smile at Ingeborg. 'Have you considered buying a hat, young lady?'

Ingeborg was not sure how to respond. She momentarily studied Florence's enigmatic smile. 'No.'

'Well, you should. You'd look a peach in one.'

'Thank you.'

'You're welcome.' Florence waved a limp-wristed goodbye, as though her past might have included membership of some noble class.

'We'll not be long,' Fortunato shouted after her. 'We'll take our friends as far as the nearest taxi rank.' He turned to Ingeborg. 'Those fascists are getting bolder; they might be hiding around the first corner.'

She forced a smile. In Leipzig they did not hide on street corners they strutted on the main streets. In Leipzig, people like Fortunato Picchi, who sensed the world had lurched to a bad place, had not yet found the courage to confront their would-be oppressors with only a disarmed pistol and an associate bearing a rolled-up leaflet warning of fascism. She hoped some version of the Picchi code would show up soon in Leipzig.

8

ART APPRECIATION

St Martins Lane, London.

Florence headed to the Empire and fretted over the remark of the pretty German girl: *Fortunato's mother?* And she fretted too over Fortunato's reaction. Or rather his inaction. She had pretended not to hear the girl say it, nor to hear Decio put the girl right.

But Fortunato had said nothing.

She picked up her pace and carried on her conversation with herself. *Yes, yes, I got married young. I had a child straight away. But I'm single now.* She had not hidden any of those things. She had not volunteered her age. What's more, Fortunato had never asked her age. Why should she volunteer it?

Anyone over forty years of age must seem old in the eyes of that young blond girl. It was the poor light. Sometimes the light worked against you. Anyway, what could any younger woman offer a man like Fortunato? Nothing that Florence couldn't. She knew everything about him that needed to be known. She understood all that he desired. It was not all to be found in the bedroom. She knew how to listen to a man who woke at night in tremors, a man who imagined himself back in the trenches eating rats and stepping over the corpses of other young comrades. Florence was still cogitating when she arrived at the Empire Café

'*Ciao, dove sono gli altri?*' Maria asked her — hello, where are the others?

It pained Florence to have to hide from her friend that Renzo was at that moment either walking around London being followed by *Ovra* agents or was dropping off anti-fascist leaflets at the Labour Party Offices. She sidestepped Maria's question. 'Fortunato and Decio are accompanying some tourists.'

'What tourists?'

'A couple of tourists they saved from a beating.'

Maria snorted and looked unsure of what she had heard. For a short fellow of thirty-five-years of age, it was likely Fortunato could take care of himself, but Decio was well past his fighting best. 'Are you sure?'

'I saw it for myself. No doubt they'll tell you all about it when they get here. They shouldn't be long.'

'And Renzo and the others?'

Deflection no longer practical. A half-truth was necessary. 'Last I saw, they were still at *La Società*,' Florence said absently and reddened. 'They're maybe waiting for Dorothy.'

'Dorothy?'

'Yes,' Florence replied and leapt into this digression without hesitation. 'Dorothy asked to come along tonight.' Florence wondered if Dorothy would come after all. Or would she go and see Charlie Churchman instead. She felt a little twang of remorse in having directed Dorothy toward Charlie Churchman. Seeing that Maria still looked puzzled about Renzo's absence, she was relieved when the sounds of voices arrived at the café door. 'There they are,' she exclaimed as Renzo, Giovanni and Dorothy entered.

Giovanni grinned and seemed bursting to recount how he had outwitted the *Ovra* until he seemed to remember where he was and as he looked around the café realised that there was no sign that his son, Ernesto, had safely arrived amongst them.

Renzo greeted Florence and Maria with the slightest of kisses before he scurried guiltily into the kitchen.

'I'm pleasantly surprised to see you here, Dorothy,' Maria said.

'I thought I ought to see what my mother gets up to every month.'

Whilst Renzo busied himself in the kitchen, the others set their places around the dining table.

The café door opened and Decio and Fortunato entered. 'Sorry we're late,' Decio announced as he and Fortunato joined the others around the dining table.

Fortunato poured water for Florence and Dorothy and passed the jug to Giovanni.

'We were delayed, busting some Buffoons on the way here,' Decio said.

Dorothy's eyes bulged as her mouth gaped wide open. 'Pardon?'

'They rescued a beautiful, young German damsel,' Florence mocked.

'One of the Buffoons had a knife,' Decio said. 'But Fortunato happened to have his old army pistol in his pocket.'

Florence signalled for Dorothy to close her wide eyes and guppy mouth.

Dorothy covered her mouth with a hand. 'You're not serious?'

Fortunato reached into his jacket pocket and removed the pistol. 'I brought it for tonight's lesson.' His leg brushed against Florence's.

Florence smiled and left her limb where it was.

'As chance would have it, I had brought my weapon too.' Decio held up his impromptu pistol barrel of tightly rolled brochures.

'You scared them off with a pamphlet?' Dorothy led the group in its laughter at Decio's ludicrous act of daring.

Renzo opened the kitchen door and entered into the salòtto,

empty plates judiciously piled in one bent arm, and a serving dish full of risotto in his free hand. From the kitchen, a high-pitched wail of a two-note progression on a piccolo could be heard as his six-year-old son continued his practice, which had been set by his godfather, Fortunato.

The kitchen door swung closed and the strident sound of the piccolo became muffled and then was gone.

Renzo circled amongst them and served the risotto.

Fortunato looked anxiously across at the empty seat next to Dorothy. He locked eyes with Renzo as Renzo replaced the lid on top of the steaming meal.

Giovanni sniffed and shrugged with pretend nonchalance. 'He better show up soon, otherwise it'll be his loss.'

As though in divine reply to his father's hopes, Ernesto sauntered in. 'Sorry I'm late.' He circled the table and kissed everyone. He sat next to Dorothy and exaggeratedly raised the lid on the serving dish then raised his eyes to the sky. '*Tante grazie.*'

'You can thank Renzo,' Giovanni said. 'He was the one who made sure we left some for you.'

'*Grazie* Renzo.'

Later, when everyone had taken or refused a second helping and Renzo had left the table once more to check on the children and the next course, Florence was fearful that Maria would start probing Ernesto about why he had been delayed. She took the situation in hand. 'Wait until you see what Dorothy brought as an example,' she said. 'You do have it with you, Dorothy?'

Dorothy laid the pocket-watch on the table. 'My grandad gave me this.' She deftly inserted her thumbnail and opened it up: she exposed its front and back, its inner workings, all oiled and fully functioning. And she named the parts.

It was some minutes before Decio, despite his awe at Dorothy's knowledge of the inner workings of a pocket-watch, inevitably brought the conversation back to the heroic rescue of the German damsel and the refugee medical student who was currently moonlighting in England as a potato picker. 'What I'd like to know,' he asked earnestly, 'how is it that the Buffoons are allowed to dress in uniform and roam in gangs?'

Under the table, Florence nudged Fortunato in the calf of his left leg with the tip of her right shoe.

'You know the rules, Decio,' Fortunato answered the nudge. 'Tonight is art. If you want to talk politics then you'll need to come back next Wednesday.'

'What would be the point?' Decio's disappointment revealed itself in his tone. 'Apart from you, no one bothers to come.'

'Precisely,' the others chimed.

Decio stared at Ernesto who returned the stare and gave a thumbs up. Decio might have been on the cusp of making another attempt at talking politics but the kitchen door swung open and Renzo re-entered. Once more, strangled notes from a piccolo drifted into their space. Renzo placed a tray on the table. The kitchen door closed slowly and the sounds of the lone piccolo were smothered once again.

'They invited us for drinks later at their hotel,' Decio said.

'Who did?' Maria asked.

'Those German youngsters,' Decio answered. 'I told them we couldn't go. Although it might have been interesting to have taken Ernesto along.'

'Why me?' Ernesto asked.

'She's an art teacher.' Decio winked. 'And attractive too. I thought you'd get along.'

'If she's already teaching,' Giovanni asked, 'isn't she going to be a bit too mature for my boy?'

'I don't know.' Decio shrugged. 'What do you think Florence? Would age be a barrier here?'

Florence tutted, and slowly shook her head. If she had not known that Decio's own wife was fully fifteen years younger than

Decio she may have wondered whether Decio was masking a reproach of some kind. 'No, I don't believe it would,' Florence replied. 'However, I believe she already has a boyfriend.'

'True,' Decio said. 'I'd forgotten about that.'

'What age did you say she was?' Ernesto shifted in his seat as though intrigued.

'I don't know, exactly,' Decio said. 'Early twenties.'

'Not prehistoric then,' Ernesto answered.

Florence smiled. She imagined that for a young man like Ernesto even Dorothy would appear prehistoric.

'She's staying at the Savoy,' Decio said between mouthfuls.

'Imagine that. Does she know that you work there?' Florence addressed Fortunato.

'I might have mentioned it.'

'Mum's been wanting to go there for ages.' Dorothy sounded younger than her years.

It was true. Florence had been wanting to there, but only with an insider. Someone who knew all the band-leaders and could introduce her to them. Someone who could ask for particular dances to be played. In short, she wanted to go there with Fortunato, and as fate would have it, he had already asked her.

'Who's playing tonight?' Florence asked.

Fortunato grinned widely. 'Well, Geraldo will be, for one thing.'

Florence shrugged. 'And Al Collins?'

'Yes, he's back for a week,' Fortunato replied.

Florence was unable to contain her enthusiasm. Her grin was a crescent moon. 'How about you, Dorothy, would you have come along for a little dancing?' She already guessed Dorothy's answer. It was one thing to come along to the art club but another to overcome an innate dislike for dancing.

'I have to be up early in the morning for work,' Dorothy answered flatly.

'I'm going to take your mother there,' Fortunato said. 'That's a promise.'

When Renzo brought the dessert Florence was confused. 'Tiramisu?'

A grin appeared on Renzo's face. 'Fortunato came by earlier.'

'Finally, you've shared a recipe!' Decio cried out.

'It's about time. When are you going to share all your recipes?' Giovanni asked.

Fortunato grinned enigmatically.

'When he's found the perfect woman,' Decio said.

'Better get a move on.' Giovanni vigorously inserted a spoon into his dessert.

Florence was grateful that the kitchen doors swung open and Renzo and Maria's children entered. The girl sat on Maria's knee whilst her brother stood in front of Fortunato, and after several attempts eventually managed to sound a two-note progression.

Fortunato smiled widely and Florence herself led the clapping.

When the children left, Decio seeming more motivated than before, tinkled a fork against a glass. 'Now, if I may.'

He was clever at getting the conversation back to politics. He had helped save a German damsel and there could not be a better moment than that to discuss what was happening in Germany. But Florence wanted to avoid politics. 'No, you may not,' she answered. 'It's Ernesto's night.'

Decio puffed and blew his cheeks.

Under the table Florence felt a hand rest on her thigh as though to say well done.

Ernesto stood up. 'I have a treat for you all tonight.'

'Yes,' Decio said without enthusiasm and sat back down. 'You're going to reveal everything about Dürer's portrait technique.'

'Correct.'

'Would anyone like to know what Dürer's art has in common with Hitler?' Decio looked around the room.

The others groaned.

'No, we wouldn't,' Giovanni answered for them all.

'Well, I'll tell you anyway,' Decio insisted. 'They both learnt their art from Italian masters.'

Fortunato leant close and whispered to Florence. 'We Italians invented everything.'

Florence felt Dorothy's eyes burn into her own.

'Do share it with the rest of us,' Dorothy said.

Before Florence could respond, Fortunato replied, 'I was thanking your mother for her offer of accommodation.'

9

ALLES GUT

Savoy Hotel, London.

Ingeborg wrote her epistle in green ink because green ink meant *alles gut*, whereas red ink would have meant something entirely different. The card was addressed to Clara. And thus began Ingeborg's colourful bending of the truth.

— Dear Clara, what can I tell you about London that you have not already imagined? London is exotic. Everyone we met here is adorable and we wish we could stay forever. She signed for herself and also for Günther before adding: PS: we met with Friedrich. He is safe and happy and sends his love. And then PPS your cousins are adorable. It was part lies. Part truth. Part omission. She blew the ink dry and handed the card to the hotel concierge.

The concierge's regard was starched and polished like his dazzling uniform and shoes. 'Urgent?' he asked.

'Yes'

The concierge took her card and glanced at it whilst he gave a secret concierge hand-wave to a scaled down version of himself.

Ingeborg did not have time to catch the mail-boy's name,

etched on the badge above his breast. The boy clicked his heels and took the card and spun through an impressive revolving door appearing briefly in the courtyard outside and then vanished. Aware of the concierge's stare, Ingeborg smiled and once again had the impression the man was on the brink of saluting her.

'Your postcard will be in Leipzig before you are.' The concierge puffed himself up.

Ingeborg did not doubt it. Nor was she surprised to learn he had read the destination. She expected no less from the Savoy.

'Anything else?' he inquired.

'Could you see that Mr. Picchi gets this?' She passed an envelope intended for the man who had saved her and Friedrich.

'Fortunato Picchi?' the concierge sounded surprised as he read the addressee. 'Our Mr. Picchi, of the Savoy?'

'Yes, that's who I mean.'

'Certainly, madam.'

'That's all, thank you.' She waited by the revolving door for Günther and Bert to show up. She thought of all that had happened and wondered how much she could say to Clara, who at that precise hour, would likely be leaving her home on her way to her work at the Academy of Fine Arts and possibly wondering whether Günther had proposed and if Ingeborg had accepted. Clara would have spent the weekend busily constructing fresh veneers upon her idealised picture of London. Veneers that Ingeborg dared not tarnish. Thus, a little epistolary embellishment had been essential. In order to keep Clara's dreams intact, it was necessary to excise certain uglier Londonien truths. But Clara was a dreamer not a fool and upon Ingeborg's return to Leipzig there would be many questions.

Deflection would be necessary. She would rely on art. She might commence by the unusual light conditions she had found. From the moment the sun had pierced the famous London brume to when it set above the river Thames. She could go on lyrically bending the truth. Painting with green words: the city sunsets, that peculiar Londonien luminescence quite unlike Leipzig and their conversation would flow naturally from that:

— Tell me more about the colours, Clara would probably ask.

— A dozen shades of brick reds and yellows and monumental drab grey stones. Some odd golds and ochres, and at a certain moment of the day, blues and blacks jutting from the shoulders and sharp edges of self-important dark buildings.

— I can see it.

— And at twilight a *chiaroscuro* not seen anywhere else.

And then Clara would likely sigh and push back her long hair with her freckled skinny hand and laugh until her mouth wrinkled at the corners. Then she'd shake her head in that sad way she had taken up and say — Oh, Ingeborg, I wish I'd gone there with you.

— Me too! Ingeborg would blurt out — I thought of the two of us, setting up our easels in Regent's Park and if we had gone there early morning, around six and waited, we'd have been bombarded by light and colour and movement. Then later still, people, a mass of them, walking and picnicking and cycling and juggling. People everywhere.

— What are they like?

— Londoners are like Leipzigers used to be, Ingeborg might say.

And Clara would nod as though she knew what Ingeborg had meant — you mean to say everyone there is still kind to each other? They are not yet suspicious of each other?

Ingeborg would have to think quickly. She could change the subject and say — Did I mention the level of hubbub?

— Noisy?

— All kinds of clamour. Buses honking horns and people shouting and selling newspapers, or theatre tickets, and dozens of street musicians coming-and-going and mostly playing out of tune.

— If only I could have gone.

— But you did the right thing to stay in Leipzig, Ingeborg would insist and smile, but her eyes would speak for themselves and they would say, *we both know it was safer for you to stay in Leipzig*.

It had been Clara's dream to visit London. But no one risked time-off from work when the *Gesetz zur Wiederherstellung des Berufsbeamtentums* committee were due to show up searching for Jews in the ancestry of the teaching staff.

Apart from Ingeborg, no one else in the teaching staff knew anything for certain about Clara's favourite aunt who had married a Jew and had "turned." Even if the committee for the Restoration of the Professional Civil Service could overlook the fact, one could not be secure. It took only one jealous ambitious junior colleague to invent a rumour.

— And is it true about the city lights?

— Yes, Ingeborg would answer, happy that Clara had herself steered the conversation back on less painful terrain. — When darkness descends, they switch on all the lights. Churches and streets, rivers and trees and acres of parks are all illuminated. Even the House of Windsor is lit-up like a doll's house.

— You mean the Palace of Saxe-Coburg and Gotha?

— Yes.

— And you visited their Parliament?

— On day one.

— And Big Ben?

— And plenty of little Bens as well.

Clara's eyebrows would likely arch at the expression.

— I mean there are clocks everywhere. Wherever you are, just pause and look around and you'll see a staring clock, some midget sentinel looking back at you.

— Lit up, I suppose.

— Or impudently mounted on a wall or upon a bridge. Even in shops and restaurants and cinemas. Everywhere, all chiming and chirping as though the whole city is communally counting down to a momentous event.

— And the National Gallery? Clara would inquire in tones that she reserved for discussion of religious matters.

— It was all that you dreamt it would be.

— I don't suppose Günther accompanied you?

She would smile in a manner that rendered words redundant. Clara would know a date could be set. She would focus upon the positive. She would tell Clara all about the friends Günther had made: the German couple and their English friends. The English sea cadet daughter that had so enchanted Günther he was compelled to propose as soon as Ingeborg returned from the National Gallery.

She would also tell Clara about the friends she and Friedrich had made: the Italians who loved art and despised fascism. She could not mention the Buffoons because that would lead to the Beretta and from there it would be impossible to leave out the part about the blade and the kippah and why she had to give away Günther's naval museum memento to Mr. Picchi.

'It has a secret code,' Günther explained.

She read it. She understood it. Clear as the lodestar. It was the Picchi code. Such a thing existed. She took photographs, front and back. Günther would get a photograph of it when they returned to Leipzig. And on that subject of photographs:

— Did you take many photographs? Clara would ask without fully revealing her anxiety.

— A few, she would say. — But don't worry I'll develop them myself and there's nothing compromising amongst them.

It was another small but dangerous lie.

PART II

NAVIGATORS

1940

Crossing the Bar

Sunset and evening star
And one clear call for me
And may there be no moaning of the bar,
When I put out to sea.

— ALFRED, LORD TENNYSON.

10

KNOWN PAST POSITION

Princes Quay, Liverpool.

In Falmouth docks, Edgar looked on nervously when a dozen Royal Navy engineers encircled the *Arandora Star*. They welded enormous stanchions to her starboard and port sides.

'What's that for?' he asked.

'Anti-torpedo nets.'

In the six months since he had disembarked her last paying passengers and brought her from New York to Falmouth, the Royal Navy had boarded up her portholes. They had replaced her pleasure deck with a gun-deck and then painted her a shade they called battleship grey and his chief engineer and closest friend, Bob Connell, called *pallor mortis*.

All of this because Europe's helmsmen had not learnt the lessons of history. Thus, for the second occasion in Edgar's lifetime, the world tilted askew on its gyroscope and he, along with his ship, his crew, and his middle-aged merchant navy friends, many of whom were berthed adjacent, had been "requisitioned." He circled Falmouth Bay for several weeks testing those nets. When it had been determined that the nets worked, Royal Navy engineers reappeared, raised the nets and severed the stanchions.

He asked, 'why?'

'Military secret,' a supervisor replied as navy engineers dragged the debris off the main deck. 'All you need to know is wherever your ship is sent she'll sail as fast as she always has.'

They made it sound like she was a speedboat, not a fifteen-thousand-tonne transfigured pleasure cruiser. The war got closer. They sent him a gun-crew. His ship was now fully fitted for war, she was now a carrack. Two days later he was told to prepare for imminent sailings.

According to his informal ship-to-ship channels, they would all be headed for the coast of France. But Edgar's instructions were to set sail in a different direction. The *Arandora Star* joined a convoy to Norway where planes rained bombs, battleships blasted canons and from several kilometres away unseen *unterseeboots* fired torpedoes.

His ship was net-less, his crew were daunted. But due to the enemy's barren targeting and Edgar's fertile navigating the *Arandora Star* remained untouched. They plucked sixteen-hundred battle-worn survivors from off the Norwegian shores. Many were mutilated. Most were traumatised. They departed the scene at fifteen knots leaving other carracks and crews in their wake, some of whom Edgar knew he would never see again.

He was ordered to sail to Greenock, where they disembarked their rescued military assets, including men who were destined to be bandaged and sent out to fight another day. On arrival, neither the smell of flesh wounds nor the sight of fifty ambulances lining the quayside dampened the mood of chief engineer Bob Connell. Edgar knew the reason why. It was because they were unexpectedly in the proximity of Bob's home city and had forty-eight hours for refuelling and restocking before they would receive their new instructions.

'You'll be staying at my Ma's place, right, Captain?' Bob reminded Edgar.

In the three years since Bob had joined the *Arandora Star,* he had talked with pride, or sometimes when inebriated he had sung with delight, about how nowhere was like "Dear old Glasgow town." According to that song, Glasgow was a place that went "round and round." A dozen times, Edgar had promised Bob he would visit his home city but until now they had never found the moment.

Whilst Bob passed the night with his wife, Jenny, at their small fat in the less fashionable East End, Edgar passed a comfortable first night on the couch of Bob's dainty eighty-one year old, twice widowed mother in Byres Road.

The next morning, Bob appeared with a borrowed black car, an Austin Seven, and they took a drive into Bob's past. They drove to Clydebank. On the journey there, Bob spoke quickly, as though there was not enough time to retell the missing parts of his story.

'I upgraded the engine for him.'

'For whom?' Edgar tentatively asked.

'For the guy who lent me this car.'

Edgar looked around the immaculate interior. He approvingly sniffed particles of polish that saturated the air. He guessed what would be coming next and he was unsure if he would be able to feign an interest.

'From seven bhp to ten-and-a-half,' Bob continued.

'That much?' Edgar hoped his astonishment seemed authentic. 'By the way, what's our future bearing?' he added in an attempt to steer the conversation somewhere else.

'A place of learning,' Bob answered cryptically. 'You'll like it.'

They parked outside a technical college whose circular library was constructed of granite with splendid arches and pillars that rendered it oddly Grecian. Bob was correct, it appealed to Edgar's sensibilities. He would have been happy to spend the remaining duration of their shore leave right there if Bob had wanted to.

An aged librarian asked, 'can I help ye, gentlemen?'

'I'd like to show my friend around,' Bob said.

'Why?'

'Old times sake.'

Thirty-five years previously that place had been Bob's alma mater.

'We shut at five,' the old librarian declared.

'We're not planning to stay that long,' Bob answered.

'Pity,' the old librarian replied, disappointment in his voice. The geriatric warden of wisdom rubbed his ancient chin and mulled things over whilst Bob signalled and led Edgar away to a seat that had once been a preferred spot.

Tall windows poured daylight in through a domed roof. Edgar was delighted to learn that the technical college also held a humanities section and he shuffled off to find it whilst Bob disappeared to rifle amongst engineering books and journals.

Edgar returned with a copy of *Salt Water Ballads* by John Masefield.

Meanwhile, Bob had found what he was looking for and he had returned with the journals held open showing rediscovered notes made in the margins years before. 'I was seventeen, when I wrote those solutions.'

Edgar consulted Bob's notes of mathematical and scientific formulae. He tried to recall what journals he had read and what margins he had written into at that same age. He could not have written as elegiacally as Bob had about steam engines. Nothing about steam engines merited the effort. He recalled once having written in response to something about steam. Not about an engine, *per se*. It had concerned a steam leviathan that relied upon its inventors; little men who were masters of the gigantic. It must have been a poem, otherwise it would not have fluttered his mainsail. 'Do these adolescent epiphanies still make sense?'

'They're not epiphanies,' Bob said gruffly. 'It's science.'

It was clear to Edgar; his friend was retracing his steps for one reason: Bob was looking for a "known past position." Whilst Bob turned pages in a distant part of his own soul, Edgar sat quietly adjacent to him and flipped through *Salt Water Ballads*, only looking up from the yellowed sheets when Bob politely coughed.

'We should leave now.'

'Why?'

'I could do with a smoke.'

'Where to?' Edgar asked and took a last glance at the final stanzas of *Sea Fever* before he quietly closed the book.

'Somewhere they'll remember me more easily.' Bob closed the journal with a clap. 'By the way, an extra three-and-a-half bhp means we'll get there much quicker.'

'Well, that's good.' Edgar's enthusiasm shone authentically.

In the car park, Bob smoked two cigarettes, after which they drove for fifteen minutes and parked outside a boxing school where a sprightly pensioner remembered an evening when "knock-kneed" Bob Connell got his first flattened nose. They remained a while. They drank honeyed tea. The darkest and sweetest tea Edgar had tasted since his four-person wedding reception.

When Bob Connell and the wiry pensioner had run out of things to remember they pretended to shadow-box and then finally took their leave of each other. Bob held the old man a long time before letting go and Edgar was reminded of another place and time in his own story. It occurred to him, not for the first time, who should accompany him to Wavertree if he should ever get the chance to go back there.

'What is he to you?' Edgar asked.

'He's part of my story,' Bob answered and looked at his watch and announced, 'we have to drop the car back.'

'Fine, I'm happy to try out your buses.'

'We can easily walk to the place I have in mind.'

'Even better. Lily likes it when I walk.'

They returned the car with its augmented cylinders and extra speed to its owner who adoringly patted its roof and asked Bob, 'did ye smoke in it?'

'No,' Bob answered and looked at Edgar for a witness. Bob looked sad to be handing over the car and when his car owning friend drove away, he breathed deeply and did a few stretching movements. 'Guess where we're going next.'

Edgar was less supple than Bob; nevertheless, he made a few stretching movements of his own and answered Bob's question. 'I know where we're going. Wales and then back to Falmouth.'

'I meant right now, this moment.'

'No idea,' Edgar admitted.

'My part of the city; the East End.'

'I wondered why you live there and your mother lives in the West End.'

'That's another story.' Bob playfully slapped Edgar on the back. 'Anyway, let's get going.' He took out another cigarette.

They walked to the far end of Byres Road and crossed a bridge over the river Kelvin. Fifteen minutes later Edgar found himself accompanying Bob and the river Clyde, eastwards.

'Where exactly are we going?'

'A bar I know.'

'How far?'

'I can walk there in half an hour,' Bob said. 'Probably take us forty-five minutes. Maybe longer.'

'You think I can't walk as quickly as you?'

'It's not that,' Bob answered, 'I know what you're like. We're going to have to stop half a dozen times whilst you study the tide, estimate the water depth, and calculate the surface light.'

One and a half hours later, they arrived at Bob's favourite East-

End pub. They sipped their grog of choice whilst some old timers regaled them with stories of folk they knew that had avoided being requisitioned.

An elderly gentleman whose hands trembled said, 'some folk are that desperate they'd do anything.'

'Aye, they would,' a chorus of pensioners agreed.

'I read about a "conscientious objector" from Mull who swapped jobs with the lighthouse keeper to avoid being called up,' a pensioner said.

'Being a lighthouse keeper seems a reasonable alternative,' Edgar said. 'I'd do that.'

'Not if you're an acrophobic,' the pensioner guffawed and the others, despite probably having heard the story a dozen times, laughed anyway.

On the walk back to Byres Road they bought fish and chips from Bob's "favourite" East End chippy and Bob hung around and chatted a considerable time to a striking, dark-haired woman and her stout, grinning, red-faced father. Eventually, Bob delivered his farewells, in Italian, to the enchanting lady and her father.

'I didn't know you spoke Italian,' Edgar said when they were back in the street.

'I get by.'

'I think I can guess why it's your favourite chippy.'

'Don't you start. Her oldest brother and I are friends.'

'That's all?' Edgar teased.

'I might have had a little crush. But you've nothing to say on that subject to Jenny when you see her, later.'

'Where's her oldest brother now?' Edgar laughed as he elbowed Bob in the side. 'Not here to chaperone her?'

'In the Royal Highland Fusiliers. Wherever they are right now.'

As they walked back to Byres Road, Bob Connell, with vinegar running off his puffy lower lip, slipped another secret into their conversation. 'Perhaps it was more than a little crush, but it could never have gone anywhere.'

'Why not?'

'For a start, apart from not being Italian, I kick with the wrong foot. You must remember?'

'Weren't you willing to become a Catholic?'

'Maybe. But depending on how you look at it, I was practically already engaged to my sister.'

Edgar spat a chip. 'What?'

Bob grinned. 'I don't think I ever told you about me and my sister.'

Edgar would have remembered a tale of incest. 'No,' he said coldly. 'I don't believe you ever mentioned that.'

Bob wiped his lips with the back of his hand. 'It's not as bad as it sounds.'

'How's that?'

'We're not biologically related,' Bob clarified. 'Jenny's my step-sister.'

'Still,' Edgar answered. 'Is that legal?'

'It certainly is.'

Edgar chewed overlong on a chip and finally swallowed it. 'But complicated.'

'That's why we moved to the East End.' Bob lit a cigarette. 'It was my mother's fault. She's too, how do your lot say it again?'

'My lot?' Edgar asked. 'You mean in Welsh?'

'Aye.'

'Stubborn?'

'Aye.'

'*Styfnig.*'

Edgar chewed on several chips and reflected upon his own *styfnig,* mule-headed mother. It was past time to pay her a visit. He sighed. It was especially past time to pay his respects to his sister, for whom he had placed two lines in the local announcements column, five months ago.

Bob waved a small fat chip in the air. 'I told my mother, "Ma, if you marry her father that'll mean I'll be marrying my own step-sister and you'll become my step-mother-in-law, and my father-in-law will become my step-father." You know what she said?'

'No, but I imagine she had her reasons.'

'Like what?'

'Financial security, that sort of thing.'

'No,' Bob said. 'It wasn't that at all.'

Edgar shrugged. He wondered afresh about the wrinkled lady upon whose couch he had slept the prior evening and whom he saw in a different light. He shook his head.

'She told me, "well Bob, there's an easy solution. Don't marry Jenny." Can you believe it?'

'Why would she say that?'

'I think she suspected that I had a soft spot for the girl in the chippy.'

Later, when he arrived back at his lodgings in Byres Road, Edgar prepared to take his place on the couch and Bob whispered to him, 'which of us has the most stubborn mother?'

'It's not a competition, you know.' Edgar said. 'But if we ever get to visit Wavertree you can judge for yourself.'

'If we ever get to visit Wavertree, you can count on it.' Bob switched off the light and left for the East End.

***

The following morning, they sailed from Greenock on the first tide. As they approached Liverpool Bay, Edgar stood on the castle deck and peered toward Liverpool. He remained there until the northern tip of Anglesey cut Liverpool from sight and he wondered if that was as close as he would come to visiting his sister and mother. It was whilst rounding Holyhead that he heard over the ship-to-ship about two Destroyers and an aircraft carrier that had not made it back from Norway. Also, Mussolini had declared war. Dunkirk had gone better than hoped, but thousands of retreating allied soldiers and third-country citizens had not made it there in time to be rescued. It was only a matter of time before the German land and air forces pushed through from the East and overran France. Another operation would be essential. Edgar was not surprised when instructions came through soon after to sail for the port of Brest, on the western coast of France.

Thanks to an accompanying Destroyer, their journey down the English coast and across the channel was uneventful. But as they approached the city of Brest, they saw that they were too late, the port and town were already under heavy air attack. Edgar radioed naval command: 'Destination is under attack. Unable to enter the port. What are our instructions?'

Whilst they awaited a response, Edgar's first officer spotted a small craft in the sea. It was barely moving but it was definitely heading in their direction.

'Naval command to *Arandora Star*, your instructions are return to base. Repeat, return to base.'

They identified the small craft. A rowing boat with what appeared to be British Infantrymen. Edgar responded, 'we've sighted a small craft with what looks like some of our lads. I believe we can bring them home.'

'Naval Command to *Arandora Star*, there's no air cover for you. You're on your own.'

'*Arandora Star* to Naval Command, we have an accompanying Destroyer. Believe we can collect cargo and make it back.'

Edgar sent a lifeboat to pick up a dozen wraithlike soldiers. By then, the city of Brest was ablaze, yet bombs continued to be dropped upon it. There was nothing Edgar could do except look on helplessly and be grateful that the bombers did not come out to sea.

They headed to Falmouth. Edgar felt enveloped by a heavy tiredness that he had never experienced before. His thoughts were numbed. In Falmouth he learnt their mission was not over, after all. Every ship from Falmouth, Portsmouth, and Southampton were required to get themselves urgently out to Quiberon where an unquantified number of soldiers, allies and third country citizens were amassing for rescue.

On leaving Falmouth, Edgar crossed Rudy Sharp's vessel the SS *Lancastria*, painted just like the *Arandora Star*. Every merchant navy man Edgar knew seemed to have been called-up. But Rudy was not only another mariner. They had grown up together. They had lived half a mile from each other. Rudy was nine months older and two inches taller and at Sefton Park school and the Sea Cadets, Rudy stuck up for his shorter, less toned neighbour.

'Would be nice if you could join us out here.' Edgar radioed.

'I'll be there before you,' Rudy responded.

Rudy liked to remind Edgar that the Cunard's *Lancastria* had half-a-knot extra speed. Edgar liked to remind Rudy it was not the size of the engines that counted but one's capacity to read the currents.

'I doubt that,' Edgar answered.

'Say hello to Bob Connell,' Rudy teased.

Edgar laughed. Even in war-time, Rudy had not given up trying to poach Bob for Cunard Lines. 'I'm taking him to Wavertree,' Edgar shouted, 'over and out,' and he closed the ship-to-ship radio. Perhaps Rudy will finally get the message.

When the *Arandora Star* arrived in Quiberon she was at the tail end of a group of transporters. The embarkation was almost already completed. All the same, they stuck around and picked up the last three hundred retreating soldiers. They could take more. He radioed Naval Command: 'Permission to wait for stragglers.'

'Are you planning a welcome party for the Germans?'

'What are our instructions?'

'Bring back your cargo.'

'Will we be accompanied?'

'Negative.'

As they headed out of Quiberon Bay, Edgar spotted Rudy's *Lancastria* accompanied by a Destroyer and another converted Cruiser. Edgar signalled to Rudy. 'You're too late, mate. There's no one left in Quiberon. You may as well tuck in behind us.'

'We heard about that. We've being sent down to Saint-Nazaire.'

'Good luck,' Edgar signalled. 'See you back in Falmouth.'

It was evening when Edgar disembarked three-hundred members of the British Expeditionary Forces who seemed happy to live to fight another day. No other carracks arrived in port after him. He was spent but still could not sleep. He had a presentiment and was expecting something when he was called into a meeting the following morning.

Naval Command secured the perimeters of the meeting room. Everyone was reminded of the importance of public morale. The Prime Minister had issued a D-Notice on what they were about to hear. A news blackout had been ordered. Assets would be seized and newspapers shut down if any news publisher dared defy it. Nor could any sea captain, who repeated what they were about to hear, expect to be sympathetically dealt with if they failed to respect the D-Notice.

Yesterday, in Saint Nazaire the *Lancastria* had embarked thousands of exhausted troops but was instructed to wait for more desperate terrorised civilians: young and elderly, men, women, and children and squeeze them all aboard. No one knew how many. Six thousand, a survivor had said. They had huddled together, their fearful faces turned up at the Luftwaffe who screamed over their heads and bombed for forty-five minutes.

At ten-minutes-to-four in the afternoon the *Lancastria* had taken four direct hits. She broke up and sank within twenty minutes. Six thousand heads in the sea. Impossible to know how many of those were already dead. Fuel and oil rose and turned the sea black around them. Diesel vapours hung in the atmosphere and choked many of them as they strained against currents in their short-lived efforts to resist drowning. Exhausted, they could offer no resistance as they watched the Luftwaffe turn their planes around and set fire to the sea.

'I know, many of you will have colleagues and family amongst the *Lancastria* crew,' the Commander spoke sympathetically. 'We don't know yet who or how many might have survived.'

A stranger in the room asked, 'is it over?'

'No, it's not over,' the Commander said. 'Not for us. There are thousands more allied soldiers and civilians escaping down the French coast. We'll have to keep going until we've brought back as many of them as we can.'

Edgar immediately received new instructions. They were needed in Bayonne. They steamed within a mile of where the *Lancastria* had sunk. Edgar removed his cap and recited a prayer. In Bayonne the *Arandora Star* took on five-hundred glassy eyed refugees and raced back toward Falmouth. They were en route to Falmouth when they heard France had fallen and entered negotiations on an armistice.

It had been coming.

Now there would only be the English Channel between Britain and Germany.

In Falmouth it was Edgar who wondered is it over? The clock counted time on the French surrender but Naval Command determined there was time to mount one final rescue operation. Edgar's instructions were to join a mission to sail down the West Coast of France, as far as Saint Jean de Luz near the border with Spain. This time, like the *Lancastria* had been a few days before, the *Arandora Star* would be the largest ship and the simplest target to spot from the skies.

Outside the port of Saint Jean de Luz, Edgar waited for the

winds to die in order to take the *Arandora Star* inside the breakwater. He manoeuvred her deep inside the small harbour. He watched from the Navigating Bridge as hundreds of Polish and Czechoslovakian soldiers piled aboard, and tens of tearful civilians, from places as far away as Paris and Madrid, trudged in behind them.

Like the *Lancastria,* they remained longer than they should. They risked the same end. But the Saints had sent them cloud cover and Naval Command had sent them an escort.

Bob Connell rang through and jolted Edgar from his melancholy. 'In case you're interested, the armistice has expired. We should go now. Unless you're waiting for some German friends'

'I hope my German friends are safe,' Edgar answered. But he took Bob's point. It was time to leave. He commanded the hatches battened, the deck gun manned and he gave the order to quit. It was over. There would be no more British ships coming to rescue anyone. Not for a long time.

He stood on deck. He watched the skies and he prayed. And his prayers were answered. The clouds stayed low and dark, and augured well for a safe run home.

HMS Harvester ploughed the waves alongside them.

They had gone as far as the Bay of Biscay when something unexpected happened.

11

STIMMEN HINTER STACHELDRAHT

Mooragh Internment Camp, Isle of Man.

They had published it in the upcoming events section of the camp magazine, but that was no guarantee of getting Gellhorn the audience he craved. Firstly, there were few copies of *Stimmen Hinter Stacheldraht*. Secondly, they were sometimes left forgotten for hours in the toilets of the less cultured lodging houses on the parade.

Thus, Friedrich had spent much of the prior week wandering amongst the camp lodging houses asking in English, "have you read this week's copy of *Voices Behind Barbed Wire?*" often receiving the impatient response "Yes, yes, everyone's heard, Gellhorn's giving a piano recital at your house." But simply knowing of the event did not necessarily translate to an audience.

The evening of the concert arrived and Friedrich had done what he could. He checked his watch. Only two minutes late. He splashed water over his face. He opened the bedroom door and cocked an ear to the sound that rose from the lounge on the ground floor.

Gellhorn's recital had already started.

Friedrich hesitated. The mad musician would likely not be aware if Friedrich was in attendance or not. But a promise was a promise and Friedrich had given his word to Jacob Burfeind. He and Jacob not only had mutual friends but also mutual respect. And in his own gentle way Jacob had been insistent: "Really, you have to come, Friedrich, it's essential for morale," he had said.

Gellhorn was playing something new. Or at least something Friedrich did not recognise. During the descent from his room on the top floor, he knotted his tie and buttoned his waistcoat. At least he would be dressed for the occasion.

He pushed open the lounge door. The entire boarding house occupants were present and plenty of others too. A pale grey smoke from self-rolled cigarettes was suspended over the scene like haze over a crematorium. Some of this "captive audience" had brought their own seats, others sat on the floor, with their knees pulled against their chests.

Friedrich searched for Jacob and spotted the bearded colossus surrounded by around a dozen of his crew members. He had kept a seat and gestured for Friedrich to join him and the crew. Friedrich stepped over several recital goers and took the seat beside Jacob. They sat with their backs to the large bay-window and their attentive faces to Gellhorn.

The pianist was, once again, projecting his chin out and tilting his neck back, madly compressing his vertebrae. Friedrich tutted. He had warned Gellhorn several times. What was the point in complaining about cervical pains if one did not act upon advice?

Gellhorn spotted Friedrich and he retracted his teapot neck and shoulders back to where they should have been.

'What's he playing?' Friedrich whispered.

'Something he composed himself,' Jacob answered.

'It's catchy.'

'He calls it *Cats*.'

'Why?'

'I don't know,' Jacob answered. 'You can ask him yourself.'

Friedrich stored the question away for later.

Gellhorn was into his third number when an army truck noisily pulled up on the other side of the barbed-wire fence. Friedrich turned momentarily away from Gellhorn and regarded the scene outside. Six soldiers, their bayonets clipped, streamed out from the back of the truck and formed a line near the gates. When several other internees stood up and turned their backs on Gellhorn and stared out through the bay window, Gellhorn, eyes wild at the interruption, looked over the top of the piano at Jacob as though it was in Jacob's gift to sort the situation out.

'What do you think they want?' Friedrich asked.

'We'll find out soon enough.' Jacob waved at Gellhorn to continue playing and raised his voice to the others, 'sit down, everyone.'

A sentry-guard opened the camp gates and three men, two of whom were soldiers and one dressed in civilian clothes, passed into the internees' section.

'What's happening?' one of Jacob's crew asked.

'Shhhh,' someone else said loudly. 'They've gone next door.'

One by one, the men sat down but Gellhorn was not in the mood to play. Someone volunteered to prepare tea and reason with Gellhorn.

The inquirers completed their visit of lodging house number two and pushed open the front door to Friedrich's boarding house. A current of air surged in and displaced cigarette smoke.

'Are there any doctors present amongst you?' the civilian asked.

'What kind of doctors?' Jacob answered.

An army sergeant looked over at Jacob. 'How many kinds have you got, here?'

'To my knowledge,' Jacob said, 'in this lodging house alone we have several Doctors of Law, at least one Doctor of Natural Philosophy and a Doctor of Theology.'

'We're looking for a medical doctor,' the civilian interrupted.

Jacob put his arm on Friedrich's shoulder and whispered, 'well?'

Friedrich spoke up. 'I'm a doctor of medicine.'

The man removed a notebook and asked, 'what's your name?'

'Friedrich Dabel.'

'Nationality?'

'Stateless.'

'Usual home address?'

The question derailed him. Usual? He ought to say 21, Tribseer Strasse, Stralsund, Germany. That had been the Dabel's "usual" home address for three generations until the National Socialist Government had appropriated it through the *Reichsfluchtsteuer* — they had declared families as Stateless, forced them to flee and then invented and levied their "flight tax" on everything they owned. He could give the last address of the lodgings they had fled to in Vienna. Except, now that his mother and sister had made it out of there and Bea and his father had disappeared, presumed dead, it made little sense. 'I'm not sure.'

'Well, where were you living before you were brought in here?' the sergeant asked and sounded a little exasperated.

He gave the address of the caravan in Penpell Farm.

'Date of birth?'

Finally, an easy question. 'Twenty-seventh August 1911.'

'Qualifications and Experience?'

Some of Jacob's crew stared at Friedrich as though they had not known his story. 'I studied medicine from 1930 to 1933 in Leipzig University Medical School,' Friedrich spoke as though he was talking about someone else. 'My studies were disturbed in early 1933 — for reasons you probably know.'

'I see,' said the short civilian who had continued taking notes.

'Then I came here to England. I waited over the summer until I was able to transfer to *Medizinische Universität* in Vienna.' He did not mention he spent that summer picking potatoes with surgical precision in Honiton, Devon. Nor that the British Medical Association blocked him and other trainee doctors from studying or working in England. 'I completed my studies and began an internship as a junior doctor, practicing in Nordbanhof Hospital. Until the National Socialists arrived in Vienna and put an end to that too.'

'I see,' the civilian answered and nodded as though he wanted Friedrich to continue.

'Then I had to call once again on the JRC and my pacifist friends in England.'

The civilian seemed satisfied. He appeared to be mentally checking against a list of things he wanted to know. He put away his notebook. He told Friedrich to pack an overnight bag.

They took him over to the other side of the island. He sat in a truck outside a hotel that had been transformed into a hospital. The civilian went inside and reappeared after ten minutes. He led Friedrich inside and told him to wait. Friedrich sat on a hard seat outside an office. He could hear voices on the other side of the office door but he was left alone and unguarded.

When the door opened, two women appeared. 'Sorry to keep you waiting,' the younger woman said and she reached to shake his hand. 'I'm Doctor Margaret Colls.'

Friedrich returned her handshake.

She smiled and continued looking him over. 'Welcome to Rushen Camp, Doctor Dabel.'

It was the first time anyone in England had called him Doctor. He felt oddly liberated. A weight lifted from him. The slouching of his shoulders and the stoop in his gait and the sorrow in his face, for which Jacob Burfeind had often reproached him, evaporated in that instant. For the first time since his rescuers had placed him in internment, he felt like the young twenty-nine-year-old man that he was. He smiled and followed the two women into their office where they consulted notes and asked him more questions about his training.

'Would you be willing to help take care of your fellow citizens?' Doctor Colls asked.

'You do realise I'm not German anymore.'

Doctor Coll furrowed her brow and fixed Friedrich with a look of profound sadness.

'What would I be doing?' he asked.

'The same as your colleagues.'

'Which colleagues?'

Doctor Colls looked down at her notes on her desk. 'A Doctor Scholtz has volunteered for Mooragh and a Doctor Altmann has volunteered over at Peel Camp.'

'I'd be working with Scholtz and Altmann?'

'Our needs are more acute here in Rushen at the moment,' Doctor Colls replied. 'But you'd be on standby for the men's hospitals too.'

'Who'd be supervising me?' he asked because suddenly he had an idea.

'I would. I'll not always be here, personally. But there's always at least one supervising nurse from the Royal Army Medical Corps who'll be with you.'

'Would my contribution be logged and taken into account?'

'You want to know if working in these conditions during a war could be recorded as part of an internship?'

'I don't see why not,' Friedrich asked. 'I'd be an intern and an internee.' The others smiled at his effort to make light of his situation. 'And might there be a salary attached?' He asked this on behalf of his sister and mother whom the JRC had also smuggled into England and who were in need of money.

'I'm sorry, but no,' Doctor Coll answered. 'There might be some other privileges we could work out,' she added cheerily.

'Such as?'

'You could use our telephone once a week.'

He knew there was a call-box near his sister's lodgings. Even without Doctor Colls' offer of a weekly telephone call he would not have refused. He felt elated at the possibility of being useful again. 'A deal.' He shook hands enthusiastically with Doctor Coll and the supervising nurse.

The following day, he was on duty in Rushen Camp hospital when he met Tauba Rubel.

The supervising nurse had briefed him. 'Our next patient tried to kill herself.'

When he first changed the bandage on her slashed wrist, she reminded him of Bea. Except for her silence and worried eyes, Tauba could have been Bea's older sister.

It was on his third day of working at Rushen Camp hospital that Tauba eventually spoke to him.

'I suppose you're wondering what happened?' she said in faltering English.

'I can see what happened,' he whispered in German.

'It was an accident,' she answered quietly in German.

An accidental slashing of the wrist? Friedrich was sceptical.

The medical notes stated that Tauba was at risk. Friedrich remembered his father's advice in these sorts of cases — look for a sign of what might be important because although they may not always see it themselves everyone has a reason to continue living: there might be a child's face in a locket, some unfinished business, a fissured belief in some form of religion, anything would do.

Tauba wore a silver chain with two Stars of David hanging from it. One silver, the other gold.

'The good thing is God intervened.'

'You think God intervened?' Tauba said scornfully.

When they moved out of Tauba's earshot the supervising nurse explained. It had been Tauba's landlady who had intervened. In

Port Erin, fishermen often accidentally slashed their limbs. Most landladies over there know what a square-knot is and how to stem a wound. When Tauba's landlady heard a pained scream and a thump as Tauba's body dropped onto her linoleum floor, she had the bathroom door open with a single kick and a knotted tourniquet applied in seconds. All of that before yanking Tauba's arm above her heart.

'Perhaps it was God's will that her landlady was present.'

'Who can say?' the supervising nurse conceded.

The following Sunday, in the first of his ten-minute telephone calls, Friedrich told his young sister the story of how Tauba Rubel had been saved.

'Why'd she do it?' his sister asked.

'She didn't say,' Friedrich answered. 'But she seems familiar. It's like I know her from somewhere.'

'What's she doing in an internment camp anyway?'

'How do I know?' Friedrich said. 'Very little here makes any sense. You should watch out or you'll soon be here too.'

'Is she pretty?'

'She's not ugly.'

'Perhaps she has a husband somewhere lurking in the men's camps. Maybe in your camp?'

Friedrich had not considered that possibility. 'Maybe she does.' He quietly hung up.

12

HARDLY FIFTH COLUMN

Palace Internment Camp, Isle of Man.

On Fortunato's first night in Palace Internment Camp, he sat with Renzo under their lodging house porch. They played music together for an hour and when Renzo called it a night he called it an intermission and he carried on playing until a clock somewhere chimed midnight. The next morning, he was escorted to the camp commander's office.

'I've had complaints,' the camp commander said jovially and stared at Fortunato's Arsenal FC lapel badge.

'What about?'

'About you and your friend,' the camp commander replied. 'Must you play so late at night?'

'It wasn't that late. Every artist must practice.'

'It says here that you're a head-waiter, not a musician.' The camp commander consulted a beige card in his hand.

'Restaurant manager, if you don't mind.'

It turned out, that the camp commander was a fan of a rival football club. But this did not seem to prejudice matters, because he had played flute in a brass band. The camp commander's face creased when he revealed, 'personally, I would let you play longer. I rather like the flute.'

'It's not a flute.' Fortunato scowled.

'I know that.'

They got along. They chatted about London football derbies, and the surprising versatility of the piccolo. He asked the camp commander what else was written on his record. For instance, was it written there that he was a member of the Free Italy anti-fascist association? He could tell from the camp commander's face that this fact was not noted. 'Where do you get your intelligence from?' he asked.

'MI5.'

'They don't know anything!' Fortunato shook his head. 'You've heard about the Free Italy movement, at least?'

The camp commander reddened. He cleared his throat and looked toward one of his men who volunteered, 'they had to compile everything in a hurry.'

'Do you want a list of who in here are associates of Free Italy or anti-fascist? I'll start in our house,' Fortunato recounted. 'In my room, there's me, there's my best friend, Renzo and his cousin, Pietro. Three of us in one room. In fact, our lodging house only has anti-fascists in it. You could probably form a brigade of Mussolini haters from the lodging houses on this parade.'

'Are you seriously telling me there are no fascists or sympathisers in Queen's Parade?'

'The only fascist I've come across here is my old boss from the Savoy.' Fortunato paused and pursed his lips. 'And I've met only one other like him and that was when we were interned at the satanic mills. But I can't see either of them wearing battle fatigues.'

The camp commander's assistant cleared his throat. 'We're sorry, Mr. Picchi. The complainants want you and your friend to be moved to other lodgings.'

'Complainants?' Fortunato asked. 'Who was it?'

'We're not at liberty to say who it was,' the camp commander responded, 'but they did say their nephew can't get to sleep.'

'I know who you mean.' Fortunato grinned. 'But it's not me playing the piccolo that's bothering young Conti. He's taken this whole arrest and internment situation badly. I'm surprised his uncles didn't tell you that.'

'They said he was depressed.'

'Of course, the boy's depressed,' Fortunato said. 'He's sixteen-years old and he wanted to sign up for the British army as a gunner. Like his uncle did in the last war.'

The camp commander and his assistant locked eyes.

Fortunato continued, 'they asked him to come back when he was eighteen years old and in the meantime the government has him arrested and interned with the rest of us. Luckily, he's got some relatives in here too that can take care of him.'

'Well, as I said,' the camp commander spoke softly, 'the complainants would like you and your friend to be moved further down the parade to other lodgings.'

'We like it where we are. Let me talk to them. I'm sure we can work it out.'

The camp commander looked down again at his notes. 'I see you've volunteered for the Pioneer Corps.'

'They don't answer me,' Fortunato replied. 'And it's not because I'm too young.' Fortunato grinned.

'We'll have to see what we can do about that.' The camp commander sounded determined.

The camp commander liked the flute and flute players and he agreed to give Fortunato twenty-four hours to convince the complainants.

The complainants, the Conti's were easy to convince because they were partial to Fortunato's prowess in the kitchen. Consequently, Fortunato and Renzo remained in lodging house number twelve and continued to play their instruments — "a little quieter, if possible." The Conti's were still resident a few days later when Decio Anzani waltzed in with half a dozen of the Ferdenzi tribe — who immediately began repositioning chairs and organising an italo-cockney table for themselves just between the Conti italo-taffies and an italo-scots table — whilst Decio and Giovanni Ferdenzi senior joined the hot drinks queue.

'We heard the best biscuits were baked down here,' Decio said.

Fortunato was startled to see Decio had also been interned. It meant Renzo was right. Everyone was being interned, regardless if they were renowned anti-fascists. 'I'm a little disappointed to see you here,' Fortunato confessed.

'We're not so happy to see you either,' Giovanni said. 'It's obviously a mistake.'

'Did you pass through the dark satanic mills?' Fortunato asked and wondered how Decio could maintain a cut of dignity if he had spent even a half an hour in Warth Mills.

'Yes, we darn well did.' Giovanni left to join the others in staking a table.

'We're getting it sorted,' Decio gruffly announced.

Renzo appeared at Fortunato's shoulder and was embraced by Decio.

'Getting what sorted?' Fortunato asked.

'We have a lawyer on the case,' Decio said. 'Also, you ought to know your women are doing a fantastic job of getting everyone coordinated. I don't expect you'll be in here for too long.'

'What can Maria do?' Renzo asked.

'You know how she is,' Decio said. 'Hyper-active.'

They were interrupted by the appearance of several of the Ferdenzi tribe, Giovanni's sons Ernesto and Cirillo and some cousins. They noisily greeted Fortunato and Renzo and then having been asked by another internee to "turn it down" they strolled away to talk quietly with Giovanni at his table. They returned moments later to the serving hatch where Ernesto blinked furiously as he and Cirillo took instructions from Decio, after which Cirillo spoke quickly. 'You'll need to excuse us,' he said and led several of the other Ferdenzi's out of the lodging house kitchen café.

Decio selected between several familiar biscuits and patisseries from a tray and he took his time before he leant in and informed Fortunato, 'I've sent them on a little errand.'

'I can see that,' Fortunato replied between gritted teeth and thought how typical it was of the well garbed anarchist; he had hardly arrived and was already busy.

'I've sent them to go and find out about the list,' Decio announced. 'In case you're wondering.'

Fortunato shrugged and hesitated to ask Decio which particular list he had in mind. There were so many "lists" circulating in everyone's imaginations.

Perhaps frustrated by Fortunato's lack of curiosity Decio turned toward the others in the kitchen café and asked, 'have any of you seen the list, yet?' The others collectively shook their puzzled heads but before the matter could be pursued any further, Giovanni called over to Decio, 'I wouldn't mind if some of those biscuits made their way over here.'

As Decio joined Giovanni, Renzo whispered to Fortunato, 'what list do you suppose he's on about?'

'It's probably your Maria, or Decio's lawyer that wants a list of who's in here.'

'Or maybe the Home Office are finally preparing a proper list of suspicious individuals,' Renzo speculated.

'If they are, you'll be on it,' Fortunato said jokingly.

'*Va fancullo*,' Renzo replied and laughed for the first time since he had been taken from his wife and children.

Fortunato threw a dishcloth at Renzo. He had been pleased to hear Renzo laugh. Since their arrival in the camp, his friend had grown more despondent with each day that passed. It was as though he had already given up. And it had become harder to get him to play the piccolo at nights.

'What are they doing here?' Renzo whispered. 'A few days ago, I served a priest in here and now Anzani shows up. They've decided to lock us all up because they think we're all fascist supporters. You can't deny it.'

Renzo was simply stating the situation as it appeared to him. Fortunato did not yet have the will to argue otherwise, because there was an explanation, and it was worse than Renzo had guessed. Fortunato's chat with the camp commander had shown it. It was not that the Government had imagined they were interning supporters of Mussolini, it was simply they had no idea of — nor did they care about — the character of whom they were interning. Simply being born an Italian was sufficient. Someone somewhere had given an order and someone, somewhere else, had not had the courage to say it was a bad idea.

Fortunato filled a fresh pot with boiled water. 'Let's go and chat with the new boys,' he suggested to Renzo.

As they sat down with Decio and Giovanni, Fortunato decided to test his theory. 'Seriously, do you know how you've ended up in here?'

Decio spun in his chair. 'I might ask you the same.'

'You're hardly "fifth-columnist" material, are you?' Fortunato countered.

'Do you see anyone here that is?' Decio replied and he stretched out an arm and traced a wide circle. 'All I can see is a ragged bunch of restaurateurs, pasta makers, tailors and what have you. Most of whom are or the wrong side of fifty years old.'

'If you ask me, the situation's down to dumb panic, ineptitude and rabid racism,' Giovanni added indignantly.

'Not everyone here's on the wrong side of fifty,' Fortunato said, 'and those that are, already fought a war. I'll bet they'd be handy with a rifle.'

'It's probably that thought which terrifies them,' Giovanni said.

'Terrifies who?' Fortunato asked.

'Our hosts,' Giovanni replied ironically.

'Lord Almighty,' Decio said angrily. 'None of us would be here if we liked the idea of living in a fascist country. Hasn't anyone thought about that? No one's asked why we all planted ourselves here. Why we all chose this place to grow our families. We've been here for decades. Plenty of us have children born here, including sons old enough and already enlisted in the British armed forces. The only thing that is terrifying here is the level of ignorance.'

'Blame *Il Duce*,' Fortunato said. 'There may even be some Italians that are not entirely opposed to Mussolini and his ways but he's the one that has condemned us all,' Fortunato said.

'What are you talking about?' Renzo asked.

'Think about it,' Fortunato answered. He considered his own boss a case in point and he had doubts on several others. 'I'll bet we've all come across some dangerous specimens,'

'Seriously?' Renzo said. 'Which of us knows anyone that's dangerous?'

'Talk for yourself,' Fortunato said. 'I'm dangerous.'

The others joined Renzo in laughter.

'No, I'm serious,' Fortunato insisted. 'If I get out of here, those fascists are going to see how dangerous I can be.' He made a slashing motion with his hand across his neck and the others laughed louder.

'What makes you think you'll get out?' Decio asked.

And, not for the first time, Fortunato wondered if he should tell anyone what he had done.

13

WAVERTREE

Brunswick Arms, Liverpool.

The Bay of Biscay safely behind them, they had been heading for Falmouth when Naval Command diverted them to Liverpool. Edgar could hardly contain his pleasure at the turn of events. It was the chance that he had been hoping for.

'Say what you want.' He dabbed a handkerchief at a watery eye. 'It's definitely Saint Brendan sending us a sign.' He marvelled at himself. His Liverpudlian accent unfailingly surfaced at the prospect of sailing into the Mersey. No one would imagine he had left the place a quarter of a century ago.

'Bugger Saint Brendan,' Bob Connell answered.

'A bit harsh on our worthy patron.'

'You're forgetting I'm an engineer.'

'What's that to do with anything?'

'For a start, we don't have much affinity with your bloody seafaring saint.'

A sharp intake from Edgar. Bob could say whatever he liked, but if there was a chief engineer anywhere on the world's waterways who belonged more to the sea than Bob Connell did then Edgar had never met him. 'Thanks to Saint Brendan, I'll be able to take you to Wavertree.'

'Aye,' Bob answered in one of his several registers of deadpan. 'There's always that.'

The *Arandora Star* loomed over a section of Princes dock. Her cargo of seventeen hundred evacuees from St Jean de Luz had been disembarked and her finished-with-engines bell had been rung and her main turbines quietened. All decks were unlit. The sole signs of human life aboard were the shapes of two sleep deprived men who stood side by side on top of the chart-house.

Edgar slouched against the guardrail and stared in the direction of the ship's prow which pointed balefully toward Bootle Bay. The ship occasionally lurched forward as though trying to break free and find a pilot ready to lead her up Crosby Channel and out beyond the banks and past the wrecks lurking on Burbo and Formby.

Bob stamped out a cigarette and shuffled closer to Edgar.

Both men held the rail and stuck their obstinate chins out seaward.

Edgar refastened the top-button of his pea-coat. 'Brisk for the end of June.'

'Aye, it is.'

They turned their gaze dockside. In their line of vision was a single span road bridge, and beyond it, at ground level, a dirty diesel-train kissed the buffers of Riverside Station. Further along, perched on an overhead railway, was the outline of a second railway station: Princes Dock Station. A diesel train on the Riverside and an electric train on the Overhead.

Edgar admired the pragmatism of Liverpool's civil engineers and the imagination of her town-planners that had coalesced to create the city's Light Overhead Railway. Electric trains shimmered sixteen feet above street level. At that moment, a levitating locomotive and its pilot waited patiently to squeeze aboard those hundreds of passengers brought there by Edgar and Bob and who streamed from dockside sheds in the direction of the station.

'Which'd be your preference?' Edgar quietly asked.

Bob pointed to the large diesel. 'Does that one go north?' he asked sullenly.

'Not directly,' Edgar answered. 'But it'd take you to a connection. You'd get there, eventually.'

'But would it be quicker?'

'I honestly don't know.'

'Where's this Wavertree of yours then?' Bob asked. His tone more congenial.

Edgar smiled. Wavertree was never further away than a lightly interred memory. But from the roof of the chart-house it could be plainly seen a mere three-miles away. 'Over there,' Edgar replied and pointed. He inhaled deeply and screwed his eyes tight shut. With his eyes closed the world came more into focus. They took the direct route toward Wavertree, south from Princes dock, past Wapping dock and then a canter up beyond Queen's dock and from there a brisk walk with a wind at their back would have had them scurrying the length of Upper Parliament Street.

'What more could we have asked for?' Edgar inquired. His pleasure undisguised. 'First we get diverted to Liverpool and then we get the weekend off.'

'How about a week off?' Bob countered.

Edgar ignored the bait. He turned away at the sound of several seagulls that had appeared from nowhere and swooped across the estuary to harass two small vessels. After a few moments he pulled down on his sloping cap rim. 'Does that mean that you're happy to be here?' he asked.

Bob smiled a crooked smile. 'At least one of us knows his way around.'

It was time to leave the ship for real and take the route Edgar's mind had travelled. They traipsed along the floating landing stage and down one of the half-dozen passenger footpaths that snaked out in the direction of the Riverside railway station. High above them a few gulls circled back and squawked loudly. Given that the disembarked evacuees had barely a crust to throw away and the gulls were passing for a second time, there was little left for them to make a noise over. Yet, the lack of prospects did not discourage them.

'Your Liverpudlian gulls are nasty.'

'You've just got to get acquainted with them.'

'I don't need to get to know them,' Bob answered with the conviction of someone who had spent many bracing summers walking Greenock esplanade. 'I prefer Greenock gulls.'

From the spot he was occupying, Edgar had been born three miles away and several generations of his closest family haunted these docks. He felt he ought to be defending Liverpudlian gulls but having recently passed some time in the company of Greenock gulls he was uncertain as to whether a case could successfully be mounted for the laridae of Liverpool. All the same, he was about to muster an argument when several of the Liverpudlian caste swooped in low over their heads.

Bob threw his arms in the air and shouted, 'bugger off.'

Edgar ducked. He recognised the musty smell of gulls. He turned to watch the birds as they rose like rockets and then swooped back into the Riverside station concourse where they landed a calculated distance from some evacuee stragglers.

'I wouldn't say they're aggressive,' Edgar said. 'I'd say they're being familiar.'

Bob stopped and turned to watch the gulls. In the concourse a myriad of voices rose. An assortment of languages and dialects: French, Spanish, Polish and Czechoslovak tongues. Tens of people, military and civilians, appeared from the shadows and started shooing away the hungry Liverpudlian gulls that fearlessly flapped and squawked amongst them. Bob shook his head as though in pity for Edgar's efforts to defend the gulls.

They continued walking until their attention was drawn toward a line of heavily laden, busy-faced dockworkers who carried ladders, cutting tools and rolls of barbed wire, and behind them were boiler-suited dockers who faced each other and walked sideways, like a column of crabs sharing the heavier loads. The line moved along the floating dock-way toward the steep gangway that led toward the *Arandora Star*.

'Shouldn't we go back to see what they're doing?' Bob asked.

'Unfortunately, I know what they'll be doing.' Edgar spoke plaintively and he retrieved the first page of a Naval Messenger's memoranda from his inside pocket. He handed it to Bob. 'I meant to give it to you earlier.'

Whilst Bob read the memorandum that had been signed by a War Ministry mandarin from the Cheshire Regional office, advising that "necessary modifications" would be carried out on the *Arandora Star* ahead of its next voyage, Edgar decided he could not share his own sentiments about the situation. He was captain, and he was a Moulton. It was his burden to find meaning in the midst of an incomprehensible situation.

Bob had barely read the page before he passively handed it back. 'They're turning her into a prison-ship.'

Edgar shivered. A light breeze appeared. He pocketed his cap. The immediate situation was worse even than Bob had imagined. There would be much more to say. However, it was not the moment to reveal the bleakest part of their orders. 'We'll talk about it later.'

On Strand Street, Edgar spotted a young flower-seller sitting on a seat adjacent to a wooden cart. Her cart overflowed with a mosaic of flowers and plants and herbs that stirred in the draught. Her legs stretched out from underneath a long blue-denim apron. She held a newspaper tight and appeared to be reading it. Adjacent to her, a painted board proclaimed: "prices freshly cut." Chalked on the road surface below it someone had written, "but the flowers might not be." Edgar missed the Liverpool wit.

The cart looked to be a permanent feature of the landscape. The pavement around it was an oasis of colour. Closer up, was a patchwork of scents and perfumes from dozens of haphazardly placed pots and bottles with a variety of short and long-stemmed flower arrangements. Several of the plants were marked as being edible.

'Morning,' the flower-seller announced in warm nasal tones.

'Morning,' Edgar and Bob echoed.

Edgar bent over exaggeratedly to smell and touch some of the flowers and herbs.

'What are you looking for?' the flower seller asked. 'Food or flowers?'

'Definitely flowers,' Edgar replied.

'See anything you like?'

Edgar pointed to a pail of blue posies. 'They both loved those flowers.'

The flower-seller reached into her cart and removed a bunch of blue, short-stemmed flowers from a bucket and sniffed. 'Me too.'

'Can you change a ten-shilling note?' Edgar asked.

The flower seller looked dubious. But before she could declare whether she could or could not change Edgar's ten-shilling note, Bob stepped forward. He held a half-crown between thumb and index finger. 'I'll take this.'

The flower-seller regarded Bob's half-crown with interest and she scrunched up her nose. 'Wait a minute.' She brought their attention to some daffodils arranged in the row behind. 'A bunch of daffs would be perfect company and that way you needn't worry about changing a half-crown.'

'All right,' Bob agreed. 'I'll take those as well.'

The flower-seller wrapped the two posies in fluttering pages from the *Liverpool Echo* and handed them to Bob.

The flower-seller called after them, 'if you take good care, they'll probably last a week. Maybe more.'

Bob passed the forget-me-nots to Edgar.

'These are perfect.' Edgar held the delicate posy against his chest, as though it might otherwise have flown away in the breeze.

Bob did likewise with the daffodils.

They picked up their pace beyond Wapping docks and headed up toward Queens and Coburg docks. By the time they arrived at Brunswick docks the breeze had calmed enough for both of them to re-fix their caps.

'That's where I learnt to swim.' Edgar pointed to Brunswick dock basin.

Bob tiptoed for a better look. 'You're serious?' He asked as though the opacity of the water and the proximity of vessels caused him to wonder whether Edgar was pulling his leg.

'And right over there's the church where I was baptised,' Edgar added as he slowed his pace and pointed.

'Methodist. Correct?'

'I have mentioned it before,' Edgar replied. He pointed to the building next door. 'And that's where we went to the sea-cubs and then to the sea-scouts. Me and Rudy.'

Bob scrutinised the sea-scout hall as though he expected something grander. 'That's where they filled your heads with all of this ancient mariner secret code?'

'No,' Edgar laughed. 'I got that at home.'

'I thought they taught all of this communing with the sea and sky and nature stuff at the sea-cadets.' It was difficult to know from Bob's tone whether his enquiry was serious.

Edgar knew it was hardly by accident that anyone would choose to become a marine engineer, as opposed to say an aeronautical or industrial engineer and therefore across time it had become easier to communicate with Bob about the metaphysical aspect of being a navigator. 'And I thought you understood it.' Edgar spoke patiently.

'About the kedger's code?'

'Yes.'

'Being passed down from generations of fishermen?'

It was clear that Bob was being ironic. Perhaps it was the news about Rudy Sharp. Rudy had survived the *Lancastria* sinking. Four thousand passengers had not. 'I've told you,' Edgar replied. 'It's a question of how one lives not simply how one dies.'

Bob slowed his walking pace. He sniffed the daffodils in his hand. He looked at Edgar with a regard that suggested he had, indeed, been teasing. 'Anyway, how far away is this cemetery you want to show me?'

'You mean that rich source of human chronicles and cultural anthropology?' Edgar replied in as good a Glaswegian accent as he could muster.

Bob laughed aloud. 'Did I say that?'

'Yes, you did.'

'I'm never taking you back to Glasgow.'

With his posy of forget-me-nots Edgar pointed along Warwick Street. 'Up there, past the house I was born in.' He picked up his pace as though he wanted to get there sooner.

'Are we in a hurry?' Bob asked.

'I'd like to get these flowers to them whilst they're in good health.' Edgar marched off.

Within a few steps Bob had fallen in — left, right, left, right and eyes straight ahead. It was a dance whose steps were easily absorbed. With each euphonic slap of leather on Warwick Street asphalt, Edgar silently thanked Saint Brendan again for sending him the best engineer in the whole of the Blue Star Shipping line. He could think of no other chief engineers that maintained an umbilical cord connecting themselves to the rhythm of their ship's engines. If a beat was ever missed Bob was awake to it before anyone. That was everything a captain dreamt of in a chief engineer.

They arrived in front of a modest, redbrick, two-up, two-down house. The curtains were closed. The modest front lawn had not seen a lawnmower in a year. The last footsteps on the garden path were those of an undertaker some five months previously. Edgar discreetly nodded. 'That's it.'

Bob stared, he looked surprised. 'This is Wavertree?'

'We're technically in Toxteth.'

'And you own this, now?'

'Half of it,' Edgar muttered. 'Along with my brother in Brooklyn.'

'And according to you Jeremiah Horrocks lived around here?' Bob sounded quizzical.

'I didn't say he had lived in this actual street.'

'Where then?'

'Not far.'

'But you did say we might find his grave in the cemetery?'

'It would make sense,' Edgar replied. 'He was born here and he died here. He has to be around here, somewhere.'

'But no one has found him in all these years?' Bob sounded doubtful.

It was thanks to Jeremiah Horrocks that a multitude of young Toxteth mariners and astronomers had developed their passion for the study of the skies and the seas. The lure of stumbling upon Horrocks' unknown grave was a fantasy shared by a great many of them. It has eluded all who have searched. But important others lay in this cemetery. And now, in Bob, there was someone else to know about the place. Someone else who might, should the need arise, be able to return and lay flowers. Edgar quickened his pace as he led Bob along a path toward a separate section of the cemetery. Once there, he removed his cap and pointed to the tallest and most ornate, purest white marble gravestone not simply in that section but in any section of the cemetery.

Bob removed his cap and whistled. 'That's a monument with something to say.'

'That's us Moulton's for you. Understated with our hello's and overstated with our goodbye's.'

Bob looked around. 'Why's the grave over here?'

Edgar pointed to a six-foot metal pole upon which a rectangular sign declared they were standing upon unconsecrated ground. 'I can think of one advantage,' he said. 'It makes it infinitely easier to find your way here.'

Bob shrugged as he passed the daffodils to Edgar and turned back to read the inscription:

In loving memory of William J Moulton
who died 3rd May 1892 aged 23 years
beloved eldest son of Captain John and Winifred Moulton Blessed
are the dead who die in the Lord.

Edgar knelt on the grass, which had remained scarred from January. He proceeded to remove the five-month-old, desiccated detritus from two wrong sized metal pots and he spoke whilst he worked to place Bob's daffodils and his own forget-me-nots. 'Willie was born at sea, off the Chincha Islands, near the coast of Peru.'

'Somehow, I'm not surprised.'

Edgar stood up. His trouser knees were fringed by dark patches and his eyes were moist. 'When he died, it was as though I'd lost my own father. I was five years old but I can still remember him. Whenever he was home, Willie read to me every night: adventure stories of distant islands and vicious Kraken and the occasional mermaid and some poetry too. I suppose that's where my own interest started.'

'In my family, it was me doing the reading,' Bob muttered. 'To my three sisters.'

'When Willie read it was hypnotic. He was a dashing, bearded master mariner. I can see and hear him right now.'

Bob looked wistfully at Edgar. 'I've never been good at remembering faces. Sounds are my thing. Especially when engines sing. Steam or combustion. Marine or otherwise.'

Edgar remained still, upright, head bowed. Tears in ducts.

Bob continued talking. 'Could be an aircraft, or an automobile. Wheels or wings. It always surprises me when people say they can't tell the difference between a whiny Bantam two-stroke, and a throaty Villiers. A breathless four-stroke, or a murmuring six cylinder or whispering twelve cylinder in-line motor. Every one of them has its own distinctive music: belts whirring and chains clacking.' He searched for a handkerchief and passed it to Edgar.

'Thanks.'

'What happened to Willie?'

'Father always told us that Willie had been lent to us until Neptune needed him back. He believed navigators belong to the seas and if they're special they'll find that the seas belong to them. Only the chosen, will return there and roam freely and watch over those they love.'

Bob sighed as though he would never understand and turned his attention to reading the adjacent second inscription.

Also, John Richard (Jack), Master Mariner
who was drowned in Shanghai harbour
14 April 1907, aged 36 years
He was loved by all.

Some daffodils flopped forward. Bob got to them first. He removed the daffodils and snapped their stems shorter. He replaced them in the pot. They lolled less but stuck together like a gang.

'You never mentioned you had two brothers that drowned!'

'It's not something one talks about when skippering.'

'I suppose not.' Bob nodded and remained where he was, close to the monument. He stared solemnly at the next inscription. 'And here's your dad, the famous captain of the *Pegasus*.'

Edgar had often spoken with pride of his father's long career as captain of a beautiful four masted, iron ship named the *Pegasus*. His father had captained that ship until at seventy-three years of age he was pensioned off. The *Pegasus* did not like its new master, eighteen months later it ran aground and had to be scrapped. It would be another eight years, 1920, before old mariner Moulton himself ran aground.

John Moulton, Master Mariner, our beloved father
who died 2nd June 1920, aged 82 years. His life an example.
And Winifred Hughes, our beloved mother, wife of the above
who died 6th June 1920, aged 77 years.
In death not divided.

Edgar shuffled aside to permit Bob closer access. 'Right to the end, he wanted to get up and go out in his boat.'

'And your mother?' Bob's voice sounded slightly incredulous as he knelt to better push apart the daffodils. 'I didn't know she died four days after him.' Bob emphasised the word 'four.'

'You could say she went down with her ship.'

'They had the same illness?'

Edgar grinned. 'Not unless Welsh witchcraft is a malady.'

'She took a potion?'

'She would have been capable of it. But, no it was pure *styfnig*, and it helped that she had the gift of *ragwelediad*.'

'Obstinate I know, but what's *ragwelediad*?'

'Foresight.' Edgar explained how as his father's cancer became stronger and his will had become weaker, his mother had anticipated it all. But she fooled them by appearing euphoric. Her captain was dying, and she simply concentrated on a thorough cleaning of their home. It had never looked as fresh. She sang constantly too. Not sad songs but Welsh love songs.

Edgar and his sister, Lucy, had been looking the other way. They forgot their mother's cancer was only in remission. They concentrated on their father as he became frailer. Father had stopped eating; they all saw that. But Edgar had not noticed his mother was barely eating either, until one day Lucy pointed it out. Edgar tried to talk sense into his mother: "You must eat. You have to keep your strength up." But she looked languidly across the bedroom toward her captain dying in his bed. She grimaced and turned her mulish white mop back in the direction of Edgar and Lucy. "Must keep my strength up?" she challenged them with an irritation rarely heard in the Moulton household. "It takes far more strength not to eat than it does to eat, and if you two don't yet understand this then your father and I didn't do the job we intended."

That night Edgar and Lucy went to the Brunswick Arms to thrash out the problem. "What would you do if you were in her circumstances?" Lucy asked and her question took the wind out of Edgar's sails. He searched to find a flaw in her logic. But there was none. His parents had been married almost fifty-two years. They had outlived three of their six children. They would choose the ending that they wanted, an ending where they could be together. *Styfnig* right to the end. Edgar and Lucy trooped home from the Brunswick with their heads down.

'Four days after we dropped father's coffin into the ground, we reopened the grave and placed her in beside him. As she had foreseen.'

'Welsh willpower.'

Edgar shook his head sadly and internally offered a prayer for his sister, Lucy, who had lain this past five months where his feet were planted.

'In death not divided,' Bob murmured.

'I suppose we could go and search for Horrocks' grave now,' Edgar suggested.

'We'll never find it, will we?' Bob answered and smiled wryly.

'If you're hungry, we could go directly to the Brunswick. If Saint Brendan is willing, maybe we'll come back here again one day and properly look for the great astronomer.'

Thus, each of them in their own world of turbines and tappets; tides and stars walked silently away from the cemetery. Later, in the warmth of the Brunswick Arms, they stood shoulder-to-shoulder and placed their identical breakfast orders. Edgar gazed into the long mirror behind the bar and imagined the watery reflection of the Mersey.

As if he had read Edgar's mind, Bob finally asked, 'about this conversion to a prison-ship.'

Apart from the bar keeper they were alone, but all the same Edgar raised a finger to his lips and with Bob shadowing closely he followed a signpost for The Snug, passed through half-glass doors and entered into a side lounge. He chose a table by the window and when Bob took the seat opposite him, he finally whispered, 'we're going to Newfoundland.'

'We're going to the North Pole with prisoners-of-war?'

'It's not the North Pole,' Edgar answered. 'Neither are we taking p-o-w's.'

'Who, then?'

'Alien internees.'

Bob scratched furiously at a cheek. 'What does that mean?'

Edgar sighed. Bob would find out eventually. He may as well tell him everything and be done with it. 'Our orders are to transport twelve-hundred and fifty men. Maybe fifty of those will be prisoners-of-war. But twelve-hundred are civilians.'

Their breakfast arrived in the hands of a lady who might have been the flower seller's mother. She placed a tray with two large steaming yellow teapots and matching cups on the table. 'The rest of your order will be here in a minute.'

'We're not in a hurry,' Edgar informed the lady.

'I don't know how we're going to manage this.' Bob shook his head and poured steaming hot tea for himself and Edgar.

'By concentrating on our jobs.' Edgar laboured to sound unaffected. Anyway, the Brunswick Arms was not the place to restart their litany on the stupidity of the Home Office's treatment of "foreigners." 'We'll do like we've done until now,' he added and burnt his tongue as he sipped his tea. 'I'll concentrate on the navigating and you concentrate on the engines.'

Bob Connell shook his head. 'I can't do it. And I know you don't want to either.'

'This is not the moment to be *styfnig*,' Edgar warned.

'If not now, when?'

Edgar was uncertain if the moment was "now" or had already presented itself and was now gone. Maybe it was still to arrive? He was sure of nothing except what would happen if he refused his command. Or if he allowed Bob to do so. 'You know what happens to "conchies" in the navy,' he warned.

'Maybe I'm ready to take that risk,' Bob said. 'Perhaps we should toss a coin?'

14

THE KRAKEN

North Atlantic Sea.

It was near five a.m.. The starboard sky held an impatient sun in its wing and corridors of golden light broke upon the ocean's surface. *Unterseeboot* U47 straddled the waterline and its engines thrummed in the prelude to another easy hit.

In the conning tower, Günther removed his cap and ran his fingers through his blond, prematurely thinning hair and reflected on the twenty-six days of their current patrol. In the first three weeks they had sunk three ships and killed no one. But in the last forty-eight hours they had killed three sailors. He let the ocean fill his lungs and sighed a heavy sigh.

'Is everything all right, *Herr Kapitänleutnant?*' second watch *Oberleutnant* Amelung *von* Varendorf asked.

'Why wouldn't it be?' Günther sounded irritated, despite the question having come from Amelung.

'You seem like a rat in a tar barrel.'

Günther smiled weakly. 'How do you mean?'

'I don't know.' Amelung pointed out to sea. 'You have your

sitting-duck on the horizon. We don't even need to deviate our course.'

'Your point?' Günther shrugged.

'I've seen you look happier.'

Günther's stone face returned to flesh. He spoke softly. 'Do I seem unhappy?'

'A little,' Amelung replied.

Günther put his cap back on. Amelung had said, "a little," but this was another of Amelung's euphemisms. He had certainly meant more than a little. Probably he had meant, "a lot." Günther stroked his stubbled cheeks. 'Are you going to remind me now of all the things I have to be grateful for?'

'Let's start with six patrols and you're still here.'

'You're still here too.'

'But I can think of other places I'd rather be,' Amelung quipped.

'So can I.'

'Like where?'

'You know where.' Günther lifted his binoculars for another look. 'What's the latest on U46?'

'I knew you'd ask that,' Amelung replied. 'Bert's heading home.'

'But has BdU confirmed it?'

'Not everything needs to be confirmed by Command Headquarters.'

Günther rocked on his heels. 'I'd like to be sure.'

Amelung sniffed and looked at his wristwatch and announced, 'he's in AN 2511.'

'You mean he's in Shetland sector.'

Amelung grinned mischievously. 'Sometimes, I forget.'

'What's the news on that nine-thousand tonner he hit?'

'No change,' Amelung replied insouciantly. 'Anyway, all you have to do is sink that duck out there waiting for you, and you'll be at six sunk too. That way, even when Bert's nine-thousand tonner becomes a luxury hotel for lanternfish, he'll still not be ahead of you.'

'What if they come across another target before Kiel?'

'Without torpedoes, even Bert won't be able to sink anything.'

There was something in Amelung's tone that bothered Günther. As though sinking enemy ships ought to be scorned. Or perhaps Amelung was mocking Bert. Either way, Amelung ought to take more care. This was their first mission without Bert as first watch *oberleutnant* and some of his old crew still felt affection for Bert, and they were arriving in the conning tower right at that moment.

'Tell me, Amelung, what do you think we are supposed to be doing out here?' Günther raised his palms to the sky.

Amelung hesitated, as though considering which particular thoughts he could reveal. Finally, he responded, 'some folk seem unduly enthusiastic.'

Another of Amelung's euphemisms. But did he mean Günther or Bert? Günther could get it out of him but he was not in the mood for small chat. Everyone knew that Bert's "enthusiasm" was all about eclipsing U47 and Günther. 'I don't want to speculate,' Günther said. 'I'd simply like to know if we can expect any change in his numbers.'

'I can assure you, *Herr Kapitänleutnant*, he's not going to sink anything else on this patrol,' Amelung replied curtly. 'The best Bert can hope for is six vessels sunk for forty-four thousand tonnes. Always assuming that the nine-thousand-tonner disappears with the next large wave.'

Whilst U47 pumped out the residue of her ballast, Günther's attention was drawn to something in the sea close to the bow. A seal? A mine? There had been no reports of mine sightings, but plenty mines drifted unreported amongst the flotsam out there and dozens of vessels had been hit when they least expected it. Günther sent two crewmen to the bow for a closer look.

Amelung whistled cheerily. 'Anyway, you can be proud of your pupil, he's wreaked a lot of destruction on his first patrol.'

Günther acknowledged a thumbs-up from the bow inspectors and he spoke from the side of his mouth: 'It's as well for you he's not around to hear you call him my *pupil*.'

Amelung laughed. 'It's as well for all of us.' He tilted forward and whispered in Günther's direction. 'You must admit, sir, he was more than a little brusque toward the end of that last patrol.'

Günther grinned. Yes, Bert had become intense. But he had not always been that way. Since the award of Günther's Knight's Cross a change had come over Bert. During successive patrols, Bert had become coated in self-spun threads of jealousy. Günther waited, hoping the old Bert might emerge from the chrysalis of angst. He had never imagined U47 without Bert. But Amelung was probably right, things were easier for everyone now that Bert had left. Günther stared at the horizon and their next victim. He supposed at that same moment U46 had surfaced and Bert had been informed about U47's numbers.

Almost four weeks into U47's sixth patrol and they had done well: five vessels sunk for twenty-seven thousand tones. But Bert's patrol had probably sunk six vessels for forty-four thousand tonnes and was almost safely back in Kiel. Günther imagined Bert beyond the horizon laughing at U47. He forced a smile. The "sitting duck" would at least elevate their numbers. Sink that and they would also have six vessels. But the target looked too small to bring them close to U46's tonnage sunk on this patrol.

'It's as well he's not here to see you, though,' Amelung said.

'What are you talking about?'

'You look as though you're in mourning.'

Amelung should try to stay quiet. Günther was not mourning anyone, especially not Bert. He missed Ingeborg and his two young daughters, that was all. He missed them more than he could tell anyone, even Amelung. But there was something on his mind: a shore job. But everything his family had they owed to his being out there, under the sea in a black metal cylinder. He sighed aloud and nodded dead-ahead, 'estimated tonnage?'

'About four-and-a-half thousand tonnes,' Amelung replied and continued training his binoculars.

The target was large enough to need an eel to sink it, but its tonnage was far too small to catch up with Bert. He had only two good eels remaining. 'You're sure there are no chances of U46 having taken on munitions?'

'It's possible,' Amelung admitted. 'But we'd have heard about it and we'd have had the same opportunity.'

'It's not that important, anyway,' Günther lied. 'All the same, let's try to sink this one with shells. Keep our last two eels in reserve.'

But everyone on U47 knew the truth: It *was* that important and Günther had just confirmed it.

Amelung would ensure U47's chief radio communications officer checked in again with Nauen station and ascertain whether U46 had after all taken on any eels or even deck-gun rounds of ammunition. 'I'm glad you're taking it like that,' Amelung said. 'Anyway, everyone knows who the better navigator is.'

Günther wondered, *do they?* After the Scapa Flow mission, the hierarchy had awarded him a Knight's Cross and claimed he was the most extraordinary U-boat pilot in the fleet. He had become conceited enough to believe their version of himself. But as he stood on the conning tower, he remembered a moment before all of this had begun. An old salt had explained what it meant to be a navigator. It had nothing to do with killing people. Günther was not that person anymore. It did not matter that he still appreciated aspects — theatres of dark skies and bright stars and extraverted planets that acted upon the oceans — something had changed.

From the moment he took on the Scapa Flow mission he had become an instrument to be played. He, who had once found his own words for the navigators' codex could no longer claim to be living by it. Perhaps it was not only Bert that had lost his bearings.

When they got so near to their target that they could read the ship's name, they began shelling it. But they were also low on shells. After six shells, four of which were hits, Amelung gave the order to cease shelling.

The crew of the transport ship: the SS *Empire Toucan,* lowered two lifeboats and began rowing away. Although she was on fire and her crew had vacated, the ship remained stubbornly afloat and showed no sign of taking on water. It was obvious, only a torpedo below the waterline could guarantee a kill. U47 would have to use an eel after all.

They went alongside the *Empire Toucan's* lifeboats. 'Any casualties?' Günther inquired of the *Toucan's* captain.

'One dead. One wounded.'

'Can we get you anything?' Günther asked.

'Some peace would be appreciated!' The captain spoke in a lilt.

'The *Empire Toucan*, what kind of a name is that?' Günther asked.

'It's the kind of name that the miniature man would love to hear has been sunk,' Amelung said quietly.

'We used to be called *Freeport Sulphur Number five*,' the captain answered, as though in an act of resistance.

Günther almost laughed. He shook his head and turned away from the British captain.

Bert had been the one to coin the epithet "miniature man." When the Fuhrer pinned the Knight's Cross with Oak Leaves on Günther's chest, Bert had sniggered and said, "Günther's made the miniature man very happy." Amelung was right, sinking any British ship with *Empire* in her name would please the miniature man. Certainly, it would resonate better than *Sulphur Number Five*.

'Where are you from?' Amelung asked the captain of the *Empire Toucan*.

'Wales.'

'We're going to have to sink your ship.' Amelung sounded apologetic.

The Welshman's eyes brimmed with panic. 'Wait! I've a couple of boys still aboard.'

'Radio officers?' Günther asked abruptly.

The Welshman did not need to respond. Günther knew he had guessed right but he had his own "stubborn boys" to take care of. There was nothing to be done except immediately dispatch the crippled ship. He gave the command and U47 sent its penultimate, precious torpedo directly midships into the *Empire Toucan*. The ship broke in two at its aft section and rapidly sunk. There was no sign of any stubborn boys. The ship quickly disappeared under the water line. Its stubborn boys had possibly got their message out, but they had not got themselves out. Either way, U47 could not remain another minute on the skin of the Atlantic.

At twenty metres below the surface, Günther entered the control room and asked for confirmation of their position.

Amelung cleared his throat. 'Severn section.'

Günther preferred the British shipping sector names to the *Kriegsmarine*'s own grid system. One might conclude this was a residue of his other, old, self. Neither Amelung nor Bert had ever acted as though they found his habit the least bit eccentric. Amelung had been supportive too when Bert's replacement, *Oberleutnant* Hans Werner Kraus, complained about having to log their midday positions twice: firstly, using the *Kriegsmarine* grid system and then using the anarchic British shipping sea areas that Günther insisted upon.

***

'Isn't the *Kriegsmarine* system adequate?' *Oberleutnant* Kraus had tentatively asked Günther.

'Adequate?' Günther repeated and stretched his arms up and flattened his palms against a wiring loom. 'It's adequate, but fundamentally featureless,' he replied. 'I need pictures with my coordinates.'

Kraus shook his head and looked perplexed.

'It's a little indulgence,' Amelung later whispered. 'But wouldn't you agree with him: it's less barren?'

The exchange had worried Günther. He could see that Werner Kraus was certainly competent on the vessel, but if the ocean held no pictures for him, it was unimaginable how Krauss could ever be more than simply competent. How could a fellow like that understand real navigators needed to see rivers and islands and banks and deeps in their coordinates? In Günther's eyes *Herr* Kraus was "spiritually lost." Also, the fellow was too dry, too wrapped up in his manuals and policies.

'Your predecessor had no problems with pictures.'

'I understand my predecessor had his own ambitions,' Kraus replied.

***

U47 neared optimum depth in that sector of the Atlantic. In the control room they busied themselves with their maps and their instruments in pursuit of the immediate priority: safe removal from the area of engagement. Günther cursed the diminution of his torpedo stocks, now down to one good eel, but he spared a thought for the worries of the crew. They had been on their way home, and now what? Was that paltry vessel worth it? Now their position was likely to be known to British Coastal Command. Now they had to hide, had to go deep, go slow and waste hours to improve their chances of remaining alive. Some of the crew would know, just as well as Günther and the watch officers, that Severn section accommodated two enemy coastal stations, both of which were within one hour's flight of their present position. Maybe an RAF Lancaster or Wellington had already been called up by those "stubborn boys" in a final heroic act of defiance. Perhaps a plane was above their heads right at that moment scouting for their profile and trajectory.

Amelung arrived in the control room. He had his little black notebook in his hand. He cleared his throat but Günther raised the palms of his hands, Canute-like, ready to deflect whatever current worry was on the tip of Amelung's tongue. 'We're going to continue as we were. Head home,' Günther said and traced the route on the map.

Amelung opened and closed and re-opened and re-closed his little black notebook.

Günther tapped his fingers adjacent to the map. 'Something on your mind?'

'The men are worried,' Amelung replied curtly.

'They're homesick, that's all.'

'No, it's more than that. There's a lot more talk about, you know —,'

'About what?' Günther interrupted.

'The number of *unterseeboots* that have made one-way patrols in the past six months.'

Günther sighed and he eyed Amelung's note-book. 'That's because of this morbid obsession with counting the dead. It's bad for morale.'

Amelung whispered. 'They all come to me and they talk about their families and you know —.'

Günther tutted before Amelung could go any further. He almost wished that Amelung was not as approachable as he was. But Amelung was easier to approach than any priest or minister, and, given they were all sharing this *unterseeboot*, he was always available. Bert had not needed to be approachable, and his replacement, Krauss hardly seemed to know what that meant. Thus, it was left to Amelung, who always had a compliment for you when you showed him a picture of your family and always remembered their names. He probably wrote them all down in that notebook of his. That was one of the reasons why Günther had asked Amelung to become godfather to Birgit. He was sure Amelung would always remember her birthday.

'Everyone has a family,' Amelung said. 'They're relying on us.'

'All right,' Günther spoke more harshly than he had intended. The faces of Ingeborg and his two infant daughters entered his mind. He softened his tone. 'Have you got it all off your chest now?'

Amelung inhaled deeply. 'I'll tell the lads we're going home.'

Günther hesitated to exit the control room. They *were* going home, that was true, but they could not go immediately. They had a single working torpedo left. Amelung had to know their patrol must continue as long as was necessary. Günther would not say this aloud to Amelung because, as the number of patrols increased and as they neared the end of each patrol, Amelung's mood darkened and with each mission he filled more black notebooks and descended further into a well of melancholy. Amelung became fragile toward the end of their missions.

Amelung's voice trembled as he asked, 'was there something else you wanted to say to me, *Herr Kapitänleutnant*?'

Günther saluted. 'No.' He left the control room. He was glad that their current patrol was, one way or another, approaching its natural end. But whilst Bert had sunk more tonnage than they had, and there remained even a slender possibility that U47 could do something about it, he would have to take chances with all their lives, even Amelung's.

15

STATELESS

Rushen Internment Camp, Isle of Man.

At the start of the shift, Friedrich was in the men's room changing into his clean shirt and white overcoat, when he overheard Doctor Colls. She had come to the end of her shift and her concerned voice passed through the open window of the adjacent ladies' room.

'Fixing her physical scars is not going to cure her,' Doctor Colls said. 'The cure is in here.'

He imagined Doctor Colls tapping herself on the brow.
'She's crying all the time,' the supervising nurse answered. 'And she won't talk with anyone.'

Later, when he changed Tauba's bandages, he was more insistent. 'Where are you from?' he asked.

'Nowhere.'

'We're all from somewhere.'

'Where are you from, then?' she quizzed him.

'Stralsund.'

He had noticed the absence of a ring on her finger. But he had met so many refugees who had to sell or pawn whatever they had managed to bring with them. A ringless finger was not proof of anything. 'Are you married?'

'What business is it of yours?'

'None. I'm sorry. I was making conversation.'

'Are you married?' Tauba asked.

'No, I'm not.'

'Do you have a girlfriend?' she asked him tenderly.

'I don't think so.'

Tauba sat up, poker-backed. 'She's in a camp, right?'

He fought to keep his emotions under control but his hand shook. 'I left her with my father in Vienna. Last I heard they had been caught and paraded in the street and forced to wash away pro-independence graffiti.'

Tauba placed her head in her hands. 'God help us,' she whispered.

'They were taken away,' he completed his thought and he looked Tauba squarely in the eyes. It was clear she had fully registered what had happened. She seemed to have softened, as though she pitied him now, but he did not want pity. He did not know what it was he wanted.

'Which camp?' she asked.

'Dachau.'

'But you made it out, right? The fascists lost another doctor and the British gained one.'

'Well, not exactly.'

'What do you mean?'

'I've not been working as a doctor since I arrived here.'

'What have you been doing?'

He smiled. 'This time, I've been picking apples and potatoes. And shovelling manure.'

Tauba stared unbelievingly and then grinned. 'This time?'

'It already happened to me. Last time the JRC got me away from danger, I tried to finish my medical degree here but the

British Medical Association thought I had come to steal their members jobs.'

Tauba nodded knowingly as though to say she was not surprised.

'The closest I came to practicing medicine was giving eye-drops to a dairy cow.'

Tauba tittered. Her hand suppressed an embryonic laughter.

'I don't know what you said to her,' the nurse remarked, 'but it's working.'

'Sorry,' he replied. 'Would you prefer if we spoke in English?'

'As long as she's smiling,' the nurse answered, 'you can speak any language you like.'

'They saved my life too,' Tauba said. She meant the JRC.

'Did they get you a job picking potatoes?' he asked.

'No. But they helped get me a job as a cleaner.'

'What did you do before?'

'I was a chemist. I have a degree in chemistry.'

His face folded in pity. 'They do what they can.'

Tauba's expression darkened. 'What have we done to anyone to deserve this? I had a home. A nice job. A family. Now I don't even have a country.'

The mood had changed. The supervising nurse raised an eyebrow.

'She finds it very difficult being Stateless,' he explained. Tauba's tears flowed in lines.

'Stateless?' the nurse asked. 'What's she doing in here?'

'What are any of us doing in here?' he replied without rancour.

Although he had needed no encouragement, the supervising nurse encouraged him all the same. He had become part of Tauba's cure. He wanted to know more about her. He began to wonder, would there be a way of finding her when this was all over. 'Will you tell me, where you're from?' he asked.

'I'm from Kryniczna.'

He held her wrists and slowly unwrapped her bandages. 'Where's that?' He massaged cream over her scars.

'In Kolomyia.'

'I see.' He continued to massage her scarred wrist.

'You have no idea where it is. Do you?' Tauba smiled. She was lit up again. Full of mischief.

'No, I don't,' he admitted and he might have blushed a little when their fingers touched.

'I'll give you a clue. I'm thirty-one. I've changed nationality four times, but I've never moved home.' Her tone was partly playful, partly painful. 'Now do you know?'

'I'm guessing Kolomyia is along the eastern borderland?'

'Correct,' she replied and grinned. 'I'll give you another clue. When I was born, I was Austro-Hungarian. By primary school, I was Russian. Then Austro-Hungarian again. Then West Ukrainian and after that Polish. For a little while I was German. Now I'm stateless.' Her voice cracked again.

He continued massaging her wrist, although other patients were waiting.

'Would you like some water?' the nurse asked.

'Yes, please.'

'Do you have any family left back in Kryniczna?' he asked.

She shook her head. 'Those who could escape went to Warsaw. Then they were rounded up and sent to a camp somewhere. Maybe one of my sisters and a brother got away. I'm not sure.'

'Perhaps the JRC can help you find them?'

'They already tried. They thought my sister made it to Vienna. But they couldn't get her out.'

'I might still have friends there,' he said. 'Do you know where your sister is now?'

'No.' She looked at the bed and shook her head.

'And your brother?'

'He hoped to make it to Palestine.'

Friedrich translated for the supervising nurse who sat down on the bed adjacent to Tauba and began to cry. Whilst the nurse composed herself, dried her eyes and hugged Tauba, Friedrich remembered where he had seen Tauba before.

'Did you ever go to the synagogue in Portland Street in London?' he asked.

'Sometimes. When I was lodging in Green Lane.'

'Will you go back there?' he asked a little too desperately. 'You know, when all of this is over?'

'I'd like that.' There was hope in her voice that it might be possible.

That night, back in the boarding house, he recounted Tauba's story to Jacob Burfeind. 'Can't you use your contacts to get her out of here, Jacob?' he asked.

'Do you think I'd be here if I had influence enough to get anyone out?'

'I know you have contacts,' he insisted. 'You have to try because she should not be in here.'

Over the following days he badgered Jacob until he agreed to do something about Tauba's case. Jacob showed him the letters he had drafted — one addressed to a JRC lawyer in London, another addressed to the secretary of a Parliamentary Committee on Refugees and the last one addressed to their common friend and activist, Lily Moulton. Jacob warned him, 'there's no guarantee any of these letters will get any further than the chief postal censor in Liverpool.'

He was undaunted. He already had an idea. He had Jacob write copies of the letters. There was one person he knew he could trust to get those letters out and he passed them to her on his next shift at Rushen Camp Hospital.

'You know there are random searches?' she asked.

'They'd never search the nursing supervisor.'

'Probably not. But if I get caught, I can go to jail.'

'I'm sorry to have to ask this,' he answered. 'Shall we try the normal route?'

'Leave them with me. I'll think about it.'

At the end of his shift on the following day, the nursing supervisor told him, 'they're gone.'

The day after that, Tauba, her physical scars healed, was released back to the women's camp at the Golf Links Hotel. He wondered if they should tell Tauba about the letters. Would it be wrong to raise her hopes? It could be weeks or months for Burfeind's letter to make any difference to her case. Perhaps it would make no difference at all.

A few days passed. He planned to ask the supervising nurse whether she could arrange for a message to be given to Tauba. Instead, it was the supervising nurse who sought him out. She had red blotches around her eyes.

He feared the letters had been intercepted and he had been the source of trouble for her.

She asked him to accompany her to Doctor Coll's office. Two policemen sat outside the office. He made sure not to catch their regard as he entered.

'You'd better sit down,' the supervising nurse said. She handed him a cup of tea.

He accepted the drink and sat down. 'There was nothing in those letters that wasn't true.'

'It doesn't matter.' The nurse bit her lip.

'What do you mean, it doesn't matter?'

'They found Tauba this morning at the foot of the cliffs.' The nurse sobbed. 'It was too late to help her.'

He felt his heart explode. He threw his teacup against a wall and beat his fists against his own head.

The supervising nurse placed an arm around his shoulders.

Doctor Colls entered the office and took his hands in her own. 'We're sorry,' she said.

He dropped to his knees and scrambled on the floor and started to pick up the broken crockery.

'They want you to go over to the police station,' Doctor Colls said and joined him in picking up pieces of crockery. 'They're waiting outside to take you there.'

'Why?' He asked brusquely and struggled to subdue a rising anger.

'She left a note. They want to talk to you about it.'

'Why did she do it?' He asked again.

'They hope you might be able to tell them,' Doctor Colls replied.

'I've tried to tell them,' the supervising nurse said. 'I think it was all that talk of the Deportment Notices.'

'Deportment notices?' His confusion was palpable.

Doctor Colls took Friedrich's hands in her own again and squeezed. 'Apparently, they've started deporting internees.'

'When?' Friedrich could not believe it. He had heard nothing about this.

'Some days ago,' the supervising nurse said. 'They already cleared out one of the mainland transit camps.'

'They were going to deport her?'

'No, only the men, as far as we know,' Doctor Colls answered.

'I think she was worried about someone else being deported,' the nursing supervisor said.

He sat again on the office chair. He held his head in his hands.

'We'll insist that you're needed here.'

'It's kind of you, Doctor. But I'm not sure I want to stay.'

'Think about it,' Doctor Colls answered and exchanged worried looks with the nursing supervisor.

* * *

In the days that followed, he thought about Tauba constantly. He was still thinking about her during his weekly telephone call with his sister. His sister seemed happy. She had volunteered to work as a nursing assistant and although they refused to take her on account of her coming from the German empire, the police had interviewed her and informed her she would not be interned, at least not at the moment.

'Have you found out any more about that mystery girl?' his sister asked.

He could not bring himself to tell his little sister what had happened to Tauba. His mind turned to his own interview with the police and the scrawled goodbye note and the little heirloom that Tauba had left him — her chain with two stars of David. He fingered the chain around his neck. 'I'm going to be deported.'

His sister, ten years younger, and normally brimming with unreasonable optimism, started to cry. 'Deported? I can't believe it. Where?'

'I don't know.'

'What shall I tell mother?'

'Tell her I've volunteered,' he said. 'Tell her it's what Dad would have done.'

'Volunteered? For what?' she asked. 'I thought the JRC were working to get you out?'

'That doesn't seem very likely.' He spoke quietly and was not sure his sister had heard him.

'You've become a defeatist.' She sobbed. 'Father wouldn't have approved at all! And Mother certainly won't.'

In the circumstances, he found his sister to be a little harsh. 'How is Mother?'

'She's hanging on.'

'Hanging on to what?'

'Why are you like this... angry?'

He knew he would not be calling his sister next week. They

would send him on the SS *Tynwald* and then he would be on his way to some distant place. It was time his sister and mother accepted the truth about their father. Nothing could be more certain than the fact they would never see him again. Nor would they ever see Bea. Most likely his father and Bea had not seen out their first day in Dachau. It was not right that his mother was living in false hope and did not know what was happening there. His sister refused to read any newspapers to her or translate any radio broadcasts that mentioned Dachau. His sister hid the reality.

'Don't let her hang-on.' It pained him to say it.

'Mother's a fighter.'

'What's left to fight for?'

'I think you're going through a moment of depression.'

'Making diagnoses already at your age?'

'Remaining sarcastic at yours?' What about that woman you spoke of last week? I don't remember you telling her there was nothing left to fight for.'

His little sister had hit a nerve. 'She's dead. Father's dead. Bea's dead. They're all dead.' He had not intended to say it quite so brutally, but it had to be said.

16

THE LIST

Palace Internment Camp, Isle of Man.

Fortunato considered ignoring the question, but Decio would likely ask again. Easier to answer now and be done with it. 'I've volunteered,' he said.

Several internees backslapped him.

'I'd be volunteering, if I was your age,' Decio replied and the response might have cut some men. A few of them turned pale.

'You're forgetting,' Fortunato countered. 'I don't have a wife or children waiting for me at home. I'm free to do what I want.'

'True enough,' several voices muttered.

But he did have a woman waiting for him and several of those men present in the kitchen café knew it perfectly well. And whilst it was true he had no children of his own he was known to dote on his godson as though the boy were his own.

A brief silence followed, which Giovanni eventually punctuated. 'Who's up for a round of *briscola*?'

'I'm in.' Renzo was the first to reply. His eagerness cut through the murmurs and chair shuffling.

And like when times were normal, it became pairs: himself and Decio against Renzo and Giovanni. They played cards like they played politics: himself and Decio, too defiant to be compliant, resisting fascism with every fibre. Renzo and Giovanni, so humble they rarely grumbled at the rot besetting the old country.

They improvised with a British deck of playing cards and whilst Giovanni shuffled the cards, Renzo leant in and whispered. 'Do you suppose we could organise an escape?'

Fortunato reacted in the same manner as Decio did, as though his face had been wired to an electrical circuit and some scientist had gently turned up the pain dial.

Giovanni paused his card shuffling and slowly shook his head. He passed the deck to Decio.

'Suppose you got beyond the barbed wire,' Fortunato asked quietly without looking up. 'Where would you go?'

'Home.'

His friend was in hell and Fortunato was not inclined to ask him how he thought he would get off the island.

But Decio was less considerate. 'It's the first place they'd look,' he said. Then he fell quiet and dealt three cards to each player and turned the thirteenth card face up.

It was the three-of-hearts.

'I know that,' Renzo said. He bowed his head and stared at the ground. 'It's just that I miss my children.'

Fortunato felt a pulsating behind the eyes, an empathetic headache brought on by nothing but his friend's predicament.

Giovanni noisily laid down the four-of-spades.

Decio hummed and contorted his face like a bad poker player and put a couple of points at risk by playing the jack-of-spades.

Renzo ignored them all. He studied his cards as though he had more than one *briscola* in his hand. He took his time and finally played the two-of-hearts.

Fortunato slowly placed the five-of-clubs, and quietly feigned exasperation at having lost that round. 'Your hand, gentlemen,' he said brightly. The mood lightened. 'I've heard some internees have already been given case review dates.' It was time to establish his own information-gathering credentials. After all he had been in the camp for days before Decio had shown up.

'Those will be the Jewish refugees,' Decio sounded certain of himself.

'Jewish refugees?' Renzo's surprise lifted his pitch. 'What's the point of interning Jewish refugees?'

'And placing them in the same camps as Nazis?' Fortunato added. He looked at Decio in a manner meant to suggest he had "sources" of his own.

'I told you,' Giovanni said. 'It's pure incompetence. That's why we've got ourselves a lawyer.'

Fortunato stared at Giovanni and then gave a nod in the direction of Giovanni's card-playing partner, who needed hope.

'Ah, yes. He's ready to take on more cases,' Giovanni said softly, appearing to have received Fortunato's message.

'Is he expensive?' Renzo asked but all the while kept his eyes on his cards in hand.

'Of course, he's expensive,' Decio said. 'How else do you think you'll get your case expedited?'

'I don't suppose you'll be wanting a lawyer?' Giovanni addressed Fortunato.

'Volunteering to join the army doesn't mean they'll let him out,' Decio said.

'But I'm not volunteering to be "let out,"' Fortunato said. 'I'm volunteering because I can help my country.'

'There you go again,' Decio joked. 'That Picchi code will get you into trouble.'

'Which country would that be?' Giovanni wanted to know.

'Do you think I'm going to waste my time in here and let Italy be ruled by fascists?' Fortunato bristled. 'No. Not me. I'm getting out and I'm going to fight.'

'Unless your name's on the list,' Decio said triumphantly.

'What is this list you've been going on about since you got here?' Fortunato snapped.

'The deportation list,' Decio replied flatly as though this should be common knowledge.

Renzo laid down his playing cards. 'What deportation list?'

'A ship already sailed,' Decio said.

'How come we've not heard about it?' Fortunato asked.

'Only Germans on that one. From mainland camps,' Decio said. 'We'll certainly be on the next one. Or the one after that.'

Renzo turned pallid. 'They're deporting us?' He appeared to be in mild shock.

'Don't worry,' Decio answered. 'I don't mean "us." I mean "Italians." And even if you two were on the list, I'm sure that Maria and Florence would soon get that sorted.'

'How?' Renzo asked barely audible.

'They already petitioned the Home Secretary,' Decio answered. 'Apparently, he's considered by some to be compassionate, even an understanding man.'

'He'd be even more understanding if it were him in here and his nephew was hiding in the cellar,' Renzo said.

'Let's give the fellow a chance,' Decio answered. 'He's already made a statement in Parliament insisting that married men with wives and children in this country should not be separated.'

'Then how come we're all in here?' Renzo asked, his voice broke in peeling away the hypocrisy between words and deeds.

At that moment, Giovanni's boy, Cirillo returned. The boy looked near hysterical. He placed a handful of loose-leaf pages on the table. 'You're all on this list.'

Chairs toppled, crockery cracked and disintegrated against the floor tiles. The news spread around the room and then broke through the door and out into the parade, where it sprinted madly in all directions, up and down and around the entire camp.

'Everyone needs to calm down,' Decio said and obliquely glimpsed at the list as though he were the wife of Lot and a frontal stare might be fatal. 'It's probably a mistake.'

But it was not a mistake, at least not in the sense that Decio suggested. Those men whose names appeared upon the list had been reclassified. They had progressed from being *resident foreigners* to become *resident enemy aliens* and would henceforth be considered *enemy alien deportees*.

They gathered around Cirillo and read some names from the list:

Fortunato - on the list.

Renzo - on the list.

Renzo's cousin, Pietro - on the list.

Decio - on the list.

Giovanni - on the list.

Giovanni's cousin Giacomo - on the list.

Young Conti and his uncles - on the list

Even the priest Gaetano - on the list.

And so it went. Until worse news followed.

According to Decio's "sources" the list could not be altered. Those named would be leaving in the morning for Liverpool where hundreds of other internees were being taken from mainland camps by train and where a huge, grey ship awaited them.

When everyone else had gone, Fortunato wandered around the room. He set chairs upright, he placed broken crockery in a bin, he dried spilt tea and coffee. And when that was done, he decided to go into the kitchen and make whatever he could make from whatever he could find.

17

CROSSING THE BAR

Brunswick Arms, Liverpool.

Edgar tossed a tanner in the air. He watched the silver coin spin several feet above his head, halt in flight, and then begin to fall back to earth. He caught the sixpenny on its descent, inches from the table-top, in the palm of his right hand. He deftly slapped it onto the back of his left hand.

Bob called it. 'Heads.'

Edgar uncovered the coin and the uncrowned profile of King George V duly obliged. 'Your choice.'

Bob stroked his long chin. 'I choose to be first-in-line to call home.'

Whilst Bob was absent making his telephone call and no doubt oblivious to the queue that had likely sprung up behind him, Edgar remained in the Snug and worried how, if Bob's call home went the wrong way, he could save Bob from himself.

He flicked through the lightly soiled pages of the prior day's *Liverpool News*. Some news of the war effort, apparently 10,000 more women were needed to take the positions of cooks, drivers and clerks; the British Government had accepted Général de Gaulle as the person to whom the Free French might rally around; and then there were the distractions; cinema listings: Errol Flynn and Olivia de Havilland were starring in *Dodge City,* due to screen three times in twenty-four hours in the Abbey Cinema near the clock tower in Wavertree. They could go there. *Why not?* Other options included a film called *Escape to Happiness,* starring some new actress with a German sounding name, or *Hitler, The Beast of Berlin* which sounded more pertinent but was screening late in the evening and therefore would not be a viable proposition for them.

He moved on from the cinema listings and was struck by a report of a man whose name he knew, Doctor Wilhelm Stekel. Stekel had become famous, not solely because he was a colleague of Doctor Sigmund Freud but also for his pithy aphorism: "the mark of the immature man is that he wants to die nobly for a cause, while the mark of the mature man is that he wants to live humbly for one." He had once argued fiercely w ith L ily a bout Doctor Stekel. She had read all about him in a nursing magazine and thought the doctor had reason on his side, whereas he had considered Doctor Stekel's aphorism to be very wide of the mark. It ran against the Moulton grain.

Curious, he read on. It seemed that for "reasons unknown" the doctor had overdosed on aspirin. *Immature or mature?* In Edgar's mind, the true question was an entirely different one. The doctor had found himself in a world in which the wind sat in a different corner. He had been stripped of all his possessions and had to flee the place he had lived all his life. He and his family, including his nephews escaped to London where his nephews had now also been rounded up and interned. Even his son, who had the foresight to escape to France several years previously, had been declared Stateless and rounded up and interned in that country. How could any sentient person have written "for reasons unknown?" The question burned in Edgar's mind whilst he waited and stared blankly at a smoke stained wall of the Snug.

When Bob returned from the phone-booth he smelled of stale tobacco and twitched. 'Everything all right?'

'No,' Edgar replied. 'Nothing is all right.'

'There's quite a queue building up out there.' Bob sat down. 'You'd better get a move on if you intend to call Lily.'

He passed the newspaper to Bob and hurriedly exited the Snug. He crossed the bar-room and made sure to avoid eye contact with all those who had words for him. He passed directly into the corridor which held at one extremity a doorway that led to an external toilet and at the other extremity a curtained phone booth. The phone booth resembled a church confessional. A congregation already filed toward it. He joined the pilgrims and shuffled and sighed with them and muttered and moaned with them about how long the fellow currently in the booth had been in there. A collective groan relayed down the chain when that caller was heard to push yet another coin into the slot.

'Enough already,' the mass muttered under its breath.

When it came to his turn, he understood that in this company his uniform and accent allowed him a certain indulgence. But he was not one to abuse the privilege. He spoke quietly with Lily and whispered, 'me too,' when she told him she loved him. She had become heated about the internment of foreign citizens and refugees, and especially over Friedrich. He had not run out of coins but the shuffling of feet from the other side of the curtain meant he could not respond in the manner he wished to the snuffling of her sobs emanating from the earpiece. 'We've lost our helmsmen but we can't lose our bearings,' was all he could tell her as he replaced the handset. She would know what he meant. She had to remain an actor.

He had not fully emerged from the phone booth when the next-in-line squeezed past him like a sinner in a hurry, worried that the penances would soon be exhausted. In his path, a group of stay-at-home bar-room-generals stood in a circle loudly discussing an article in the early edition of the *Liverpool Echo*: something about a bombardment. He swivelled between them and this time politely accepted their backslaps but still declined several offers of a glass of gin "in appreciation of everything you men do." He reached the bar and ordered one beer for Bob and one cydrax for himself. The barman would not accept payment.

Without spillage, he returned to the Snug and clinked glasses with Bob. He was about to ask Bob about his call to Jenny when the door squeaked open. A gaunt, elderly, weather-beaten man appeared in the doorway and surveyed the sunlit Snug. The old man held the Snug door open with an angled shoulder and grasped a half-pint glass of beer in each hand.

In the background, the bar-room generals could be heard in animated discussion over the prior night's bombardment of Jersey and Guernsey. Edgar made out the chatter of 'dozens wounded' and 'several dead' and 'what's the point in bombing those islands?' The half-in, half-out geriatric answered: 'None! No point at all. Even the Germans must know those islands are demilitarised.' Doddering eyes swivelled the Snug for confirmation or a sighting of a missing mate for the half-pints. Another disembodied voice from the bar-room answered: 'they probably got their islands mixed up, maybe they meant to bomb the Isle of Man.' A raucous laughter filled the bar-room in response.

Bob Connell pushed back his chair.

The half-in, half-out veteran decided the Snug was not harbouring whomever he searched, he completed a volte-face and let the door swing lethargically behind him.

Edgar vigorously brushed away imagined dust residue from his uniform and checked the alignment of his shirt-cuffs. In a single tipping motion, he finished his cydrax and placed his empty glass on the table.

Bob slowly tilted his glass, drained his beer and observed the ceiling. He placed his glass noisily on the table. 'Time to leave?'

Edgar nodded. 'Yes. Major Bethell will be pacing the decks.'

'Who's Major Bethell?'

'Chris Bethell. He's the fellow in charge of embarking our passengers and guarding us all.'

Bob's face twitched. His eyes darkened and his feelings were, again, no longer fathomable. 'We'll not be embarking "passengers" will we? We'll be deporting people that we shouldn't. Friends.'

Edgar sucked his teeth and led the way out. He cursed the Home Office who had taken the term foreign British resident and as though it did not already hold enough of a negative charge they had transformed it into a sinister abstraction that held a nebulous but ominous threat. Now, his neighbours were no longer simply "foreign" or "exotic." They had become "enemy aliens." And he and Lily were supposed to consider those café owners and tailors, and artists and ice-cream salesmen and priests and lawyers and teachers and engineers that had lived amongst them for generations, were enemies.

Both men sighed as they left the Brunswick Arms.

Bob patted Edgar on the back. 'It's all right.' He shoved his hands deep into his pockets. 'I know why you held it back.'

Edgar smiled guiltily.

They were approaching the *Arandora Star* when Bob asked, 'do you remember that fish and chip shop in Glasgow?'

'Very attractive woman, with a large father and a poster of Glasgow Celtic,' Edgar replied. 'How could I forget.'

'They were taken away.'

'Who was?'

'The owner and his youngest son. Jenny told me on our call.' Bob had tears in his eyes. His voice choked up. 'Their shop was ransacked. Plenty of others we know.'

Edgar could not be surprised. This war was turning out like the last one. The same idiocy. The same mistakes being repeated. There was panic and fear. But it was stoked, by the usual newspapers. And there would be worse to come. It would not stop at middle-aged chip-shop owners and their sons. Once again, the gyroscope had spun off-balance and the ships-of-state had lost their way. In a storm such as this, courageous, empathetic helmsmen were needed, but they could not be found.

'I'm sorry to hear that.' Edgar wanted to hug his chief engineer.

'Jenny says, they've already been interned.'

'Where? Lily might know some people who can help.'

'What people?' Bob's voice rose hopefully.

Edgar was not entirely sure what Lily might be able to do. During their telephone call she had sounded less confident than usual. Some of their friend's shops and cafés had been attacked too. 'She has friends and connections in all sorts of committees. Old nursing pals. Worse than fisherwomen.'

Bob sucked on his teeth and strode on, staring dead ahead.

Edgar fell in and they walked in silence, back to Princes Quay. At the sight of the *Arandora Star* and the silhouette of her ugly transformation, Edgar felt his heart drop into his boots.

They boarded the carrack silently.

Bob slid open the door to the officers' lounge.

Major Bethell was already seated at the officer's oval, teak-topped table. The Major stood up. He stuffed a notebook into a side-pocket of his jacket. He was poker-backed and wooden faced. 'Jolly pleased to meet you, old boys.'

Bob half-heartedly saluted before he stepped away and opened the forward, bow facing window and asked, 'mind if I smoke?'

Major Bethell shook his head. 'Go ahead.'

Edgar saluted energetically, as though compensating for Bob's lack of enthusiasm. He brought his hands together in a little clap before extending a handshake. 'Likewise.'

'Want one?' Bob inquired and held out a cigarette.

Major Bethell tilted back on his heels, then raised a hand and as though to push away temptation. 'No thanks.'

Edgar waited for the Major to sit back down. He took the seat directly opposite him. He scrutinised the man who would be his companion and protector for the next two months.

The Major cut a confident figure. Tall and lean and in fighting shape. Handsome in a rugged tin-soldier manner of handsomeness. A square face with embedded, alert, lively eyes. His nose was long like Bob Connell's but straighter, never broken. He sported a dark vigorous moustache that was bushy like his eyebrows. He was younger than Edgar, by five or six years. He had probably volunteered from the army reserve, not bothering to wait on being called up. His uniform was pristine and his shoes were brilliantly polished. There was something else though; the Major's odd enunciation reminded Edgar of certain distant Dukes and Lords and Earls who had, over the years, occupied the first-class cabins of the *Arandora Star*.

Major Bethell leant forward out of his seat and looked at Edgar with a certain intensity. 'Well. Down to business. I suppose.'

Before Edgar had an opportunity to reply, Bob spoke aloud. 'Can I ask, how many men you brought with you to guard our dangerous cargo?'

Edgar felt on the verge of blasphemy. He muttered to himself, 'for goodness sake.'

Major Bethell swivelled and stared directly at Bob. 'If you don't mind, chief engineer Connell you'll not refer to the passengers as cargo. At least, not in my company.'

The Major's upper class tones could not entirely conceal the undertone of a threat, a slithered vein of violence. But Bob appeared impervious to it. His eyes lit up. His lips unsnarled and his bent pugilistic nose seemed to straighten as he held Major Bethell's stare. Finally, he sniffed and said, 'I'm happy to hear that.'

'Our chief engineer's not too content about our next mission.'

Edgar sent Bob a regard that he hoped would straighten his rudder. 'He feels we shouldn't be deporting anyone, anywhere.'

'I agree,' Major Bethell said and he looked Bob in the eyes before adding softly, 'but it's not in our gift to choose.'

'You've heard of conscientious objectors, right?' Bob said.

'Your problem is this,' Bethell replied calmly, 'you'd be just another conchie, conscientiously objecting in a urinal that passed as a prison cell, whilst someone else, who did not have your principles or competence would be transporting your passengers. How would you feel if any harm came to them?'

Bob sighed deeply and stared out again beyond the bow facing window and puffed on his cigarette as though considering whether he was ready for the prison conjured by Bethell.

'Would you be happy with that?' Major Bethell asked in the same calm tone as previously.

Bob was silent, as though chewing over the question.

Edgar cleared his throat and tried to remember if he had ever seen Bob that rattled. 'I understand you've already met some of our passengers.'

'I have,' Bethell said cheerily, 'I came across from Douglas with some of them.'

'Which ship?'

'The *Tynwald*.'

'That's Jimmy Whiteway's ferry,' Edgar said. 'I should go and see him.'

'Well, if you do,' Major Bethell answered and tapped on the table with an index finger, 'remember you're not at liberty to divulge any part of your orders.'

'I don't suppose we can have the passengers knowing where we're taking them,' Bob whispered and blew smoke against the window.

Major Bethell's face at first became pale and rigid and then softened, as though he had solved some painful question or had begun to better tune in to Bob's problem. 'It would only make them more distressed if they knew where they were going.'

Bob smiled wanly and nipped the cigarette.

'Do you think they would be happy to learn it now?' Bethell asked softly.

'I don't know,' Bob answered. 'I would need to consider it some more.' Bob saluted Edgar and then the Major, this time with more vigour. 'I should go and check in with my lads.'

Major Bethell rose and limped slightly as he went around the table to return Bob's salute and accompany him toward the exit.

As he stepped away, Bob turned and in a warmer tone said, 'I'll see you at the officer's dinner tonight. Probably have an answer for you then.'

'Officer's dinner?' Bethell asked and furrowed his handsome forehead.

'My idea,' Edgar confessed.

They had become automatons. Necessity had obliged that they lose their routines. But now they had a different sort of mission. It was not the snatch and grabs of Norway and France. It was not a mission they could feel proud of. But it offered an opportunity to recover a shred of their old human habits and he was determined to take the chance.

Before the war, it had been a routine aboard their cruise-ship, like it was on every other in the line. Officers and passengers dined together. No matter if their ship was hideous with its barbed wire and boarded up portholes, he would have them do it again. It could not be identical. There would be no welcome-band on the quay. They would not board their passengers with fanfare, but neither would there be shells exploding in the near distance. 'I was thinking you'd be our guest of honour, for the first evening,' Edgar said. 'And bring a few of your own senior officers.'

'I'm not guest-of-honour material.'

'I'll be inviting some of our passengers too,' Edgar revealed.

Bethell's face lit up as though the idea had begun to appeal.

His spirits rose at Bethell's reaction. He could make the mission feel a little less depressing. They had almost two months of sailing ahead of them and by inviting a dozen different passengers to dinner every night he could meet half of the internees before they saw the trace of the coast of Newfoundland.

'Who do you plan to invite?'

'I'd like to see the manifest,' Edgar asked. 'Name, residence, occupation, that sort of thing.'

'Me too.' Bethell grinned apologetically. 'There isn't one. At least not a proper one.'

Edgar had not considered that possibility. He pursed his lips firmly and muttered. 'Without a manifest how on earth could you even know if you've been guarding the right individuals?'

'We didn't.'

'How have the passengers been selected?'

'I've no idea.' Bethell flattened his moustache. 'Nor have they.' His sympathy was palpable. 'It's all a numbers game. Isle of Man, Bury and Lingfield, it's all to get the numbers.'

Edgar shrugged. 'In that case, we'll prepare our own manifest,' he said brightly. 'About twelve-hundred of them, correct?'

Bethell slid his hand into the inner pocket of his jacket and extracted his army issue, faux-leather, pocket notebook. He placed a finger on a page. 'All told, I understand we're currently guarding one-thousand-two-hundred-and-thirteen internees.'

Thirteen more than he had been informed of. He stared at the notebook. 'And how many of you?'

Bethell flipped the notebook closed. 'Two-hundred-and-fifty-three of us. Including myself.'

Edgar had already worked out the base logistics. 'With that number of passengers, your guard detail, my crew and the deck-gun crew, we'll be over seventeen-hundred aboard.'

'I know several large villages with less people,' Bethell replied.

'Me too,' Edgar said. 'I'll call the first mate and chief steward. They're going to need to know everything.' Edgar rose and put through the calls to his two officers.

Major Bethell walked to-and-fro a little agitatedly. It was a few steps but on account of a limp his fluidity of motion was forced. He sighed as he retrieved and reopened his notebook. 'You might remind your chief steward that our instructions are to try and keep the Germans and Italians apart. On separate decks if possible.'

'You can tell him yourself,' Edgar answered and watched Bethell rotate the notebook in his hands.

'Would you like one?' Bethell asked and held out his notebook.

Edgar shook his head. 'My wife buys all my notebooks. I could open a shop with all that I have.'

'Well, if you change your mind,' Major Bethell answered and limped around the table. 'By the way, I'd be jolly grateful if your chief steward can billet me somewhere where one need only negotiate a reasonable number of stairs.'

'I imagine he'll squeeze you in up here with the other officers.'

Bethell gave out a little laugh. 'That'd be fine. As long as your officers don't mind me cursing in the night.' Bethell vigorously rubbed at his knee.

'I was going to ask you about your leg.'

'France, 1915.'

'I was in India.' Edgar felt guilty for having only suffered from dysentery and a fear that his fiancée might catch a tragic attraction to a handsome, wounded soldier.

'Most nights it's fine. Sometimes though, if I'm somewhere humid, I'll have these moments when it feels like they didn't get all of the fragments out.'

'We were strafed several times,' Edgar said. 'Lost a few staff and some of our crew had shrapnel wounds. But I've been lucky.' He looked over Bethell's shoulder toward a little concealed cabinet. 'Maybe a gin could help?'

A sound was heard from outside. Bethell grinned and looked at his wristwatch. 'Ask me again, later.'

The door to the officers' mess slid open. The first mate, six-feet tall and possessing an accent as near polished as Bethell's, bounded across the threshold with a warm contagious confidence. He shook Major Bethell's hand. The first mate and Major Bethell apprehended each other as though decrypting some implied lineage that only they could perceive. Meanwhile, the chief steward edged into the room and proffered a limp handshake and hesitant salute.

That was how the chief steward was. Despite his superior memory and being unsurpassed in logistics, he always gave the impression of being an extra in someone else's show. Particularly when in the company of the first mate.

Edgar decided he ought to put in a call for Bob. It might be helpful if Bob returned. One of Bob's officers answered and said that the chief engineer was "otherwise engaged." But if it was an emergency he would come back immediately. Failing that they could count on him to be there for dinner, like he said he would be.

During the deliberation over logistics, trajectories and security, the chief steward confirmed the obvious: 'If you want my opinion, we can't keep twelve-hundred emotional passengers waiting in a long queue to present their identity papers.'

'And?' Bethell asked as though urging the chief steward to say aloud the consequences that followed his premises.

'And, any passenger manifest is going to have to wait until long after boarding. Perhaps the next day, or even the one after.'

Bethell nodded agreement with the chief steward.

'We'll aim to establish a passenger manifest forty-eight hours after our departure,' the chief steward suggested.

'Assuming they have any identity papers at all,' Bethell said.

As the meeting wore on, Bethell seemed less aloof. Or perhaps Edgar had become used to his ways.

The chief steward cupped his chin in one hand and looked as though he had the thread of an idea. 'Remind me sir, how many Germans did you say there were?'

Bethell consulted his notebook, 'four-hundred and seventy-three,' he replied. 'But it's like I said before, old chap, they're not really German in any homogenous sense.'

'But, for the sake of simplicity,' the chief steward asked, 'I might accommodate them as though they were?'

'You mean billet them together?' Bethell almost laughed.

'Why not?' the chief steward inquired.

'It's a long journey and hate festers,' Bethell sounded serious. 'Better to find some way to segregate them. There might be a few Nazi types. Can you imagine billeting them with Germans and Austrians who've been resident in England for years and who seem more British than we do? Or billeting them with political or racial refugees from Germany and Austria and Czechoslovakia?'

The chief steward blinked rapidly and paled as the problem seemed to form more clearly in his head. 'How will I know which are which?'

'It can't be that complicated, can it?' the first mate piped up. 'We can separate those in uniform from the rest and ask the others where they're from.'

'That will take you only so far,' Bethell said. 'The merchant mariners are in uniform and I don't think we saw many, if any, Nazi types amongst them.'

'Well, how did you manage to tell them apart?' the first mate asked.

'We didn't.'

'But you did manage to keep them from fighting, right?'

'With some help,' Bethell answered.

'What kind of help?' Edgar asked.

'In stopping the arguments for a start,' Bethell said. 'One of their lot, a big-framed, German merchant navy captain, sorted them out. All of the Germans listened when he spoke, and he seemed to know who was who.'

'Well, let's find him,' Edgar said. 'What's this man's name?'

'I have it right here.' Bethell rummaged in his notebook — 'Burfeind.'

Burfeind? It could easily be another man. After all, the Burfeinds were like the Moultons, a family full of mariners. Edgar half-hoped it was Jacob but also that it was some other man with the same surname. 'Did you get his first name?' He asked tentatively.

Bethell flipped back to the page. 'I never asked him and I didn't hear anyone say it. They all called him *Herr Kapitänleutnant.*'

'What did he look like?'

Bethell shrugged. 'You lot all appear more or less the same to me.' He sounded apologetic.

'Would you say he was younger or older than I am?' Edgar asked impatiently.

'Mid-fifties, I suppose. Bearded. Friendly face.'

Edgar felt the dirty tricks of fate. He would watch the boarding from up on the forecastle deck. It would not matter that there would be more than twelve-hundred passengers coming aboard, if his friend Jacob Burfeind was amongst them he would recognise him without difficulty.

Bethell shut the notebook and pocketed it. 'Principled, salt-of-the-earth type,' he added as though a clearer picture had begun to form in his mind.

'Principled?' Edgar asked and smiled. 'How do you know?'

Bethell rotated his wedding ring around his finger. 'I'm not entirely sure. Possibly his officers said he was. Or I just figured it out when I heard how they came to be captured.'

'How's that?' the first mate asked.

'Apparently, they were pursued by a British Destroyer and

Burfeind told his civilian passengers and crew it was not their fight. He ordered them onto lifeboats and then scuttled his ship.'

'What was the ship called?' Edgar seized on that question.

Bethell reached again into his pocket and reopened his notebook. 'The SS *Adolph Woermann*.'

Edgar felt as though everyone could see right into his head. He smiled broadly. 'Put Burfeind on our list for tonight.'

'And what about the Italians?' The chief steward asked Bethell, 'I don't suppose this fellow Burfeind could help you with them?'

'No,' Bethell answered. 'But there were others who did.'

'See that they get invited also,' Edgar instructed.

'I suppose you expect me to keep all of their fascists segregated from their non-fascists too,' the chief steward asked in alarm.

Bethell laughed aloud. 'I doubt you'll have that problem with them.'

'Are you telling me there are no fascist sympathisers amongst the Italians?' The chief steward sounded both doubtful and relieved.

'I couldn't go that far,' Bethell replied. 'There are likely a few, but there can't be many. If they have any, they all kept themselves to themselves. I had the impression they would be worried about upsetting the priests.'

'Priests?' The first mate could not mask his incredulity. 'We're deporting priests?'

'Only a couple, as far as I can tell,' Bethell answered and grinned mischievously. 'And a couple of rabbis too.'

The chief steward removed his cap and tapped it tambourine-like against his thigh. 'Who can we rely on to keep the Italian factions apart?'

Bethell consulted his notebook again, and said, 'the priests for sure. Anzani and Picchi.'

The chief steward noted the names and looked up from his notes. 'Anzani and Picchi, they're priests?'

'No,' Bethell answered. 'Anzani says he's the Honorary Secretary of the British Branch of the League of Rights of Man.'

'Lord Almighty,' the first mate uttered.

'No, I don't think he's amongst our internees,' Bethell quipped.

Edgar changed his mind. He was relieved that Bob was not present to hear the fiasco of who had been interned. He wondered if Bob's local chip-shop owner would turn out to be amongst their future passengers. He hoped not.

'There'll be no handcuffing of anyone, right?' the chief steward asked hesitantly.

'Even if we had enough sets of cuffs,' Bethell replied, 'I can't see how it would be possible. Anyway, my men are all armed. I don't anticipate any problems beyond a desperate internee trying to jump overboard and swim home.'

The chief steward tapped his pencil repeatedly on the cover of his notebook. 'I'll need you to find this *Kapitän* Burfeind and Mr. Anzani and Mr. Picchi and whomever else you or they think can help us decide who gets billeted where. Bring the priests and the rabbis too. We'll need to talk with them before we can allocate spaces and start boarding.'

'Where and when?' Bethell asked.

'Back here,' the chief steward answered. 'In two hours?'

Bethell looked at his watch 'I should get started on that now then.' He saluted and stood up.

Edgar, his first mate and chief steward returned Bethell's salute. They watched him limp away to join his own officers. As soon as Bethell had gone, the first mate and chief steward muttered about all of the preparations they had ahead of them.

He left his officers to their task. He took his leave and went to his own quarters and sat at his desk and bowed his head and closed his eyes. He recalled his last contact with Jacob. Over the years they had taken the habit of snatching some time at the end of their wives' annual long-distance, short-duration, telephone calls. Like

Alexander Graham Bell they saluted each other with an "ahoy" not a hello. On their last telephone call, they promised they would meet in their old place of worship as soon as the world spun again on its true axis.

It seemed simultaneously a dream and a nightmare that by the time they would next lift anchor he and Jacob could be reunited. They may even have dined together. He turned his thoughts to the rest of his passengers. They did not know him in the way Jacob did. For them, he was simply an agent that followed orders to take them away from their families. For them, he would seem as complicit in this injustice as those fear mongering dim-witted politicians who had labelled them "enemy aliens." A pain formed behind his eyes. In a gesture of frustration, he called Naval Command one more time. 'Captain Moulton. Requesting accompaniment on our upcoming mission. Over.'

'Negative,' Naval Command responded. 'Listen Captain, there's no point in continually calling us. The answer won't change. Over.'

'How about partial cover, just until we pass Hebrides? Over.'

'We don't have spare Destroyers just bobbing around, Captain. There's nothing been sighted between here and the edge of Hebrides in the past three weeks. Over. And. Out.'

He replaced the ship to shore handset.

They would be on their own.

He felt he had no business being the master of such a mission. But he was not afraid for himself. He was a Moulton. When his moment arrived to cross the bar, he would be ready. He brooded on account of all of those that had no business to be aboard the *Arandora Star* with her *pallor grey* paint and razor-wire passageways. Fortunately, they had a gun and a gun crew, but above all they had speed. That and their wily navigating would keep them safe.

18

MOCKINGBIRD

Palace Internment Camp, Isle of Man.

It was one hour after black-out. Fortunato was alone in a corner of the lower-ground-floor kitchen. He was perched on the ladder linking the kitchen with the garden-level delivery hatch. Nothing prevented him from leaving the kitchen by the conventional route. If he wished, he could have exited through the swing doors, walked up two flights of stairs and straight out through the unlocked front door. But he had his reasons for stealth.

He stepped up a few rungs, tiptoed and opened the hatch. As though a man-sized meerkat, he popped his monk-like, tonsured crown above the hatch and scanned the grey horizon, beyond the wire fence and across Douglas Bay. He waited until the waning moon concealed itself behind a drifting cloud and he seized that opportunity to sling his beige, canvas duffle-bag over his shoulder and spring into the hotel gardens.

His presence had not gone unobserved.

From an unlit sentry-box twenty metres directly ahead a rifle-butt tapped against a wooden floor.

Thunk! Thunk! Thunk!

Fortunato froze. He knelt on the grass.

Beyond the barbed-wire enclosure, dark horses cantered out of Douglas Bay until they were recalled by the imminent reappearance of the quarter-moon and dashed for the beach, where, despite the War Office's requisitioning of the beachfront guesthouses, curious locals still congregated every weekend and left castles to be washed away.

Again, thunk! thunk!

A silver halo had been thrown across the bay and brightly illuminated the crescent sands but left the promenade and garden obscured. Fortunato rose from the dark foliage. His knees cracked and salt-spray stung his eyes. He swiftly approached the sentry-box.

Rifle in hand, the guard, an ex-soldier from the last war and as wizened looking as many of the older internees, stepped out from the sentry-box.

Fortunato stopped where he was and held his hands in the air and smiled.

'You spooked me,' the guard confessed.

'I scared you?' Fortunato asked.

'Only for a moment,' the military pensioner answered. 'Creeping out of the ground as though you were *Virgil*.'

'You know Dante?' Fortunato asked, surprised.

The sentry pointed along the Queen's Parade toward the Palace Hotel. 'That used to rival the best theatre houses in Liverpool.'

Fortunato had noticed it when his ship had docked in Douglas Bay. In the daylight, it was probably the grandest looking of all the hotels on the beachfront parade but in the evening curfew it hulked as undistinguished and forlorn as the others.

'Saw the *Inferno* there with my missus. She loved it.'

'They do Italian theatre here?' Fortunato sounded incredulous.

'Well, they did,' the sentry answered. 'In English, of course. The occasional opera too. If it hadn't been for our season tickets at the Palace, the missus would have had us off this island and back home in a jiffy.'

'I thought it was getting her job at the post-office that changed her mind?'

'How do you think she got that job?'

'You met someone at the opera?'

'Exactly,' the guard replied. 'That's how things go here.'

'That's how things go everywhere.'

'Your good lady would love it here. When this is all over you should bring her out.'

'She's more of a city type.' Fortunato winced at a raw memory. 'The seaside's not her thing.'

'You never know,' the guard insisted. 'Perhaps when she's seen it for herself.'

But Fortunato did know.

***

When it had been obvious that the war was coming and everyone knew which way the wind would eventually blow with Mussolini, he had the idea to move out of London. Somewhere quiet, somewhere less hysterical. A dozen times, the owner of the Landsdowne Hotel had offered him the position of banqueting director and a dozen times he had turned it down. The time had arrived to say yes.

'We could move to Eastbourne,' he suggested to Florence.

'Eastbourne?' Florence sounded alarmed. 'You're kidding me, right?'

'I've been offered a good job down there at the Landsdowne.'

'Have you ever been to Eastbourne?'

'The owner tells me it's a wonderful town,' he answered. 'Fresh-air, a healthy lifestyle, and best of all no one knows us there.'

'That's because they're all too old to remember who they know,'

Florence responded. 'I've been there. People go there to forget and to be forgotten. I'll never be ready to go there. Even if I live to be ninety.'

But he had convinced her. They went. They worked side by side. They lived the best few months of their lives together. They might have remained squirrelled there except their friends in London were more important than their anonymity.

***

Douglas in the dark, with its facsimile hotels running along its template parade fronting similar sunken gardens, reminded him of Eastbourne. 'Have you got anything for me?' he asked the sentry, hopefully.

'Not what you most want,' the sentry answered and grimaced. 'I'm sorry.'

'How about Renzo?' Fortunato asked. 'Any letters for him?'

'Nothing for your friend either,' the sentry replied. 'They probably don't know you're in here.'

Fortunato's lips vibrated. Almost three weeks of frustration. Their families had no idea where they were. He had written weeks ago, from the dark satanic mill — as Renzo had taken to calling Warth Mill. He had written again on their arrival at Douglas. They had done what was asked: written a single page in English. But it seemed the rumours were likely correct and neither Fortunato's nor Renzo's letters had made it much further than the camp censors.

'But I did find the almonds you asked for.'

'You may as well keep them.' Fortunato smiled dispiritedly in the dark.

'I wouldn't know what to do with them.'

'I've brought something for you, too.' Fortunato used two pillow-cases from his duffle bag. He wrapped them around his hands like bandages and created a letter-box sized gap between strands of barbed-wire through which he pushed through a brown paper bag and a small white envelope.

The sentry sniffed the paper bag and slipped the envelope into his jacket pocket. 'What's in here?' he asked.

'*Cantuccini,* directly from the kitchen.'

'Cantuwhat?' the guard asked. 'The missus enjoyed those other things.'

'You mean the *ricciarelli?*'

'She never tasted anything that good.' The sentry slipped a white cotton handkerchief, in the form of an envelope, between the wires. 'Your almonds.'

Fortunato opened the handkerchief, selected and began chewing an almond. 'How about you? Did you like the *ricciarelli?*'

'The best.'

When this was all over, he would invite the sentry and his wife to the Savoy. He would instruct the pastry cook to prepare *ricciarelli.* They would use almonds freshly brought in from Tuscany. Then his new friend could honestly say he had tasted the best.

'When do you think you can despatch my letter?' Fortunato asked.

The sentry patted his pocket. 'Providing there's no funny business in there, it'll go on Monday.'

'Are you sure your sister won't mind delivering it personally?'

'Don't worry. Your lady's going to get her letter and no one will be any the wiser.'

'I owe you.'

The guard rubbed an eye. 'No, you don't.'

'I'll miss you.'

'Are you going to be playing that flute of yours tonight?'

'Probably.'

'Remember, not too loud,' the sentry muttered and shuffled back into his sentry-box.

Fortunato remained alone. Once more, he looked out into the bay. Dark forms bobbed happily on the horizon.

He returned to his lodgings and sat under the doorway porch on a damp step. He removed his piccolo from his duffle bag and placed his lips over the embouchure and his fingers along the body and formed a note. He blew hard and tunelessly. He blew again. Between notes he gasped. Above his head someone slammed a window shut and drew the curtains closed.

The will to play the instrument ebbed away from him. He sat motionless with it on his knees. He wiped the head-joint and was about to return the piccolo to its case when the lodging-house door opened and a dozen men approached. Each of the men carried a lit candle. Renzo was amongst them and had brought his piccolo.

They played the *Mockingbird* and were accompanied by the low humming of internees. A haunting sound carried along Douglas promenade in a way it would never be heard again.

The next morning, lodging house number twelve was emptied. The internees were marched out at gunpoint on to a thin strip of esplanade. Despite their lack of energy, they stood to attention and awaited the residents of several other lodgings. Guards unlocked the barbed wire gates and the internees filed out one-by-one, across the promenade and onto the canvas-backed army trucks which awaited them with its engines running.

In the distance the SS *Tynwald* blew its horn.

19

EDGE OF SEVERN

North Atlantic Sea.

It was approaching the changing of crew shifts when Günther sauntered into the control room. He found Amelung bent over a map, whispering and laughing with Wilhelm Spahr, U47's chief navigator. Thirty-six-year-old Spahr, a northerner with the complexion of a leatherback turtle, had also been with U47 from the first day. Spahr tended to be blunt with his words but sharp in his intuition. Günther appreciated Spahr.

'What's so amusing?' Günther asked.

'I was asking Amelung how he is getting along with Krauss.'

Günther checked the hour. 'Where is Kraus anyway?'

'I expect he's on his way,' Spahr replied.

Günther dropped his voice, 'I had meant to ask you too, how are you getting along together, now?'

Amelung's eyebrows arched. 'He's not the most humorous man I've ever come across.'

'We shouldn't judge everyone by Bert Endrass' standards,' Spahr said.

'You have a gloomy tendency yourself at the moment, Amelung,' Günther added. 'Which reminds me, how are we for power?'

'We'll likely need to surface to recharge,' Spahr replied.

Amelung stroked his chin contemplatively. 'You must agree things were easier when Bert was first watch officer.'

'Bert's ego was getting far too large,' Spahr answered and glanced at Amelung guardedly. 'It's as well he got his own show.'

'I suppose,' Amelung answered. 'But did we have to end up with a ghoul like Kraus stomping around constantly citing procedures?'

Günther held back a smirk and Spahr's shoulders still shook with laughter when first watch officer Hans Werner Kraus entered the control room.

Kraus saluted and asked, 'what did I miss?'

'Amelung was just making plans for his father's birthday party,' Spahr answered and grinned.

'Do you realise how fortunate you are *Oberleutnant von Varendorf*?' Kraus said.

'How's that?' Amelung asked.

'As soon as we tie-up in Kiel you can slip off to your father's pile and eat cake.' Kraus pretended to be tugging his forelock. 'Whilst the rest of us will be tucking into crackers on board the quarter-ship or eating dry toast on a third-class train trip home.'

Günther saluted his men and returned to his own quarters. He lay upon his thin mattress whilst U47 remained submerged and crawled northwards at 70° and her first and second watch *oberleutnants* completed their hand-over procedures.

At midday, Kraus logged their position: BE3544. He puffed noisily when Spahr suggested they might pencil the British equivalent. They had only covered twenty-four nautical miles and Kraus became anxious that the falling battery-charge levels could result in their suffocation. He ordered U47 up to periscope depth and seeing she had the visible ocean entirely to herself he commanded that she be brought fully on to the surface, just until batteries were recharged. No more. No less.

Several slow, uneventful shifts later Kraus was back on shift, the sclera of his eyeballs reddened by poor sleep, his eye-pouches were deep enough to accommodate billiard balls. They were nearing the end of that shift when he asked Spahr, 'our position?'

'Edge of Severn,' Spahr said.

Kraus snapped, 'I meant our proper position?'

'BE3511,' Spahr replied and grinned.

'We're still in BE3511? How bloody large is this quadrant?'

'Enormous,' Spahr answered. 'We'd make better time if we remained longer on the surface.'

Kraus shook his head. 'Too risky.'

Spahr sucked his cheeks, exhaled and muttered something unintelligible.

'What were you saying?' Kraus asked.

'I was just saying it depends how you look at it.'

Krauss had to have known how Spahr looked at it. Spahr was one of Prien's Scapa Flow crew. Everyone in the *Kriegsmarine* had heard about Scapa Flow. Everyone in Germany had heard about it. Even the enemy side, including bloody Winston Churchill, had had something to say about it.

In the eyes of some people, Günther and his Scapa Flow crew had been lucky. Günther had been the first *unterseeboot Kapitän* to win a Knight's Cross. He and his crew were amply rewarded, they ought to be content with that.

'There's calculated risk and then —' Kraus stopped himself.

'You think the Scapa Flow mission was not a calculated risk?' Spahr asked gruffly. He could have added that despite Günther's alleged interest in the pecuniary bonus that came with accepting the mission, Günther had made it clear to Admiral Dönitz that he was volunteering only himself. The crew were free to accompany him or remain in Kiel as they wished. But Spahr and the crew of U47, even Bert Endrass at the time, would have followed Günther anywhere.

'You tell me,' Kraus replied.

Spahr folded his lips into his mouth. There was plenty he could tell Kraus: Nearly nine months had passed since U47 had sailed right into the middle of the British fleet moored in Scapa Flow and sunk an enormous battleship. Some might agree with Kraus's unspoken assessment of the whole endeavour; that it was not a "calculated" risk but rather luck and fearlessness over procedure and calculus.

However, even Kraus would have to admit the Scapa Flow mission could not have succeeded without an abundance of skill, professionalism and that mysterious something else that only true navigators had. It may not have been "calculated" in the way that a man like Krauss calculated risk, but if they had stopped to evaluate the risk would they have gone there in the first place? When they returned from Scapa Flow, the Ministry of Public Enlightenment had hailed them all as heroes. The entire crew received promotions. The officers were invited to Berlin where Günther, Bert and Amelung had medals of rising class pinned on them by the miniature man. On the way back to Kiel, Günther let Bert wear his Knight's Cross. That was when Amelung reminded them that eight-hundred mariners from the *Royal Oak* had died in the Scapa Flow attack. Men like themselves. Bert had shrugged and said, "so what?" Some crewmen said that was when things started to change between Günther and Bert. Who knows?

But Kraus was right about one thing: luck had played a role. Not only in Scapa Flow but in all of their missions. And after Scapa Flow, their luck began to change. They always worked with the same diligence, but on the patrol immediately following Scapa Flow, they tracked an enormous British cruiser, they had a perfect line on it. They fired a torpedo but missed. They tried the same with a British Destroyer. They had a direct hit, but the torpedo was a dud. By the end of that particular patrol, they had to settle for an unaccompanied mail-steamer, a mis-identified Dutch tanker, and a Norwegian steamer. The Ministry of Public Enlightenment didn't call them for any more pictures, nor pin any medals, nor offer any more secret missions.

On the next patrol Günther screamed at Bert: "How's it possible to miss?" And Bert screamed back, as loudly: "I don't personally manufacture these fricking eels you know!" Spahr had smoothed the situation. He reassured them that U47's problems of misfiring eels and nearly getting hit by depth-charges and suicidal ramming ships that emerged out of the fog, were not unique to them. Nor were the bomber-planes that arrived from nowhere. The entire seventh flotilla was suffering in the same way.

Back in Kiel, Günther calmed down and took his complaint to BdU *unterseeboot* command, who could not deny that the number of defective torpedoes was increasing. The news seemed to calm Günther and Spahr had been present when Günther apologised to Bert. But it was already too late. Bert's transfer request had been sitting with BdU since U47 had docked.

That was the end of a friendship. A great pity, because Günther and Bert had sailed both worlds together: charted and uncharted. They had been through a sinking together. They had spent six months living hand-to-mouth in a single room in Dublin, listening twice a day to the British shipping forecast. Bert had been present in London when Günther had proposed to Ingeborg.

Now Bert was out there, somewhere on the bitter ocean captaining his own *unterseeboot*.

Spahr cleared his throat and was on the verge of explaining all of that history to Kraus when they were interrupted by a squeal from the adjacent listening-room.

20

HERDED

Princes Quay, Liverpool.

The SS *Tynwald* was a large ship. Amongst the internees who crossed the Irish sea from Douglas, only Fortunato had sailed before on a larger vessel. When they disembarked from her they found themselves back in Liverpool.

They were herded on the quay and told to form a column of two abreast.

Up ahead, other columns of internees had already formed similar queues. Some of them had apparently been waiting several hours already. Many men had already taken to sitting on top of their battered suitcases. Messages flowed up and down as internees asked for news of relatives who might or might not be in the herd.

Fortunato sucked on his teeth but otherwise was silent as he stood beside Renzo and wondered if families would be joining. Immediately behind him in the queue were Decio and Giovanni and right behind them came a bunch of the Ferdenzi's and behind them the remainder of their boarding house.

Berthed further up Princes Quay was a ship that dwarfed even the *Tynwald*. It seemed to be on a different scale. Fortunato was not alone in presuming it would be their fate to sail on it.

'They're waiting for us. Right?' Renzo asked and nodded at the large ship.

'I suppose so.'

'Ever worked on a ship that big?'

It had been twenty years since he had served on the cruise ships. He shook his head. 'No.' This carrack had the look of a cruise ship that had once been very luxurious, much more luxurious than those he had sailed on.

'It's enormous,' Decio said over Fortunato's shoulder. 'It can't be only for us.'

On the crossing a rumour had broken out that they were being sent to Italy. It had caused panic. Decio had asked Fortunato to help snuff out that fear. Fortunato said to whomever was willing to listen that it made no sense to send them to Italy. They would have had to round up their families, including sons that were serving in the British forces. Even the most insular Englishman knew it made no sense to "repatriate" civilians who had either never lived in Italy or had left thirty or forty years ago.

He had said that, but buried inside him was the germ of a doubt. Had he granted too much common sense to those who had interned thousands of friends?

Up ahead, four soldiers headed down the line. Occasionally they stopped to question some of the internees.

'Looks like they're searching for someone,' Renzo said quietly. As the soldiers got closer, Fortunato heard an internee ask, 'why, what's he done?'

'Nothing.'

An internee pointed down the queue, 'you see the fellow there, in the crumpled suit, shiny shoes and the red hanky in his breast pocket?' The soldiers continued down the line. For a moment, Fortunato wondered if Decio's lawyer had saved the day. Perhaps the lawyer had vouched for them all. Might they all be going home?

The soldiers arrived and Fortunato continued eavesdropping as they spoke with Decio.

'Are you Decio Anzani?'

'Yes,' Decio replied.

'You're to come with us.'

'What for?'

'We're not sure,' the older of the guards replied. 'But you've to come straight away and bring the priests.'

'Which priests?'

'I dunno,' the soldier sounded perplexed. 'Those two that came over with you.'

Decio tapped Renzo on the shoulder and asked him to go down the line and locate the priests.

'Bring them straight aboard,' the older guardsman instructed and left with Decio and one of the soldiers.

Renzo left, accompanied by the remaining two soldiers.
Fortunato watched Decio walk sedately up the quayside, a soldier at either side of him. And despite the many hundreds of his countrymen who surrounded him, he felt himself to be quite alone on the quay.

Soon, Renzo's place was occupied by Giovanni, who asked, 'what do you suppose is going on?'

'I don't know. Let's wait and see.'
Ahead of them some men smoked and exchanged words with the patrolling guards. Some men asked for water. Some men grumbled about the heat. Whispers came down the line that there were Germans queued up nearby. Others apparently herded on the platform of a train station. Whispers too that there were other Italians herded in a customs shed.

'I can't swim,' Giovanni anxiously admitted.

'I wouldn't worry about that,' Fortunato reassured. 'Wherever we're going we're not going to be swimming there.'

'It's fine f or you t o m ake fun,' Giovanni s aid. 'You've spent years aboard these things. I'll bet you can swim like a fish.'

'I get by,' Fortunato admitted and reassuringly added, 'there's nothing to worry about. I'll be there to take care of you.'

'It's not right,' Giovanni said. 'None of this is right.' Giovanni seemed on the verge of some form of a breakdown.

Fortunato agreed with his old friend. He could hardly do otherwise. He turned away from Giovanni and caught the attention of his yo u n g er brother, Giacomo Ferdenzi and asked him, 'what about you?'

'What about me?'

'Can you swim?'

'Are you joking?' Giacomo answered. 'When would any of *us* have learnt to swim?'

Fortunato shrugged. He regretted asking the question. 'Well, there's nothing to worry about. I'll be there for you too.' He peered down the queue, hoping he might see Renzo coming back with the priests. No sign. He presumed Renzo had located the priests and found another path.

21

INTERNEE REPRESENTATIVES

Arandora Star.

Some time later, Edgar descended the starboard staircase that led from his own quarters down to the officers' quarters. He saluted Bethell's man posted by the door, and with a mixture of curiosity and trepidation peered in through the door window.

Nine people sat around the table. The chief steward, and eight "internee representatives," as Bethell had taken to calling them. Four representatives for the Italians, and another four for those considered to be German.

At the far end, another guardsman had been posted.

Jacob held sway. He was wearing his naval uniform and was easily spotted. Aside from a sprouting of grey in his hair and beard he appeared unchanged from the last occasion Edgar had met him, two summers previously. He had prepared himself for Jacob's presence and was not shocked at his presence. However, he was entirely unprepared to see Friedrich.

Edgar stepped away from the window and slowly circled around the deck.

'Is everything all right, sir?' the guardsman asked.

'Yes,' Edgar lied. He forced himself to return and look again.

Jacob was in animated discussion with a dapper older Italian, who was dressed in a crumpled dark suit from which a blood-red handkerchief stylishly peeped out of the front breast pocket. Meanwhile, Friedrich Dabel gazed intently at Jacob's interlocutor, as though he was trying to place the man.

The well suited Italian spoke animatedly. On his right flank a younger, unshaven and by comparison, casually dressed man sat quietly nodding. On his left flank sat the two priests whom Bethell had spoken of. One of them was ancient looking, the other, less creased but hardly youthful either. The cassocks of both priests were faded.

All the time the dapper Italian spoke, Jacob maintained a look of interest and concentration and his posture afforded and simultaneously demanded respect.

Edgar smiled ruefully. He felt that he had solved the mystery of how his own brother, Willie, might have looked had he lived to Jacob's age. He waited for a lull in the discussion, which arrived at a moment when the senior Italian paused to locate his words. He opened the door and all present turned to face him.

'Captain Moulton,' the chief steward said.

'I know who that is.' Jacob stood up and grinned. 'Ahoy, Captain,' he added and stepped toward Edgar.

'Me too.' Friedrich also stood up. 'I know who that is.' Bethell's guardsman stepped forward.

Edgar smiled and discreetly pointed an index finger at the floor and the guardsman relaxed. He returned Jacob's salute and then embraced Friedrich. He watched as confusion brimmed within the chief steward's eyes.

'I knew they'd not have requisitioned the ship without requisitioning you,' Jacob said gruffly.

He restrained himself from another crude blasphemy and

shook his head in incredulity at Friedrich. 'I heard from Lily that you'd been interned, but what are you doing here?'

Friedrich shrugged. 'Apparently, I present a risk to the country.'

'Where have you been?'

'In a camp not far from the farm and then another one on the Isle of Man,' Friedrich answered.

Jacob gestured for Edgar to sit between himself and Friedrich.

'I'm sorry about all of this.' Edgar looked around the others in the room. 'We all are.' He especially thought of Bob Connell when he added, 'if it was up to the crew, we'd not be part of this.'

'It's not our war,' Jacob answered jovially. 'We'll all have to make the best of it.'

'Well, that's changed the mood in here,' the chief steward said.

'How far have you got?' Edgar asked.

'For a start, they know they're all invited to the officer's dinner.'

Edgar looked around and acknowledged the internee representatives who had begun nodding and muttering their thanks. 'Obviously, it can't be as fancy as it once was. But it's a tradition.' He paused his gaze on Friedrich who looked far too lean. 'I think you'll enjoy tonight. We've some decent cooks aboard.'

Jacob turned to introduce the others on his side of the table: 'Well, obviously you know Friedrich.' He pointed to the others: 'This is Rabbi Schoenthal. And this is Rabbi Moser.'

Neither Rabbi wore any religious sign. They both could easily have passed for legal or bank clerks. Edgar was unsure how to greet a pair of religious refugees that had ended up on his ship. For that matter what might he say to the Italian priests who sounded as though they had lived their entire lives in Britain. Once more, he wished Bob was present. Bob always seemed at ease in the company of Catholics. Indeed, Edgar had taken him for one when they first met. And, of course, there was that moment when Bob probably had considered joining their ranks. Bob would know what to say. But Bob was busy in the engine room getting the ship ready for departure.

It was the chief steward who took the initiative of introducing the Italian side of the table to Edgar. 'This is Mr. Anzani.' He indicated the senior, impeccably draped, gentleman.

Edgar reached across the table and shook Anzani's hand. He was on the point of commiserating with Anzani when Friedrich blurted, 'Mr. Anzani? I know you.'

Decio Anzani looked at Friedrich for a few seconds and then shook his head slowly before answering, 'I think you may be mistaken.'

Friedrich insisted. 'About seven years ago. In a back-lane in London. I was with a friend. We were ambushed by some Buffoons. And there was another man with you. He had a pistol and you also pretended you had one in your pocket,' Friedrich spoke quickly.

A light seemed to have clicked at least dimly on for Decio, who had begun nodding as though he was trying to dislodge a memory.

'You saved my friend from being disfigured and me from a beating, or worse.'

Decio snapped his fingers. 'Yes. I remember you and your friend. An art teacher. Ingrid, right?'

'No. Her name is Ingeborg. She said that you and your friend were musketeers.'

'Fortunato,' Renzo spoke quietly. 'That fellow with the pistol, the one who saved you, that was Fortunato Picchi.'

'Do you know him?' Friedrich asked.

Renzo grinned. 'A brother of mine.'

'He's a lot shorter than you.' Friedrich shook his head doubtfully. 'Is he here too?'

'He's not far away,' Decio said. 'He's on the quay, waiting with the rest of the unfortunates.'

Renzo shook hands with Friedrich. 'I'll tell him you're here.'

Edgar turned to Renzo and the priests. 'We have a small room here on the ship,' he said. 'A quiet place for prayer. Maybe you'd like to see it?'

The priestly duo nodded in agreement. The elder of the two gestured toward the rabbis on the opposite side of the table. 'I suggest we share it.'

The rabbis smiled their accord with the idea.

Decio returned to his previous train of thought: 'We were in the midst of agreeing with your chief steward where and how he might accommodate us, italo-brits.'

'Italo-brits?' Edgar echoed.

'Or brit-italos, if you prefer,' Decio said in an odd accent that seemed a blend of Romford and Rimini. 'You can choose to call us whatever you prefer, Captain. As long as you don't call us enemy aliens.'

'I was asking Mr. Anzani,' the chief steward said, 'if he could tell us how many fascist sympathisers there might be amongst the Italian passengers.'

It was Renzo who laughed hardest. 'If you can find a dozen fascists you'll have done well.'

'Apparently we're going to be more than eight-hundred Italians aboard,' Decio said. 'There could be a few fascists. What do you think *Monsignóre*?' Decio asked the elder of the priests. 'What would you say, perhaps about twenty?'

'I heard there were some in Lingfield and Bury camps,' the priest rasped. 'Plus, any that came across on the *Tynwald*.' His voice sounded as old and irritable as he looked. 'But you needn't worry about them. They're harmless windbags. You can billet them in the same place as the rest of us.'

Edgar was unsure whether it was a good idea to leave suspected Italian fascists with the others, but he determined he should leave that for Major Bethell and the chief steward to decide upon with Decio Anzani and the priests.

'It'd certainly make the situation more manageable if we didn't have to segregate them,' the chief steward answered.

The old priest pointed to the guardsman at the back of the room and the guardsman snapped out of a slouch 'We'll call on him if we need to.'

'Good,' the chief steward concluded. 'That's sorted then. Italo-brits to the lower decks.'

'Why there?' Renzo asked as though he had a fear of being assigned there.

'That's where most of our accommodation is,' the chief steward explained. 'There's a lot more of you.'

'And us?' Jacob asked.

'Since there's less of you, you'll be in the upper decks,' the chief steward answered. 'Less private accommodation up there, but we can squeeze you into the communal spaces.'

Friedrich whispered something in German to Jacob Burfeind, who shrugged.

'Any ideas on how we should segregate your lot?' the chief steward directed his question to the German side of the table.

Rabbi Moser was first to respond. He spoke in a heavy accent that Edgar guessed might be Polish or Czech. 'You could start by separating the refugees from the others.'

'How many are there?' the chief steward asked.

'I'd say around two hundred,' the rabbi answered.

'Two hundred refugees?' The chief steward asked and his disbelief in the stupidity of their mission temporarily froze his jaw open. 'Two hundred German Jewish refugees?'

The rabbi looked confused.

'Not all refugees are German or Jewish,' Jacob explained. 'There's plenty of German Jewish refugees out there' And with a thumb he signalled to the quay. 'But there are plenty of Austrian, Polish and Czech Jewish refugees too. Then there are those German refugees that are socialists, or trade unionists, or perhaps even the odd communist they had not got around to killing. Also, if I may adapt signor Anzani's phrase there are the others, germano-brits, or austro-brits, you must not forget them. They might or might not be of Jewish faith but given they have been resident in Britain for many years they are not refugees.'

'This is a mess.' the chief steward rubbed his forehead with the palm of his hand.

Once again, Edgar was relieved that Bob was with his crew preparing for that night's departure and it would be some time before he got wind they would be deporting not only elderly men who thought they'd be safe in Britain, but refugees and priests and rabbis too. As if all this was not bad enough, they would also be deporting socialists and communists. Edgar imagined that Bob would take all this as badly as he was taking it himself.

'How about the German prisoners-of-war we're supposed to be transporting?' the chief steward asked.

'Depends, if you mean me and my crew,' Jacob answered. 'Are we prisoners-of-war?'

The chief steward looked at Edgar, as though in search of the answer.

Edgar cleared his throat. 'Did they convert your ship for some military service?'

'Would have been difficult for them.' Jacob laughed heartily. 'I sunk it and surrendered to the British.'

'How about captured aviators and *Reichsmariners*?' the chief steward insisted. 'There must be some dangerous characters amongst them.'

'I think they already left last week.' Jacob grinned.

'Aren't there men in uniform?' the chief steward insisted.

'Perhaps you mean us?' Jacob said. 'There's plenty of merchant mariners, engineers and cooks lined up outside. I doubt whether many of their hearts skip a beat for the *Fuhrer* or whether many of them are genuine party members.'

The chief steward scribbled more notes. 'This is going to be more complicated than I thought.'

From the corner of the room, a loud ringing startled everyone. Bethell's man stared at the telephone as though surprised he had not spotted its presence earlier.

With a hand movement, the chief steward indicated to the guardsman he should pick up the telephone.

Even before the guardsman picked it up, Edgar knew who would be on the other end. He felt it in his gut. He pictured Bob Connell, six-decks below on the orlop, nonchalantly holding the telephone hand-piece with one hand and tapping away cigarette ash with the other.

The guardsman picked up the receiver.

'Who is it?' the chief steward asked.

'Engine room, sir.' There was a short delay whilst the guardsman listened. 'It's a message from the chief engineer. He says Captain Moulton and Major Bethell need to join him in the engine room. There's a problem.'

Edgar knew this was coming. There was danger in it for Bob and perhaps for himself too.

22

EDGE OF SHANNON

North Atlantic Sea.

Chief navigator Wilhelm Spahr opened the door of the listening room, second watch officer Krauss stepped past him and squeezed himself into the room. The seated communications-officer turned to acknowledge and salute both Kraus and Spahr.

'Was there something you wanted to say?' Kraus asked.

'Hydrophone trace,' the senior communications officer answered.

Kraus stiffened. 'Of what?'

'A single vessel, sir.'

'Distance?'

'About fifteen kilometres.'

'What type of vessel?' Kraus asked hopefully and appeared to have relaxed.

'Can't say for certain,' the senior communications officer answered. 'Definitely steam driven turbines, probably four.'

Kraus rubbed his chin and turned to Spahr. 'Suggestions?'

'Perhaps go up and take a look?'

Maybe it had been all that talk, several shifts back, of Scapa Flow or the fact that on this patrol his own numbers trailed Amelung's, but Kraus did not immediately reject Spahr's suggestion. 'Take her up to periscope depth,' he ordered.

Spahr winked at the communications officer and asked, 'shall I instruct the torpedo room to warm up our eel?'

'I'll take care of that,' Kraus said. 'If it's necessary.'

As U47's observation periscope pierced the surface of the ocean Krauss commanded that her last working torpedo be warmed-up and asked confirmation of their position.

'Edge of Shannon,' Spahr answered, forgetfully.

'Just give me our bearings the same way every normal *Kriegsmarine* watch officer would want them.'

'Sorry.' Spahr sniffed. 'Force of habit.'

Kraus waved away Spahr's apology and pressed an eye to the observation periscope.

'All clear to surface?' Spahr asked.

'Yes,' Kraus responded.

U47 rose and made toward her target at eighteen knots. By the time her prey was two nautical miles distant port side they had identified her as an underpowered merchant ship of over 4,000 tonnes. Entirely oblivious to U47's proximity, the merchant ship had not even begun to attempt a zig-zag manoeuvre.

'Should I wake the *Kapitänleutnant*?' Spahr asked.

Kraus consulted his wristwatch. 'There's no need,' he answered, seemingly acutely aware of the approaching roster change. 'Let's get the matter done on this watch.'

Sea conditions were between smooth and slight. From the conning tower, Kraus trained his binoculars on the steamer. 'Yes, this will do.'

'We could get closer,' Spahr said.

Kraus turned to look doubtfully at Spahr. 'We could but we're already well in range.'

Spahr read back their coordinates, the calculated firing distance, the trajectory angles.

Kraus gave the command, 'away-when-ready.'

Their last torpedo exited and cut a trough at thirty knots. In four minutes, the starboard side of the steamer would be ripped open, and Kraus could notch up his own contribution to U47's sixth patrol.

Four minutes passed.

On the conning tower, Kraus turned pale, and beads of perspiration trickled. He turned to Spahr and then back toward the steamer. Somehow, the torpedo, their last, had missed. He shook his head in resigned defeat only to hear in that same instant an almighty explosion.

'A little error in our calculations, sir.' Spahr grinned. 'Probably that steamer was further away than we thought. But it's our lucky day, it's a hit.'

Kraus stiffly put out a hand to Spahr.

Spahr reciprocated.

Around them the other crew members on the conning tower also exchanged handshakes.

Günther emerged on the tower, Amelung two steps behind.

'What's going on?' Günther asked.

'We're registering a kill,' Kraus said.

Amelung trained his binoculars on the steamer approximately two kilometres dead-ahead at 90°.

Kraus grinned and kept his eyes on Günther.

Günther, forgetting to congratulate Kraus, asked, 'tonnage?'

Kraus's eyes took on a sheen of disappointment. 'About four-thousand tonnes, *Herr Kapitänleutnant.*'

'That puts us a kill ahead of U46,' Spahr said cheerfully.

Günther nodded. 'Our last working torpedo, too. Well done, *Oberleutnant* Kraus,' Günther attempted to make his tone as encouraging as he could.

Amelung continued focusing his binoculars on the stricken steamer. 'It's still afloat,' he said. 'I suppose we should go over there.'

Günther almost asked, what for? He stopped himself. He knew Amelung's pretences, perfectly well. Amelung pretended to be saying "let's go over there and finish the job," but what he meant was something entirely different. What he meant was "they probably have casualties let's go and help." 'All right,' Günther said and smiled as he caught Amelung's attention, 'let's finish the job.'

U47 had almost reached the steamer when a message was passed to Amelung and then relayed to Günther. A dazzling British navy Destroyer, packed with anti-submarine weaponry was streaking through Severn sector, possibly on course for Shannon. According to Günther's mental map, they had plenty of time to salve Amelung's conscience and still, easily get away. 'Continue on full power, dead ahead,' Günther commanded.

The cargo steamer was called the SS *Georgios Kyriakides.*

Amelung spoke to its bemused crew. He passed wine and sausages to thirty merchant sailors in their two small lifeboats.

'Anyone left aboard?' Günther asked.

'All hands are on these lifeboats,' the captain of the *Kyriakides* answered.

'Good,' Günther said. 'Keep rowing, because we're going to make sure your ship doesn't delay on its visit to the seabed.'

U47's deck gun crew turned their 88mm cannon on the *Kyriakides* and the ensuing boom and rip rhythm lasted several minutes until the *Georgios Kyriakides'* entrails were visible. Her descent along with her cargo of several thousand tonnes of sugar was watched in silence by Günther, Amelung, Spahr and the rest of the crew on the conning tower. In the meantime, the *Kyriakides'* lifeboats were frantically being rowed in the opposite direction, toward Ireland.

Kraus cleared his throat and broke the silence. 'We shouldn't

Forget there's a Destroyer or perhaps two of them heading this way.'

'What's our position?' Günther asked.

'Shannon Sector,' Spahr replied and grinned at *Oberleutnant* Kraus.

'Where exactly within Shannon?' Günther asked.

'50°25N, 14°33W,' Spahr replied.

Kraus grinned and seemed happy. From those coordinates he could work out which grid he was in.

'Can we go now?' Günther directed his question to Amelung.

Amelung nodded.

Minutes later, the conning tower and deck had been cleared and U*47*'s main hatch was sealed. U*47* dived. Soon, they were gone from the skin of the Atlantic. They were invisible to anyone aboard the *Kyriakides'* lifeboats. In fact, they were a spectre to all, except for any British Navy Destroyer or Coastal Command submarine-hunter in the vicinity, appropriately kitted and interested enough to locate her.

In the control room, Kraus appeared to be preparing to recite the weaponry of the putative pursuer, a gesture which was unnecessary because they all knew, and they could all recite the weaponry a Destroyer would come at them with: twin racks of depth charges, 530 mm torpedoes, 120 mm canons and 40 mm pom-pom guns.

Günther held up a hand. 'The Destroyer was barely out of Severn sector, and it is not even sure that its direction was Shannon.'

'I wish I had your confidence.' Kraus sounded anxious.

'I sense it's not going to be our turn today,' Günther replied.

Spahr bent over the map and muttered aloud. 'Even if she was coming for us, would she be ready to chase for days on end, all through Shannon into Hebrides and around Shetland? I've a good feeling too. We'll have Amelung back in Kiel in plenty of time to light his old man's birthday candles.'

At the mention of his name, Amelung turned to Spahr and bowed like an eighteenth-century music conductor.

Kraus held up a finger and as though struck by a brainwave he declared, 'Herr Kapitänleutnant, by my calculations, I believe we can confidently say that U47 has now surpassed U46's number of sunk vessels.'

'Do you think that's all that matters?' Günther answered and left the control room.

Kraus eyes spoke of his discomfort.

Spahr regarded Kraus with what could have been sympathy. 'It matters. But he wished it did not,' he said softly. 'You'll have to be patient *Oberleutnant* Kraus, this situation with Bert and U46 has created a confusion and a great number of doubts in his mind.'

23

ENGINE ROOM

Arandora Star.

Edgar made his way to the Docking Bridge to find Major Bethell. He found Bethell loudly instructing several of his Sergeants on how to handle the boarding of twelve-hundred internees.

'Yes, yes,' Bethell said, 'patting down does need to be done. But only the bare minimum.'

'It's not right,' one of Bethell's younger sergeants answered. The fellow looked distressed.

Edgar stood a discreet distance away and busied himself with inspecting some deck fittings.

'Why not?' Bethell asked.

'For a start, they're not enemies, sir,' Bethell's man replied his voice strained.

'Well, I know that.' Bethell spoke calmly and pressed his hands together against his lips as though praying. 'So, you recognised a few internees down on the quay?'

'Yes, sir.'

'Who did you recognise?'

'Neighbours of mine.'

'Welshmen?' Bethell asked doubtfully and cocked his head.

'Yes,' the guardsman answered but seemed less sure of himself.

Bethell scratched the side of his head. 'From where?'

'From Neath.' Bethell's man appeared on the edge of tears.

'I don't know what to say about that,' Bethell answered and he turned to Edgar. 'Maybe Captain Moulton can tell us something about why your neighbours are here.'

Edgar stepped closer. He understood what Bethell needed from him. But he was not confident he could reassure the guardsman. He had hoped that no one would expect him to try and impose any meaning on this mission.

The entire situation scraped a level of stupidity that could not withstand the least scrutiny. He reached for the simplest of platitudes: *there was a war on*; *mistakes happened*; *an invasion was imminent*. This was all true, and he could have ornamented those excuses: *decisions needed to be made in the heat of the situation*; or *the situation was worsening by the hour*. That was also true.

But ever since his telephone call with Lily, a chasm of incoherence had hollowed him out. It had been made worse by what he had come to learn about the identities of his passengers. The "aliens" were tenured or even second generation italo-brits long since striated into the fabric of British society. Priests from the north and chip-shop owners from Glasgow and ice-cream makers from Manchester and tailors and restauranteurs from London. They were boys barely out of school. Fathers with sons in the British forces. Grandfathers, whose British born grandchildren waited at home for news of them. And even the Honorary President of the League of Rights of Man.

What of the "Germans?" They also were a mixture of tenured and second generation germano-brits and stateless refugees whose ranks were filled with men like Friedrich: doctors and artists, musicians and teachers, and rabbis. Who had imagined they had escaped fascism when they had fled from their annexed countries. Even the "prisoners-of-war" were not what they had been made out to be.

Bethell's man from Neath stared at Edgar as though he saw the fugue tumbling around inside Edgar's mind. A couple of Bethell's sergeants came to stand beside him and they all looked at Edgar and waited for the answer.

Even Bethell looked at Edgar.

Edgar had never felt that degree of loss in his own bearings.

Bethell sighed and finally asked, 'what are we to make of it all?'

Edgar did not know what they should make of it, but he reached for his most trusted consolation. 'At times like this, I search for an answer in someone else's experience. Often in poetry.' No one snickered and no eyes rolled. 'Do you know any poetry,' he asked Bethell's man.

'I know some *Hedd Wyn*,' The Sergeant said. 'From *Rhyfel*. "Why must I live in this grim age."'

'Good choice,' Edgar said.

Bethell cut in: 'Or how about, "Ours, not to make reply. Ours, not to reason why,"' he recited solemnly.

'Tennyson,' Edgar said. 'I was thinking of him too.'

The sergeant seemed not to have been succoured by any of that. 'Could I be put on another detail, sir?' he asked.

Major Bethell sighed again. 'I'm afraid it's too late for that.'

Edgar considered how to get himself and Bethell out of the situation. 'We'll all have to handle this in the best way we can.' He turned back to Bethell, 'Bob Connell wants us to go and see him. It's urgent.'

'Is there a lift?' Bethell asked.

'Not all the way down.'

***

They arrived in the engine room where they were quickly greeted and led into the adjacent Boiler Room. Given their intended sailing time, the warming-through phase should have been well underway, but the ambient temperatures and noise levels were less elevated than Edgar expected.

Something seemed off.

Surrounded by several of his "lads," Bob stood adjacent to a turbine engine casing. In one hand he held the engine room logbook and in the other hand he held an empty half-pint glass.

'Something up?' Edgar asked above the sounds of gentle whirring and banging.

'Aye,' Bob said and a shifty smile incongruously crossed his face.

'Something serious?' Edgar added.

'Well, I thought I should let both of you know straight away.'

'Let us know what?' Bethell asked.

'We're not going to be able to heave anchor,' Bob spoke matter-of-factly. 'Not tonight, and maybe not for a while.'

'Why not?' Edgar's concern was clear. 'What's the problem?'

Bob stroked his nose and grinned at Edgar and handed him the engine room logbook. 'Take a look for yourself.' He raised the drinking glass and placed it against the turbine casing. He leant in until his ear covered the thick base of the drinking glass. He had the air of a doctor with an improvised stethoscope. He appeared to be listening attentively as the turbine communicated some message to him through the drinking glass.

Edgar glimpsed summarily and tried to make sense of the logbook, but like Bethell he was drawn to watch Bob.

Bob's eyes animated in close rhythm with the loud *umms* and *ahhhs* he made. A couple of his lads stood nearby and wore expressions that suggested some dire news was being relayed. Finally, Bob stepped aside but he held the beer glass in position with a single finger. 'Go ahead take a listen.'

In their time together, Bob had never once asked this of Edgar.

Edgar placed a finger on the centre of the glass where Bob's had been. Then rested an ear against the glass in the same way he had seen Bob do it. Odd sounds came through the glass but they were strangers to Edgar. He had no means of decrypting the diverse groans and occasional glugs and unrelenting whizzes that merged with the background whirring and whistling. Eventually he asked, 'what am I listening for?'

'You're not listening. You're feeling.'

'What am I feeling for?' Edgar asked.

'Vibrations.'

'What sort?'

'The wrong sort.'

'And how will I know they're the wrong sort?'

'You'll know them all right,' Bob insisted. 'Listen for the loss of equilibrium.'

This was Bob's protest. His moment of *styfnig*. He had invoked the navigator's *cri de coeur*. Edgar had known it was coming. But protest could not be possible. People faced court martial and jail for less. In the presence of the Major and Bob's own "lads" Edgar would not take the risk of confronting Bob. Instead, he puckered his cheeks and stared hard at Bob. 'Maybe it's not as bad as you think. Perhaps there's a little problem in the quality of fuel. And we can always fix that, right?'

Bethell closely followed the entire scene. He seemed to grow more bemused. 'How long do you think we might be delayed?'

'A while.' Bob replied and defiantly smirked as he added, 'I wouldn't go boarding any internees if I was you.'

'Why not?' Bethell answered.

'For a start there's the loss of equilibrium I mentioned.'

'Could it be the turbine blades?' Edgar feigned a modicum of engineering know-how and gently tapped on a turbine casing, not caring how ridiculous he might seem to the engine room crew.

Bob pursed his lips and looked away as though he was in danger of laughing aloud.

Bethell rocked impatiently on his feet and occupied himself by looking around the boiler room. There were three other equally enormous casings with numerous tubes and painted pipes that made the space appear complex yet magisterial. Bethell stared at some yellow painted piping which led away toward a tunnel like a giant fallopian tube connecting the boiler room to some hidden and mysterious placenta.

Edgar wondered how long Bob expected him to pretend to know how compromised turbine blades might sound. In the background, thunking and booming noises picked up a louder and faster rhythm.

'I should point out there's also a problem with the lubricating system,' Bob added and almost smirked in delivering that news.

Bethell sighed and bent to massage his knee. 'Your half-pint beer glass told you all of that?' Bethell's irony was, by then, unfiltered.

Bob looked nonchalantly toward a thicket of pipes and valves and indicated a bell-shaped jar, half-full of golden oil and a horizontal slit of black oil in it, like the eye of a serpent. 'No. She did.'

Edgar raised an eyebrow. 'Are you saying you have doubts about our seaworthiness?' He watched Bob closely for any flicker.

'I don't like the way the dog-vane is pointing, Captain. For this particular voyage I doubt we are seaworthy.'

Edgar did not like the way the wind blew either, surely Bob could see that.

'I'll tell you what,' Bethell said, 'we'll go ahead and board the internees, because we don't have an alternative.'

'You're not getting it,' Bob half-shouted above the turbines which had now become louder as had the temperature in the room, 'we're not transporting anyone, anywhere.'

'Listen old chap,' Bethell spoke loudly but calmly, 'I think you're the one who doesn't get it. I never said anything about transporting internees, only about boarding them.'

'Why even go that far?' Bob's tone fell back and he crossed his arms over his chest. 'If we've no intention of transporting them?'

'You'd prefer to leave them standing around outside where they are?' Bethell asked. 'Like battery hens. Some still stuck in holding cells, or sat around on the goods yard of the station terminus?'

Edgar hated to see Bob placed in this predicament. Perhaps Bob was counting on the fact that the *Tynwald* was still tied up. She had plenty of seats and benches and even a small lounge. But she wasn't designed to hold passengers overnight and maybe he imagined the internees would be sent back over to Douglas, back to their camps on the Isle of Man. But Edgar knew this could not happen. Too many political reputations were at stake. He was on the point of saying this when Bethell intervened and placed an arm around Bob's shoulder.

Bethell pulled Bob closer. 'If they don't leave with us then they'll simply have to wait where they are until a reserve transport ship comes to fetch them.'

Bob folded his arms. He sighed deeply. He gazed at Edgar as though to say, I'm fine with that.

'And if my information is correct,' Bethell continued, 'it's probably going to be the SS *Dunera*.'

Bob grinned and unfolded his arms. 'What if it is?'

'You want these fellows to be transported by the brutal brigade?' Bethell's response to a question was to ask his own question.

Bob tilted his head like a curious owl and his eyes revealed he was not going to be taken in with any of it. 'What do you mean, brutal brigade?'

'Don't you chaps get to hear anything?' Bethell said.

On the edge of firing a riposte, Edgar stopped it in its breech.

He did not want to say, as a matter of fact he was in the habit of getting to hear plenty. And he was certain he heard more gossip than Bethell. For instance, did Bethell know that the SS *Duchess of York* had left Liverpool on her way to Australia only six days ago? She had been stuffed with German internees. That news was "unofficial," but the harbour master and harbour pilots know everything and Edgar knew them. And did Bethell know that the SS *Ettrick* was on her way right now to Liverpool and she would be transporting the next wave of internees and refugees already on their way to be dumped on Princes Quay? Well, Edgar knew all of this. He leaned in between the Major and Bob and curtly asked, 'what is it you think you know, Major Bethell, about the *Dunera* that we don't?'

Apparently, equally wary of the other crew members in the vicinity, Bethell replied quietly, 'better not to talk here. I propose we chaps go up to your quarters and continue our little chat up there.'

Bob seemed relieved by the turn of events. He pointed over the top of Bethell's shoulder. 'Straight down there and up the staircase on your left.'

They moved along the orlop deck like three Indians. The Major took the lead, Edgar a few steps behind and then a few steps further back came Bob Connell calling out instructions for the Major. They had not gone far before Edgar felt a tug at his coat collar.

24

A SILVER BOX

Princes Quay, Liverpool.

Whilst Fortunato waited on the quay for news and the return of his friends, clouds drifted freely away and the sun began to beat harder. The guardsmen herding them on the quay did not object as their charges drifted closer to the water's edge and the shady relief of the ship's berth. He shielded his eyes as he stared ahead at the looming ship. Around him some countrymen, who had never been so close to a ship of such enormity, expressed their awe and wonderment.

The heat, the smell, the sound, transported him back in time, twenty years previously to Southampton when he had worked on cruise liners. He recalled the excitement of families when they saw close up and anticipated boarding some gigantic liner which would be their home for weeks to follow. They were passengers who had dreamt over months of some exotic destination selected after having seen an advertisement or having studied a brochure. Their ship was immense but it did not make them feel small. They were passengers who had strolled leisurely along the quay and anticipated the pleasure of reaching the landing stage where they would be met by Fortunato and his colleagues who would hand out complimentary drinks and instructions on how to find their cabin. Their walk felt like the beginning of an adventure not the end of a misadventure. They were passengers who travelled in families and left their cares and woes behind them, whereas Fortunato and his friends would travel with their cares and woes and leave their families behind.

In the near distance, he heard church bells ring out. Stupid, cheery church bells whose happy ding-dongs peeled out until a dog could take no more. It barked. It kept barking, and some strangulated laughter could be heard. Even the guards seemed to have sensed the absurdity. The dog's yelping had reached a crescendo when an internee down the line acclaimed, 'you'll have to excuse us, we're being invited to a wedding over there at Saint Nick's.'

Like the others around him, he laughed aloud and looked back in the direction of Saint Nicholas' Church. Near the pier head he caught a glimpse of its church steeple. At this hour on a normal Sunday, he would be headed to church. Florence would be there, Renzo and Maria and their two children too. He searched in his wallet for his thin silver medal of *Arcangelo* San Michele that his mother had given to him. Same as she had given to all of them. It had brought him luck in the war. He removed the medal and held it in his clenched fist and was silently muttering to San Michele when Giovanni interrupted him.

'There they are.' Giovanni pointed along the quayside.

Accompanied by four guards, Decio, Renzo and the two priests were headed back down the quay. They seemed in no hurry to return. Decio had an air of a school master inspecting his pupils. The group occasionally stopped as Decio was permitted to exchange a word with someone he recognised in the line-up. Renzo strode along beside him like a suffering assistant headmaster and occasionally glanced down the quay as if searching for someone.

'This will do, leave us here,' Decio said when the group finally reached Fortunato and Giovanni.

Fortunato watched the soldiers turn around and march away back up the quay before he inquired, 'well?'

'The captain was most agreeable. He seems to be a very decent man,' Decio answered. 'And there's something else.'

'And he's a pacifist,' Renzo added.

'How does that matter to us?'

'Well, he said he was sorry,' Renzo replied and he looked directly into Fortunato's eyes. 'No one else has said that to us.'

'Did he say where they are taking us?' Fortunato asked.

'Or why they have needed to keep us hanging around out here for hours?' Giovanni added.

'He can't tell us where they're taking us,' Decio said. 'But I've a feeling we'll get it out of him at dinner.'

'We're having dinner with the captain?' Giovanni asked doubtfully.

Fortunato did not find the idea to be odd. The liner had obviously been commandeered and likely its crew had too. Dinner with the captain was a custom and probably all they had left of their old lives. 'Why did the captain want to see you?' Fortunato asked.

'Logistics,' Decio replied curtly.

Some lost clouds passed over their heads and offered relief.

'You said there was something else?' Fortunato asked.

'Do you remember, years ago, when we stopped some fascists from cutting up a couple of tourists?'

He remembered it clearly. Florence had been there. Later, she had made a fuss about something the girl had said. Her distress gave him the moment to reassure her that he neither knew nor cared what difference in years they had between them. He had never been happier. Before he could respond to Decio on whether he remembered that evening or not, Giovanni tugged at his sleeve, the column lurched from some collective anaesthesia as depressed internees picked up their bags and suitcases.

'We're moving,' Renzo said.

'Finally,' replied Giovanni.

Guardsmen at the head and sides of their column set the pace as they walked up the quay. Slow and steady. After perhaps two-hundred-metres, they stopped. From that vantage point he saw the others, queued up in the vicinity of the railway and customs shed. Hundreds more internees as ragged and tired and dispirited as Fortunato and those who walked alongside him.

The process of boarding had begun.

'Yes, I remember it,' Decio said.

'You recall the student doctor?' Decio asked then added incredulously, 'he's an internee too. He's being transported along with us.'

'Jesus wept,' Fortunato answered.

'Move along,' a guardsman shouted.

From time to time, sounds could be heard of men or boys refusing to step off the quayside and on to the walkway toward the hulking great ship. It always ended the same way, no matter if a boy cried out for his mother, or a man cried out for his wife and children. The guards and other men in the queue would take the internee to the side, give them a drink of water, calm them, and then look for a friend, or someone willing to board with the reluctant internee. It was explained, no one wanted to go, but there was no choice.

He was approaching the boarding point when a large black saloon car pulled up on to the quay. The curiosity of everyone in the vicinity was aroused as two uniformed policemen and a tall thin man in a brown gaberdine coat stepped out of the car. The trio strode to the head of the queue and spoke to the guards.

He was not close enough to hear what words were exchanged and thus was startled when the trio, accompanied by a soldier from the guard, came down the file and the thin man began asking, 'do you know where we'll find Fortunato Picchi?'

He stepped out of the queue. 'That's me.'

The thin man spoke quietly. 'Good. I've got your application here.'

'What application?'

'Don't play games,' the thin man responded. 'Do you want to help or not?'

'It's a bit late, wouldn't you say.' Fortunato stepped back into the queue toward his friends.

'I've gone to a lot of trouble to come here.'

Renzo asked, 'is everything all right at home?'

'It's not that,' Fortunato answered. 'It's my application to join the Pioneer Corps.'

'Who are you?' the thin man asked Renzo.

'I'm his friend,' Renzo answered. 'Are you taking him home?'

'Apparently he's reconsidered his alliances.'

'It's not that at all,' Fortunato replied. 'These are my friends,' he added. 'I should stay here with them. They might need my help.'

The thin man shrugged. His expression seemed to say he might know what Fortunato was going through. 'You'd be helping everyone a whole lot more if you didn't spend the war interned thousands of miles from the action.'

'If you do go, tell Maria and the kids I'm ok.' Renzo took his piccolo out from his pocket. It was tucked up in its silver box. 'And give this to my boy.'

The thin man watched Renzo hand over the box. He nodded to Fortunato, as though to say, yes whatever that is, you can take it.

Fortunato and Renzo embraced.

Decio said, 'well done!'

'Don't worry about us,' Giovanni sounded sorrowful. 'I'll get myself a life jacket, like you said.'

He bid his farewells and took his place in the car, in the back seated, between the thin man and a uniformed policemen. Whilst the thin man passed a note out of the car window, Fortunato caressed the silver box and looked up at the liner. He thought he could make out the silhouettes of three men standing on a platform high above the last deck of the ship.

'Take good care of my friends,' he muttered.

25

A SMALL PROMISE

Arandora Star.

Edgar fixed his collar back in place and turned briefly to reproach Bob with the power of a cold stare.

Bob whispered, 'what do you suppose he thinks he knows?'

'The man is not a fool. He can see the same as anyone else. He knows everything you did back there was a sham.'

Bob's face-mask of *who me?* appeared and he whispered in reply, 'no, he doesn't know anything.'

'He knows all right.'

'What if he does. Do you want to be remembered for this?'

'What choice do you think we have?'

'Everything all right back there?' Bethell shouted.

'Fine.' Edgar pointed beyond Bethell. 'Carry on, straight up.'

'Have you wondered what your brother would do,' Bob whispered as he stepped past Edgar. 'Or your mother come to that.'

Edgar sighed at the price of fraternity. It was a low shot.

Bethell stepped on to the main deck and bent to massage his knee. 'Damn humidity.'

'You'd better get used to it,' Bob answered. 'If you're planning two months with us. Anyway, it's not far now, sir. Straight ahead, take that first corridor and then out through the doorway you see there on your left.'

Edgar picked up the pace and stepped wordlessly past Bob and Bethell. 'I'll take it from here.'

They ascended the dregs of their journey in silence and arrived at the door of the captain's house. Edgar opened the door and stepped inside.

Bethell followed him in.

A cough from outside. Bob's hand wave informing them that he would remain on the outside, in earshot, but for the moment staying put on the other side of the open door.

Edgar watched Bob light up a cigarette.

Bethell wheezily announced, 'I think I'm ready for that gin.'

Edgar poured two tumblers of naked gin and a glass of cydrax. He passed one gin tumbler to Bethell and sat one on the counter in front of the captain's bridge. The cydrax he kept for himself.

Bethell held his tumbler aloft as though saluting the majestic Merseyside skyline, seen through the panoramic windows of the captain's bridge. 'Cheers.' He clinked Edgar's glass. He picked up Bob's tumbler and made his way to the open door and stood, a tumbler in either hand. He addressed Bob quietly. 'I can't say I blame you, chief engineer Connell. But I don't believe you have thought this through.' He handed Bob his glass.

Bob inhaled and held his breath for as long as his lung capacity granted him. Eventually a waft of cigarette smoke punctuated out through his nostrils and rose like exclamation marks.

From his position near the window, Edgar smiled and envied but quietly saluted Bob's *styfnig*.

Bethell sipped on his gin and continued. 'All you'd achieve is a tiring delay. You'd have our passengers wait around on the quay and in sheds until the *SS Dunera* comes for them. No one is going to thank you for that.'

Edgar searched his memory to find the place where ships and captains and crews were filed away. 'What's wrong with the *Dunera*?'

'Nothing, I suppose,' Bethell said. 'But I'm not talking about the *Dunera*, I'm talking about her guard.'

Bob blew circles of smoke. Thin spectral donuts floated and stacked one upon the other before dispersing one by one. When the last circle had gone, Bob asked pointedly, 'what's wrong with her guard?'

Bethell leant in and quietly said, 'keep this to yourself, but they're made up mostly of rogues, thugs, and bigots expressly released from prison. I've heard very bad things and I'd hate to think of that kind of guard escorting any friends of mine. Especially if it was unnecessary.'

Bob smiled a pained smile. He flicked his dying cigarette and sipped at his glass of gin.

Edgar swilled his drink. The game was up. Bethell was on to Bob. It was time for Edgar to do what was necessary, even if it upset Bob. 'I'm going to assume it's too late to sort our turbine problems in time for our scheduled departure on tonight's tide,' he said. 'I'll come up with some excuse, as long as we're ready for first tide tomorrow.'

Bethell raised his glass and stared into Bob's eyes. 'That sounds like an offer. And if that were to happen, there'd be no need for anyone to come over here snooping. Nor would my guards have to keep our passengers waiting around.'

Bob pinched the near dead cigarette tip between his thumb and forefinger and crushed the remnant in his hand. He stepped past Bethell and entered the captain's house where he threw the remains of his cigarette into a small metal bin. He met Edgar's gaze full-on and finished his glass of gin in one mouthful. He placed the glass on the counter and spoke in a hush. 'I'm sorry about what I said.'

Edgar finished his own glass and placed it back on the counter. He patted Bob affectionately on the shoulder. 'It would be a difficult journey to make without you.' Then more loudly, for Bethell's ears, he said, 'we'll set sail in the morning.'

'I'm glad that's sorted,' Bethell answered. 'Especially, as we already started the boarding.'

Bob scowled in Bethell's direction but his eyes bore no malice.

'Let's go up top and see how that's going, then,' Edgar said and led them across the navigating bridge and up the near vertical staircase to the chart-house.

Atop the chart-house, Bethell leant on the handrail and stared ahead into the wind. Edgar and Bob took a 360° look around themselves.

Internees were already lined up along the footbridge seven decks below. If despondency had a shape, Edgar believed he was looking at it right then. Hundreds upon hundreds of internees: two-abreast. Some carried small, battered looking suitcases. Others held the stays of duffle-bags or bundles tied-together. It was a wretched sight. A shameful shuffling of human desperation accompanied by hollow sounds of resignation. These were not the faces of relief, nor joy, nor hope. This was the opposite of a rescue, and he was its navigator. He shook his head in sadness.

Bethell stepped closer. 'You'll see, things will improve.'

'I can't imagine them being any worse.'

'I'll make you a small promise. As soon as we're far enough out from here, if you told me that you needed to take down that bloody barbed wire then I'd certainly have to listen to what you had to say.'

Bethell had raised Edgar's spirits. He realised once more how glad he was that it was Bethell who was with them.

Bob remained mute and looked intensely through binoculars at the sad line of humanity.

Edgar could not say if Bob had even heard Bethell's promise to help rid them of the barbed wire. Perhaps Bob was busy searching in the crowd for an elderly Glaswegian chip shop owner and his son.

'Take a look at that.' Bob handed the binoculars to Edgar and pointed at the front of the boarding line. 'Looks like the War Office are here after all.'

Edgar saw that a large, black, saloon car had parked on the quay. Even from a distance it was an officious picture. An officer, by the look of him, spoke to a squaddie and sent him aboard, no doubt to find and deliver a message to Edgar. 'I wonder what they want?'

'I wouldn't worry,' Bethell said. 'It's too early for them to start poking around asking serious questions.'

They could ask whatever they liked. Edgar was not concerned. In order to figure out that there was no technical obstacle as to why the *Arandora Star* would not part on the scheduled evening tide, they would have had to send a navy man aboard; someone capable of examining Bob Connell's logbook and Edgar Moulton's conscience.

But they had sent a squaddie with a message.

When the squaddie arrived he did not ask what tide they would be leaving on. 'They're removing an Italian internee, sir,' he announced and handed Edgar a memorandum signed by a Brigadier Gubbins.

Possibly on account of his relief that he would not have to explain his own culpability in a delayed sailing or perhaps on account of the solemn manner in which the squaddie announced the news, even Bethell laughed aloud.

Edgar did not inquire what the man had done to warrant his treatment. Neither did he reveal that given the lack of a meaningful passenger manifest, they would probably have been none the wiser had the squaddie not bothered to come aboard and inform them. He read the memorandum. Apparently, Mr Fortunato Picchi would be removed from the line. It seems he had volunteered for bomb and mine disposal and his services were now considered "essential."

Edgar whistled softly and felt grateful to this anonymous Italian. 'Tell the Brigadier on my behalf, it's lucky we had not already left.' Then, looking directly at Bob, he added, 'you can also tell him we had a technical problem but we've resolved it and we'll be sailing on the morning tide. If there's anyone else he needs to take, then he'd better do it soon.'

Edgar watched the squaddie return to the quay with his message. They took no one else from the line. He waved when the black saloon car flashed its headlights and pulled away from Princes Quay. He had the sensation someone in the car waved back.

26

LUCKY, LUCKY GÜNTHER

North Atlantic Sea.

The North Atlantic Ocean rippled one hundred metres above their heads. U47 traced a line as close to the seabed as Günther dared to take her. Every *unterseeboot Kapitänleutnant* knew that over the course of time the probabilities tilted one way. But, if they were good at their job and battery conditions and their luck favoured them, an *unterseeboot* could remain hidden for hours. He felt it was not the day for his good fortune to desert him. And yet it was obvious that every *Kapitänleutnant* likely felt that same way on the day of their death.

It had been his intention that they would surface sometime around dusk. They would recharge their batteries and continue the journey home. In the secrecy of his own quarters, he permitted the gloating face of Bert Endrass to materialise in his mind. The image had no sooner formed there when its antidote entered his quarters. But even in the dim light, Günther apprehended Amelung's anxiety. Günther held up both hands. 'I suppose you've been talking with Kraus?'

'Yes.'

'We don't know for certain there are any pursuers. If there were, Nauen would have let us know, right?'

Amelung's smile seemed forced. 'I imagine they would have. But I wasn't thinking about that.'

'What were you thinking about?'

'Those sailors.'

'Don't worry about them, Amelung. They've probably been picked up by now.'

'I mean those stubborn boys. Those two young radio-officers we drowned.'

'Well,' Günther rasped, 'we don't know if they drowned.'

'They drowned.'

'It'd be their own fault if they did. They should have left with the others.' He waited for Amelung to find argument with his conclusion, but Amelung shrugged, defeated, and Günther wished the captain of the *Empire Toucan* had not revealed his radio-officers had been seventeen and eighteen years old. Amelung had likely already added these particular stubborn boys to his list. Günther tutted and looked at his wristwatch and happily realised it would soon be time for Amelung to go off duty. 'Isn't there somewhere else you should be?'

'Sorry, sir.' Amelung saluted and turned away, leaving Günther to cope with his own grey guilt.

He imagined Amelung passing amongst the men of second watch as they completed their shift in the radio communications room, the engine room, and the weapons room. In due course their collective whiff, an odour which owed its distinctiveness to the fact they were almost all partial to onion, would be replaced by that of Kraus' men. The crew of first watch were mostly partial to pickled cabbage and had their own signature scent that, this far into the mission, was no less distinctive nor pungent than Amelung's watch.

Günther closed his eyes and breathed thin air. He pictured the pallid blue tinged skin of the men of first watch. Their hands and faces as though life had leeched from them during their shallow sleep. They were all Günther's boys. He had to keep them safe and he had to keep their morale high. Tasks rendered increasingly difficult on account of probabilities and suffocatingly omnipresent on account of Amelung's obsession with numbers.

It was not as though Günther needed Amelung and his statistics to remind him that the British were getting better. He knew it as well as Amelung did. And he had tried to do something about it. Ever since the Scapa Flow mission he had the ear of Admiral Dönitz. Dönitz had a direct line to Grand Admiral Erich Raeder and Grand Admiral Erich Raeder defecated in the same pot as the miniature-man. Thus, Günther had done what he could do to trumpet a warning.

On his last shore-leave, he met privately with Dönitz and Dönitz assured him that he would pass the message to Raeder and was confident that Raeder would personally inform the miniature man. The miniature man would listen because he knew who Günther was. Günther's message was blunt: "If we can't build safer replacement *unterseeboots* faster than the British sink them then this war will end in eighteen months, when the last *unterseeboot* is sunk." Günther had not yet told Amelung about that discussion. He had been too wrapped up in the situation with Bert to say anything to Amelung. It occurred to him that he ought to tell Amelung now. Who knew when there might be another opportunity?

He went to find Amelung. He followed in Amelung's trail, through the radio communications and listening rooms, through the control room and mariners' quarters until he reached the engine room where a cluster of electric motors whirred and odd words were being exchanged. Amelung was not present. It took Günther a moment to realise the engineers of second watch had been making bets on whether U*47* would surpass U*46*'s figures.

'How many patrols have we made?' Günther asked of no one in particular.

'This would be our sixth, sir,' a worn-looking engineer said. It was apparent, by the paper slips he held, that he was the book-runner.

'Anyone can get lucky on a single mission,' Günther said.

'Good point, sir,' a Bavarian further down the line quipped.

'No one's as lucky as us,' another crewman rejoined.

Günther smiled and shrugged his shoulders. He had heard the crewmen say that several times before. They had learnt it from Bert: "Günther Prien the luckiest sailor there's ever been." Another quip from Bert's bank of quips. "Günther found the honey when Günther found the money." Of course, Bert had never acknowledged that it was thanks to Günther that he too also "found the money." If Günther had not attested to Bert's credence in the party's values, it is unlikely Bert would have found himself in the higher paying officer class. Günther had told the lie with fingers crossed behind his back, just the same as he had when he attested his own credence. He shook his head and asked the book-runner, 'what odds are you giving here?'

'Evens we'll sink more tonnage than U46 during this patrol.'

Günther shook his head in disbelief. How could the book runner expect anyone to take that bet? They had no working torpedoes left and barely any shells. There could not be a full witted soul aboard who did not understand the odds were stacked.

'Are we including merchant ships,' the Bavarian asked.

'Of course, everything counts,' the book-runner answered. 'Tonnage is tonnage.'

Günther chuckled as he left the engine room and passed back through the mariners' quarters. He would return to his own quarters, forget about their bets, forget about telling Amelung about his conversation with Dönitz. He would lay down and talk to Ingeborg and his daughters. Their photograph was taped to the bulkhead. When he got back to Kiel, he might call Ingeborg and say he was ready to request a shore position. He would ask her if it made her happy. Then he would reveal the decrease in salary that went with a shore position. He imagined her reply: "Who cares? You said you'd always be by my side." It was true he had said that but before they had had two children.

* * *

They had met at a wedding. A portent he had once wondered about. It was the wedding of another teacher at the Academy and Mother had asked Günther's stepfather to accompany her.

'Lots of your students will be there, dear. Not my thing,' his stepfather had replied.

'How about you, Günther?' his mother asked.

Günther shrugged.

'You can bring Bert too, if you like,' his mother said.

That had been Günther's first ever moment in the company of Ingeborg. She was blond. She was popular. She had serious wealth in her past and looks in abundance, but most importantly by some tilting of the planets she had been assigned to his table.

It had seemed to Günther that all of the guests knew each other. Thanks to a student named Bea they all seemed to have several names and nicknames for each other. He was not even sure if Ingeborg's real name was Ingeborg. The clear night-sky, the music, the mood had all been suggestively seductive, and when he finally got to dance with her she seemed content not to change partner at the end of the number. By then he had been a little drunk. He considered he was not ugly. He knew he had ambition in his veins and a *Reichsmarine* career was around the corner. She let him do all the talking. 'I'll call you Celeste,' he slurred. 'Sculpted by the stars.' And then asked her, 'do you have a boyfriend?'

She did not answer.

'Whatever. I'd like to see you again, Celeste,' he asked instinctively. 'If you like.'

She shrugged.

And perhaps because all that night he had seemed to be the only guest unable to distinguish Symbolism from Cubism he decided to pedal a persona of being otherwise exotic. 'I suppose I'm not arty like you all are, but I'm definitely interesting and not as impoverished as I seem.'

'Is that a fact?'

Thanks to the Merchant Navy he had not lied. He *was* interesting. Despite not being wealthy in the way they all were, he had seen a lot of the world, considerably more than her and a great deal more than the stiff, grey, financier who sat growling at an adjacent table. Günther had made up his mind and despite what Bert would later say, "luck" did not enter into this, only opportunities and perseverance mattered. There was an opportunity and he persevered with it. 'I'm a qualified navigator,' he said and could see she had no idea what he meant.

'What do qualified navigators do these days?'

'Read signs.'

'What signs?'

'We reckon the charts.'

'And what does that mean?'

'It means we can see into the future. For instance, I can see myself never leaving your side.'

At last, she smiled.

He gambled: 'And I see us together this Saturday.'

Perhaps as a dare, she replied, 'let's make it Tuesday, at seven p.m.' She had slurred a little too. 'We need a model for our life-class.'

The following Tuesday, despite Bert's incredulity, Günther garbed as though a bare chested Centurion attended Ingeborg's art class, and he went back every week until the end of term.

'You're not as tall as I remembered,' she said on the first Tuesday. 'More handsome though,' she let slip on the second Tuesday.

It took two months of modelling for their "life-class" before she said she admired his resolve.

Günther might have been lacking a fat wallet but he had one supreme advantage over any monied dull banker or would-be wealthy boyfriend, something that money could not buy. He had Clara for a mother.

Clara was not only artful, open, and sincere, but was Ingeborg's art teacher and adored by Ingeborg.

***

He lay on his bunk and stared at Ingeborg's photo and waited for Kraus to arrive and express concern about how little charge they had got into the batteries prior to diving, and how travelling at four-knots praying to avoid suffocation on the seabed worried the men. Kraus was correct to be concerned, because although BdU tried to suppress the statistics, unfortunately *unterseeboots* were not the only things that leaked. That was the thought that slipped into Günther's mind seconds before *Oberleutnant* Kraus, his face creased with apprehension, arrived in his quarters.

27

RECOVERED HABITS

Arandora Star.

They had queued near Princes quay for many hours. They were subdued by the loss of what it meant to feel human, but occasionally some men were buoyed by finding old friends and relatives in their midst. Despite having wanted to leave the internment camp, Friedrich stood in line and willed that he would never reach the head of the throng. But sometime after eight p.m., he and the rest of his group were herded aboard the enormous grey ship, by sullen-faced soldiers with guns.

A rumour circulated that the ship had already missed the evening tide. Someone suggested it was on account of an engine room problem, others had heard it was due to a disagreement. There was gossip that they might not leave at all. Some men in Friedrich's group invented their own near futures but Friedrich preferred to find other internees who were better informed.

Not long after boarding, he found them. Hundreds of internees, italo-brits formed a queue adjacent to germano-brits who formed a smaller second queue. They were lined up like cast members in some vast portrayal of an apocalyptic tragedy. They waited for palliasses to put on the floor of cramped cabins or communal spaces, and plates and pitchers to balance on their knees, and food rations to distribute amongst their groups. Despite the absurdity of the situation, they displayed no enmity for each other, or their guards, and in the usual sense of the word they were far from "alien."

Friedrich was billeted with other refugees and Jacob and a number of German Jewish sailors. A spontaneous camaraderie broke out within the confines of their sheds and spaces. They kept their doors open, hundreds of men sat in corridors, some were lucky enough to sit at long tables near the kitchens. It had been midnight before Friedrich had been able to lay down and attempt to sleep on the floor of a shed on an upper deck.

They slipped out of Liverpool on the morning tide.

Friedrich was permitted to stretch his legs. He stood on a deck and looked through the barbed wire atop the railings. He waved goodbye to Liverpool. His sole regret? There had been no way for any of them to get a message out to relatives. His sister and mother would have to wait to hear from him.

That evening, Edgar kept his promise of having internees dine with the captain and officers. He had clearly thought about the seating arrangements. Friedrich had the honour of sitting between Edgar, whose wife, Lily, had twice found him safe harbour, and Decio the dapper Italian anarchist who had once helped rescue him from a beating. There was no trace of Fortunato Picchi. Friedrich would learn the reason for this omission later. Next to Decio there was Renzo. And on Edgar's other flank, Jacob sat as though he was a brother. Next to Jacob there were the priests and rabbis and adjacent to them another Doctor of Medicine, an Italian from Harley Street.

Despite the conviviality of the seating arrangements, the evening began as though it might be tense. Earlier that day, an internee had tried to hang himself and had to be cut down by one of Jacob's men. This was on Friedrich's mind. He supposed it was on other minds too because they had barely taken their seats when Decio spoke out forthrightly.

'We passengers deserve to know where we're going,' Decio said. 'What can you tell us, Captain?'

Edgar looked around the table into the faces of his senior officers.

The chief engineer nodded eagerly as though he wanted Edgar to divulge their destination.

Edgar looked toward the army men, Major Bethell and his officers. They all puckered and shrugged. None of them seemed to see any problem in Edgar divulging the destination.

Edgar had his elbow on the table. His hand covered his mouth.

Friedrich felt sure there was something that held Edgar back. It was as though Edgar worried they would be disappointed to learn of where it was he was taking them. Had they been alone he would have told Edgar wherever it was they were going it could not be worse than the wild fears that had circulated. There were rumours they were to be handed over in a prisoner exchange: a death sentence for them all.

Edgar spoke tentatively. 'To a place you'll be well treated.'

The assertion triggered some relief even though they still did not know precisely where they were being taken.

But Friedrich believed in Edgar. He raised his glass of water. 'I'll salute to that.' The others joined him.

'How do you know?' Decio pressed Edgar.

A momentary hush was re-established.

'My wife has some informal but reliable sources.'

'Bravo for Lily,' Jacob said loudly. 'I for one, can confirm her credentials in these matters.'

'Me too,' Friedrich added and with that remark it seemed all the tension of the prior thirty-six-hours was siphoned out to sea.

The chief engineer asked, softly, 'I suppose they might like to know specifically where they're going.'

Edgar locked eyes with his chief engineer for a moment before he smiled and looked around at several passengers. 'A country ready to welcome you all. But, in the circumstances you find yourselves in, perhaps none of you will welcome it.'

'What choice do we have?' Decio said. 'We're nationals of a country that we fear, and residents of a country that fears us.'

'And we're being shipped to a country whose name you've not yet told us,' Friedrich chimed in as cheerily as he could.

'Canada,' Edgar revealed. 'We're taking you to Canada.' He placed an arm around Friedrich.

'Well, cheers to Canada.' Jacob raised a glass, others joined and rationed liquids sloshed over the table.

'It's a pity Fortunato is not here,' Renzo said. 'He's been to Canada. He said he felt at home there.'

'Which reminds me,' Decio said. Let's raise a glass to absent friends and family. May they stay safe.'

That is when Friedrich learnt that Mr. Fortunato Picchi was not coming with them. Seven years had passed since Fortunato Picchi had rescued Friedrich. He could not claim to know the man in a profound way, but he felt a debt and an affinity. He cheered and he saluted the good health of "absent friends," especially Fortunato Picchi. Now that he knew where he was going, even though it had not been in his plans when he fled for the second time, and despite the presence of Major Bethell's armed guardsmen in the corners of dining room; who continued to look on and listen attentively to everything that was said, he began to imagine his nightmare was coming to an end.

When the dinner was over, he thanked Edgar for helping to banish, at least for an evening, the incubus of war. He was tired of living like a wretch, fatigued by the regret of having been born into the wrong tribe, in the wrong place, at the wrong point in history. But, for the first moment in a long time, he felt almost cheerful. He returned to the shed and lay on his palliasse and closed his eyes.

In his half-sleep he wondered about Canada. He knew little about it, except that it was very far from Stralsund. Very far from anywhere he had chosen or been chased to. It was a place that he had never thought of in the past. If it was a place that had touched Fortunato Picchi, perhaps it would touch him too.

He thought, they could probably use a Doctor of Medicine there. Perhaps Canada was a place that he could remain in. His fiancée was dead. His father was dead. His mother was on the brink of dying from heartbreak. All he had left to worry about was his sister, who was likely in a camp by now.

He stirred sometime after midnight when the ship passed the Isle of Man. He was glad to be leaving it behind. He felt pity for those he saw around himself, in the shed and in the cabins and on the floors. They were not glad to be leaving. They had lived most of their lives in the country that was deporting them. Now they had only the nightmare of being separated from their families, whereas he had the dream of restarting a life in Canada. He would send for his sister and his mother too if she made it and they would set down new roots and the horror would one day be over.

28

FROM SHANNON TO HEBRIDES

North Atlantic Sea.

Kraus wrung his hands. He said he regretted having wasted the last good torpedo to attack such a small vessel. He was sorry for having put his own ambitions above those of Günther.

Günther scratched his forehead and then rubbed the back of his neck. 'There's no need,' he assured Kraus.

'But if I had waited,' Kraus insisted. 'Maybe we'd have come across something larger.'

Günther placed a hand on Kraus' shoulder. 'To catch up with U46's tonnage we'd need to have come across a ship of at least fifteen thousand tonnes,' he looked Kraus in the eye. 'Do you know how many times that has happened?'

'No, sir.'

'Once, in six patrols,' Günther answered.

Kraus gazed at the floor of Günther's quarters and then at the photo Günther held in his hand.

'Where are we?' Günther asked.

'Crossing from Shannon into Hebrides.'

Günther grinned. Kraus was adapting. Perhaps he needed to reconsider his assessment of the man.

'I heard U46 tied up in Kiel yesterday morning,' Kraus said.

Günther reached for a flask of water and finished its contents. 'Any other news from BdU?'

'Yes, but it is not good, sir. It seems there are now two Destroyers within three to four hours of our current position.' Kraus delivered the news flatly as though he had already run his own calculations.

However, even assuming one or both Destroyers were heading directly for U47 and accepting their surface speed advantage there were plenty of options Günther might consider. He reflected on what was worse, that Bert had arrived in Kiel with his superior tonnage, or the possibility that the British Navy had sent two Destroyers to find U47.

'There's something else, sir,' Kraus added. 'I've been thinking about why all but one of those type G7a's has turned out to be a dud.'

'That's how it is,' Günther replied. 'Ask Amelung. Sometimes a batch will be fine, sometimes not.'

'I think I might know what's wrong with them.'

Günther knew this was Kraus' way to try and make up for having used the last working torpedo. But if anything could have been done to fix the problem then U47's weapons engineer would have already done it. It seemed implausible to Günther that Kraus could have anything to offer beyond contrition. He put an arm around Kraus' shoulder. 'We've kept the last dud from the batch. We'll know what the problem is when we get back to Kiel.' They stepped out of Günther's quarters and Günther smiled and added. 'Take your break and I'll see you in Hebrides.'

Kraus headed away toward the stern muttering about an idea he had and how he had not always been a sub-mariner.

Günther intended to go directly to the control room but on his route there he came across Spahr in deep discussion with the radio communications officer.

'They're getting a faint hydrophone trace,' Spahr said.

Günther grimaced. 'Already?'

'What do you mean, already?' Spahr asked.

'Kraus told me that there might be two Destroyers on our tail.'

'This trace is ahead of us,' Spahr answered.

'Ahead of us?' U47 had nothing but Günther's guile to defend themselves with. He swapped places with Spahr and stepped into the listening room. If there was a Destroyer ahead of them, the sooner he confirmed it, the better were their chances of escape. 'Any idea what's in front of us?' he asked.

The communications officer shook his head. 'Whatever it is, its path is erratic.'

'Is it a single vessel. Could it be a Destroyer?'

'Yes, sir,'

'Or it could be a very large merchant ship,' Spahr said over Günther's shoulder.

'Or maybe a troop-transporter,' the communications officer contributed his own idea.

'A troop carrier?' Günther laughed. 'Where would they be going?'

Amelung appeared in the corridor. 'Or it might be a lure, sir.'

'Might be,' the communications officer sa id in support of Amelung's theory. 'We know they have an anti-submarine operation in Fermanagh.'

Günther rolled his eyes, he was unconcerned about the possibility of an ancient aeroplane trundling out from Fermanagh and blindly dropping bombs into the sea. But the idea of U47's position being passed to a couple of putative Destroyers worried him. He checked his wristwatch and cupped his chin in his hand. 'Are you sure there's only a single vessel?'

'It's possible there might be more,' the communications officer agreed. 'It could explain the erratic course.'

'Right,' Günther spoke quickly, 'continue on our present path and keep listening.'

Amelung exhaled, his relief was undisguised. 'I thought for a moment you'd want to surface for a visual or an attack.'

Günther tutted and shook his head. 'Yes, let's sneak up on an armada and throw second watch's laundry at them. That would immobilise any crew that had not built up tolerance to toxins.'

Amelung grinned and had sufficient self-awareness to hold his nose. 'By the way, Krauss is in the aft torpedo room bothering the weapons engineer.'

Günther shook his head and sighed. He headed for the torpedo room and when he arrived he found Kraus sprawled flat on top of the last dud G7a torpedo and the weapons engineer standing by, watching intently.

The weapons engineer cleared his throat and stared vacantly at Günther. '*Oberleutnant* Kraus has an interesting theory, sir. But I've informed him that you already decided a post-mortem should wait until we're safely back in Kiel.'

'If we wait for Central TD to tell us, it'll be months before we know what the problems are,' Kraus answered. 'Assuming they ever tell us.'

'What idea do you have?' Günther asked, his interest piqued.

'Before I became a sailor, I worked at A.G. Weser,' Kraus answered. 'We used to design and manufacture these things.' He climbed off the torpedo. 'I'm almost certain there's excess pressure in the balance chambers.'

The weapons engineer nodded. 'It makes sense.'

Kraus slipped a long-bladed screwdriver inside an open section of the torpedo. 'See here?' He beckoned the weapons engineer and Günther to step forward, then pointed to where the tip of the screwdriver was resting. 'You see that?

'What is it?' Günther asked.

'That, sir, is the hydrostatic depth-control valve.'

'What about it?' the weapons engineer asked doubtfully.

'Take a look at the gauge. You can see that it's not right.'

The weapons engineer looked closely at the gauge, he ventured no theories of his own.

'That's why the G7a's have been useless,' Kraus suggested.

'Six G7a's fired on this mission,' Günther said. 'Five duds. That's why we have to take that one home.'

'I reckon they've been running at least twenty metres under the target and out the other side,' Kraus said. 'A factory fault, but rectifiable.'

Günther asked, 'are you saying you can fix it?'

Kraus shrugged. 'Probably.'

The weapons engineer shook his head and tutted. 'It's too unstable to try anything remedial here.'

'Are you saying it's dangerous?' Günther insisted.

'I wouldn't recommend it,' the weapons engineer answered.

'I'm not asking if you'd recommend it,' Günther answered with greater irritation than he intended.

Meantime, Kraus had located a circuit diagram and was turning it in circles and seemed almost to salivate over it.

'Say our lives depended on it,' Günther insisted.

'Do our lives depend on it?' the weapons engineer asked quizzically.

'They might.'

'I hope they don't sir,' the weapons engineer sounded matter-of-fact, 'because this batch is the worst I have seen.'

'Kraus thinks he can fix it.'

'Even if Oberleutnant Kraus thinks he could fix its depth running problem, it could explode in the tube, or circle-back like the others.'

Günther shook his head dubitatively. 'What'd be the odds?'

'I couldn't reckon them,' the weapons engineer answered

'Everything can be reckoned,' Günther replied. He saw that Kraus was eager to remain and work with the weapons engineer. 'If it's unstable, wouldn't it be better to get it out of U47 than go all the way back to Kiel with it? Even a dud might ward off a Destroyer. Why don't you and Kraus see what you can do about it?'

Günther left before the weapons engineer could argue further. In the control room he told Amelung and Spahr that he had left Kraus and the weapons engineer with a conundrum.

It was almost time for Kraus to come back on shift when Günther received a call from the weapons room.

'I've done what I could with the balance chamber,' Kraus said. 'And it's armed now.'

'We have a functioning torpedo?'

'I don't know, sir.' Kraus sounded subdued.

'By the way,' Günther said, 'we have a confirmed target in our path. And it's probably fifteen-thousand tonnes.' There was a smile in his voice. He replaced the intercom and turned to recognise a regret in Amelung's eyes. 'We won't even be delayed.' Then with the gesture of an under-arm pitcher he swivelled his fist through an imaginary sea surface. 'We'll rise up like the Kraken, get rid of that torpedo and be gone.'

Amelung turned away.

At around six a.m. German time, U47 was deep inside Hebrides sector when her observation periscope broke the surface of the Atlantic Ocean. Günther confirmed the hulking, twin-funnelled grey transporter on the horizon. The great grey ship zig-zagged at a regular and predictable rhythm. Her speed and course were not overly complicated to plot: bearing, estimated ten nautical miles, at 313°, bow right, target angle 45°. Quite catchable. In due course he would take up position at the attack periscope and began calibrating and shouting projections.

Amelung stood adjacent. 'I wonder where they're heading?' he asked barely audible.

'Same place we all are,' Günther replied, his voice louder than Amelung's but empty of sentiment.

Amelung sniffed as though unconvinced.

But Günther was not to be distracted. If this was not a trap. If the transporter did not sight the eel and turn its great mass away from the torpedo's trajectory. If Kraus and the weapons engineer had been lucky, then their last eel would skewer the starboard side of that grey hulk and rip a hole as wide as a galley and cripple its engines. After which U47 would disappear once more into the stillness.

But suppose it was a trap, or the ship's lookout had already spotted them and messaged coastal command. Perhaps anti-submarine forces were already on their way. Maybe his weapons engineer was right to warn him and the faulty torpedo would explode in its tube. Perhaps Krauss' recalibration of the hydrostatic depth-control valve was ineffectual. Always questions. Always doubts.

What was worse? Fire and miss and they would return to Kiel and suffer Bert's arrogance. Fire and hit and if he was "lucky," they might sink that ugly transporter and Bert's gloating would have to wait for another day. There was another outcome, fire and auto-destruct U47. In which case Bert would be drowned in grief, real or imaginary it would make no difference to Günther and his crew.

Two chances from three.

They were all going the same place, anyway.

U47 got closer. He saw a large deck gun fitted to the grey transporter, but he was still unconcerned; because although the transporter was in range of U47 and Günther had spotted it, the reverse was evidently not true.

He checked his wristwatch one final time. He signalled for silence.

Amelung broke the silence and he asked something most odd. 'You know what I'm looking forward to?'

'What?' Günther replied impatiently.

'Hearing how my beautiful little goddaughter is doing.'

Even the mention of little Birgit did not jolt a cautionary reaction from Günther. He pushed his fingers under his cap. He looked into Amelung's eyes and he sighed heavily, but he did not see Brigit's reflection there. He saw Bert, already laughing, already back in Kiel.

He gave the command. 'Away.'

When he looked again in Amelung's eyes, Bert's reflection had gone. He thought he saw others reflected there, children crying but none he recognised.

29

CONVERGENCE OF THE TWAIN

North Atlantic Sea.

Edgar had tossed and turned in his cot. From his window he saw a sky which was cloudless and star filled. He searched in it for constellations that were steady and reliable. He hoped this would bring the tranquillity that was missing. His conscience was not clear, it was overcast. He replayed several of his dinner conversations and wondered how it was possible he could have come to be where he was.

It had gone beyond midnight when they passed the Isle of Man. He imagined the *Arandora Star* listed slightly to port as hundreds of passengers moved to gaze in bewilderment at the outline of the distant island. Edgar and the island had something in common. They had been requisitioned. Some of the men aboard had been interned there in one the ten camps, penned behind a barbed-wire stockade, only to now be penned on the *Arandora Star.*

He rose at six a.m. and checked their position. They were ninety nautical miles west of Malin Beg.

In awe, he watched an orange and red sky plunge into the

tranquil cobalt Atlantic. For three weeks, no British ship traversing this stretch of the Atlantic had met the shadow of an enemy vessel, so he had been told. All was quiet on the surface. Could be that all was quiet in the deep too. But there were thousands of souls aboard who relied on him, thus he took the precaution of zig-zagging.

In another two hours they would waken their passengers, those that had slept. They would begin morning routines. Feeding seventeen hundred mouths was something that had never been done before on their ship.

Two hours after that, if Bethell was to be believed, work could begin on removing some of the barbed wire that had transformed the *Arandora Star* into a floating internment camp. They would have access to the lifeboats. They may never need them but simply knowing they could reach them would ease many minds.

Conversations from the prior night, feeding regimes, exercise, access to the light, to the air, to peace of mind, these were the mundane matters he was mulling over on the cusp of a bright day when seven decks below the aft funnel, just beneath the water line, a torpedo ripped through the ship's starboard skin into the entrails of the ship's engine and boiler rooms.

The destructive force boomed its potency and rocked the huge ship such that its violence touched every shadowy corner of the *Arandora Star* and in Edgar's own heart.

A wave of disbelief swept over him.

Provoked by oil and fuel stores located under the boiler room, a secondary detonation was triggered. He heard the sound of electrical systems dying and if he could have looked into the engine room at that moment he would have seen his chief engineer arrive to discover that the main and back-up generators were already destroyed.

* * *

Bob arrived in the spot where moments earlier a trio of his lads had been obliterated. Others of his crew were nearby. They were torn apart. Fragmented body-parts had been transformed into bloody projectiles and had flown in a violent fury across the confines of the engine and boiler rooms smashing instruments and wounding colleagues.

The darkness was pierced by the faint illumination of battery powered lights, a peculiar stream of daylight filtered in from a gash in the ship and blue flames flickered from the boiler room. Bob moved fully into the boiler room and the cold ocean lapped around his ankles and an acrid odour of burnt flesh filled the air. The Atlantic deafened him as seawater poured into the *Arandora Star* in a frenzy, as though the ocean wished to silence the moans of several dismembered engineers who had begun to recover whatever of their senses remained.

***

Back on the bridge, Edgar scanned the scenes in every direction. He wondered when the ship's deck gun would retaliate. But the deck gun remained silent. He expected to hear a shout from the ship's lookout. But the lookout remained mute. Their attacker had to have been an *unterseeboot*. Had it already vanished so soon from the surface of the sea? Was it leaving the scene or getting closer for another shot to finish them off?

From below decks, a hail of panicked, distraught voices.

He handed control of the bridge to his first mate and made his way down to the boat-deck. On his way there, gunshots rang out as Bethell's men shot into the air in an attempt to impose order. For a moment it worked. But the ship listed abruptly by five-degrees. The ocean was mighty and impatient to receive them.

Distressed fearful voices rose up again from below decks in primal cries of 'Mother of God, help us. *Aiutaci, Madre di Dio.*

Hilf uns, Mutter Gottes.' Passengers streamed up from the lower decks and struggled to maintain their balance.

On the boat deck, he saw a large scene of chaos and tucked in corners several pockets of people praying, spots of surreal calm.

He saw Jacob and some of his men, their hands protected by jackets, talking, not shouting, simply working at removing barbed wire from the least impeded lifeboats.

Further along the boat deck, sixty people had somehow swarmed onto another lifeboat that was still attached to its station. He sent a young crewman to explain to them that if the lifeboat were to be released from its fixing, most of them would die on impact when it smashed into the sea or was crushed against the side of the ship.

From one deck below, he heard internees wail for assistance and he saw them turn in circles whilst in their midst some of Bethell's guardsmen handed out life jackets. Elsewhere, other guardsmen tried unsuccessfully to marshal internees who had emerged from corridors and stairwells that otherwise would have trapped them like rats in a maze.

'We have to get everyone to stop panicking,' he shouted to those officers closest to him. But there was no means for ship-wide communication. He sent a crewman to search a megaphone. In the meantime, it was impossible to establish ship-wide calm. He went to talk with Jacob and found some of his own crewmen had now begun assisting Jacob and his men in manhandling life-rafts and throwing them into the sea.

Several confused guardsmen arrived and pointed their rifles at a trio of Burfeind's men further down the deck. One of them asked Edgar, 'Captain, what do you want us to do about them?'

'Do any of you know how to release the lifeboats?'

Silence. Followed by a shaking of heads.

'They do,' Edgar said. 'Let them get on with their work and get yourselves onto the lower decks and try to keep everyone calm. See that everyone has a life jacket.'

The guardsmen had barely darted away to do as he had instructed when another explosion sounded from the lower decks, and there was no longer any calm to keep.

The ship had already begun its irreversible journey.

Hundreds of terrified internees fled the rising water on the lower decks. They swarmed onto the boat deck. Hardly anyone amongst them wore life jackets. Many of them wandered hopelessly around saying they were looking for their father, or their brother or their uncle or for a friend.

'You have to leave,' he pleaded with every passenger whose path he crossed.

Some of them said they would not leave the ship without their missing family members. Others said they were too afraid to leave because it was too far to the surface, or they could not swim.

'You won't need to swim,' he implored them. 'Get yourself a life jacket and go onto the lower decks and organise jump offs.'

Another group of internees emerged. Led there by a priest whom Edgar had met the prior evening. Edgar stood beside the priest and his flock. The more elderly passengers amongst them remained terrified, frozen to the spot.

Bob appeared on the boat deck. He was bloodied but carried life jackets which he handed to the flock whilst asking Edgar, Jacob, and the priest why none of them wore life jackets.

'We don't need them,' Jacob replied.

The ship listed further. She would soon be gone.

'I think you do,' Bob argued. 'There's an enormous hole on the orlop deck.'

The lowering mechanism of another lifeboat jammed and a commotion broke out on the port side. That lifeboat swung uselessly from side to side and around seventy occupants howled in fear. The situation had not fully been brought under control when the *Arandora Star* listed heavily again. The violence of the listing caused a dozen terrified internees to jump from the lifeboat into the sea. But most remained seated, ashen faced, their hands gripped upon the swinging lifeboat's side-ropes. A crewman finally unjammed the mechanism just as the ship's prow rose abruptly and dozens of internees careered over the side.

Yet another explosion was heard from within the guts of the ship. Edgar knew it was over. He hunkered and linked arms with Bob, Jacob, and the priest.

'There's nothing more we can do here,' Bob announced as though he had read Edgar's thoughts.

Edgar loosened his grip on Bob's forearm. 'There's nothing more *you* can do here,' he replied and nodded toward the sea. 'They'll need you down there.' He unlinked arms with Bob and pushed him away.

Bob stared hard at Edgar.

The ship groaned. Its resistance almost entirely exhausted. 'Hurry up,' Edgar insisted. 'You'll be more useful on the lifeboats.'

'Don't worry about us,' Jacob said. 'We'll see you later.'

Bob moved crab-like toward starboard. He removed his shoes and tightened the cords on his life-jacket. He saluted Edgar. He looked over the side of the ship and jumped feet first from the *Arandora Star* and was gone. Into the chasm.

***

He plummeted sixty feet like a sack full of lead. He gasped when the shock of cold sea-water hit him. He kept his mouth closed tight as the sea swallowed him. Despite wearing a life jacket he travelled deep into an ice-cold darkness. A quietness enveloped him. For a moment he forgot where he was. Suddenly his descent came to an end. His lungs felt raw and ready to explode. He flapped his arms and cantilevered from the knees. He propelled himself upwards, again and again until he pierced the calm flat surface of the ocean. He gulped and filled his lungs and he thought he screamed but no one heard him in that vast concert hall of desperate sounds.

Around him, there were hundreds of men in the ocean. Though some were in the process of drowning and would soon be finished, many remained alive. He did not recognise faces, neither amongst the living, nor amongst the corpses that floated, some of them with broken necks or bloodied heads.

He searched the surface for the nearest lifeboat, life-raft, or piece of floating debris. He found a lifeboat and turned on his back and thrashed his legs and made toward it. As he moved away from it, he saw the prow of the *Arandora Star* protrude awkwardly. She pointed to the sky. Some figures had clung on to her forecastle, their arms linked but still not a life jacket on any of them.

The sea remained calm but seemed colder. He continued with his thrashing. He heard oars slice the surface and voices call out. He did not know if this was his lifeboat attempting to get closer or to take distance.

He heard the remainder of the *Arandora Star* groan and heave in a dying spasm. He turned in the water to face her as several figures stepped off her prow and into the ocean. Meanwhile, around him, those men who had squeezed onto lifeboats, or like himself, floated on the surface of the Atlantic holding onto debris or rafts, howled a primal, mournful farewell to their kin.

She slipped below. A final whimper and a submerged explosion before a widening slick of oil appeared on the surface, like black blood to mark where the *Arandora Star* had once been.

She was gone.

And so too was something in him.

PART III

SUNSET

LATER

30

JENNY'S CALL

Honiton, Devon.

The second month my eyes were sunk
In the darkness of despair,
And my bed was like a grave
And his ghost was lying there
And my heart was sick with care

— ALUN LEWIS

Seven-thirty a.m. in the Moulton family kitchen and the habitual weekday domestic drama was in motion. There was the clang and hurly-burly of pots and pans. The whistling of their outsized kettle and scraping of toast accompanied by morning chatter. The pouring of tea and clatter of cups. The opening and closing of stiffly hinged doors as Lily and two of her three daughters entered and exited the kitchen.

The morning argument had already begun with the squeaking of twelve-year-old June's finger on a steamed-up kitchen window that asserted her fifteen-year-old sister, Cilla, "loved" a certain Egon Silbernagel.

'Tell our June to mind her own business,' Cilla whined as she ran across the kitchen and rubbed the window with the sleeve-cuff of her bright yellow flannelled pyjama top.

Lily surveyed the kitchen and winced. Like their lives, the place was dishevelled. 'Mind your own business,' she told June.

Meantime, twenty-year-old Elisabeth, who had earlier taken occupation of the bathroom, slid open its noisy barrel-bolt. It was a signal that she had finished her ablutions and was liberating the facilities.

That sound triggered a race between Cilla and June.

Cilla had tried asserting seniority as second daughter in the family. But this supposed prerogative over who got to use the bathroom in what order had not yet been conceded by June. Therefore, it was safer for Cilla to rely upon her superior speed and get there first. She was out of the kitchen, her left-hand on the bathroom doorknob, her right-hand clutching a make-up bag, before June had scrambled down from the kitchen stool.

June fizzed but calmly crossed the kitchen to renew her graffiti.

Elizabeth appeared in the kitchen. 'Bye mum.' Then as though an afterthought she added, 'bye, June.'

June waved goodbye without turning to face her sister.

'Bye dear,' Lily answered. 'When will you be home?'

'I don't know,' Elizabeth replied. 'Around blackout. Will that be all right?'

'I suppose,' Lily conceded.

'I did mention it yesterday. I'm working late.'

Lily tightened the lid on a jam-jar. Working late? Had it been mentioned? She dropped the crusts from several slices of toast into a brown paper bag, which also contained yesterday's crusts.

'Is Gordon Stringer working late too?' June asked in her telling-tales tone of voice.

'That's none of our business,' Lily admonished her youngest.

Elisabeth mimed "*is Gordon Stringer working late too,*" and shook her head before she quit the scene.

Meantime, June stuck out her tongue and turned her attention, once more, to her other sister's reputation. 'And Cilla's in there, putting on her make-up to look good for E-gon Silber-nagel,' she said, elongating Egon's name and rendering it more foreign sounding.

Lily liked Egon Silbernagel. His parents had got him out by pretending he was protestant. "I'm sending you a young lad from the kindertransport programme to help out," Lily had told her mother. "Send me as many as you like," Mam had answered. An extra pair of hands was always useful, especially now that Lily's brothers were no longer around to help. Egon milked cows and collected eggs and went to church on Sunday, after which Cilla gave him English lessons and he taught her German.

It was thanks to Cilla that Egon's English had improved "beyond everyone's expectations." He had adopted several of Cilla's expressions and according to the vicar he even forgot to say his "aitches" and sounded everyday more like the grandson of a farmer. Given how much the boy had been shuttled around it was a wonder he spoke at all. He was a remarkable boy, and despite his situation was often seen smiling. According to Mia Woodruff, the whole Kindertransport gang were like that. They kept their tears for those moments they were alone.

Fresh squeaking of June's fingers on the kitchen window brought Lily back to the present. *EM loves GS.* Lily smiled. If it was not for June's nosey-parkering Lily might not even know GS' name. Why was Elizabeth hiding Gordon Stringer away? 'I hope there's no hanky-panky,' she said aloud.

June asked in puzzlement, 'hanky-panky?'

Lily blushed and placed the last remaining dishes into the large sink. She glanced sideways at the clock above the cooker range. 'None of your business.' She raised her voice enough to be certain she would be heard along the corridor, 'and don't think you can stay in there all day, madam.'

'I just stepped in,' Cilla shouted back. 'You never tell our Elisabeth to hurry up.'

'I'll ask Elizabeth,' June said defiantly.

Lily prepared to respond to both Cilla and June but the telephone rang. Tring! Tring! Tring!

A telephone call that early in the day meant one of two possibilities: either the caller had money to burn or they had a message that could not wait for the cheaper call tariffs.

Lily hoped her caller was wealthy.

She hurried out of the kitchen into the hallway where their deluxe model, black bakelite telephone hung on the wall adjacent to a gilded rectangular mirror.

Before she reached it, the telephone warbled another cycle: Tring! Tring! Tring!

It seemed to Lily that their telephone took on a different sound depending upon the day of the week and time of the call. Sometimes it summoned the household ominously loud and fast. Occasionally, it sounded tired and rendered a lethargic Tri..ing, Tri..ing as though some electrical connection was dying.

This morning it was full of vim.

As Lily picked up the telephone, she braced herself for an emergency at the hospital. 'Hello, Bournemouth, four-seven-one-six.' She spoke in a moderately posh register, midway between the one she used with her extended family to mark the fact that she was no longer a farmer's daughter and the one she used when informing relatives of patients what they most dreaded to hear.

'Mrs. Moulton?' the caller asked doubtfully.

The caller was female. A Scottish accent, probably Glaswegian.

One that Lily had heard before. 'Yes,' Lily affirmed and searched her memory. 'Who's speaking?'

'It's me, Jenny Connell.'

'Bob's wife?'

'Aye, that's right,' Jenny spoke softly. 'Bob asked me to call you.'

Jenny Connell could be ringing her for one reason only: Bad news.

'Bob asked? Where is he?'

'He's in hospital.'

'Edgar's in hospital?'

'No.'

Lily let the telephone handset slip. The handset hung from its cord and swung to-and-fro. She was on her knees when June emerged from the kitchen.

'What's wrong, mum?'

Lily stared at the handset.

June reached out. She held the receiver close to her ear. 'Hello.'

'Is your mum still there?'

June nodded and held the telephone out to her mother.

Lily accepted the handset. She stood up and whispered into the mouthpiece, 'sorry, Jenny, I dropped the telephone.'

'They were torpedoed. It's probably going to be in all the newspapers.'

'It's not possible. I spoke with him only recently.'

'You spoke with Edgar?' Jenny sounded surprised and relieved. 'When did you speak with him?'

Lily's hands shook. She bit her lip. 'I can't remember.'

'They were torpedoed two days ago,' Jenny spoke quietly. 'Have you spoken to him since then?'

Lily shook her head and whispered, 'no.'

June stared at Lily.

'Bob last saw him two days ago. On the boat deck.'

There were questions she could have asked but June was sat

on the floor with her arms wrapped tightly around herself. There were words Jenny Connell had not yet pronounced. Lily need not, and would not ask her. Nothing need be confronted. Her chest tightened. Her throat dried. She breathed raggedly into the telephone mouthpiece. Around her waist, she felt the warmth of June's arms and her fingers which were clasped against her stomach.

'Apparently it sunk quickly.'

June tugged at Lily's sleeve.

Lily did not respond. She preferred a silence to establish itself. This telephone call might all be a figment of her imagination.

'Hello. Are you still there?' Jenny asked.

June had returned to sitting on the floor and sobbed quietly.

Lily wondered why her daughter was already sobbing when Jenny Connell had not yet given them cause to cry. There had been a rescue of some kind. After all, Bob had asked Jenny to call. It had only been two days. For everyone's sake, Lily remained objective. In her mind's eye she had a vision of her younger self on the *Salta* and all the chaos and death of that sinking. 'How many were rescued?'

'Bob's not sure. Hundreds of them drowned. More than half of them. He's searched all over for Edgar.'

'But they got their lifeboats launched, right?' Lily said dryly. She had heard stories of survivors sitting on lifeboats in the middle of the ocean for days, or weeks. She wondered how long it might take for all of the lifeboats of a large ship to be accounted for. June still clutched tight on Lily's legs. Lily could not dare to utter Edgar's name.

'Edgar's missing.'

'Missing?' Lily echoed.

'Bob said to tell you that Edgar was Edgar.'

Lily pointed a finger at June and then directed her toward the kitchen. 'You go there, you remain there and neither you nor your sister move until I say so.'

June bit her lip but did as she had been instructed.

Lily turned it over. "Edgar was Edgar." She knew well what that meant. The bloody Moultons always remained on deck until the last. Undoubtedly, he would have waltzed into the water as though he had no one else to think of. Probably justifying it by thinking his family would understand.

'They walked into the sea arm-in-arm,' Jenny said.

'Who did?'

'Edgar and that friend of his.'

'Which friend.'

'That German sailor friend of his.'

'Jacob Burfeind? I don't understand,' Lily answered. 'What was Jacob doing there?'

'Apparently, he tried to help Edgar get the passengers off the ship. But there were too many of them and there was panic.'

'Panic?' Lily repeated. 'Edgar?' she asked, disbelief in her voice.

'No. Not Edgar,' Jenny said. 'The internees, especially the older ones. Bob says, most of them couldn't swim.'

'I have to hang up now,' Lily blurted because she had once lived this herself, and the thought of hundreds upon hundreds of desperate folk drowning, Edgar among them, was filling her own lungs with water, causing her to gasp and panic. 'June has to go to school.'

'I'm so sorry,' Jenny said.

'Thanks for letting me know,' Lily answered and before Jenny could say any more, she clicked and ended the call. She remained with the telephone in her hand and listened to the beeping dead telephone line. She slowed her breathing. She thought of what should happen next. Sometime later she would receive another telephone call. An "official" call from a Ministry or from the Admiralty. Or perhaps even a Blue Star officer would call her. She would not answer to any of them. She would wait for Edgar to call her. But what if they sent a telegram?

The Admiralty would do that. They would send her a

telegram and they would say what Jenny Connell could not bring herself to say; that Edgar was "missing presumed drowned." Well, they could stick their telegram. She would not open it. Furthermore, she would keep the radio turned off. The newspapers in Devon might not even report it. To be safe, she would not buy any of them.

Except, the story would probably appear in the newspapers in the big cities. The *Liverpool Echo* was likely already working on it. The provincial newspapers would pick up the story and print it a day or two later and then someone would tell her daughters that they were fatherless and then she would be a widow. She cried on the inside but got her daughters out of the house without revealing the entire content of the phone call.

Later that same morning, a telegram arrived. It came from the Blue Star Line: "We regret to inform you we have received advice of the sinking of the *Arandora Star* by enemy submarine. Survivors now being landed and others coming in. Will advise immediately names come to hand."

Lily called the Admiralty. 'Have any names come to hand?'

'No.' They were sorry that they had not already been in touch. She should not tell anyone for the moment but yes Captain Moulton was among those missing, presumed drowned. She sobbed and they said he might "come ashore." As though his body floated around the sea contemplating whether to wash up on a cosy spot.

'Come ashore? Where?'

They did not know where. Nor could they say for certain when. But if he did come ashore they would let her know because someone would have to identify him.

That night, she gathered her girls in the kitchen and broke the news: 'Your father is missing.' They wept for Edgar. 'But the Admiralty say he could still come ashore.' The girls wept some more. Lily held her tears back because she had to. It would become a routine for them. Congregating in the kitchen, her daughter's weeping, Lily holding her tears back.

***

Four weeks later, the second month of Edgar's disappearance, a man from the Admiralty called Lily early one morning. 'A body has washed up off Scotland,' he told her as though she should be relieved to hear this.

'Edgar's body?'

'No.'

'Then why are you calling me?'

'The corpse was wearing a life-jacket from the *Arandora Star*.' The Admiralty mandarin sounded morbidly surprised.

'Who was it?'

'We don't know,' the man said. 'Young fellow. About sixteen or seventeen.'

'How awful.'

'An alien. Not one of ours.'

'What does that mean?' Lily snapped.

'Well, it means we know it was a civilian.' The man's tone turned dispassionate as he added the revealing detail: 'Difficult to identify because the corpse was only partly dressed.'

Lily had known even before she picked up the phone that it would be the Admiralty and it would not be Edgar that had "come ashore" because he already had. His ghost had been with her every night since Jenny's call. That night she told Edgar's ghost about the Admiralty man's empty voice telling her over and over "not one of ours, not one of ours."

She went to the kitchen on her own and made tea. She lit a cigarette. Then she stubbed it out. Tears ran warmly down both cheeks. She found herself grieving not only for Edgar but for the young man. Who was he? Was his mother lying every night with her son's clothes next to her in bed, like Lily was with Edgar? Was his mother sitting in her kitchen right at that moment wondering where her son was? *It's awful.* It was no different to Lily and her girls, waiting and desperately hoping for some news. Any news. She thought of Edgar turning up unrecognisable on some distant beach and someone there saying, "not one of ours." There had to be something she could do.

The next day, she rang her friend Mia Woodruff and said, 'I want to do more.'

'You're a teaching nurse. Aren't you already doing enough?'

'I'm not teaching every day. I have to stay busy.'

'We can use some help up here at Hobart House.'

The following day, to numb her pain, she took her overnight bag and travelled to London.

31

FROM HOBART TO EMPIRE

Hobart House, London.

Florence had arrived early, but it was nearly four p.m. when she got close to the entrance. She craned on tiptoes and gandered over the head-scarfed woman one place ahead of her in the queue. Behind her, the wretched procession twisted, serpent-like for several hundred yards winding its way around Hobart House and stretched beyond the adjacent London streets. But she was confident. This would be the day she would get inside Hobart House. This would be the day she would return to the Empire Café with an answer.

The cortege contained a few sad-faced, elderly, frail looking men. They were lost amongst several hundred women, many of whom carried babies tightly wrapped in shawls resembling papooses and others who comforted infants in prams, but most of the women were accompanied by pale and tearful children who held onto their hands.

Some women, like Florence, had come alone.

They queued in line to learn whether their loved one, or loved ones, were simply "missing" or "missing presumed dead." They gathered with the same apprehension and waited to discover whether their capacities for grief would be overwhelmed.

'This is my third day.' The woman one place ahead, declared.

Florence smiled wanly. 'We're near the front.'

'I'm not leaving until I get an answer,' the woman replied. 'I'll sleep here on the pavement if I have to.'

A queue marshal appeared from inside Hobart House. It would be the same routine as yesterday. He would walk down the queue and decide where the tail would be.

'Would you like an apple?' the woman asked and held out a shiny apple, vivid green like her headscarf.

'Thanks.' Florence kept her eye on the queue marshal whilst she bit into the apple and deposited a red lipstick slash across its belly.

The woman slipped off her headscarf. 'I'm Anna Guidobaldi.'

'I'm Florence Lantieri.'

'Who's missing?' Anna asked.

'My man.' Florence felt a bloom on her cheeks. 'And his best friend and his best friend's cousin and, you know.' She stopped herself. It would have been simpler to say, "everyone."'

'I see.'

The human chain shuffled several links forward.

Florence's hopes sank when the queue marshal stopped a few feet ahead of her and counted the line of prospective widows. She wrapped the apple core in her handkerchief and dropped it into her pocket and willed the queue marshal to carry on walking and counting. She held her breath. After a moment, the marshal started up again and walked past her.

'I'm afraid that the rest of you will have to come back tomorrow,' the queue marshal announced.

Florence exhaled. Behind her the queue sighed, some women grumbled but their protest was subdued.

'You can try calling the telephone number in the poster,' the queue marshal said sympathetically.

'But they don't bloody answer,' Anna responded. 'That's why I've been here three days in a row!'

'I thought I'd seen you before,' Florence said.

Anna's tears welled, and her face crumpled. 'I'm not usually like this.'

Florence hugged Anna and Anna reciprocated. They decided they would go in together and comfort each other when the news, whatever it was, would be delivered.

When their turn arrived, Florence stepped forthrightly into the office and proffered a fake smile and was taken back in time twenty-five years. It felt like she was visiting the office of Dorothy's headmaster. The queue tail was out there in the corridor watching her through the narrow window in the middle of the door. Undaunted, Florence let her question fall quickly from her lips. 'I'd like to know the whereabouts of Mr. Fortunato Picchi,' she demanded from the two well groomed "volunteer" ladies who sat together on the other side of a trestle table.

'Are you a relative?' the lady in pearls asked.

Florence glanced at the name on a hand-written white card placed on the tabletop; pearl woman was Mrs. Mia Woodruff. Meanwhile, the other lady, a Mrs. Lily Moulton according to her name card, scanned a typewritten list of names.

'Fortunato Picchi, you say?' She ran her pencil up and down the pages.

Florence watched as Mrs. Lily Moulton hesitated and occasionally stopped the pencil at a name. She cursed herself because she could not stop tears from running hot down her face. She had promised she would not let that happen. She reached into her handbag and rummaged. 'I'm also asking about my friend's husband.' She held out Maria's power of attorney.

Mrs Lily Moulton looked at the document but did not take it

away from Florence. 'How long have they been missing?' she asked and her voice was mellow and gentle, like she understood.

'Two months.'

Anna Guidobaldi hovered at Florence's shoulder and seized that moment to step forward and lean over the desk. 'They were probably on that same ship. The one that sank.'

'You mean the *Arandora Star*?' Mrs. Lily Moulton asked.

Anna nodded. 'Yes. My husband, Filippo, was on it. I know that for a fact.'

Mrs. Lily Moulton bit her bottom lip. She looked down at the desk. 'My husband was on that ship too.'

Florence felt her throat tighten. She raised her eyes to Mrs. Lily Moulton and everything that needed to be communicated passed in the glance between them. Mrs. Lily Moulton was a "presumed" widow. Yet here she was, comforting others. 'I'm sorry to hear that, Mrs. Moulton,' Florence said acknowledging the name on the badge.

'Lily. Just call me Lily.'

'How do you know that your husband was aboard the *Arandora Star*?' Mrs. Woodruff asked.

'He sent a letter home from Glasgow,' Anna answered. 'Luckily a nurse put a stamp on it and posted it.

'One of those rescued and hospitalised,' Mrs. Woodruff said, and she smiled in a way that made it clear she was pleased to have found the wife of a survivor. She picked up a separate list from her side of the table. 'What's the family name?'

'Guidobaldi,' Anna spoke with urgency.

Florence twisted closer to get a look at the list in Mrs. Woodruff's control. She made out some of the headings: "name, address, last known contact, destination." But the list was too long.

Mrs. Woodruff arrived at the G's and stopped her finger at a name. 'I believe Mr. Guidobaldi might have been transported elsewhere.'

'Transported elsewhere?' Anna's voice stretched to a high note.

'You'll need to fill in some forms,' Mrs. Woodruff said. 'Can you pass those forms dear?' she asked Lily.

Lily handed Anna some forms and a pen.

Mrs. Woodruff sat back on her swivel seat. She clasped her hands on top of the desk. 'Most of the surviving internees from the *Arandora Star* were transported on the next available ship.'

'Transported? Anna snapped in her normal voice.

Mrs. Woodruff soothed. 'Those hospitalised are a little dispersed. If you could fill in the form we'll let you know as soon as we trace him.'

Anna fell silent. She stepped aside and began form filling.

'And what about Mr. Picchi and Mr. Musetti?' Florence asked. 'Have they been transported elsewhere?'

Lily looked down her lists and lowered her head. 'I'm afraid Mr. Musetti is missing, presumed drowned.'

'Do you mean Renzo or Pietro?' Florence asked.

'Both,' Lily replied. 'I'm very sorry.'

Florence held on to the chair and sobbed. '*Il mio Dio,*' Florence said. 'I don't know how I'll tell Maria.'

'Would you like a drink of water?' Lily asked. 'Here, have a seat.'

Mrs. Woodruff took up the lists. 'There's no mention of a Mr. Fortunato Picchi on this list.' She shook her head. 'But the lists are being updated every few days. If you could leave your details.'

Florence drank the glass of water offered by Lily. She sat the empty glass back on the table and Anna, her form filling duly completed, held out a handkerchief to her.

Meanwhile, Lily wrote on a pad and tore the page out and handed it to Florence.

'What's this for?' Florence stared at the note.

'The foreign legation will sometimes receive information before we do. You know, I think I can help you and your friend. There's a lot of formalities that will need to be taken care of. Shall we talk more privately?'

Lily shepherded them out past other pale faced women to an empty office. Frosted windows and thick striped curtains helped dull the senses. They sat on leather armless seats that squeaked and faced each other. They drank tea. They shared stories and they made plans. By the time Florence had left Hobart House she had given Anna and Lily an invitation to attend that evening's meeting at the Empire.

Florence waved goodbye to Anna at the entrance to Saint James' Park. She entered the park and twice circled the lake. Tearfully she sat on the bench where she had sat many times before with Fortunato. She held several photographs in her hand and asked, 'where are you?' She waited. Tears flowed. No one answered.

When she arrived at the Empire, she found Maria in full-flight preparing for that evening's meeting, pushing rows of tables together and bossing her two children. '*Ciao tutti,*' Florence said and tried hard but could not make her voice sound cheerful.

'*Ciao Florence,*' Maria replied and then turned away to continue scolding her son. 'No, not there!'

'I managed to get inside today,' Florence blurted. 'I had a long talk with a very understanding woman—'

Maria cleared her throat and cut Florence off in mid-sentence. She probably saw in Florence's regard everything she needed to see. She looked to her children but carried on lifting and moving tables. 'We'll talk later.'

'But you said to put them there.' The boy pointed in front of the bar and he looked to Florence and shrugged his shoulders.

Maria shook her head in exasperation. 'Are you two not going to say hello to Aunt Florence?'

'Ciao *zia,*' the children echoed.

'What I meant was for you to push the tables against the bar,' Maria explained to her son and pushed. 'Like this.'

In the same way that Fortunato was not their real uncle, Florence was not their real aunt. But she had been around since before the children were born. They had learnt to call her *zia* and she liked it that way. She watched her twelve-year-old niece shake out tablecloths and roll her eyes at her brother who was only one year older but already much taller. 'I'd be happy to help you with that,' Florence said to her niece. And when her nephew looked at her doubtfully, she added, 'don't you need to go practice your flute or something?'

'It's not a flute, *zia*,' the boy answered. 'It's a piccolo.'

'Don't be rude,' Maria said.

'He's right,' Florence answered, 'Fortunato's always correcting me too.'

'All right you two. Time for you to go upstairs.' Maria finally shooed her children out of the café.

As the children ascended the internal staircase, Florence fretted over the words to tell Maria that Renzo was missing, presumed drowned. As was his cousin, Pietro. What should she say of Fortunato? The children's voices trailed away and Florence steeled herself for the conversation to come but the café door was pushed opened and Lily Moulton arrived, a little earlier than expected.

'Hello, I hope it's all right.' Lily stepped in and pulled at the strings of a green, duffel bag strapped over her shoulder.

Maria looked quizzically at Lily Moulton. 'I'm sorry but we're not open tonight.'

Lily stopped in her tracks and glanced at Florence.

'This is Lily,' Florence said. 'She's the woman I mentioned.' It was clear that Florence had not yet had the time to share with Maria all that she had learnt whilst at Hobart House.

'Shall I come back later?' Lily asked.

'Stay, please,' Florence said. 'But Maria and I need a moment.'

Maria froze. Her pallor turned grey. She looked at the floor.

'Perhaps I can help here?' Lily looked around the café.

'Sure, you could unstack some of those chairs and carry on laying table-cloths,' Florence suggested.

Maria walked quietly into the kitchen. She left the door open.

Florence followed her in.

Maria sat on a kitchen chair. She held her head in her hands and asked softly. 'And Pietro?'

Florence hugged Maria. 'Yes, Pietro too.' She placed her hands on top of Maria's and squeezed. 'I'm sorry.'

'Fortunato and the others?'

'His name is not on any list.'

'He's alive?'

'They don't know where he is.'

Maria washed her face at the kitchen sink. 'We can't say anything to the children. Not yet.'

Florence sighed. 'You should take tonight off. I can take care of the meeting. Or we can cancel it.'

'People are expecting us.'

Florence was sure that Maria would insist upon carrying on. But she was also certain that Maria's stoicism could not last. Carrying on was a way to remain on the rails for now. That was all. When they emerged together from the kitchen, their faces were red but dry and neither of them spoke about their men, missing presumed drowned or simply missing.

Lily continued covering tables but she stared at Florence as though startled by the women's composure.

'Florence has told me everything,' Maria said. 'Thanks for coming.'

Lily stopped stacking chairs and hugged Maria.

'How many of us are we expecting tonight?' Maria asked.

Florence played along with Maria's fortitude. 'About thirty, I suppose.'

'Those leaflet drops of yours are working.'

'They seem to be,' Florence answered. 'But some women say they'll come and then they start to worry about making a fuss.'

'A fuss?' Lily asked incredulous. 'We must all make as much of a fuss as we can!'

Florence knew she had done the right thing in befriending this woman. She expected Maria would agree.

The others began to arrive. Anna Guidobaldi was amongst the first and she swept in with several newcomers.

Maria seemed to be grateful for this chance to lose herself in the hubbub. She showed Anna and the other women where to place the food they had brought with them. She fussed over them as they stood around unpacking their contributions and whispering awkwardly to each other. The door opened again and other arrivals streamed in. Amongst them were the regulars: widows, mothers, sisters. Maria greeted them all as warmly as she always did.

There were already forty women present in the Empire Café when Florence clapped her hands together. 'Thank you all for coming again this week. Before we start, I'd like to thank Maria for lending us the Empire.'

'Hear! Hear!'

'And I'd also like to introduce a special guest.' Florence indicated Lily. 'This is Mrs. Lily Moulton. She's come here directly from Hobart House.'

At the mention of Hobart House, a hush fell over the group until Lily, herself, spoke. 'I'd like to thank Mrs. Lantieri for inviting me. I'll be joining you here as often as I can. If you can't get to Hobart House then Hobart House will get to you.'

Everyone present gave up a little, polite, applause.

Although she crisped when anyone addressed her as "Mrs. Lantieri," Florence also forced a smile. Lily did not yet know, the idea of giving a pain-free divorce to her estranged swine of a husband was anathema to Florence. She had applied for a divorce but even if it meant he could be free to marry his floozie, Lantieri did not wish to pay. Therefore, she had to put up occasionally with hearing herself being addressed as "Mrs. Lantieri." She would find a moment later to take Lily aside.

That night there were more women attending than she expected. It was mainly thanks to herself. She had printed the leaflets and knew where to leave them. The Home Office had closed down *La Società*, but a visit to the church in Clerkenwell Street had been sufficient to find plenty of potential italo-brit widows. And once she had had that idea it was obvious she should visit a synagogue and ask the same question; "has anyone here had a member of their family interned and had no news since?"

That evening there were Austrian and Hungarian and Czechoslovakian women present: refugees who had also never imagined their husbands and sons would one day be considered "enemy aliens." The women had brought enough food for a battalion. It was piled high in vessels of different colours, shapes, and sizes. Florence would have been hard pressed to give a name to some of the hotchpotch of cold meats, fish, vegetables, rice, and pastas placed upon a row of tables which sagged under the weight.

She watched Maria move amongst other presumed widows, like the Ferdenzi's — one of whom came from Kings Cross and the other from Soho. Then there were those women like Anna Guidobaldi who did not yet know where their husbands were, but at least could take comfort in them not yet having been presumed dead.

Also present was Mrs. Guidobaldi's next door neighbour, Mrs. Harris. Mrs. Harris' husband was a journalist. He was English and he was alive. Lily had been most happy to discover this during their chat in Hobart House and it was she who had encouraged Anna to enlist her neighbour in their quest. "It's always helpful to know people," Lily had confided.

It was clear to Florence that Lily "knew people." For a start she knew her colleague at Hobart House, Mrs. Mia Woodruff, who wore pearls and knew a fellow in Scotland Yard, who knew several King's Counsels who knew several Lords and Ladies. Lily also knew how to ask questions of these people and could continue asking them, again and again and again, until clues slowly emerged: of a husband, brother, or father who might have been seen in this-or-that internment camp, might be rumoured to have embarked on this-or-that ship, might have been sent to this-or-that distant colony.

Florence tinkled her glass with a fork. 'Thanks to our friend here.' She nodded to Lily. 'We've come into possession of several lists, including embarkation lists.' Florence spoke grimly. 'Mrs Moulton has some information for us concerning the *Arandora Star.*'

A murmur spread around the café. The women stopped eating. Drinking glasses were placed back onto tabletops.

Lily stood up. 'I'm afraid the completeness of the lists can't be guaranteed.'

'In what way?' A Miss Dabel asked.

'We know there are persons whose names do not appear on the list as having boarded but who did indeed board the *Arandora Star.*' Lily clarified and looked around the room. 'And vice versa.' She pushed her reading glasses right back to the bridge of her nose. 'I'm afraid the situation will remain unclear until we can obtain a roll call from the camps.'

Anna Guidobaldi piped up, 'when might you receive a roll-call from the Isle of Man?'

'We already have our first one,' Lily answered. 'But most of the men were taken from the mainland holding camps, and there's been a great deal of movement there. Anyway, I have a list from Palace Camp.'

The room had deflated, but at the mention of Palace camp, Florence had felt her own pulse quicken. Some women, non-Italians, groaned, but several Italian women looked on hopefully.

'We're trying to get lists of all the camps. And we will, eventually.' Lily sounded assured.

Anna leant forward and sipped her water. 'Presumably you'll be able to share this particular list tonight?'

'Anyone here who believes their relative might be in Palace Camp on the Isle of Man or was on the *Arandora Star* can come and see me.' Lily motioned with a regard toward the small table she had set up at the back of the café. 'I'll be right over there for as long as you need me.'

'I heard some men survived the *Arandora Star* but have been sent away on another ship somewhere else,' Mrs. Anzani said. 'Is it true?'

'Yes, it is,' Lily answered.

'I heard some men were rescued from the *Arandora Star* but have suffered concussion and don't remember who they are,' one of the Mrs. Ferdenzi's said.

'Or perhaps they don't want to say who they are,' someone else said.

A nervous laughter passed through the café.

'Which reminds me,' Lily Moulton said, 'It'd be useful to write down as much as you can about your missing relative.'

'Such as?' Mrs. Anzani asked.

'Their height, their build, their hair colour, and eye colour,' Lily responded. 'Also, is there something they always carry with them? Anything else that can help identify them.'

Florence understood that Lily was not asking this so as to identify concussed survivors. They all understood that. She thought of Fortunato's identifying features: five-feet-seven-inches tall, balding, a little corpulent. What else? Frequently carries a small wooden flute. Missing molar number thirty-two. Has a birth mark the size of a sixpence under his left ribcage.

Later, Lily took up her post at the back of the café. She removed a bottle of smelling salts from her handbag and placed it on the table next to her drinking glass.

Mrs. Anzani was the first to be brought around by Lily's smelling salts. Decio had joined the "missing, presumed drowned," along with four-hundred-and-forty other Italian internees.

When everyone else had gone home, Florence and Lily sat for a while with Maria, they held her hands until Maria properly surrendered to her loss.

Maria's desolation was total. She wept so much that handkerchiefs could not absorb her tears, and her blouse became soaked. She cried with such violence that her heart broke in an instant and passed out of her body in small pieces which rolled down her face. She sobbed so convulsively that her face was not recognisable as her own.

Lily sedated Maria and Florence helped lay her on a couch.

Florence poured a grappa for each of them, and she and Lily sat on the floor in front of Maria. Finally, she asked Lily about her own loss.

'Edgar's missing, presumed stubbornly dead,' Lily said. 'We've been waiting for his mortal remains to come ashore. My girls seem to need that.' She shivered in that manner one does when a spirit trespasses over a grave. 'I suppose that's what we all want now. We just want to get them home. Right?'

Florence put an arm around Lily. Whatever else happened in their lives they would remain friends. 'I hope when you're up here at Hobart House, you'll stay at my place,' she said.

'Of course.'

Several hours later, Florence, accompanied by Lily, went in search of other lachrymose ladies.

The news was late, it was was unwelcome but families awaited it.

32

AMORPHOUS SILHOUETTES

Honiton, Devon.

The third month of his going
I thought I heard him say
'Our course deflected slightly
On the thirty-second day – '
The tempest blew his words away.

— ALUN LEWIS

When sleep came to Lily, she would take it. But in those first weeks it had not called often. Others called instead: the Devon Voluntary Aid Detachment needed another pair of nursing hands. She went wherever her services were needed. Teignmouth or Exeter, it made no difference to her. And when her presence in Devon was superfluous, even though the journey took seven hours, she returned to London. Back to Hobart House. Back to her friends in the Empire Café. Back to those who waited for the same sort of news she did. At least she had a place to rest in London and a host who understood her when she walked the floors in the twilight.

Some weekends, she persuaded Florence to travel back with her to Honiton. "We both need the company," she had said to Florence. And when Florence expressed a doubt, she reminded her "Maria's got her sister-in-law. And my girls like it when you're here."

So, they developed a routine: she, Florence and the dog, Billy. They took the ten-thirty Cornish Riviera from London Paddington to Exeter via Bristol. They pretended they were going on a seaside trip. But their conversation always returned to their missing men.

This particular Saturday, the train picked up speed outside London and rocked them side-to-side. 'Any news about Edgar?' Florence asked.

Lily blew a raspberry. Only a few days previously she had pestered the Admiralty and the Home Office for news. They told her one of the *Arandora Star's* empty lifeboats had been sighted seven miles off the coast of Donegal. But she already knew that. She read the newspapers. Her children read the newspapers. Her friends read the newspapers. 'Nothing new,' she answered and opened her satchel. 'Shall we get down to business?'

In London, they had purchased a batch of newspapers. They had a fresh consignment of letters to write to lawyers, members of parliament and religious leaders. Their missives would keep them busy. By the time they arrived at their stop-over in Exeter they would have several letters ready to take to the post office. And that would help to fill the time whilst they hung around and waited for the local train to Honiton.

'How's the little one been this week?' Florence asked.

She put down her pen and a half-completed letter to the editor of the Torquay Herald. 'I'm worried. This week she says that she dreamt Edgar and Jacob were on the seabed sitting at a table playing cards and laughing.'

Florence folded her newspaper and placed it on the adjacent empty seat. 'It's good that she's talking again. Maria's two still won't talk about their father's drowning. And she can't properly explain to them why their father was interned in the first place.'

'It's not only June. I've been having my own nightmares too,' Lily admitted quietly. 'I wake up pleading with Edgar to "come ashore." I tell him if he would only "come ashore" I'll take him up to Wavertree and place him with his stubborn parents.'

Florence leant down and stroked Billy.

Lily reflected on what Florence might conceivably tell her nephew and niece that could ever make any sense. Nothing could heal their pain. Not even Edgar's explanation about the world's navigators having lost their way. Perhaps it could help in the future when they became adults. But children always asked, why? Again, and again: "Why?" It always came down to the same question: "Why do the adults let themselves be led by people who have lost their way?" Lily never had an answer to that.

When they arrived, they found all three of the Moulton daughters in the kitchen. June was at the sink running water over her face and wiping it away with a kitchen towel. She blinked profusely for a few moments then said 'hello' to Florence and left the kitchen. Cilla was seated at the farmhouse kitchen table engrossed in her open notebook. She looked up and waved. Elizabeth was seated opposite Cilla and already had a glass of home-made gin in front of her. 'Let me get glasses for you both,' Elizabeth offered.

'What are you two up to,' Lily asked.

'Talking about graves in Scotland,' Cilla replied.

At times their conversations had become too estranged and morbid. A psychiatrist at the hospital had assured Lily that this detachment was their defence. A semantic shield protecting their fragility. "Let them be," the psychiatrist had said. Their plotting of winds and calculating where the tides ran, and maintaining lists of names and addresses of coroners and meteorologists and co-ordinators of coastal lookouts allowed them to maintain a kind of purpose. They needed that whilst they waited for their grief to become exhausted.

'What about them?' Lily asked.

'He could already be ashore,' Cilla whispered. 'In one of those.'

Lily stroked her chin. She had wondered about that too, but she had not felt it in her bones.

'I'd say, he's more likely to be in Ireland,' Elizabeth retorted and placed two extra glasses on the kitchen table.

'We need to write to the County Coroners again.' Cilla opened a newspaper at a page she had already marked with a red circle. 'Listen to this — "a man wearing a naval uniform and an oilskin coat was found washed up on a West Scotland beach. The badly decomposed body was found among the rocks and was buried yesterday at a local cemetery" — That's it. Can you believe it?'

Florence looked benevolently over the top of her glass. 'I agree it's disappointingly lacking in information.'

Cilla shook her head defiantly. 'It's worse than disappointing. How are we ever going to find Dad if that's their best? And how can we possibly help you and all those women from the Empire?'

Lily took a sip of her anaesthetic and sat her glass down. She placed a hand on top to prevent Elizabeth or Florence from refilling it. 'You know, it's not necessarily the coroners' fault. The newspapers don't always pass on everything that the coroners have told them.'

'Well, we can write to them too,' Cilla answered and held her hands out as though accepting an offering on behalf of the church. 'Insist a little.'

Lily hesitated to say any more on the matter because of what she had been holding back from the girls and Florence. The

Admiralty had told her they believed any remains washing up now would be in a state of advanced decomposition. They asked did she still wish for a telegram in the event they ever found something that might be Edgar. By "something" they meant, something bloated, eyeless, and limbless. A piece of watery flesh they could pass off as being Edgar's mortal remains. Then they reminded her that Bob Connell had volunteered to identify Edgar's remains, should they ever be found.

'I've been thinking,' Lily said and licked her bottom lip. 'After all this time it might be better if we never received a telegram.'

'What are you talking about, Mum?' Cilla said.

'I think I prefer to remember your father the way he was.'

Florence purred a little. She put her arm around Lily's shoulder and pulled her tight.

Cilla shook her head. 'No, we can't give up now, Mum.' She stared at Lily and then at Florence. 'You promised you'd bring him home. It's not too late. Don't you remember the report of that body that washed up after three years, tossing around the Solway Firth?'

'I never heard of that case,' Florence said.

'A pocket-watch was enough to identify it. That man's family could at least bury something and put up a stone.'

June entered the kitchen and then sat on the floor next to Lily. Lily wondered how much June had heard. She leant down and kissed June.

'Three years in the Solway Firth.' Florence said. 'Goes to show you,' she added. There was surprise in her voice.

'That was a case of a coroner doing his job properly,' Cilla said firmly. 'He found a way to identify the man and he made sure it was publicised. That way the man's relatives had a chance.' Cilla held up the same newspaper as before. 'Unlike in this case.'

Lily stole a sideways glance at June. She had not flinched but

Lily whispered to her, 'Perhaps it'd be best if you went to your room, darling.'

June rolled her tongue around the inside of her mouth and then cleared her throat. 'Mum, we talk about this all the time when you're not here. We're just trying to find dad's cadaver.'

Lily felt her blood freeze. She had never heard June say "cadaver." She let out a gentle gasp and squeezed her daughter's hand. 'But didn't that report say that the body was badly decomposed?' Lily addressed Cilla. 'They were fortunate. Not everyone has a pocket watch and chain, you know.'

Cilla stared back hard. Then turned her attention to Florence. 'What about dentistry?' she said defiantly and consulted her notebook. 'Tooth fillings. Missing teeth. False teeth. Straight teeth. Buck teeth. Gold teeth.'

'As unique as a fingerprint,' Florence spoke with authority. Her experience as a dental nurse was, by now, well known to the Moulton girls. She smiled as though unsure whether she ought to feel guilt or remorse for her answer. She let her drink roll around her mouth.

Lily did not dare reveal the admiralty had told her there were many headless and limbless bodies that had washed ashore. They could all have been from the *Arandora Star*. Edgar might already have come ashore, unannounced. Or he may have become one of those amorphous silhouettes he often spoke of, who drifted in the sea, following mariners in the hope of keeping them safe. Shouting warnings in the wind, hoping their words would be heard. She wiped a tear and stared at Cilla who stared back at her with eyes red and vacant.

Cilla shrunk from her mother's stare as though the unsaid had reached her. She looked back at her notes. 'Let's suppose a torso washes up,' she said as though hypothesising about the weather. 'Who ever met a sailor without a tattoo?'

'What if it's an internee and not a sailor?' Florence asked.

'Plenty other men have tattoos.' Cilla looked at Florence. 'You remember that list your friends gave us?'

Florence nodded. It would be unlikely she could forget it. She spent hours every week cross referencing it with the newspapers. Searching for husbands, fathers and brothers washed ashore and comparing that with the lists of identifying elements.

'We need more detail.' Cilla looked at her sisters in turn. 'More than pocket-watches, wristwatches, wedding rings, lucky charms, and musical instruments.'

'Dad wore a watch,' June said under her breath. 'And a wedding ring with a date on it.' June shifted position but remained on the floor near to Lily.

'That's right, he did.' Lily felt her chest tighten.

'And he had a medal on a chain around his neck,' June added.

'That too,' Lily agreed and her tears reached her throat.

'When they find Dad's body would we all have to look at it?' June asked.

'No, we wouldn't.' Lily swallowed her emotions.

'Clothes,' Cilla interjected as though to stop June. 'Bodies are washing up still wearing the clothes they left in.'

'But they never say much about that,' Florence replied. 'Except, if it's a uniform.'

Cilla raised a finger and consulted her notebook before she spoke again. 'Yes, but even then they still don't say enough about the colour of the uniform or the types of buttons or insignia.'

Lily stared at Cilla. It was as though her daughter had taken a distance from grief by transforming into a forensic detective.

'About that report,' Florence gestured to the newspaper Cilla had shown. 'That man had both a uniform and an oilskin, right?'

'Correct.'

'Then, he must have had a shirt and a vest and underpants. Why haven't they said anything about those?'

'That's my point!' Cilla replied. 'What about those clothes? Colours, materials and textures and labels could tell us a lot.'

Lily was not sure if she welcomed Florence encouraging Cilla in that way. But maybe it could help. 'I suppose they don't mention clothes too much because the colours are likely to be faded.'

Cilla shook her head as though to say, no, that's not it. 'Also, foot sizes and shoe types. And coins and crosses. And photographs and receipts, and postcards, even cheques and envelopes.'

Elizabeth stood up lethargically. She sighed and refilled the gin glasses for all three adults and said, 'it's hardly worth listing anything made of paper. What use would that be?'

'That's where you're wrong,' Cilla seemed on the verge of tutting. 'Anything held in a watertight wallet can help. Unsaturated legible photographs have been found and even a cheque was deciphered.'

'Dad has photos in his wallet,' June spoke once again as though to herself. 'I don't know if it's watertight.'

Lily looked away at the wall and managed to refrain from letting out a sob. She was glad Elizabeth had refilled her glass.

'I read last week, that nine people washed up across two beaches,' Cilla said. 'Three of them were identified through the papers they had on them.'

'Where did you read that,' Florence beat Lily to the question.

'I can't remember. I can find it if you want.'

Lily wondered how she and Florence could have missed it. They had meticulously gone through the newspapers. There had been plenty bodies washed up but none of them had been identifiable.

Cilla had her own pile of newspapers that she kept in a linen bag. 'Here it is,' she said and handed Lily a cutting from the *Londonderry Sentinel*. It was two weeks old.

'How did you get this?'

'I already told you mum,' Cilla sounded exasperated. 'I've been in touch with a coroner over there. He takes cuttings and sends them to me.'

Lily skim read the cutting and muttered: 'Nine bodies washed up. Two British soldiers and one Italian internee had been identified. Another two bodies wore uniforms but could not be identified. Two civilians were thought to be Italian, because of religious signs, but could not be identified. Another body was thought to be German — on account of having a document with Germanic writing — and the last cadaver was too decomposed to accord it any form of identity.'

'Dad has a poem in his wallet.' June traced a circle on the floor.

Lily stared at June and handed the newspaper cutting to Florence who, on hearing an Italian had been identified, gestured eagerly to have it. Whilst Florence read, Lily stared at June who had drawn her knees up and rocked back and forth. 'It's *Crossing the Bar*, right?' Lily said quietly.

June continued rocking back and forth and then stopped and added a head nodding motion: 'yes.'

'My God.' Florence blurted. 'Giovanni's turned up. If he's turned up…' Florence stared at Lily. 'I have to call his wife.'

Lily looked at Florence in alarm. 'No. You can't. It would be better if a nurse or doctor were present.'

It was one thing to learn that your husband was missing and presumed drowned it was another to know for certain he was dead and lay in the ground far from home. Lily would be present when Florence broke that news.

Florence could not take her attention off the newspaper cutting. She read and re-read. 'They don't say anything else here about the others,' Florence complained. 'Not their build, shoe size, colour of hair, or whether they were bald. Nothing!'

'That's what I've been saying,' Cilla replied. 'We ought to write to some of these coroners,' she alternated her attention between Lily and Florence, 'and remind them about all those things that would give us a better chance of knowing if a washed up body belongs to us.'

Lily nodded enthusiastically. 'Of course. We'll write.'

'Look at this,' Cilla held up another newspaper, one of those brought from London by Lilly and not yet exhaustively combed. 'This is what I'm talking about.'

The newspaper reported that more bodies had recently come ashore in Scotland. This coroner had understood the pain of anxious relatives waiting for clues. He had listed the possessions found on the body in question:

A small black leather purse,

a soft striped collar,

two handkerchiefs,

a large spoon,

two propelling pencils,

a tin of fifty cigarettes.

This man was not Edgar.

'Did you know,' June said, 'that the oceans are made of tears?'

'My nephew recently told me the same thing,' Florence replied.

'Last night I dreamt Dad was in a little boat on a stormy sea and he was shouting something,' June said. 'But I couldn't hear what he was trying to tell me.'

For the first time since the sinking Lily cried openly in front of her girls.

33

AN ALIEN COMES TO DANCE

Sussex Gardens, London.

It was Christmas Eve and Florence was alone in her apartment. She was rifling deep in the pockets of her memories whilst the BBC Radio Home Services broadcast the Savoy hotel *Orpheans*. They were playing *These Foolish Things*. She turned the radiogram up louder, then kicked off her thick corduroy carpet slippers and waltzed around the room. In her mind she waltzed with her man.

Her doorbell sounded.

She expected it.

She had recently acquired a new neighbour. He was elderly but not yet hard enough of hearing. Likely he had come to complain again about the volume. Dressed as she was, in her dressing gown and with her hair enmeshed in curlers, she hesitated between answering the summons or simply turning down the volume. She chose the latter. She turned the volume down low and continued waltzing around the radiogram. Friendly neighbourly relations were worth preserving, especially in these times. But her doorbell sounded once more. This time longer and more insistent.

Perhaps it was Dorothy coming to check on her. Would that girl never learn? She had specifically told her not to come around. She had explained that Dorothy absolutely must spend Christmas Eve with her shiny new fiancé and his family. She decided not to answer the door. She turned the radiogram even quieter and poured herself a bootlegged vodka. She sat her drink on the small drum table. She lay back on her settee. Her head rested on its arm and the Savoy hotel *Orpheans* band quietly but melodiously carried on with their repertoire.

The doorbell rang again.

She steadied herself and strode toward her front door. 'I told you not to come here today,' she shouted as she approached the door.

The bell ringing stopped. 'I think I would have remembered that, *amore,*' a male voice responded.

The hairs in her neck rose up. Some cruel charlatan was pretending to be Fortunato. She held her shaking hand on the door latch and asked, 'who's there?'

'It's me.'

'Fortunato?' She asked and was already weeping before she undid the latch.

'*Si, sono io,*' Fortunato answered. 'Open the door, *amore.*'

She opened the door, not caring which curious neighbours might have been around to see her embracing her "*eytie.*" She threw her arms around Fortunato. She sobbed into his neck and pulled him into the apartment. Somewhere in the background her radiogram chimed of *ties that bind us.* Once inside, she composed herself and stepped back. It was not a dream.

Fortunato closed the door and placed a small valise on the floor. 'I'm sorry, but I couldn't contact you.'

She forgot that she was not looking her best. She stared at him.

He was thinner. His suit hung as though embarrassed. Tears flowed. 'You look like a sparrow. Where have you been?'

'I'm not able to say much about that. But if everything goes well, I'll have British nationality by the time I'm back.'

She was confused. Back? Back from where? She wanted to know where he had been for the past five-and-a-half months but she had a more urgent priority. She could not remain in his presence looking the way she was. 'Can you prepare us something to eat whilst I transform?'

Fortunato grinned. 'I'm not so hungry. And I think I like you the way you are, natural.'

'It'll not last. Trust me, I need to get redone.'

In the background The Savoy *Orpheans* had begun to play *A voice in the night.*

'Wait a moment.' He put his arms around her.

They danced. He must have felt how lightweight she also had become, but she did not care. He must have seen how her hair was now flecked in grey, but he had the grace not to mention it. When the dance was over, she kissed him and pushed herself free and went to her bathroom. Whilst she performed her ritual she could hear him making himself at home. Placing his shoes in the hallway, turning the radiogram volume back up, and unzipping his valise.

She sat beside him on their settee. 'None of your clothes fit.' She placed her palms on his face. 'But you're in good shape.'

'I've been in training.'

'We thought you had drowned,' she answered. 'You've been in training? What for?'

He tapped the side of his nose. 'Can't say.' He placed a finger to his lips. Then sipped his tea.

'You can't tell me what happened?'

'You know what happened. We were picked up. Then we were moved. Then we were moved again. Then we were brought back and lined up and herded toward a ship.'

'But we thought you'd drowned,' she repeated.

'I wasn't even boarded.'

'But I received a letter from you, saying you were on some deportee list.' She wiped a tear. 'A retired lady brought it to me. She said her brother had become friendly with you, but you had left with all the others.'

'I did. But they took me out of the line.'

'Why?'

'I had tried to enlist in the camp. First they said no. Then they said yes.'

'You enlisted in the British Army?'

'You can't be surprised.'

'You know what happened to our friends?'

'We're in a war, Florence. It was a fascist U-Boat.'

'They shouldn't even have been on that ship.'

'I know that.'

'Well, how can you fight for them?'

'It's not that kind of a battle. Do you think Renzo would want me to fight for fascism?'

'Don't be stupid,' Florence spoke softly.

'How's Maria coping?'

'It's been difficult.' Florence shook as sobs coursed through her again. She signalled for him to pass her a handkerchief. 'Some days she acts as though Renzo is not lost at sea. She talks as though she expects to see him again. She's going to be shocked to see you.'

Fortunato held her tight. 'We heard how you all made a fuss on our behalf.'

'What did you expect us to do?' She brightened.

'That you'd forget all about me.'

She had never punched him before, not even playfully, but she did it then. '*Non mi scorderò mai di te!*' she said with tears in her eyes. 'One day we'll tell the world. One day I'll place an advertisement in the *Times of London*.'

Fortunato smiled. 'I wouldn't be surprised if you did.'

***

They arrived at the Empire Café by the back entrance. She stepped ahead and had almost reached the door when it was flung wide open and Maria's boy emerged carrying a mid-sized household bin.

The boy stepped into the yard and looked beyond her. He gingerly sat the bin on the ground and stared at Fortunato. '*Sei tu zio?*' the boy asked tentatively.

Fortunato held out his arms to his godson.

The boy crumpled into Fortunato's embrace. 'Is my dad with you?'

Fortunato stroked the boy's cheek.

Florence suppressed her sobs and watched the boy grip Fortunato tighter.

Fortunato's eyes met hers as he removed Renzo's piccolo from his jacket pocket.

'He wanted me to make sure you got this.'

The boy stared at the piccolo. He trembled as he reached out and took the instrument. His lips closed over the embouchure and he breathed in deeply. His upper body shivered and he blew into the instrument.

'Your dad wants you to continue practising, a little every day,' Fortunato said.

Seemingly summoned by the notes of the piccolo, Maria appeared in the doorway. She took a moment to absorb the scene then covered her mouth with a fist. 'Florence, my God,' she said and ran to hug Fortunato. 'You look malnourished.'

Florence cleared her throat and walked to where the bin had been placed on the ground.

'Let's not stand around out here,' Maria scolded. She looked around, as though expecting others to be in the vicinity. Seeing there was no one else, she uncrossed her arms and asked, 'you're coming in, right?'

'If you'll let me cook dinner,' Fortunato answered. He kept an arm around his godson. 'I've only got two days leave. It'll be a little while before I'm back. At least let me cook.'

Maria shrugged. 'Why? Where are you going in two days?'.

'I'll be re-joining my unit.'

'I wish that Renzo had enlisted,' Maria said.

'Seriously?' Fortunato asked. 'How could he? There was no time for anyone to take anything in. He thought he'd be back home in a few days. He'd never have left his family just like that,' Fortunato answered.

'But he left us anyway.'

'He didn't ask to be transported.'

They stepped inside. Florence recalled the last occasion she and Fortunato had been there together. The windows had been smashed and graffiti daubed on the wall. They had gone there together to help Maria and Renzo clean it all up. The next morning the police had knocked on Florence's door and said they had come for her "lodger."

Over dinner, they talked of Fortunato's trim figure, they talked of foods that were rationed, and places that had been flattened. Only when the children had gone to their room did Florence allow the conversation to return to the internment. She had instructed Fortunato not to talk of the knifings, the suicides or escape attempts. He should only describe the long beachside promenades, the quaint holiday hotels requisitioned by the government. "Go easy on the barbed-wire fences, watch-towers, searchlights and sentry posts," she had said and bless him, Fortunato did as she had asked.

'What was the internment camp like?' Maria asked.

'I've stayed in worse places,' Fortunato answered.

Florence knew it was true, for she had seen him relive being in the trenches in another war.

'What's next?' Maria asked.

'If everything works out, they'll finally process my application for British nationality.'

And if things don't work out?' Florence asked.

'A certain Pierre Dupont is going to be very disappointed.'

'Who's Pierre Dupont?' Florence asked.

'I've already said too much,' Fortunato replied and again he tapped the side of his nose. 'It's this wine of Maria's.' He held the wine glass by its stem and rotated it.

Florence and Maria raised their glasses and toasted loudly to Fortunato's good health. The sounds brought Maria's son from his bedroom. The boy arrived with his father's piccolo attached to a string hanging from his neck. He pattered quietly over to Fortunato and sat on his knees.

'Zio, did my dad play in the camp?'

'He did.'

'What did he play?'

'Mostly, he played the Mockingbird.'

Florence felt a lump arise in her throat as it became plain to her that the boy had been crying.

'I knew he would,' the boy answered and solemnly tried out several notes for himself.

Two days later, Fortunato returned to his unit.

34

OPERATION COLOSSUS

Naples

In Naples, the German S.S. interrogated Pierre Dupont. He frustrated them. They became angry and split his lip. When the Carabinieri arrived and took over his interrogation, Pierre Dupont knew the game was up. He could have gone on confusing the Germans, but not the Carabinieri.

Within minutes of having swaggered into his view the interrogator and stenographer circled him and read his arrest notes. Several concentrated glances later they had seen right through the short, unshaven, and unlikely "Pierre Dupont," whom the Germans had tied tightly to a chair.

'*Chi-sei-tu?*' the interrogator demanded to know who he was.

Pierre Dupont stared at the floor and pretended not to understand.

The interrogator impatiently swung out an arm and the crack of nasal cartilage accompanied the same question in French this time. '*Qui êtes-vous?*'

He screamed with pain. Then answered: 'Pierre Dupont.'

The interrogator laughed and asked, '*da Parigi, vero?*' From Paris, correct?

Warm blood trickled through Pierre Dupont's fingers as he rearranged his nose.

The interrogator whispered: '*Vedremo.*' We'll see. He asked Pierre Dupont to talk about his district. He wanted street names. He wanted the location of the town hall. He wanted the name of the nearest church and the best baker shop.

From his training, the prisoner remembered a few street names, no bakers and had no idea of where the nearest town hall was, or which saint had lent their name to the local church. Pierre Dupont proffered some answers, as fake as his French accent that came and went like that of an enthusiastic American tourist. On the other hand, there was his inexplicably perfect Tuscan locution that the Carabinieri had heard all about.

'Look,' the interrogator said. 'I'll tell you my name, if you tell me yours,' and his widening grin conveyed all the hurt that was to come because of Monsieur Dupont's woeful command of spoken French and deep ignorance concerning the topography of his putative district. The interrogator then brought his face up against Pierre Dupont's and quietly explained he and his stenographer would go out and have a little "chat" with some of the other "comrade" prisoners. But they would return in one hour. And they would give Monsieur Dupont one last opportunity to tell them his real name or they would cut off his testicles.

'Not as though a guy like you needs them,' the stenographer scorned on his way out and the interrogator laughed.

The Carabinieri left him tied to his chair.

The German armed guards remained inside the office and grinned vacantly.

Pierre rocked on his chair. They could question his comrade prisoners for as long as they felt like it and they could cut-off as many of their testicles as their barbarism dictated but none of them would give up Pierre Dupont's real name. Such sentiment was not borne out of an unshakeable belief in the heroism of Pierre Dupont's comrades, but rather because none of them knew his real name. Special Operations Executive had kept his real identity a secret from all the other team members. Everyone on the mission knew he was an Italian, not a Frenchman, but no one amongst them knew his real name.

Blood trickled from his nostrils and splashed on his boots and dripped on to the flagstoned floor. He considered his choices. He could tell them his real name. He was unafraid of whatever they would do to him. But there was his mother and siblings to think about. They would be targeted. He could prolong the charade by insisting he really was Monsieur Pierre Dupont. Or he could invent another name, something English this time and more plausible than Pierre Dupont. But that long march, that tiresome wait, that truck ride and then the train journey to Naples, followed by a humiliating march at the end of a bayonet, all conducted in a country that had become unrecognisable, had exhausted him. And an entire day had passed since he had last eaten. Whatever identity he might invent it would have to resemble a truth and be simple to remember.

He could say his name was Wilf Pearce. Close enough. He could say he was born in London and lived there in Sussex Gardens with his Italian lover. He worked at the Savoy. He supported Arsenal — he could name their team, their manager, their league position. He could say he had a dog, a German shepherd named Billy whom he walked in Hyde Park. The story coalesced in his mind, it gathered substance, it took on a solidity and he was almost ready to risk his testicles for it until he saw the enormous lacuna in his own story. Why would Wilf Pearce be in possession of an ID tag and papers presenting himself as Pierre Dupont? A man named Wilf Pearce would jump from a plane as himself. Only a British spy or an Italian anti-fascist would parachute into Italy wearing a

British army uniform and pretend to be French. In fascist Italy, neither of those options were to be spared. Therefore, who was he? What was he?

From the moment when, kitted out as a British paratrooper, he had rushed into the farmhouse adjacent to the targeted viaduct and startled the residents by screaming at them in mother-tongue Italian to scarper from the imminent explosion, everyone had figured him for what he was. No doubt they had described him in precisely those terms to the Carabinieri; he was an Italian anti-fascist dressed to look like British military.

His nose had stopped bleeding when the Carabinieri showed up one hour later. 'My name's Fortunato Picchi,' he told them cheerily. 'I'm originally from Carmignano,' he added before he noticed the interrogator held a razor in his hand. 'I've been living in London twenty years. I went there because my family are all fascists,' he lied. 'Can't stand any of them.'

'Pity. I was looking forward to cutting off your balls.'

They did not cut off his testicles. Instead, they kept him awake for another seventy-two hours. They tried to get the truth from him about his family. But they could not. And when they had finished their questions they told him he would be sent to Rome where he would be judged and sentenced.

'Tried by whom? *Il Duce's* lackeys?'

'By the Special Tribunal for the Defence of the State,' the interrogator answered.

'Have you ever thought about that?' Fortunato rasped to the man who broke his nose, 'our Government's in such a state of decay it needs a Special Tribunal to defend itself from its own citizens.'

'In case you're wondering who broke your nose,' the interrogator said, 'the name's Major Fioni.'

'You broke your country, you halfwit,' Fortunato replied.

The Major slapped Fortunato once more.

The next morning, four guards took him on a train from Naples to Rome Termini. The train made several stops and other prisoners joined and sat in the same carriage. Like Fortunato, they were handcuffed to a seat rail. Like Fortunato they were told to look at the floor and shut their mouths, and like Fortunato on arrival in Rome they were marched at the end of a bayonet out of the railway station, past hundreds of German soldiers.

They pushed him into the back of a waiting black prison-wagon. They kept the engine running and pushed in another four prisoners. The wagon doors were locked and a thick metal bar slid in place. Only when the wagon pulled away from the station did one of the others, an elderly man, break the silence. 'Pigs,' he said whilst he comforted and stroked the cheek of a boy not much older than Fortunato's own godson.

'Why is he here?' Fortunato asked.

'They accused him of assisting the commando unit that tried to rescue his father from the local jail,' the elderly man answered.

'Your father must be proud,' Fortunato said.

The boy remained mute but the old man leant into Fortunato and whispered, 'they already killed his father and his brother.'

Fortunato felt his stomach churn and his breathing pause.

'Why are you here?' the old man asked Fortunato.

'I was in a British airborne commando unit,' he answered. 'Thirty of us. We blew up an aqueduct at Tragino.'

The old fellow stared at Fortunato in disbelief.

Fortunato regretted that in Naples they had taken his British Army uniform and given him someone else's baggy clothes to wear. He wanted to let this old patriot know that the fight would go on. Everywhere, there were others, young, old, and middle-aged men like himself: a balding, previously overweight, forty-three-year-old restaurant manager who would not watch those thugs destroy Italy. A movement was forming to free Italy from fascism and Fortunato was part of it. In twenty-weeks he had become fitter than any time since he had moved to England. He had re-learnt how to handle explosives. He had jumped dozens of times from a plane. There would be others like him.

'Only thirty of you?' the old man whispered. 'How did you expect to get away with it?'

'There was a plan, but it didn't work out.'

That was as far as their conversation could go. They had arrived at Regina Coeli and were taken to separate areas of the jail. Fortunato never saw the old fellow nor his grandson again.

In Regina Coeli, they battered Fortunato and bruised his ribs. They took him from his cell and asked him all the same questions they had already asked in Naples. They enjoyed checking his answers against whatever they had noted down in Naples and took pleasure in punching or slapping him when his response did not satisfy them. He stuck to the truth as best as he could recall it. When they asked him about the internment camps he admitted he had been sent there. They understood him less. He did not tell them about his friends who had been deported from the camps and were missing, presumed drowned. Nor did he tell them about the English section of the *Italia Libera* movement. Then, one day, after weeks of questions and light beatings, his interrogators stopped coming to his cell. A few days later, the jailer told him charges had been raised against him.

'Shall I be needing a lawyer?'

The jailer laughed as he lifted the hatch in the door and pushed a food tray and an envelope in. 'More likely you'll be needing a priest.'

'Seriously, what happens next?'

The jailer spoke softly through the hatch. 'They'll assign an advocate to you. Open your envelope and you'll see who they've assigned. He'll show up here. You two talk and then you'll be taken to the Palace of Justice for judgement.'

'When?'

'April fifth. See for yourself.'

The Special Operations Executive had issued a watch to him, but the Carabinieri had taken it. There were clocks and calendars and routines tucked around the prison but none in his cell, nor in the humiliation room where they took him for questioning. He had asked for a pencil and notepaper, but they refused. He had considered scratching discreet notches on a wall and keeping count, but they had taken away his belt, his shoelaces, and his coins. Apart from his fingernails and the buttons on his shirt there was nothing left to scratch with. He was uncertain of how many days had passed since he had arrived in Regina Coeli. His cell had a window, but they had boarded it up. Only the screams of other prisoners, the noise of pain travelling differently at night gave any clues as to whether it was day or night. He might get close to guessing which day of the week. It had been three days since the other prisoners had attended mass and their muted mutterings were heard throughout, even in Fortunato's wing.

'What date are we now?' Fortunato asked.

'March, twenty-sixth.'

Ten more days. The news rendered Fortunato optimistic. They would have to keep him alive until then if they wanted their little theatre. Probably there would be no more questioning or beating. He opened the envelope and read the charges. 'Are we Tuesday or Wednesday, today?'

'Yes,' the guard conceded. 'One or the other.'

They let him sleep whilst he waited for his trial. He got himself into positions where his exhaustion trumped the pain in his rib-cage. He pulled his rough, wool blanket over his head and screwed his eyes to shut out the electric light. He surrendered his mind to whatever thoughts wished to enter, as long as they would be positive. Sometimes he imagined himself tiptoeing backwards through the cell door like a wraith through corridors and descending stairs and passing right through the giant doors which led out of the prison to the riverside. In this fantasy he travelled back to Rome Termini in a taxi-cab, not a jail-wagon, and the streets were empty of soldiers.

Several days later, Fortunato met with the tribunal appointed defence lawyer in a small parlour. A diminutive bird-like man with a vivid orange shirt. Everything else about him was black: black suit, black gloves, black scarf, even black eyes. He reminded Fortunato of a sad finch in winter. He wondered how the lawyer had been chosen. Probably on account of a long-held party membership. Or perhaps he had a connection. Whatever the reason, he did not seem entirely happy with his lot.

'You joined the British Pioneer Force?' It could have been a question, or a search for a justification, but it sounded a flat reproach.

Fortunato grinned until his ribs hurt. The fools had believed him when he told them he had joined the Pioneers. They had no idea of the SOE. 'You understand. I was not happy in internment. My lady-friend was worried about me.'

'I thought you were single?'

At least the legal finch had read the file. 'Unmarried. Not single,' Fortunato clarified. He shrugged and added, 'only because my lady-friend's divorce has not yet come through. I've explained all of this.'

The lawyer sniffed. 'You do know you can appoint your own defence lawyer?'

'I doubt the money they took from me would cover the cost.'

'These charges are serious,' the lawyer reproached. 'It says here you gave assistance and collaborated with enemy forces.'

'I acted as interpreter. Does it say I saved Italians from being blown up?'

'You admitted to being an anti-fascist.' The lawyer's glasses rode his nose as he turned over testimony.

'I'm anti-authoritarian,' Fortunato replied. 'Aren't you?'

The lawyer sniffed again. 'You'll have to say they forced you.'

'They broke my nose and bruised my ribs.' Fortunato raised his handcuffed hands and pointed to his nose. 'Quite a forcible manner to obtain a confession of being anti-fascist.'

'No,' the lawyer replied, 'I meant you'll have to say the English forced you to join their mission.'

Fortunato smiled bitterly and shook his head, as though he was sorry for the lawyer's stupidity. 'Will it be a public hearing?'

The lawyer scratched nervously at his neck. 'No press allowed.'

'How about members of the public?'

'Places are limited,' the lawyer said. 'Usually all taken by the *Milizia Volontaria per la Sicurezza Nazionale.*' He snapped closed his notes and added tight lipped. 'Perhaps a close family member, but not usually.'

'Blackshirts?' Fortunato did not hide his disgust. 'The *Mvsn* pass themselves off as the public now?'

'Anyway,' the lawyer pressed on, 'you'll have to say the British forced you to join them, and I'll ask for the Court's leniency.'

'What kind of leniency?'

'Life imprisonment. If you repent and show remorse and get the right judge.'

He could not promise the lawyer anything. They shook hands and the sad little lawyer fluttered out, with a promise not to be seen again until Saturday 5 April.

Fortunato returned to his cell and contemplated whether he could repent. He was sorry for many things in his life, but he could not bring himself to repent having tried to fight fascism. Perhaps Decio was right, he could not stop himself from looking down dark alleys. But that was the way things were. He knew if he had another opportunity he would do the same again. Maybe this time they would succeed in escaping too. He wondered about the others. Where were they? In Regina Coeli? Or had they been killed? Or shipped to some distant internment camp?

They came for him early on the morning of Saturday 5 April. The guard delivered a small pile of clothes; clean and freshly pressed. The pile included a pristine collar, a tie, socks still in their packaging, a hat, a coat and even a pair of gloves.

'This is how it works.' The guard winked.

'How what works?'

'Fascism.'

'What if I preferred to go there dressed as I am now?'

The guard opened the cell door and revealed four militia-men there to accompany him.

'You're up early,' Fortunato addressed the Blackshirts.

'Follow us,' a Blackshirt spoke.

They took him to an empty cell in a lower wing of the prison. They watched him shave and dress. They searched him. They took him to another wing, through a courtyard and into another internal bay, where a van waited. 'Shouldn't I have my lawyer with me?' Fortunato asked.

'You'll find him at the Palace of Justice. You're lucky you've got him,' the Blackshirt said.

'Why's that?'

'Half of his clients get away with life imprisonment.'

Fortunato considered the odds. Life imprisonment hardly seemed like "getting away." In either scenario the prognosis was the same. There would be no more walking with Florence and Billy around Hyde Park. An escape from Regina Coeli would be "getting away." He wondered how many of the finch's clients had managed it. In his dreams he had managed to escape on several occasions.

35

AFTER NOON NEWS

Leipzig

The flying fish like kingfishers
Skim the sea's bewildered crests,
The whales blow steaming fountains,
The seagulls have no nests
Where my husband sways and rests.

— ALUN LEWIS

Ingeborg crossed rooms. Back and forth. She opened and closed
doors. She had the feeling she was running late for something.
Would it make any difference if she could remember? She clapped
her empty coffee-mug into a full sink. The mug clinked as it settled
adjacent to other heaped up dirty crockery and cloudy schnapps
glasses. She stood with her arms outstretched in front of her and
she leant on the sink and stared in, puzzled to see numerous empty

vessels piled up there. How long have they been there? she wondered.

Yes, yes, all of this debris was entirely of her own making. But it would soon be cleaned up: a clear-out is coming. She looked once more into the sink: but not now.

She returned to the sitting room and switched on the radio because she had to be there if she wanted any news. When it came, the early broadcast was like the one of the previous day. Full of descriptions of how the Luftwaffe's bombing of London had "pummelled" their Houses of Parliament and would soon turn their Westminster Abbey to dust and their British Museum and National Galleries too. She cried about that. She hoped it was another lie and she wondered if the news in England was full of talk about how Leipzig would be pummelled.

All this talk of pummelling. Her thoughts scuttled sideways toward the oak chest where they kept their photograph albums. The Houses of Parliament, Westminster Abbey, The British Museum. She had photographed all of those places as well as the back of a cafeteria menu given to Günther. She had promised to return to those places with Günther and Clara. Now there would be nothing to see, only ashes. She wished she could remember where she had hidden those photographs; the synagogue, Friedrich, Günther's cousins twice-removed and those others.

She slumped deeper into Günther's black leather armchair adjacent to the radio and had a peculiar premonition. This would be the day. She speculated which radio news broadcast would carry the message to her. Probably it would be the *After Noon News Broadcast*. Hardly anyone listened to it. Not the "patriots," because they would be in their factories "contributing to the war effort" listening to *music-for-work*. Only people like Ingeborg would be at home palpitating over the *After Noon News Broadcast*.

They could slip it in whenever they wanted to and no one except for Ingeborg would be the wiser. It would probably be

Joachim: the broadcaster with the high voice, who would announce it. Joachim talked excitedly and fast. It made sense he would be the one to announce it. And then everything would return to its prior calm and Joachim would play something from Deutsche Masse and when that had finished Joachim would be the one to trot out their usual eulogy: blah, blah, blah, hero, hero, hero, and something about a memory that would live in the hearts of every German for all time.

On Günther's last furlough they had listened to the radio together. Günther was a hollowed-out impostor of himself. But they had managed to laugh at Joachim and the *After Noon News Broadcast* and she had been reminded of the man she had spited her own mother for. Günther had also shown her how to move the aerial around in search of a clearer signal.

'Stay in range,' he reminded her when he was leaving. 'If necessary, move the aerial around.'

'You too.'

She liked the idea of staying in range. On that furlough he said things would change, as though he may have meant it. He said he had requested a shore position and there was a chance. All he wanted was that chance to live in a different way. That was the last she had heard. He had not come back. He was no longer in range. She felt it. He was in a place where the sky could not be seen and birds did not fly. Every day, for weeks she had called BdU offices in Kiel. She was happy to make their lives a misery too. She asked to speak to Günther or to Bert or to Amelung.

One day she told them about the leaflets from the sky and they put her through to Amelung.

Amelung sounded surprised. 'Hello Ingeborg. I've heard you were looking for me.'

'Then why haven't you called me back?'

'I've been waiting,' he spoke quietly.

'What for?' Ingeborg snapped. 'Permission from BdU's propaganda puppet-masters?'

Amelung promised he would come to see her. He did not say much more, but she perfectly understood he could not say everything he wanted to say on the telephone: BdU did not deal in truths. Whilst she waited in Günther's chair for Amelung to show up, she closed her eyes and drafted a letter to Clara: it would be in red ink.

She had no sense of how long had passed when loud bawling and a shrill voice from the children's room woke her.

'Mam, mam!' Dagmar called.

Ingeborg rubbed her eyes and snapped the radio off.

'Mam! Mam!'

She pushed open the door to their daughters' bedroom. Identical pinewood cots on opposite ends of the room. In one cot lay Birgit. Dark haired, olive skinned and not quite a year old. In the other cot lay, blond and pale, two-and-half years old Dagmar,

As soon as Birgit saw Ingeborg, she increased the volume of her bawling.

'Shhhh. Shhhh,' Ingeborg said.

When Birgit first arrived a mongst h er blond-haired, light-skinned antecedents, Günther had remarked: "Well! Well! What are the chances of that?" Brigit started bawling right there and then and she had barely stopped bawling since. Today, Birgit was dressed in Dagmar's faded, brown, one-piece, which had a little rip in the side that Ingeborg intended to get around to sewing. She smiled at Birgit and Birgit turned down her bawling but turned up her bleating, as though she was famished.

Ingeborg looked at her wristwatch. It had been six hours since the last feed. Now she remembered what it was she was late for.

36

VIVA L'ITALIA

Rome

When Fortunato arrived at the Palace of Justice, the sad little lawyer was already located in the "secure room." For the occasion, the lawyer had changed to a dark grey suit, with matching dark grey waistcoat open at the bottom button, and he had changed his orange shirt for a white one. He resembled the junco bird.

'How was the journey?' the lawyer asked.

'Short,' Fortunato replied.

'Have you considered what I suggested?'

Fortunato had indeed considered it. But was still unsure if he had any intention of supplicating himself for the fun of the fascists. They would let him repent and beg leniency and then they would probably pass whatever sentence they already had in their mind.

'Sure, I've thought about it.'

The little lawyer sighed. 'Good. We've got Tringali today. Go heavy on the repentance and look as though you are praying for yourself and *Il Duce* .'

The Blackshirts lead him through an elegant wood-panelled

corridor into a lavish ornate courtroom. The "public spaces" were already filled with militia "volunteers."

Doors opened behind him and the militia's legal counsel, of five men, paraded into the room like peacocks. Their chests buckled under the weight of their medals of vivid ribbons and various metals struck for imagined heroism in some mythical battle against anti-fascists.

The magnificent five took their places in the sumptuously upholstered arc set aside for them and awaited the arrival of the military prosecutor and, on an even more elevated position, the sublimely well preened President of the Court who, as the junco bird had said, was none less than the lieutenant general of the *Mvsn*, signor Tringali, himself.

The reading aloud of the "facts" was swift. The sad lawyer fluttered when they asked Fortunato whether he would stand by all he had previously said concerning his "acts" even the part of his having been "entirely satisfied with enrolling for the enemy army?"

Fortunato smiled. '*Si.*'

The lawyer put his head between his knees.

'Have you anything to say for yourself?' the military prosecutor asked.

The little lawyer looked up expectantly at Fortunato and then bowed his head and placed his hands as though to pray.

'*Viva l'Italia*,' Fortunato said loudly and then repeated it '*Viva l'Italia.*'

'Indeed.' The military prosecutor said and puckered his lips before he continued in a dull monotone to read aloud the previously typed sentence: 'for offences under article 242 of the penal code: life Imprisonment.'

The junco fluttered and Fortunato stuck out his chin.

'For offences under article 247 of the penal code,' the military prosecutor smiled, baring his perfect shiny teeth as he looked at Fortunato and announced, 'death by firing squad.'

The five peacocks saluted and shouted, '*Al Duce*,' and they saluted a larger than life picture of their *Duce*.

'To be carried out tomorrow at 7am.' The prosecutor added.

In a blur they returned him to Regina Coeli. They insisted he change back into the old clothes. He learnt that they intended to publish the details of his arrest and sentence on the door of every town hall in Italy. This would be a disaster for his family. There were fascist groups in every part of the country who took a pleasure in smashing windows, or painting the walls of homes, or doing even worse to families considered to have harboured or ever had an anti-fascist in their family.

He appealed again for a sheet of paper and a pen. They told him he could write one letter. It would be delivered anywhere in Italy. There could be nothing for Florence. There could be nothing for Maria or his godson. He wrote a letter to his mother.

Sunday 6 April 1941

My Dearest Mother,

After many years you receive a letter from me. I am sorry, Dear Mother, for you and for everyone in the house about this misfortune and the pain it will cause you. Now all that remains in this world of both pain and pleasure is over for me. I don't care much about dying, I regret my action because I, who have always loved my country, must today be recognized as a traitor. Yet in conscience I don't think I am. Forgive me, Dear Mother, and remember me to everyone. Above all, I ask you for your forgiveness and your blessing, because I need it so much. Kiss all my brothers and sisters and to you, Dear Mother, a hug, hoping, with God's help, to join each other in heaven.

with many kisses,
Viva l'Italia, your son,
Fortunato.

***

Later, a priest arrived. He was tall, young, and looked worried. They prayed together. Fortunato confessed his sins, of which there were many, but they did not include trying to fight fascism. They did not include volunteering for the parachute regiment. The priest reassured Fortunato that he would see to it that the jailer kept his word concerning the letter. He remained long enough to share a meal with Fortunato, and they talked.

'Is God watching us, Father?'

'God sees everything.'

'Does God believe I'm a traitor?'

'God knows your heart."

'They said I was a traitor to Italy.'

'They live in a different Italy from the one you remember. There is a temporary darkness.'

'If he knows the heart of men, why do I have to die?'

'Your courage and your bravery are needed to help light the path.'

When the priest finally took his leave Fortunato remained awake and considered everything that had passed in his life. He had been a soldier in two wars. They had said the first had been "a war to end all wars," but that was a lie. Here he was, in another war and sentenced by his own countrymen who said he was a traitor, and that was a lie too.

***

They came for him at six-fifteen a.m. They handcuffed him and placed him in the same van as the previous day. The priest from the prior night was already in the van. He looked as though he had not slept either and his regard was of someone worried that the Blackshirts could mix up the prisoner and the priest.

'Shall we go for a nice drive in the country, Father,' Fortunato joked half-heartedly.

The priest smiled in pain.

'Do you know where they're taking me?' Fortunato asked.

'Forte Bravetta,' the priest replied. 'It's not too far.'

Indeed, it was not too far, and indeed it was in the countryside. Thirty quiet minutes in which Fortunato remembered the things he'd never see again: Florence, his godson, his dear friends, his mother, his brothers and sisters, his nephews and nieces, his beloved German shepherd. In the absence of his piccolo, he whistled as the van slowed and turned right into an unmade road.

Shortly thereafter, the van stopped moving but the engine continued running. *Never too late for a rescue,* he thought. Doors opened and slammed closed. The van moved again, slower, and rocked from side to side as it went.

They stopped the engine, opened the doors, and removed him from the van. It took a moment for his eyes to adjust to the bright daylight. He found himself standing on a dirt track surrounded by four guards. He turned at the priest's voice and saw that the track inclined and then bent away around a corner. He was sure his fate lay there, beyond that corner, hidden from sight by trees. He felt the air on his face. He could smell recently cut grass. The priest came to his side, and he followed the priest's regard past the guards, down the dirt-track which continued for one hundred metres before it cut through a hill creating an embankment on both sides.

A squadron of Blackshirts stood on the left edge of the dirt track road. They formed a semi-circle, their rifles draped loosely from their shoulders. Cigarette smoke hung in the air above them. Some of the Blackshirts chatted amongst themselves. None of them looked up the track toward Fortunato.

Ten paces away, at the foot of the opposite embankment, facing the Blackshirts, sat what appeared to be a farmhouse kitchen seat. It was painted white, like a forgotten prop from an outdoor drama and part of its back had been awkwardly hacked away.

A guard placed a black bag over his head and several hands gripped his shoulders and someone pushed him forward. 'Keep walking,' a voice in his ear said and its owner's alcohol infused hot breath touched Fortunato's cheek.

He did as he had been commanded. He felt someone steady him and he understood it must have been the young priest. As they approached the firing squad, he heard the movement of limbs and cessation of chatter. Hands stopped his forward momentum.

'Turn here,' the same warm breath as before instructed him.

They rotated him and pushed him forward several more steps and then they removed the black bag.

'No, looking back!' The guard barked.

He had his back to the Blackshirts. He stared ahead at someone who was in the midst of hammering small wooden supports into the ground adjacent to the legs of the hacked kitchen chair. He watched the man tie the chair-legs to the ground supports. The securing was barely finished before they pushed him forward once more and he found himself sitting the wrong way round in the chair with his elbows draped upon the top of the chair-back.

He felt the cord cut into his flesh as guards tied his ankles to the chair legs. They looped a rope around the chair and tightened it around his back. They pushed his head forward, his chin rested on the hacked out seat-back. Behind him, he heard sixteen Blackshirts cock their rifles. He would have been happier to stand and to face his executioners. He thought they might have been happier too. There was no dignity in this for anyone. In the distance, he heard the engine of a truck. He heard the song of birds in nearby trees and saw some small animals play in the grassy embankment.

He hummed the Mockingbird.

The command to shoot did not come. Perhaps it would never come. Maybe *Il Duce* had decided no more Italians should be shot in the back by his firing squads. Or was it simply not his time?

He felt the warmth of the young priest's hands upon his forehead. Together they recited *Our Father* and he accepted the viaticum and he shut out every sound until all he heard was his own thoughts. He felt sorry for the execution squad. They did not know him and he did not know them. He supposed they had not all volunteered. He supposed too that they could never speak of what they were about to do or at least could never speak of it to their mothers.

'It's time,' a guard said.

The priest slipped away into the wings.

***

If he could have seen it, Fortunato would have seen how the firing squad had arranged themselves: eight kneeling, eight standing. He would have seen a hearse had arrived and looped around the field such that it faced up the incline ready to collect his mortal remains whilst they were still warm.

If he could have seen it, he would have seen the hearse doors open and a simple unmarked coffin being removed and lain out on the ground. A fellow with a spade stood next to the hearse.

If he could have seen it, he would have seen that some members of the execution squadron had already decided to miss. It was difficult to miss and also considered an offence against the state, but some of them would miss, all the same. Sadly, there were in the midst of the execution squad some members who considered that the man tied to the chair was not a good man. They had no knowledge nor interest in knowing that this was a man who had fought in a war to protect ideas and freedoms, so they might enjoy them. They did not know, nor did they care, this was a man who was always ready to look down dark alleys, no matter the fear in his heart.

***

'On my command.' The guard looked at his left wrist. At these moments, in the fascist world, fastidious timekeeping was not the single solace available to them, but it was important.

'Fire.'

Sixteen puffs of smoke.

Fortunato was no more.

They brought the undersized coffin alongside the white hacked kitchen seat and untied the body. The cadaver was contorted, bullet-riddled and was missing part of the head. They pushed it into the coffin, as though closing a jack in its box.

Some of the firing squad lit up cigarettes and laughed. Some members seemed pale and sickened. Someone bragged about having hit the traitor in the head.

A few could not find words.

The captain delivered a pep talk to the squad. They must think of the man they had executed not as a comrade, not as an Italian, not as "one of us." He was to be considered rather as an "enemy alien." None of them could have understood the irony in the captain's choice of words, not even the captain.

The news of the execution was published later that morning and transmitted to London by an American press agency operating in Rome. A few weeks later a prematurely aged woman placed an advertisement in the *Times* newspaper and relocated to Eastbourne.

37

PINK LEAFLETS

Leipzig

We never thought to buy and sell
This life that blooms or withers in the leaf,
And I'll not stir, so he sleeps well,
Though cell by cell the coral reef
Builds an eternity of grief

— ALUN LEWIS

Ingeborg felt Dagmar stare with her father's eyes and Dagmar's frown seemed to say, Mother, can't you hear us anymore? My sister's starving. Ingeborg looked into Dagmar's eyes and sighed aloud. 'Sorry, I've been a little out of range, my darlings.' She turned her back on Dagmar and undid four buttons and opened her blouse.

She lifted Birgit from her cot. The baby fed with a greedy

haste and for a moment it sounded like she might choke, but instead she jerked her head away from the nipple and gasped for air. An image of Günther emerged in front of Ingeborg's eyes. Günther choking in his airless submarine. She forced herself to think of Amelung, on his way with news. He was likely wandering some station platform, perhaps dressed in civilian clothes with a little flower pinned to his lapel. The other passengers would all be watching him. He would smile at everyone and would probably reach inside his jacket pocket to reassure himself that his train ticket was still there. Then he would do it again and again. They all had their twitches now. For that, they could thank the BdU and living their lives in a metal tube under the sea.

She looked at the clock in the children's room. The train from Kiel would have deposited him in Hanover forty minutes ago. He would be waiting on his connection. He would kill the time by walking around the perimeter of Hanover Central and probably pay over the odds for a schnapps. The next train for Leipzig was scheduled to depart at 12:20. He should arrive at Leipzig Central at 15:39.

She had been calling them for nine weeks before Amelung answered. How long could they maintain a patrol? Not that long. They could have said something to her before now. At least, with all that time to kill Amelung could have thought of something to say to her that might comfort her.

In a haze, Ingeborg found herself carrying Birgit, as though the infant was a parcel. She massaged her tiny back. The child burped and fell quiet. Birgit smelt milky and was as light as one of those packages of newly knitted baby cardigans that Clara kept sending over.

A seasonal zephyr pushed the bedroom window wide open. Her mind elsewhere, Ingeborg hesitated in front of the flapping curtain. She opened the window fully and thought I already threw something from here. She gazed from the window and recovered her memory of the remainder of her phone call with Amelung.

***

'Where the hell is he?' she had asked.

'Officially?'

'Don't do that.' Ingeborg had been unable to stop her anger rising.

'I can only tell you what is already in the public domain. You know that.'

'It's all in the public domain. The British have been dropping leaflets like confetti. It's everywhere.'

'That's pure propaganda.'

'That's the truth,' Ingeborg snapped. 'For Christ's sake, Amelung, even Dagmar picked one up off the street. It's lucky she can't read.'

'I'm not in a position to comment on any of that,' he whispered.

'Why not? What are they waiting on?'

'If there's something official to announce then it will be heard through the authorised channels.'

'It's been two months. I can't go on like this.'

'You do know there are forty-four sub-mariners in every *unterseeboot* don't you, Ingeborg?'

'I'm not married to them. And, as far as I know, you're not godfather to forty other children. Are you?'

Amelung sighed a deep, long, sad sigh.

'You're supposed to be his friend.'

There was a long silence before Amelung spoke again and she heard a distant click, click, click of the telephone connection. 'I'll talk with BdU.'

'Don't do that to me.'

'I'll come to Leipzig and we can talk about it.'

'What will you say to BdU?'

'I'll say your family are connected with the hoi polloi, and that you're all very arty and flighty and not entirely stable.'

'Arty and flighty,' Ingeborg repeated, and she had almost laughed for the first time in months.

***

'Mamma,' Dagmar said and Ingeborg was brought back to the moment.

'It's nothing darling.' She continued to stare out of the window at a woman who had appeared in the street with a letter in her hand.

Ingeborg had already checked her own mail that morning. There were no letters or leaflets for her. And thankfully no parcel from Clara either. Not that she was expecting any since Clara had a new tactic to distract her. Clara had begun sending photos and postcards instead of knitted cardigans and bootees. It was all intended as an antidote to the stomach churning provoked by the frequent arrivals of anonymously sent malignant mauve envelopes with their pink leaflets inside.

Clara had read the pink leaflets and must have craved the same end of torment as Ingeborg ached for. If it arrived, Ingeborg would be a widow and Clara the mother of a dead national hero.

The woman across the street disappeared from view. Ingeborg remembered what it was she had thrown out of the window. It was Clara's last parcel. She had stood in the same spot and watched as the parcel fluttered and then for a brief moment had seemed to resist its destiny before it twisted this way and that way and finally dropped like a young bird leaving the nest too early and died on the pavement, five floors below. She had tried to retrieve the parcel. But by the time she got to street level all that remained of it was a looted brown paper bag with a tear in it.

Birgit started bleating and Ingeborg felt a wetness in her blouse and on her cheeks. She closed the window and returned to sit in the rocking chair next to Birgit's cot. She reopened the buttons of her blouse, pulled up her brassiere and this time offered Birgit the left breast, not because it felt fuller but because that nipple felt less raw. Still, she winced and quietly cursed when Birgit sucked too hard. Across the room, Dagmar sat down in her cot and played with her soft toy boat. Her father's last gift.

Birgit stopped for an intake of air. In the peace of the moment Ingeborg rested her head on the chair-back and closed her eyes and wondered how Amelung would react when he saw with his own eyes the pink leaflets, which asked:

"*Wo ist Prien?*

Schepke, Kretschmer, Prien, what has become of these three officers, the most famous German U-boat Commanders, the only ones on whom Hitler has bestowed the Oak Leaves cluster? They sailed against England. They are not coming home. Schepke is dead. German High Command had to admit it. Kretschmer is captured. German High Command had to admit it. And Prien? Who has heard anything of Prien recently? What does German High Command have to say about Prien?"

That was all she wanted to know. "*Wo ist Prien?*" Where was her husband? She had been asking for months but it had taken the British to tilt the truth out of their airplanes. They littered Berlin, Frankfurt, and Munich and finally even Leipzig with their leaflets.

When Amelung called her from Leipzig Central Station, he sounded relaxed, as though he had consumed a schnapps, or two. He said he was authorised to tell her as much as any wife should want to know. Enough to be able to "move on." It had sounded cruel, but he had only cited what she had said herself. Now, she wondered how much detail a wife needed to know about a missing

325

husband. Certainly, more than the bare impersonal facts required for a death certificate. She needed more than hearing he was "formally listed" as missing. She already knew that. Where was he? Drowned? Well, obviously. Or was it more accurate to say suffocated? She expected Amelung could tell her all she needed to add to her memories of Günther. That would allow her to move on. But what about Clara? What would a mother "need" to lubricate the path from hope to grief?

It was one minute to six p.m. when Amelung rang the doorbell. He had brought cognac and flowers for Ingeborg, and a doll for his god-daughter, and a yellow bonnet for her sister. Ingeborg settled the children in their bedroom whilst Amelung poured for himself and Ingeborg. As soon as she returned, he talked nervously about the risks they all took. Then he rambled on about the "probabilities" associated with commanding an *unterseeboot*. 'I don't want to hear your blah blah,' she said. 'I want facts.'

'BdU's last contact with U47 was 03:54 hours, 7 March,' he said abruptly. 'Tenth patrol.' He placed his glass of cognac firmly on the table. 'Not many make it that far.'

'What was he even doing on another patrol?' she asked. 'Why didn't he get a shore job like you did?'

Amelung shifted his position on the couch. He uncrossed his legs. 'My shore role is only temporary, you know. I'll soon be back out there again.'

'Or do like Eckerman and Kretschmer did and manage to get his *unterseeboot* away?'

Amelung did not answer, and his eyes spoke of his regret for having told her about Eckerman and Kretschmer.

'Or keep U47 on the surface like Matz managed to do?'

Amelung flinched. 'He would have tried to bring U47 to the surface,' Amelung spoke quietly. 'But if she was damaged it would have been impossible.'

'I've been having nightmares about how he suffered.'

'Without oxygen, we sub-mariners simply go to sleep,' he explained.

'Is that the truth?'

'Yes.' His tone seemed intended to assuage her. 'We lie on our bunks and never wake up.'

'I don't believe you. Someone once told me that when they're holed, the hull collapses and the mariners all die an excruciating death and then become food for fish.'

'I wouldn't pay any attention to Bert's little euphemisms.'

'How do you know it was Bert?'

'You forget we were all on U47 together,' Amelung said.

'It's awful. Knowing he's never coming home.'

'Lately, Günther had another way of looking at it,' Amelung answered.

'How did he look at it?' Ingeborg wanted to know.

'More spiritual, less food-chain. He always said that navigators belonged to the sea and if they are lucky, they'll return there and roam freely, always watching over those they love.'

Ingeborg smiled. 'Where did he ever get that idea?'

'Some old merchant navy man he once met in London.'

It had been their only trip outside of Germany. Günther had proposed to her there because the wife of the ancient mariner told him he had better get a move on. They promised to return. They had planned on finding the old merchant navy man. They had kept his telephone number. And she would have found those crazy Italians that had rescued her and Friedrich. And Friedrich, where was he now? 'I remember,' Ingeborg said, sadly.

'What?'

She remembered where she had hidden the old photos: she had wrapped them in tissue paper, inserted into a false lining of her cloche hat acquired in London and safely stored in the third hat box on her side of the walk-in wardrobe.

LATER STILL

But oh, the drag and dullness of my Self;
The turning seasons wither in my head;
All this slowness, all this hardness,
The nearness that is waiting in my bed,
The gradual self-effacement of the dead.

— ALUN LEWIS

38

LANDFALL

London

In a brightly lit cafeteria overlooking the arrivals hall at London Airport, widow Lily Moulton had found the perfect place to mark the minutes. Certain that no one could hope to pass unobserved, she waited patiently for Mrs. Sturm, the still pretty German lady whose first husband had killed Edgar, and whom she had befriended some years ago after receiving a long distance telephone call.

She placed her weekend valise on the floor at her feet and sat her well stocked handbag on the adjacent seat. She checked her wristwatch against the large circular clock perched high above the arrivals board. She adjusted in her seat and maintained a clear line of sight of the board until she found the incoming flight she was interested in: British European Airways from Frankfurt.

She regarded around herself. She located the emergency exits. The cafeteria was half full and lively. Everyone else was around her own age, except for four younger customers tucked in a far corner discussing the offerings of a juke box. A waitress arrived and Lily ordered a pot of tea and settled absently back and wondered if she had correctly divined Ingeborg Sturm's "incredible" news.

***

Ingeborg had dropped clues during their telephone call, especially near the end when Lily had pressed the point.

'As I said in my letter,' Ingeborg yielded, 'it's a little windfall, but enough money for me to keep my promise.'

'Hmmm, did you sell a picture?'

'No, it's not that. I'm often selling pictures. But you know how it is. People won't pay more than twenty Deutschmarks.'

Twenty Deutschmarks; close to two pounds. In Devon, you could buy a lot for that. Lily's curiosity had continued to gnaw at her. Perhaps Ingeborg had been left something of value by a deceased relative. Money or jewellery? Her curiosity was worse than any itch. But it would have been indelicate to ask directly.

'What kind of a little windfall?'

'You'll never believe it,' Ingeborg said and chuckled.

Lily ruled out a bequeathal because Ingeborg sounded too happy. 'In that case you'll have to tell me.'

'I'd rather keep it a surprise. Also, I'd prefer for Florence to hear it directly from me.'

'But what if I guessed?' Lily spoke quickly because she was unable to hide her impatience and also because she expected to hear the voice of the operator cutting in to ask if her friend was willing to pay for another three minutes. 'If I guess correctly, will you say?'

'Let's not start guessing,' Ingeborg said coyly.

Lily pretended to agree but her curiosity had been stoked beyond reason and as soon as she replaced the receiver, she called her three daughters and asked them to guess.

The Moulton family consensus was that Ingeborg had found a

wealthy patron. But Lily was dubious. There had been no sniff of that when she had asked Ingeborg if she had sold a painting. Lily called Florence, partly to share the news: Ingeborg had confirmed they would stay in the Savoy hotel after all, but also to swap gossip.

'I know all about it,' Florence said. 'We had a very lively chat about an hour ago.'

'You know about the Savoy hotel?' Lily's surprise sounded in her voice,

'I thought about talking her out of it.'

'I can call her and say you don't want to go to there.'

'I think she knows how I feel about the Savoy.'

Lily liked the idea of the Savoy but was not without sympathy. She knew that Florence's memories remained raw even after all this time. On the other hand, Ingeborg's own reasons for going back there were strong too, and she was paying. 'Where do you think Ingeborg's windfall has come from?'

'I never asked. I suppose she's sold her story.'

'Sold her story?' Lily wondered why she had not thought of that herself. 'You mean sold Günther's story.'

'It's as much her story.'

'And ours,' Lily said. 'But everyone knows Günther's story. The man wrote an autobiography. What's left to say?'

'Plenty.'

'You think so?' Lily asked and wondered what had remained unsaid of Günther's exploits that could possibly be worth enough to pay for Ingeborg's flight to London and a weekend's stay at the Savoy for the three of them.

'Or she's met a young, fancy-man,' Florence said suggestively.

'You're forgetting she's married.'

'Wouldn't stop me.'

'You're being ridiculous.'

'I've got form.'

Lily had laughed loudly at Florence's flagrant falsity.

***

The young lady at the travel agent had managed to dissipate Ingeborg's residual worry by telling her, "It's like taking a bus." Her nephew had said as much too when she shared her plans with him. But the price was something else. Her nephew had an altogether different opinion on that.

'How much!' her nephew sputtered.

'Four-hundred-and-eighteen marks.'

'Jesus. Aunt Ingeborg, they saw you coming.'

Ingeborg hated that her nephew blasphemed all the time. Nowadays, all young people seemed to do it. She had heard they even did it whilst at work.

Her nephew was employed as a clerk by the Federal Employment Agency in Leipzig. For a young fellow he seemed to be terribly well informed. Especially about the price of things and the lack of skilled labour in the country. Ingeborg did not deny that four-hundred-and-eighteen Deutschmarks was indeed a tidy fortune. It was not far off her monthly salary of five-hundred Deutschmarks. She was uneasy at maybe having been taken advantage of.

'It was either that or take the train and add two days to the journey,' she explained.

Her nephew likely sensed her discomfort. 'Yeah, it's the market, Auntie Ingeborg,' he said with the sagacity of a seventeen-year-old who had survived a war. But at least he did not blaspheme on that occasion. 'Hopefully you'll be able to take a Juncker,' he added. 'They're a lot less noisy.'

They all seemed sure of themselves these days. Even her own daughters tell her they would never be manipulated like her generation were. She hoped they were right and prayed their confidence would never be tested. Anyway, even if the travel agent had "seen her coming," thanks to her little windfall Ingeborg could afford it.

'Actually, I don't care how much it costs,' she told her nephew. But she was careful not to tell him how much she had handed over for the triple room accommodation in London.

Ingeborg returned and inquired of the travel agent whether one might choose to travel on this-or-that plane. Could she take a Juncker? The travel agent laughed and explained that all flights from West Berlin — as they had taken to calling it — were operated by British European Airways and you took whatever plane they, with their pleasant burgundy lettering, offered you, and you paid whatever price they asked of you.

Before departing Templehof for Frankfurt, Ingeborg had taken a few grains of methyprylon. A first for Ingeborg. At least with that particular sedative. But whilst she waited for her second flight of the day the calming aura of the sedative tapered off. She had no other choice but to slip into the ladies' room and consume her plan b; a decent swig of forty-two-per-cent proof *Long Horn* schnapps.

They called out the imminent boarding of her plane. Feeling bolstered, she crossed her fingers and then the departure lounge. She joined the queue to ascend the stairway. Despite the warm flush of courage from the schnapps, she almost turned back. Only the knowledge that her long-distance friends were waiting for her in England prevented her from bolting.

She traversed the plane threshold and grinned inanely at the free-smiling Fräulein hostess and held out her crumpled boarding-pass in her outstretched hand. She took her allocated seat and rifled nervously in her weathered brown leather satchel that covered her knees. She retrieved a magazine and buried her head in it.

In the midst of nonchalant pretence at reading an article in *Der Spiegel*, somewhere in the periphery, she registered several passengers who huffed and sighed and moved around and generally occupied themselves with "what-to-do-in-an-emergency." She insouciantly hummed a nonsense lyric. She had made the mistake of listening attentively on her earlier flight From Templehof and had concluded the instructions were entirely useless; *Who ever heard of anyone-surviving an airplane-crash?* She continued to flip and re-flip the pages of *Der Spiegel* and barely noticed the plane had begun its sly, creeping forward motion, until passengers around her had begun noisily buckling themselves in.

She discreetly tugged at her own twisted seat belt and realised that her youthful suited up neighbour was sitting on part of it. She tugged harder and he gazed distractedly out of the porthole window. She gave up on the idea and theatrically pushed her outstretched hands against the dorsal of the seat in front and sank herself firmly into her seat until she felt the pointy knees of the passenger behind her push like lances into her kidneys.

Her young neighbour finished gazing onto the runway. He angled his prim posterior and untwisted Ingeborg's seat belt. 'It's optional,' he said as he handed the belt to her. 'But it'll make you feel better.'

Ingeborg smiled, and noticed that, optional or not, he had fastened his own belt.

The plane picked up speed. It hurtled faster and faster as though a gap in the clouds had to be attained before cloud-closing time arrived. She gripped her satchel between her knees. She kept her eyes closed tight for an eternity and when she finally reopened them, she found the attractive Fräulein who had earlier smiled freely and falsely now stood in the aisle holding a silver tray with cigarettes, exactly like in the advertisement in the travel agent's office in Leipzig.

'Would madam care for a cigarette?'

On her earlier domestic flight, she had not been asked that question. That hostesses had also spoken perfect English, but this particular Fräulein sounded different. Ingeborg mulled over the accent and wished she had been asked instead whether she would like a sedative. She stared vacantly at the air hostess and admired her immaculate smart military style cap and burgundy suit with its BEA logo and lapel name-badge. She tilted her head to read the badge but before she could answer or make out the hostesses' name, the address system crackled and the captain spoke above the engine noise. He welcomed them all aboard this DC3.

The hostess re-presented the tray and the question, 'would madam care to smoke?'

Ingeborg mildly waved a hand. 'I'm trying to give it up.'

The hostess barely listened to Ingeborg's response and had already stepped forward and smiled vacuously at the man in the seat behind. Meanwhile, the plane rattled and its engines reached a crescendo and then fell alarmingly quiet. The plane made a sudden descent as though the air below it had been sucked away. Several passengers groaned fearfully. Ingeborg heard one of them muttering a kind of a prayer.

'Happens a lot,' her co-passenger said as he stretched his legs out below himself.

'I don't travel much by plane.'

'Some passengers get a thrill from it.' He shook his head. 'Not me.'

Ingeborg pursed her lips. She examined her fellow passenger more closely. He seemed an anachronism — this young man in his dark, pin-striped suit, with matching waistcoat, and white well-starched shirt. His hair was shiny and flattened. She knew what he was: another of those English family banker fellows that had popped-up all over Germany. The plane was almost full of them. Most of them were awkward looking and barely of shaving-age, but toward the front of the plane a few older-looking, more wizened men sat, similarly dressed.

She reached into her satchel and rummaged for her rolled up collection of letters and photographs of her friends and those photographs she had taken herself when she had last been in London. The plane dropped lower and Ingeborg heard odd noises emerge from underneath. The plane levelled out, stopped shuddering and everything quietened.

'Would you like a cigarette,' her co-passenger asked.

Ingeborg wondered if the fellow was pretending to be deaf. How could he not have heard her earlier? She stared at him as though he had presented her with a conundrum.

'We're in the smoking section,' he added.

'I'd prefer a schnapps.'

The fellow grinned. 'Me too' and then he lit up for himself anyway. He turned once more to stare out of the porthole window and remained like that, pivoting around occasionally to flick ash into the tiny ash-tray in the arm of his seat.

Ingeborg sniffed and discreetly used one of Lily's envelopes to divert little plumes of tobacco fumes.

The captain's voice came over the address system. He apologised for his earlier manoeuvres. He seemed to enjoy talking. He talked about what his passengers might see on the opposite side of where Ingeborg was sitting. That airspace over there was under Russian control. The captain blathered on about "the convention." Ingeborg knew people who lived over there. She would have liked to visit them but it was simpler now to go to London and visit acquaintances from twenty years ago than it was to travel twenty-kilometres from West into East Berlin.

She stopped listening to the pilot and swapped Lily's letter for one of Florence's. They had been going to make a movie about Fortunato. A film company had it all in hand. A writer had been assigned and the lead actor too. But then it was all off. Florence had never said why they had not made the movie. It ought to have been made. What were they called, that film company? She agonised over it: What were they called? She scanned the letter and found it: *Crown Films*.

She rummaged amongst her photographs of her friends. Her favourite of Lily was not a recent one at all. It was when Lily was plain Miss Priscilla Jane Selfe, farmer's daughter recently turned nurse. She wore a white bonnet and her abundant black hair was bunched up under it. A determined and sassy pale smile. A young nurse ready for anything. Ingeborg sighed. It was easy to see why Günther had been smitten by Lily. Even by the older version. Who could have known what lay ahead: 'what a mess,' Ingeborg muttered.

'Pardon.' The young banker stubbed out his cigarette.

'Sorry,' Ingeborg answered. 'Not you, I was thinking aloud.'

'She's something else.' He looked again at the photograph.

Ingeborg smiled. 'This was taken a long time ago.'

'Oh,' the young banker sounded disappointed.

Bar one, she returned all of the other photographs safely back in the satchel. She stared intently at the one photograph that most linked the three women. It was the photograph of the back of a strange menu upon which Edgar Moulton had once written his telephone number and Günther had substituted half a dozen terms on the definition of Dead Reckoning.

The day after she had almost had an eye carved out, she had given away the original coded menu. She had scrawled on it, "This is the Picchi code. It was written down," and she folded it up, inserted it into an envelope and left it with the concierge for Fortunato Picchi. Of course she had taken a photograph of it for Günther. And when it was time to keep a promise, she called that number; Bournemouth, four-seven-one-six and asked to speak with Edgar Moulton. It turned out, Edgar was also out of range.

***

The thought of passing even a few days in the Savoy hotel had caused Florence considerable heartache. But she would have the compensation of meeting with Lily and Ingeborg. Real contact this time, not letters or telephone calls or postcards and photographs.

She found her journey less tiring than she feared. As soon as her train departed from Eastbourne, she felt herself metamorphose and with each passing mile and with each look in her compact-mirror she became younger. At the end of an almost two-hour journey, she stood in the concourse of London Victoria train station and felt she had unwithered by a decade. She was a modern day feminine Juan Ponce de León who had unexpectedly discovered the font of youth on a train journey.

However, as she sat in the taxi-cab outside Victoria train station, she had a disappointing realisation that in several days she would likely re-wither on the return journey. She frowned when it came to her turn.

'Long journey?' the driver asked.

'Ten years.'

The driver chuckled and asked, 'where will it be today?'

'The Savoy hotel.' Florence leant forward. 'Take your time, young man. I'm not in a hurry.'

The driver reduced speed and asked, 'would you like to go the picturesque route?'

'Yes, I would.'

'You from around 'ere?' he asked.

'What's it got to do with anything?'

'Fair 'nuff,' he replied. 'Sounds like you are.' He whistled rather tunelessly for a few minutes.

'Would you mind piping down?'

'My mother hates it when I whistle. You remind me of her.'

When they arrived at the Savoy hotel, she politely refused any help in carrying her luggage. She tipped the driver generously, after all, he could have said she reminded him of his grandmother.

She had never imagined going back there, but Ingeborg could not imagine them staying at any other hotel. She stood a polite distance away from the revolving door, her valise at her side. She was clammy hot. She turned to watch pedestrians wander by in the distance. She heard taxis overshoot their stations and seagulls squawk on their way back to the river. She opened her coat and breathed deeply and was serene. Nevertheless, when she turned to the hotel, she still imagined Fortunato's smiling face on the other side of the revolving door.

'Are you sure I can't take that for you, madam?' the doorman appeared from nowhere and asked again.'

She shook her head. 'No.'

Other guests arrived and disembarked from their taxi-cabs and engaged the willing doorman. She watched them pass inside. Finally, upon a slow revolution of the spinning door she shuffled inside whilst the doorman was busy elsewhere.

Despite all that had happened the place had barely changed. The colours of the livery, the sounds of polite commerce and huddled chatter. Even the soapy smelling porters in their unchanged uniform looked familiar. There was one important matter that could not be the same. She considered asking who is running your kitchens now? Where have all the Italians gone? It would have been taken for madness to ask that. She supposed no one spoke about it, although everyone knew the answer.

She approached the check-in desk. The reservation was in Ingeborg's name — a triple room at seven-guineas a night. Florence must have looked harmless to them: a scrawny, albeit elegant, pensioner in need of a decent meal.

'I'd like to go on ahead and rest a little,' she informed them.

They had no hesitation in telling her the room was ready, she could go ahead without the main party and lie down.

Accompanied by the porter, she stood in the lift. He looked about her own age, and he fitted in as though he might have been there for some years. But she did not recognise him. On arrival at her floor the lift-bell chimed a familiar chord and tears welled in Florence's eyes. She choked them back. She was on the verge of asking the porter if he had known of Mr. Picchi and all the others.

'Have you stayed with us before, madam?' the porter asked.

'Yes, I have' she said. She might have blushed. 'But it was years ago.' Her tired eyes managed a mischievous glint as she recalled how Fortunato had taken her there and shown her all the places the public never got to see. She had heard the commotion and felt the heat of the white-tiled kitchens. She had looked inside stores and cupboards and once or twice had a sweaty entanglement in a suite kept for VIP's and then taken a shower before going down to the bar where she got to mix and taste Harry Craddock's cocktails and dance in the vaulted ballroom, like a paying guest.

'Welcome back.'

'I'm glad to be here.' She understood she would never stop grieving, but she was at peace to be in London. Even happy to return to the Savoy. She would stay there for the prospect of seeing her nephew and niece and of course for the sake of Lily and Ingeborg who had come into money.

***

Lily spotted Ingeborg as she meandered behind the luggage porters who, themselves, followed a crowd of suited men. She was dressed frumpier than Lily had expected but she was nevertheless unmistakable and good looking. Ingeborg clutched an unfashionable brown leather satchel to her chest. She wore a red headscarf and shoulder-length hair. Not quite as blonde as the photographs, but still not a grey streak to be seen.

Lily crossed her legs, sipped her tea, and congratulated herself on her foresight. Only a few days before, she had asked her eldest daughter, 'do you think I'd look silly if I dyed my hair?'

Her daughter had struggled to force herself not to giggle. 'Mum, why on earth would you want to dye your hair?' And then covered her mouth with a hand. 'Are you meeting a man?'

'Don't be ridiculous,' Lily snapped.

'I suppose I could do it for you.'

'Make it look natural,' Lily said.

On the bus from London airport to the city, Lily and Ingeborg were loud and hugged constantly. Some passengers stared at them, some tutted at them but most read newspapers or whispered to the people nearest them.

'Have you thought of all the places we might go this weekend?' Ingeborg asked.

'Anywhere you'd like to.'

'All the places they went to last time.'

'The naval museum?' Lily laughed. 'I'm not sure I want to return there.'

'Günther told me you were like a queen there.'

'He said that?' Lily smiled. 'Well, it couldn't be the same.'

'What about Florence?' Ingeborg asked. 'Maybe she wants to visit some of her old haunts.'

'She did mention the Empire and her old apartment and her daughter and her nephew and niece and some friends.'

'We probably should not pack too much in,' Ingeborg said.

'Don't worry about Florence,' Lily answered. 'She's as sprightly as we are.'

***

Florence was awoken by laughter from the corridor outside. She hurried from her bed and pulled open the curtains. She flew to open the bedroom door but, as she reached it, someone opened from the other side.

Lily and Ingeborg stepped into the hotel room.

A porter looked on bemusedly as the women greeted each other and hugged and sobbed in unison. When it looked as though the women had paused, the porter discreetly placed two large suitcases in the room and vanished.

'And they say English women are not tactile,' Ingeborg remarked.

'A popular myth,' Florence said. 'Spread by English men abroad.'

Lily and Ingeborg set about arranging their clothes and testing their beds, whilst Florence wandered into the bathroom.

'By the way, we were right,' Lily shouted.

'What about?' Florence asked.

'About Ingeborg's windfall.'

Florence stepped out of the bathroom and asked Ingeborg, 'you found a rich fancy-man?'

'No,' Lily interjected. 'She sold her story. It's going to be a movie.'

'Günther's story,' Ingeborg corrected. 'For four thousand Deutschmarks.'

'Four thousand.' Florence whistled and wandered back into the bathroom. 'Sounds like a lot of money.' Her voice tightened. 'Is it?'

'I'm planning on having a lot less by the end of the weekend.'

'But it's expensive here,' Florence said. 'We could have gone to Eastbourne.'

'I'm sure Eastbourne's wonderful,' Ingeborg answered, 'But you know how much I've been wanting to come back here to London. And you can see your nephew and niece.'

'Do you know who's going to play you?' Florence asked.

'Some young actress.' Ingeborg exchanged glances with Lily.

Florence gargled before asking, 'Should we know her?'

'I wouldn't think so,' Ingeborg said. 'But Udo Wolter says she has a great future.'

'Who's Udo Wolter?' Florence asked.

'He's the one that bought the film rights. He has a very active imagination. It was his idea to insert a minister into the story.'

Florence came back into the room, she wore perfectly applied mascara, vivid red lipstick, and a matching dress. She sat on her bed. 'Why would they insert a minister into the story?'

'Udo thinks it'd explain the change in Günther's outlook.'

'What change?' Florence's expression was puzzled as she examined her reflection in the full-length mirror.

'Father Kille. He'll be a childhood friend of Günther. It will be an anti-war message.' Ingeborg shrugged as she replied. 'You look young in that dress. It suits you.'

'It's quite daring,' Lily said. 'I could never get away with a red dress.'

'It's fuchsia,' Florence answered. 'Don't they want your film to be truthful?' she asked. Her tone piqued in puzzlement.

Ingeborg cupped her face in her hands and shrugged. 'Udo said it's a device. Like in a Shakespearean play.'

'How are they handling the *Arandora Star*?' Lily asked.

'I don't think they're including that particular episode,' Ingeborg said quietly.

Lily sat on the edge of her bed. 'I see.' She sounded deflated.

'Pity. It's as though everyone wants to keep it quiet.' Florence held her lipstick out to Ingeborg. 'Would you like to borrow this, dear?'

'No, thank you.'

Florence held out the lipstick a second time. 'We'd not have to buy a single drink if you wore it. Believe me.'

'Remember, Ingeborg's married,' Lily said.

Florence smiled mischievously. 'Excuse me, Ingeborg.'

'What happened to that movie they were planning to make of Fortunato's exploits?' Ingeborg asked. 'You never said.'

Florence was distracted. She looked at the bedroom door. She thought she could hear something beyond it, a noise in the corridor outside.

'Didn't they say that the timing wasn't right?' Lily answered in Florence's place.

'Yes, that's how they explained it,' Florence said quietly.

'Who explained it?' Ingeborg asked.

'Someone from the Ministry of Information,' Lily, again spoke for Florence.

'That's right,' Florence said quietly. 'They felt the public were not ready.'

'Ready for what?' Ingeborg asked.

'To be reminded about the internment camps,' Lily said, angrily, and she looked eye-to-eye with Florence. 'Right?'

Florence shrugged. 'I suppose.' And again, tilted an ear toward the door and corridor.

'And the deportations,' Lily's voice rose again. 'No one wants to remember those.'

'I wouldn't say that *no one* wants to remember them,' Ingeborg said. 'It's sometimes less painful to efface the past than accept the shame of one's own culpability. Wouldn't you agree?' Ingeborg asked loudly.

Florence was reminded of something Fortunato had often said about the past. There was a danger in trying to efface the past. Try to, and you will deface the present and menace the future. Yes, that was it. She smiled at her friends and wondered who would remember any of that when they were no longer around. Who would have the courage to walk down dark alleys? She might have asked the question except that right then the sounds beyond the bedroom door soared and the music of a piccolo levitated until she recognised a perfect rendition of a tune she had not heard in some time.

ACKNOWLEDGMENTS

BOOK COVER

The jacket cover is derived from a 1929 poster of the *Arandora Star* and licensed from Alamy, UK. The image has been reworked by the graphic artist Audrey Beauhaire of Anythink, Paris.

FRAMING POETRY

The poem *Convergence of The Twain* was written by Thomas Hardy in 1912 as a commemoration of the loss of the RMS Titanic that same year.

Alfred, Lord Tennyson wrote *Crossing the Bar* in 1889 and it was first published in the Lloyds Weekly London Newspaper on 15 December of that same year.

The wonderfully talented and tragic young war poet Alun Lewis wrote *Song* upon seeing bodies in the sea. The poem was first published in 1945 by George Allen & Unwin in Lewis' second poetry collection, *Ha Ha Among the Trumpets*. Later published material from this writer can be purchased from Seren Books. (www.serenbooks.com)

RESEARCH APPROACH & MATERIAL

In the course of seven years researching this novel, I have largely eschewed engaging with other historical fiction texts which took the sinking of the *Arandora Star*, Operation Colossus, or Alien Internment in Britain as a principal topic.

This was a simpler task to accomplish than might be imagined because unlike USA, where an entire literary canon exists around the internment stories of "enemy aliens" and in particular of Japanese-Americans the same is not true on this side of the Atlantic. The casual observer of the British literary scene would be forgiven for believing no such event as the mass internment of foreign civilians ever occurred on British soil.

The imbalance in awareness may owe something to the readiness of Americans to confront their past and the reticence of us British to do the same. Whereas a book by Jeanne Wakatsuki Houston and James Houston entitled *Farewell to Manzanar* was published as early as 1973, went on to sell over one-million copies, and was introduced into the school curriculum of several states.

There exists nothing equivalent in UK. There is no novel entitled *Farewell to Metropole* or *Farewell to Mooragh* to name but two of the internment camps established off the coast of Liverpool on the Isle of Man.

It is thanks to this thriving literary canon in USA that even today it is relatively easy to find readers of American Historical Fiction for whom the term "Executive Order 9066 of February 1942" will elicit a recognition of a wartime order that led to the internment of many thousands of civilians. They might even be able to cite *Snow Falling on Cedars* by David Guterson or *When The Emperor Was Divine* by Julie Otsuka as examples from the literary canon. It seems fanciful to imagine an equivalent proportion of British citizens could do the same if one cites the term "The Aliens Order 758 of May 1940." Yet the impact upon internees and their families is no different

Whilst eschewing fiction on the topic, I have had the privilege to engage with a substantial amount of non-fiction material in several languages and of various types. This includes, but is not limited to, written forms of a biographical or genealogical, as well as an impersonal nature: such as academic journals, government records, and newspapers. Also, audio-video material including movies, and , and newsreel, documentary, and audio recordings. All of this material has been informative, much of it has been heart-warming, but sadly it must be acknowledged that a certain amount was harrowing.

Therefore, I wish to graciously acknowledge those individuals, academics and journalists who trod this same path, long before me. Their dedication and skill in recounting their own lived experiences, or their curiosity and perseverance to ensure that the lives of others were not forgotten has informed my own approach. To the extent that my novel feels historically "authentic" it is thanks to them all. To the extent that my novel occasionally places some obscure literary aesthetic over an authentic historical fact I have only myself to blame.

SUPPORT

Net proceeds of this first edition of the novel will be donated to local associations in Italy and UK for the exclusive purpose of maintaining the memories of victims who drowned whilst being deported on the SS *Arandora Star*.

I wish to take the opportunity of thanking Comitato Pro Vittime *Arandora Star* di Bardi committee members: Giuseppe Conti, Romeo Broglia, Pier Luigi Previ and the Istituto Italiano di Cultura, Edinburgh for their warm support in helping increase the awareness of this story Italy and UK respectively.

AFTERWORD

Lily Selfe remained a widow and died in Cornwall in 1969 at eighty-one years old.

Florence Lantieri allowed her divorce application to lapse and she relocated to Eastbourne in East Sussex where she died in 1970 aged ninety-one years old. She took out an advertisement in a London newspaper and publicised Fortunato's sacrifice for the country.

Ingeborg Prien remarried in 1943 to Paul-Heinz Strum and lived out the war with her two daughters.

Some eye witness reports state that Edgar Moulton along with Jacob Burfiend, Major Bethell and the priest Gaetano Fracassi walked arm in arm from the prow of the ship. The sea has not given up any of these four men. Edgar was posthumously awarded the Lloyd's War Medal for bravery at sea for his conduct in helping to save lives.

Whilst every member of the Colossus Operation was captured, only Fortunato was executed for his role. His body was dumped in a mass grave near the spot at Forte Bravetta Rome where he was killed on 6 April 1941 and it lies alongside the many martyred political and resistance fighters. Crown Films, the British wartime propaganda film unit ultimately decided against making a film of Fortunato's exploits in 1941 as it was considered likely to increase fascist attempts to target *Libera Italia* resistance efforts.

There remains some doubt over whether U47 was destroyed by HMS Wolverine, or by hitting a mine, or due to an auto-destruct on account of a faulty torpedo. However the date and location of the last message from U47 is well documented as 7 March 1941 south of Iceland. Günther and the crew of around 45 are believed to have perished on 8 March 1941.

Renzo Musetti and his cousin Pietro both drowned. They were among the estimated 442 Italians from a total of around 740-748 persons that died (source is Alfonso Pacitti's updated research due for publication in 2024). Whilst this novel is in memoriam to all the victims of every nationality that were killed as a result of the unnecessary policy of internment and deportation of resident foreigners and refugees, it is particularly dedicated to Lorenzo Musetti and especially to his son, Antonio Musetti.

Maria Marioni (wife of Renzo) was naturalised in 1955 and remained a widow. She died in 1988 aged eighty-nine years old.

Decio Anzani's body was never recovered.

Giovanni Ferdenzi's corpse was one of the twenty-two identified Italo-Brits that washed up. In his case on the Irish coast in August 1940. He is buried in Clomany cemetery.

Friedrich Dabel, a medical doctor and Jewish refugee aged 29 years old, was one of the 150 plus "German" A Class (high risk) internees that drowned. His body had never been recovered.

Tauba Rubel, escaped to the UK in 1939 and had found accommodation and work before she was rounded up and interned in Rushen Camp on the Isle of Man. Her desperation was one shared by many who ended their own lives in the internment camps or on the transport ships. She is buried in the Jewish cemetery in Douglas, Isle of Man.

Amelung Von Varendrof, left U47 ahead of her last patrol. He took command of U213 and made three patrols during which he hit no enemy boats and killed no enemies. He was killed on 31 July 1942 when U213 was sunk and all-hands-lost. His body has not been recovered.

Bert Endrass, captained U46 for eight patrols and then moved to captain the more modern U567. After three patrols U567 was sunk with all hands, on 21 December 1941. His body was never recovered.

STATUTORY RULES AND ORDERS

1940 No. 758

ALIEN

THE ALIENS ORDER, 1940

At the Court at Buckingham Palace, the 17th day of May, 1940.

PRESENT,

The King's Most Excellent Majesty in Council.

His Majesty, in pursuance of section one of the Aliens restriction Act, 1914, as amended by any subsequent enactment, and by any provision of the defence (General) Regulations, 1939(a), and of all other powers enabling Him in that behalf, is pleased, by and with the advice of His Privy Council, to order, and it is hereby ordered, as follows:-

1.   This Order may be cited as the Aliens Order, 1940.

2.   After paragraph (5) of Article 12 of the Aliens Order, 1920 (b), there shall be inserted the following paragraph —

" (5A) Where a deportation order has been made with respect to any alien, and, in the opinion of the Secretary of State—

(a) the deportation of the alien would be impracticable or prejudicial to the efficient prosecution of any war in which His Majesty may be engaged, and

(b) the detention of the alien is necessary or expedient for securing the public safety, the defence of the realm, or the maintenance of public order, the Secretary of State may direct that the alien be detained; and an alien detained in pursuance of any such direction shall be deemed to be in legal custody and shall be detained in such manner as the Secretary of State may direct."

Rupert B. Howorth

a) S.R. & O. 1939 No. 927   (b) S.R. & O. 1920 (No. 448) I, p.138

Empty Seat

They asked for nothing except for the chance
To show the content of their foreign minds.
Now there's a void, empty seat at the dance.

You might wish you'd taken another stance,
Asked forgiveness, admitted you were blind.
They asked for nothing except for the chance.

And hoped you'd be capable of nuance
In your fear of aliens, folks of that kind.
Now there's a void, empty seat at the dance.

Yes, shrill voices urged your reflex adherence
Poisoned you against your fellow mankind.
They asked for nothing except for the chance.

- Interned! transported! They dared a last glance
In the direction of "home" this island.
Now there's a void, empty seat at the dance.

Years and tides mark their sad disappearance
But mothers and children still bear it in mind
They asked for nothing except for the chance.
Now there's a void, empty seat at the dance.

— Lawrence Battersby

ALSO BY LAWRENCE BATTERSBY

THE PROVIDENTIAL ORIGINS OF MAXIMILIANO RUBIÍN

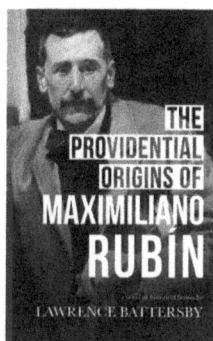

An assassin on Spain's version of death-row becomes a cause célèbre as two men: a famed writer and psychiatrist, take opposite sides in the free will argument.

KIRKUS REVIEW

INDEPENDENT LITERARY REVIEW

"Engrossing story ... brings a little known tragedy to vivid life."

"Set in 19th-century Spain and offers a trove of philosophical, social, and political clashes.

CADENCE   Short Story Collection

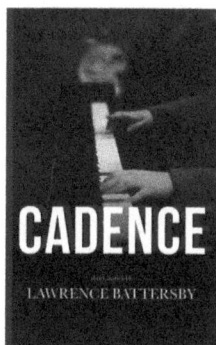

12 short fiction pieces including, 'fan fiction' reprises of work from several of my favourite writers - such as Julian Barnes, George Orwell, and Don Delilo, as well as several semi-biographical historical fiction shorts.

This collection is scheduled to be brought together under the title Cadence for publication in Summer 2025.